THE EMPEROR'S SWORD

Christian Cameron is a writer and military historian. He participates in re-enacting and experimental archaeology, teaches armoured fighting and historical swordsmanship, and takes his vacations with his family visiting battlefields, castles and cathedrals. He lives in Toronto and is busy writing his next novel.

The Commander Series
The New Achilles
The Last Greek

The Chivalry Series
The Ill-Made Knight
The Long Sword
The Green Count
Sword of Justice
Hawkwood's Sword

The Tyrant Series
Tyrant
Tyrant: Storm of Arrows
Tyrant: Funeral Games
Tyrant: King of the Bosporus
Tyrant: Destroyer of Cities
Tyrant: Force of Kings

The Long War Series
Killer of Men
Marathon
Poseidon's Spear
The Great King
Salamis
Rage of Ares
Treason of Sparta

The Tom Swan Series
Tom Swan and the Head of St George
Tom Swan and the Siege of Belgrade
Tom Swan and the Last Spartans
Tom Swan and the Keys of Saint Peter

Other Novels
Washington and Caesar
Alexander: God of War

THE EMPEROR'S SWORD

CHRISTIAN CAMERON

ORION

First published in Great Britain in 2024 by Orion Fiction,
an imprint of The Orion Publishing Group Ltd.,
Carmelite House, 50 Victoria Embankment
London EC4Y 0DZ

An Hachette UK Company

1 3 5 7 9 10 8 6 4 2

A CIP catalogue record for this book
is available from the British Library.

ISBN (Hardback) 978 1 4091 8028 9
ISBN (eBook) 978 1 4091 8030 2
ISBN (Audio) 978 1 4091 9997 7

Typeset by Deltatype Ltd, Birkenhead, Merseyside

Printed in Great Britain by Clays Ltd, Elcograf, S.p.A.

MIX
Paper from
responsible sources
FSC® C104740

www.orionbooks.co.uk

To Craig Renaud, Tailor and Knight

PROLOGUE

Calais, June 1381

Sir William Gold stood in his arming clothes in the common room of the tavern, surrounded by pages, while his noble squire, John de Blake, coached them on the intricacies of Sir William's beautiful hardened-steel harness. Against the wall that supported the inn's magnificent mullioned windows stood a row of wicker baskets, each containing pieces of armour polished so brightly that Aemilie, the inn-keeper's daughter, could see her face distorted and reflected a hundred times in a helmet, a cuisse, a vambrace.

She loosed a long sigh.

'Monsieur is leaving us,' she said, in a voice that she hoped hid her sadness.

Sir William favoured her with a smile and held out a long arm to have an arm-harness buckled on. His arming coat was covered in a fine silk brocade better than any dress she had, a sharp contrast to the great knight's arming hose, which were padded and quilted, but had definitely seen better days.

'Would that I could stay forever, lass,' he said. 'But ...'

De Blake made a very quiet sigh and took the arm-harness from a page before the boy could maim his master with it. He and Sir William exchanged a look, and the young squire was just pointing the top of the rerebrace to Sir William's arming doublet, pulling the laces through the maille with care, and he grunted, as he was holding a great deal of Sir William's weight.

'Ah,' Sir William said, looking past de Blake to the stairs that went up to the private rooms. 'Master Chaucer.'

'No *sauvegardes*, then?' Chaucer said from the base of the stairs to the upper floors.

'And no likelihood of any,' Gold said. 'You have it easy, going to Paris. I have to cross the Channel.'

'And you're going to take all of your men out into the pouring rain?'

'I am, Geoffrey.' Gold managed half a shrug as his squire began to work on the second arm. 'I pinned a great many hopes on this voyage to England, but I've had disappointments before ...'

'Some angry peasants ...' Chaucer said with a courtier's smile.

'I've seen a dozen popular risings, from the Jacquerie in France in '58 to the wool workers in Siena last year. They're no joke.' William's eyes fell on Aemilie. 'When the workers and the peasants work up to revolt, they are very dangerous.' He shrugged against the weight of his armour. 'And they have reason.'

Chaucer sneered. 'Reason?' he asked. 'This from you, William? The noted professional routier?'

Aemilie had been with the two men for days, and she had begun to understand the rhythm of their conversation. Chaucer would provoke and William would retaliate. It was their way.

The other famous gentleman residing at their inn appeared from the stairs.

'Oh,' he said. 'My lord! You are not leaving?'

'This very hour,' Sir William said. 'I have sat long enough, Master Froissart, for all that I enjoy the pleasure of your company.'

'But ...' The Hainaulter looked at Chaucer. 'You were going to tell us of Sir John Hawkwood and his wars! And your adventures with the Tartars!' He paused. 'And the Great Raid in Tuscany! A great *empris*.'

Sir William looked at the Hainaulter a little too long, and Aemilie felt the same discomfort she felt when her brother was rude to her friends.

'I can tell you about Tuscany in a sentence,' the knight snapped. 'The companions treated Tuscany as if it was France, and reaped a great many florins. I promise you, Master Froissart, that there were absolutely no deeds of arms.'

Froissart shook his head. 'But when great knights—'

'Great knights like money, just like everyone else,' Chaucer said. For once, he and Sir William were eye to eye, and in agreement.

A very foreign-looking man with a scraggly beard appeared by Sir William's elbow. The man had hundreds of folds on the skin of his face; indeed, when he smiled, which he did often, his whole face looked as if it was made of old leather. His eyes had a wicked slant, and Aemilie had, at first, thought the man looked like the Devil, but his French was impeccable and he was courteous. It was obvious that Sir William thought highly of him, foreign devil or not.

'John,' Sir William said. To Aemilie, he said, 'John is a Tartar.'

The other man gave a familiar head nod. Then he leant in and spoke into Sir William's ear, and William's eyes came up.

'Master Chaucer?' he said.

'William?' Chaucer answered.

Sir William, halfway into his armour, turned to her. 'May we have a private space, lass?'

She looked back to the bar for her mother or father, but she was the only authority.

'Yes,' she said, with as much cheer as she could manage. She liked the old knight, but she found him ... fearsome. 'Yes, you may have the solar at the head of the stairs.'

Sir William led the way, clacking slightly, and leaving his squire standing by the window with a cuisse in his hands. Froissart was a little annoyed that they didn't invite him, and he scowled, and she nodded at old Bill, her father's most reliable server.

'Hippocras for Master Froissart,' she said, with her mother's snap of authority. She made a quarter of a courtesy to the squire, whom she knew to be someone's son – someone important. 'May I fetch you anything while Sir William is about his business?' she asked.

The boy smiled. He was cradling the cuisse like a baby, and he suddenly realised what he was doing, blushed, and put the piece of armour back in the basket. 'I think John and I would be happy with bread, cheese, and small beer. We have to ride.'

John, the man with the wrinkled face, smiled his devil's smile, and Aemilie wondered how long you had to stay in the sun and wind to get a face like that.

'Not riding today,' he said. 'I'd bet my bow against your small beer.'

The squire's eyes widened. 'But Sir William said ...'

John, better known as John the Turk, nodded. 'God takes a hand.' He crossed himself, which Aemilie found reassuring.

Froissart put a hand on the foreign man's shoulder. 'You say Sir William is not leaving?' he asked, with hope in his voice.

John the Turk turned, his eyes narrowed, and Froissart hurriedly withdrew his hand.

'Best ask Sir William,' John said.

'But ...' Froissart said.

Providentially, old Bill appeared at Froissart's elbow with a heavy cup of steaming hippocras. Its aroma of spice and heady wine turned many heads.

John grinned, showing several gaps where teeth were gone. 'I'd take the same, mademoiselle,' he said in his excellent French.

She nodded, and motioned to Bill, and hoped her mother would appear. There was a tension she couldn't trace, and she knew that these men frightened her father. Bill gave her a wink and moved back to the kitchens, and there was a loud crash.

She favoured all the men with another courtesy. 'I must see to my kitchens.' She slipped away behind the bar and into the controlled chaos of her inn's vast kitchens: two great fireplaces, a spit, an open hearth, two enormous tables, and a hundred smells.

A small fortune in copper pots was strewn across the stone floor like looted armour on a stricken field. Blanche, the morning cook, stood with her hands on her hips, glowering at a pair of spit-boys who looked both aggressive and ashamed. Blanche defied her type by being as slim as a reed, as if the vast amount of pastry she consumed didn't ever reach her body. She had a harsh voice and a strong arm, and she struck one of the spit-boys a ringing blow to his ear.

Aemilie stood perfectly still for a moment, and Blanche looked at her.

'They were screwing around instead o' doing their work. An' this one tipped all the clean coppers—'

'I didn't!' the boy said. 'Marc did.'

'I never!' Marc proclaimed.

Aemilie took a breath. 'Silence,' she said.

Everyone froze.

'We have guests – noble, powerful guests. Men who are used to being served flawlessly in great houses. I will speak to each of you later.' She took another breath. It was the threat that she and her brother feared most: the threat of 'later' punishment.

And it worked. The two boys flushed and stared at the floor; the morning cook straightened her back and met her eye.

'Sorry, mistress,' she said.

Aemilie almost let herself feel a glow of satisfaction.

Then she turned on her heel and walked back into the common room, where Sir William was back from the solar, and having his arm-armour taken off.

Despite having an arm on his squire's shoulder, he managed something very like a bow.

'If you will have us, we'll stay another day,' he said. 'Perhaps two.'

Chaucer nodded to her. 'As will I.'

Froissart wriggled with suppressed curiosity, but he didn't speak. Aemilie felt for him. She made a deep courtesy and then met the wolfish eyes of the knight.

'Does that mean you will favour us with more stories?' she asked.

Froissart beamed his thanks.

Sir William glanced at Chaucer. Chaucer grunted. Both men seemed more relaxed.

'I suppose I can go to Mass in my arming clothes,' Sir William said. 'Belt, dagger, no sword.'

His squire put a belt around his hips. Archers were already carrying the armour away. They were in full kit, and some looked sheepish to be armed in her inn's parlour. But out in the yard, horses were being unsaddled in the light rain. John the Turk was out there, giving orders as if he was a great lord.

'Gentlemen?' Sir William asked. 'Mass?'

Froissart nodded. 'And perhaps afterwards you will favour us with another tale? The voyage to Trebizond, perhaps?'

Chaucer laughed. 'Mass, and then one of William's tales? One implausible story after another. Perhaps we might hear of Prester John after Trebizond ...'

Sir William looked at him, mildly enough. Froissart winced at the blasphemy; Aemilie stopped moving.

But Sir William merely took Chaucer's arm. 'Come, brother,' he said. 'If you have no need for God's grace, I will take your share.'

Chaucer sighed. 'No, no, you have the right of it,' he said, and they trooped out into the light rain.

An hour later they were back, damper but milder, somehow. Froissart had passed from being an outsider to being at the centre of their conversation. He was telling them a tale about a Breton captain, and Sir William nodded while Chaucer made a note on the wax tablet that always hung at his belt.

'De La Salle?' he asked.

'God's mercy, we faced him in Tuscany a few years back,' Sir William said.

Just as on the other days, Sir William took a spot near the big hearth, and Chaucer and Froissart sat with him. The other guests and most of Sir William's men crowded onto benches, squeezed into tables, or stood against the walls.

By then, Aemilie's mother was back from market, and her father back from taking hard currency to a banker by the walls, and the work of the inn was rolling along, and she could return to her duty as personal servitor to the three famous men. They had a pitcher of small beer on the table, and Sir William had his book of hours open, his rosary lying across his rondel dagger that lay across it, pinning it open.

'You will not favour us with tales of the Great Raid on Tuscany?' Froissart asked. 'For my part, I have always wondered if there was policy involved – if Sir John Hawkwood was serving Bernabò Visconti or the Pope in weakening Florence ...'

Sir William nodded. 'No,' he said. 'We hadn't been paid, and as I keep telling you, even a few lances are very expensive to maintain. Five hundred lances? Without a state to support us? It was a terrible time.' He shrugged. 'But the raid did depend on the events before it. I saw some of them, and for others ... why, I was in Outremer.'

Froissart nodded. 'But Sir John Hawkwood is surely one of the greatest knights of the age. Tell me more of him.'

Aemilie noted that once again, Chaucer and Gold exchanged a glance, and were in agreement. Froissart ignored them. 'You served him through every campaign ...'

'Hmm,' Sir William said. 'As I say, I wasn't with him in '74, when I was in Greece. Now that was a great *empris*, though I had little idea of it at the time.'

Froissart nodded. 'But tell me of these exploits ...'

Sir William leant back.

Chaucer leant over and spoke softly, but Aemilie heard every word. He said, 'Was there more to the matter of Prince Lionel?'

Sir William sat back and smiled grimly. 'And Robert of Geneva. Cardinal Robert.'

'Pope, now,' Froissart said.

'Not to us,' the two Englishmen said together, and then Sir William said, 'I will never acknowledge that spawn of Satan as pope. His so-called election was a farce.'

'Come,' Froissart said. 'Spawn of Satan is a trifle—'

'You weren't at Cesena,' Sir William snapped. 'If you want to hear about the massacre of innocents, forget Limoges. Cesena was ... terrible. Shall I tell you about that?'

His eyes were hard, and the other two men sat back.

'But first,' he said, relenting, 'I'll tell you of two of Sir John's greatest victories, and our voyage to the Euxine and the Tartars.'

PART I

ATHLETE OF GOD AND FAITHFUL CHRISTIAN KNIGHT

Northern Italy

1372-73

A KNYGHT ther was, and that a worthy man,
That fro the tyme that he first bigan
To riden out, he loved chivalrie,
Trouthe and honour, fredom and curteisie.
Ful worthy was he in his lordes werre,
And therto hadde he riden, no man ferre ...
As wel in Cristendom as in hethenesse,
And evere honoured for his worthynesse(;) ...

Geoffrey Chaucer, *The Canterbury Tales*, 'The General Prologue'

In the spring of the year of Our Lord 1373, it seemed as if the world had been turned upside down, and all the players in the great chess game of Italy had been shaken in a hat and placed on the board in different colours – red was suddenly white, and white red.

If you recall, and I have to look at notes to remember myself, the summer of 1372 had placed Hawkwood, with his company, on the side of Milan against the new pope, Gregory, the eleventh to take that august name on climbing into the seat of Saint Peter, or at least the Avignon substitute. Gregory was an inveterate enemy of the Visconti of Milan, who reciprocated his hatred with their own vipers' venom. And the war they fought wandered between hot and cold like a sword blade being forged and quenched, forged and quenched. You may recall that I saw the results of Albornoz's defeat of Hawkwood in '68, and then later, we stood with Bernabò of Milan against the Pope and the Emperor at Borgoforte. Through all of this, I was serving with Hawkwood, but I was serving my feudal duty for the Count of Savoy, who was, and remains, my feudal lord, despite some bumps and mishaps.

Regardless, we gave good service to Bernabò, and he returned our service with promises and very little gold. And I will probably repeat myself a hundred times on this subject, but it is very expensive to keep a company in Italy, or France, or any other theatre of war. It beggars belief how many iron buckles, leather lace points, feed bags, and scabbard tips a company can use – aye, and lose – in a month.

Listen, friends, because this is the essence of my tale. There are really two kinds of companies, and they are much the same whether they fight for a great lord for feudal duty, for a town for pay, or for themselves as 'Free Companies'. That's correct, Master Froissart, and I will insist on this point. Either they have the training and discipline to maintain themselves, with regular food, good forage for horses, new iron buckles for well-worn harness, scabbard tips on scabbards and rust polished off armour ... Either they have pride and discipline, or they don't, and they are a mob of dangerous rogues bent on murder, rape and destruction. It is the great pity of our time that most employers care not a whit which kind they employ, as either will do in many situations. And it is the sin of my life that, having led the first kind of company, I almost let my lances become the second kind, as you shall hear.

And sadly, Master Froissart, it's all about money. Of course, it's about chivalry and training, too, but ultimately, if you don't pay your hired killers, they tend to take what they need, and that way crime and mindless war lie.

So, in the autumn of the year of Our Lord 1372, Sir John Hawkwood, by then one of the most famous captains in Europe, gathered his two hundred unpaid lances and left the armies of Milan, and joined with our army for the winter. I was there ahead of him by arrangement, as you may recall. I even played a small role in getting him to come over to the Pope, although, to be fair, he was inclining that way all summer, even as we won a great victory at Rubiera over Galéotto Malatesta and Niccolò d'Este. A great victory that harmed the Pope and seemed to suggest that victory was in the grasp of Milan.

Right? Everyone caught up? I promise, a cup of wine helps. Italy wasn't a cesspit like France, but it was complex enough, for all God's love – and it still is. Consider, gentles ... Florence, Milan, Genoa, Rome, Bologna and Naples, every one of them as rich and powerful and populous as London or Paris – more so. Venice and Genoa are richer than England or France. Milan is richer still. The Pope is made of money – imagine having one tenth of all the minted money in all of Christendom. And the smaller cities like Verona, Pisa, Siena ... almost as rich as London. So imagine ten Englands and ten Frances packed into a very small area, and you have Italy, with all the money, and all the war.

And in the winter of 1372, we were laying out the board for a fresh round. You'll remember that in 1368, everyone thought we were headed for the 'Great War' of our time – a war that would engulf all the cities in Italy, as well as the continental powers and England. It started ... and then fizzled.

Just before Christmas of 1372, the Pope excommunicated all the Visconti. And if you were listening, you know how richly they deserved it, and how happy it made me, and I saw the hand of Isabella of England in it. Daughter of King Edward the Third, sister of the murdered Prince Lionel, Duke of Clarence, wife of Enguerrand de Coucy, reputed Europe's greatest noble and our commander in the field, Isabella had the political power to attack the Visconti, and thanks to a few of us, she had the proof she needed to know how her brother died. I said all this last night, but I want you to remember, because the ripples of that murder roll on like waves from a storm, to this very day, and because my refusal to forgive the Visconti led ... Well, you'll see.

At any rate, one more time. At Christmas of 1372, we were preparing a great army for the Pope. I was still serving as a feudal lord for Amadeus of Savoy, but my lances were in the pay of the Church now, serving directly with Hawkwood. I had fifty lances of my own. Every lance had a fully armoured man, an armoured squire with most of the harness of a 'man-at-arms', an archer or crossbowman, and a page. The core of my people had been with me since Jerusalem – Marc-Antonio, my former squire, Pierre Lapot, a close friend, Etienne l'Angars, my corporal, Gaillard de La Motte, Grice and John Courtney, Father Angelo and a dozen others. I still had some of my veteran archers, too – Ewan the Scot, Gospel Mark, Sam Bibbo, my master archer, and even Witkin, a strange man who had nonetheless become one of my most trusted companions.

And I had relatively new men, too – the Greek archer Lazarus, a Cumbrian veteran named Dick Thorald whom I could barely understand, Greg Fox, a London tailor's apprentice, and Tom Fenton, once a penniless young man and now a fashionable man-at-arms. I still had Benghi and Clario, the incorrigible Birigucci brothers, and their terrible page Beppo, and a dozen more, including Christopher, my squire and master horse thief, a dark-skinned man who claimed to be from Aethiopia.

And Janet. Lady Janet, Ser Janet – a woman in the world of chivalry. Janet and I had been together as comrades since the days of the 'White Company'. She liked to fight, and she liked to be a knight, and she was a noblewoman where many of us were the merest routiers. She could do figures and cast accounts, and she kept my lances paid and fed. Which was wonderful, nigh on a miracle, because it's not my strongest suit, I confess it.

And Pilgrim. He scarcely comes into this story, but he had become my company's dog, not just mine, and he was gaining weight as fast as he made new friends at camp fires.

And Fiore? You might well ask, as he was close to being the best friend I'd ever had, saving perhaps Richard Musard. But Fiore was back in Udine, a mountain town whose populace was renowned throughout Italy for violence. He'd promised to join me 'in the spring' with a few lances of his own, but I hadn't seen him in months, and had received no word.

Fifty lances! I was just learning how much hay fifty lances could consume – and how much grain, and how much meat, and how much wine. I'd never really had much more than twenty lances, and the potential for profit was magnificent, but the potential for financial ruin was just as great. If you imagine that a lance was paid twenty florins a month – sometimes less and sometimes more – then my fifty lances were due a thousand florins a month, from which they were expected to find their own food and fodder, except that … ahem … it didn't usually work that way, and we tried at all times to feed ourselves from the enemy. To increase profit, and discomfit the foe. Naturally.

A thousand florins a month was perhaps ten times my monthly income from my estates in Savoy. I did receive occasional incomes from Cyprus and Lesvos, but they were infrequent and didn't amount to much.

I'm being long-winded, but here's my point. I had reached a stage of my career as a knight – as a soldier – when I could no longer easily support my own men out of my pocket. Even my beloved Emile would have struggled to pay fifty lances for a whole campaign season.

As a side note, Catherine of Siena, the most blessed woman in Italy and a living saint, often demanded that all of the mercenaries and Companies of Adventure go on crusade. Holy woman that she was, she didn't understand that such armies would have to be paid for – not so much because of the greed of mercenaries, but because men and horses have to eat.

I'll be returning to this point many times, because until the Christmas of 1372, my own company had been small, and it had always been paid well by Nerio, and by the Count of Savoy, and protected from starvation by my magnificent wife, who *did* have the estates required to cover all of their expenses. But she died of the plague in a church in Piedmont, and I left the direct service of Savoy to serve John Hawkwood and the Church. I had more than doubled my numbers – with good men, veterans, carefully chosen with Janet's help, and Bibbo's, and l'Angars's.

So as the Pope's army gathered around Bologna, my thoughts were increasingly in the account books that Janet carried in her saddle malle. While I took every opportunity to play at lance and sword with my people, I was becoming accustomed to reading numbers and shopping for forage. Because that is the real life of a captain at war – every day, it's food, forage, shelter.

Bah. You want to hear of battles.

Well. 1373 was a very good year for battles, as you shall hear.

We were on the Pope's payroll, and we'd been promised double pay for the first two months of our contract. I myself was receiving almost three hundred florins a month as a chief officer under Hawkwood, and we were brigaded with, of all people, Niccolò d'Este, the lord of Ferrara, who had just been our opponent the year before. In fact, we had in the same army – or at least on the same side – Malatesta, Este, Hawkwood, Amadeus of Savoy, his cousin the Count of Turenne (no friend of mine), Otto of Brunswick, and a small host of Gascons under Amanieu de Pomiers. And our commander, Enguerrand de Coucy. I mention the last, because we'd become friends – at least as much as a great noble and a former assistant camp cook can become friends. He kept magnificent state in the camp, and I was welcome at his table, and I often took Janet with me, as she knew everyone in France.

You might have thought we'd be unwelcome with Este and Malatesta, as we'd pinned their ears back at Rubiera the year before, but in fact, there was no such rancour, beyond Malatesta's slowness in paying his ransom. I'd taken him at Rubiera and sold him to Sir John, who still hadn't paid me.

Sic transit gloria mundi.

We were under the walls of Bologna in late winter, and Coucy had the most magnificent tent I've ever seen – really more like a castle in miniature, with three great pavilions joined by halls of double-walled canvas lined in tapestries and carpeted in Turkish rugs. He had a hanging bucket by his bed for water, and lanterns of brass and bed hangings of velvet, and the prettiest Madonna hanging by his bed. Altichiero had done her, and she was magnificent, and also bore a stunning resemblance to Lady Isabella, the King of England's daughter and Coucy's wife.

His pavilions were studded with braziers that were kept lit by a horde of servants and burned incense as well as charcoal. Janet and I spent so much time there because it was warm, in addition to the pleasure of his company.

We were sitting at his long table – I believe we'd all just celebrated the Feast of Epiphany in Bologna. Coucy had the biggest, longest camp table I've ever seen, five or six ells long, kept for his 'peers', the name he had for his intimate friends. This was a man who had friends – his social skills were on a par with his military prowess. He had friends who were brilliant knights, and friends who were poets, and friends who were simply travelling. Janet and I were lucky to be admitted among them. It was at that table that I met Altichiero, the Veronese artist. I've been told that Boccaccio sat there glowering one night, sad and ruffled, like an old hawk, because he was on his way home from Petrarca's funeral.

And Hawkwood. As was the way in those days, Coucy, as one of Europe's greatest noblemen, was the commander of the papal armies of Lombardy. The Green Count, my sometime feudal sovereign, was away in the north, fighting the Visconti from his own lands, but Hawkwood might have resented Coucy getting the command, as he was older, and at that point he was at the height of his military powers. But the Pope liked aristocrats, and felt that mercenaries were untrustworthy, which was, I suppose, both naive and foolish. But in 1372, no one appointed a mercenary as commander, although all that was to change.

Coucy had the good grace to make light of it, and to consult Hawkwood on almost every issue – and not just Hawkwood, but Malatesta and Este and others. He had the gift of making every man feel singled out, included, consulted. In many ways he was the antithesis of my Count of Savoy – where Amadeus pronounced, Coucy enquired.

Let me add that both leadership styles appealed to me – they both work. One might even argue that the Green Count consulted in private and pronounced in public, where Coucy consulted in public and pronounced in private ... a mere matter of style.

But, as usual, I digress. It was early January. The Magi had found the Christ child, and we'd all exchanged gifts. Janet and I were still on edge with each other, tempted by carnality and fully aware what the costs would be. Otherwise, my life was as happy as it could be with Emile gone. Janet and I were seated, as I say, at Coucy's long table, and it was warm. My Turkish kaftan lined in wolf fur was hanging off my shoulders, and I was playing with Charny's dagger, when Hawkwood leant over the table. We'd recently been joined by an exile from Piacenza, Dondazio Malvicini Fontana, who was to ride with Hawkwood. He was a little too angry for my taste, but I barely knew him, and he'd begun to harangue us all in his enthusiasm for what he called the 'liberation of Piacenza', and my attention wandered as I thought about things. Mortality. My dead wife. My children, growing up without me. My son by Emile, being raised in Savoy. I needed to ... to ...

'Gold, are you asleep?' Hawkwood snapped at me.

Coucy smiled.

I could hardly say, 'I was thinking about my dead wife and my failings as a parent,' so instead I apologised.

'I was just saying that I thought we should make a run at the Via Emilia, and Sir John ...' Coucy waved at Fontana.

'You came down the Via Emilia in summer, young William. What do you say?' Sir John asked.

I had a glass of very good wine. It was a beautiful glass that came in a fine leather case, and had been my Christmas gift from Janet. It was a pleasure just to hold it. I looked at Fontana, and then at Sir John.

'If we sent an advance guard to seize the bridges,' I said, 'I think we could move quite rapidly.'

'Just so,' Coucy said. 'You can repeat all your exploits of summer, but going in the opposite direction.'

Malatesta, who was present, roared a laugh. He was easy to like, for a big bruiser of an Italian knight.

'For my part ...' Sir John said carefully. He looked around, to see if all these great nobles were listening. It was fascinating to see Sir John hesitant. I was used to him being unafraid of anything, but he genuinely seemed to desire Coucy's good opinion – perhaps because he was King Edward's son-in-law, or perhaps merely because Sir John was a little in awe of his rank and repute. 'For my part,' he said again, 'I worry that as we move on Visconti lands, they will come at us.'

'Surely they will face us in Lombardy,' Coucy said.

'The Visconti have very little chivalry to begin with, and it's spread thinner when they're losing, like too little butter on too much bread,' Sir John said. 'I think you'll find they'll ignore us and raid the Pope's lands, rather than facing us in the field.'

Malatesta shrugged. 'It may be as you say,' he said, indicating how little he cared for the peasants and merchants of Papal Lombardy.

Este made a face. 'You think that if we march to the gates of Piacenza, Bernabò will simply ignore us?' he asked.

Sir John smiled his fox's smile. 'Do we have a siege train? And the men to take Piacenza?'

Coucy remained silent, but at this sally his eyebrows shot up.

'What do you mean?' he asked.

I thought Fontana was going to explode. 'The city will fall into our hands like a ripe plum as soon as we approach,' he said.

Coucy's look was perfectly bland, but I knew the man well enough to know that he didn't believe this any more than Sir John.

Sir John looked at me. I thought he deserved some support.

'My lords,' I said, 'I am the least commander here, but as a swordsman I know that if my point does not truly threaten my opponent, he can ignore my blow and work his own will. I think Sir John merely says that if we lack the means to really hurt the Visconti, they are free to ignore us. I can say from experience that outside their personal fiefs, they care very little what happens to their subjects.'

Malatesta winced.

Este shrugged. 'Who cares?' he asked. 'I mean, does the Pope really expect us to destroy the Visconti?'

Silence greeted this sally, as Este had committed the social sin of speaking a truth we all understood but none of us was supposed to say aloud. The war was devastating the peasants of one of the richest places in the world, but the two contestants, the Pope and the Visconti, were almost impossible to injure, and that meant the war was being fought by proxies like us, with money. The peasants were doing all the bleeding.

Ugly. I saw it quite clearly, and it made something go hollow in the pit of my stomach.

Janet laughed. 'Why bother?' she said. 'I mean, we could simply sit here, and let them sit there. Everyone would be happier.'

Coucy smiled at her. 'You always were a clever one,' he said.

She shook her head. 'The most expensive war in my generation, and what have we accomplished?'

'A little too honest,' snapped Sir John, as we rose to leave. 'Janet, these are great lords ...'

'Yes, John,' she said. 'I grew up with them.' *Unlike you*, she left unspoken.

Two days later, Hawkwood led us – by which I mean all the English and some of the Italians – out of comfortable winter quarters, and we marched west, on the Via Emilia. It was like a re-creation of the year before, except that this time we were the papal forces, and we had all the major towns – Modena, Reggio Emilia, Parma. Bernabò's forces were nothing to sneer at, as he had most of the good German captains, but they retired steadily as we moved along the road, our horses' hooves ringing on the frozen ground like an armourer's hammer on the anvil. At first we had food everywhere, because Bernabò's men had made themselves thoroughly disagreeable all winter. While Bernabò was personally a beast, I suspect the Germans behaved badly because they hadn't been paid.

If raiding peasants reminded me a little too much of France in the fifties, and made my stomach feel empty, unpaid bills left much the same feeling. It was Saint Crispin's day, according to the mark in my book, and we'd just missed another pay day. That is, Sir John hadn't been paid, so that I hadn't been paid. I arranged with my bankers and Janet's good offices to pay everyone else in my fifty lances, and I did so in Castelfranco, on the road to Modena, because my little company was being sent to grab the bridges. I took a risk and moved my money there to pay everyone, away from Sir John's much larger company. Sir John had been joined by one hundred lances under Sir John Thornbury, a solid man with an excellent reputation, and Sir John, through his various contractors like me and Thornbury, had almost six hundred lances – two thousand mounted fighting men of his own. By contrast, Coucy had a few more than three hundred lances.

I'm leaving my road again, but all this matters, because I was paying my people from my own estates in Savoy so that they weren't tempted to rape, murder and rob. Sir John affected not to care for such niceties, but I noticed that he happily used my troops for his advance guard. And the point is that I paid out a little more than fifteen hundred ducats in gold. That's about a year's income from my estates, or one sixth of my worldly goods in 1373, to pay my lances for one month. Just one.

However, we left Castelfranco with the whole company, from Witkin to Janet to Christopher, by my side. We were in fine fettle, with good plumes in our helmets and big new wool cloaks over our bright armour. Lombardy isn't big on snow, but it is cold enough, by the Virgin. And as we rode out, I had a happy meeting, because there was my friend Sister Marie on a mule, with a dozen churchmen around her and an escort of Papal men-at-arms, all of them moving to protect their charges with drawn swords from my *compagnia*. We were, after all, the notorious 'English'.

But Sister Marie called out, 'I know these men,' and Father Angelo rode forward from our ranks with his rosary wrapped around his hand.

We shocked the priests and monks with a hug.

'Where are you bound?' I asked.

She nodded. 'I'm joining these worthy men to examine an early gospel,' she said with a brittle smile.

'Sister Marie's Latin is surprisingly good for a woman,' a Benedictine said. From his tone of voice, you might have thought he meant a compliment.

A Dominican friar in a spotless white robe merely glared. 'Son of Belial,' he spat at me. 'Get out of the road.'

Ah, the Church does excel at making itself loved. All those servants of the gentle Jesu.

'Are you going west?' I asked.

'To the monastery of San Raimondo in Piacenza,' she said.

'You're riding into a war,' I said.

The bishop, who I had taken for a captain of men-at-arms, pushed his horse through the press.

'Who are you, and by what right do you delay us?' he snapped in aristocratic Roman-Italian.

I bowed. 'I am sorry to delay you,' I said. 'This esteemed sister and I made the Camino di Santiago together.'

By then, Sister Marie was embracing Lapot, and I had spotted

Michael des Roches, attired in a severe brown cote. I went forward to clasp his hand, but the bishop grabbed my arm.

'I find you shockingly rude,' he said.

I turned, brushed his hand off my arm, noting that he had rings *over* his gloves. I thought of many things to say and do, but I suspected that Sister Marie would be made to pay for any display of temper.

'I'm sorry, my lord, but these are dear friends. We will clear your way in moments.' I smiled, kept my hand from my sword hilt, and turned my horse.

But the bishop insisted that his party ride on, and he was loud and angry and got his way. The religious troop vanished up the road to Crevalcore, and we turned due west towards Modena. Sister Marie rode past me. Her extended arm blessed me, and I was pleased to see that she had a sword strapped to her mule's saddle under her thigh.

'I have someone for you to meet!' she called out.

The bishop glared at her, and Michael des Roches smiled. I remembered that smile from great days and great conversations – a smile that announced that the scholar had something interesting to say.

I saluted him, and we rode on.

We rolled west, with our prickers out ahead, covering the miles. I had a dozen guides, all kept separated and all reporting to Sam Bibbo and Lapot, and flankers out as far as the villages to east and west, watching the cart-roads and the lanes. Lapot took a dozen archers, a few old routiers like himself, and my squire Christopher and rode well ahead. We'd find his people left as guides for us, or we'd glimpse them on a hilltop to the north, but that was seldom. Usually we just knew they were 'out there'.

Modena, Reggio Emilia, and right to the walls of Parma.

Outside Parma, my people made camp on the west side of a big ditch – whether a stream or an old irrigation ditch, I don't know. Janet proceeded to set up a market to purchase grain and fodder, which was our method of gathering information, and also keeping supplied. The local peasants had borne the brunt of the war, as armies slogged up and down the Via Emilia, and they were shy of coming into our camp until guarantees were made, a process in which Father Angelo played a role. He had declined to return to being a minor priest in Verona, especially as his family were on the outside of the local politics, and he had in effect adopted Sir John's entire army as his 'parish'.

All this to explain that it was evening and my people didn't have fodder for their horses yet. I walked into the 'market' to find out what was holding up the feeding of horses and cooking of soldiers' food, to find some very angry peasants haranguing Father Angelo and Janet.

I was in my usual evening campaign attire – an ancient wool gown that couldn't even remember better days, arming hose so worn that they were more stuffing than quilting, and shoes so light they were like slippers. After a day in armour, I just wanted to be light as air – ageing, I suppose.

Regardless, I slipped in with the farmers unnoticed.

'Maybe if we didn't feed the bastards they wouldn't come back,' a young, angry man said.

'Ye're daft as a newt,' said an older man. 'If'n we don't come sell 'em our grain, they just come an' take it, like.'

A dozen mounted archers sat on their horses at the back of the queue of wagons – and explained the surliness. I pushed through to the table where Janet sat with our notary.

'Trouble?' I asked.

She looked up. 'They really don't want to sell us grain,' she said. 'Bad harvest, and last year's campaign stripped a lot of these farms.'

One of our new Italian knights was a cousin of Father Angelo – Giorgio Cavalli. He was young and a 'true believer', by which I mean he was a political adherent of the Pope and hated the Milanese. Ser Giorgio was standing armed behind Janet, and he heard the bickering of the farmers.

'We are soldiers of His Holiness the Pope!' he roared. 'We are come to protect you from the Viper of Milan!'

He was met with the sort of stony silence usually reserved, among farmers, for tax collectors.

'Are you fools? Can't you raise your noses above your dung heaps to see that—'

Father Angelo rose from the table and clapped a hand over his cousin's mouth.

'They are angry enough already,' he spat.

The older man who'd spoken out in favour of selling us grain now looked at me. 'You're all the fuckin' same to us,' he said. 'Bandits with armour.'

Stung, I pointed at Janet's table and the piles of silver coin – *my silver coin*, let me add – waiting to pay for the forage and grain.

'We pay for what we take,' I said.

'Aye, at Bologna market prices. And if this empties my barn, where do I get more?' the man asked. 'Four fewkin' years o' war, mate. Four years you've cleared me out. My woman an' I ate onions last winter. Fuck you, and fuck the Pope. And the Vipers. Hope you all burn in Hell for eternity.'

I was rocked back as if he'd hit me. For a moment, all I could think of was the nuns screaming at us in France, a long time ago – a moment that is still with me, by the saints. I was, by 1373, a knight of some renown – a man who'd made pilgrimages and a crusade, fought in tournaments, fought under the eyes of my prince. I was no longer a routier, a brigand.

Was I?

It hurt, and troubled my sleep, as well. But in the end, they sold us their grain. The next day we were moving before dawn, heading south around Parma and looking to seize the bridges over the Taro.

Somewhere to the east in the dawn, a German captain was determined to stop me. But he'd never fought the Turks, and his pickets weren't aggressive, and before the winter fog burned off, I knew from Christopher that the southernmost of the three bridges was the lightest held. He had two dozen barbutes, or German lances, holding the southern bridge. A pair of low-born pickets shivered in the winter mist, and the rest were mounted in front of the bridge.

Sam Bibbo rode up with forty of my archers, dismounted, and cleared them in a minute. He didn't kill a man, although there were two dead horses on the bridge, but the Germans ran. Mercenaries can't afford to lose horses.

The second they turned their backs, we were moving across, spreading north, cutting the little garrisons at the other two bridges off from their main body. We took four ransoms, let a couple of penniless squires go after we took their horses, and watched the rest of the Germans ride away north. I agree, it wasn't exactly Poitiers or Brignais, but it was very satisfying to take all three bridges in an hour with no loss whatsoever. I later learnt that the German captain had two hundred lances to my fifty.

Greg Fox had taken one of the German men-at-arms, who proved to be a knight, and a valuable one at that. In less than a week, before Hawkwood and Fontana had even caught up with us, a Genoese banker had arrived, negotiated the ransom with our notary, and handed Fox a signed and sealed contract for payment of a ransom. It was more money than my former tailor's apprentice had ever had in his life, and I stopped at his wattle and daub hut to congratulate him. He was drinking with the other archers, and his eyes were fairly glowing from the wine, but he shook my hand.

'Are you going home to England with your winnings?' I asked.

Sam Bibbo put an arm around him. 'Never in life, Sir William. He's going to buy himsel' a nice harness and ride with ye as a gentleman.'

Greg flushed, but nodded. 'An' so I am, if you'll have me,' he said.

I clapped him on the back and then looked over the archers. 'At this rate I'll have no archers,' I said.

'Aye, well,' Bibbo said, 'we can always send for more lads from home who want to get rich.'

It was a raucous evening, and a pleasant one – success has a good taste. But when I left, Janet left with me, and she walked with me as far as my pavilion, which, I was pleased to note, had a brazier lit inside. In the orange light of the burning charcoal, I could see the demonic face of Beppo, page to the Birigucci brothers.

'Thanks for keeping the tent warm,' I said.

Beppo laughed. 'Mostly Beppo was keeping Beppo warm,' he said.

Janet leant down and warmed her hands at the brazier. In the archers' hut, the close press of a dozen or more men and women kept it all comfortable, but in my pretty canvas pavilion, one brazier barely took the sting out of the air.

Janet smiled at me across the brazier. 'Fox gets rich off one ransom,' she said. 'But the farmers here are losing everything.'

I had seen how many farms on the western side of the Taro were empty. I knew that the thatched roof on the archers' hasty long hut had been lifted entire from an empty farmhouse.

Beppo grunted.

'What, Beppo?' I asked.

He had become one of the most important men in my little

command – he seemed to know everyone, and he must have ridden on every road in Italy.

'North of here, it's worse,' he said. 'Around Cremona, babies starve. Beppo sees.'

'And for what?' Janet asked.

She wasn't bitter – surprisingly, her love of knighthood had endured past her own experiences of hell. Her question was like one of Fiore's. Come to think of it, the two of them had a great deal in common, and he did love her for years. To no avail, as you will have heard.

I shook my head. 'I'm not sure any more.'

Beppo grunted again. 'Men say Beppo looks like Satan,' he said. 'Beppo say many men act like fucking Satan and look very nice.' He pointed with his chin towards distant Pavia. 'The Visconti are much worse than the Pope,' he said. And shrugged. 'And yet ...'

Janet smiled at him. 'And yet, on the ground, there's not much to tell the difference between them.'

'Beppo wants a sausage,' the man said suddenly.

'Are you going to grill it here?' I asked.

'Eh, Capo, I built the fire.'

'Fair enough,' I agreed. 'So yes.'

Janet waved, indicating that she, too, wanted a sausage.

Beppo ducked out through the tent's door, and a rush of icy air reminded me of how much more pleasant it was *inside* my pavilion.

'A lady wishes she thought it was a good idea to share a nice warm bed with a gentleman,' Janet said. She shrugged. 'But the lady thinks that it is a terrible idea.'

I nodded mutely, unable to say anything. But when the silence stretched too long, I said, 'Perhaps the lady has spent too much time with Beppo if she refers to herself constantly as an absent person.'

She smiled a twisted smile. 'You are a good man, Guillaume d'Oro,' she said.

Well. Not really. But it's nice to be told so. Then Christopher came in and set about some housekeeping, and I offered him a cup of wine and a sausage.

We all ate our sausages, hot, and so warmed, went to our separate beds.

*

25

I waited a few days for Sir John to catch up. He certainly didn't seem to be in a hurry to get to Piacenza, and so I dawdled, keeping a screen of archers on good ponies watching the flat plains to the north, but the weather closed in, and we were happy for a snug camp and a few stolen roofs. When I knew that Hawkwood was at Cella, west of Reggio Emilia, I moved further west, although I was cautious now, because we were – at least technically – in enemy territory. I moved up to Fidenza, a fortified village about four miles from Parma to the west, and halted, reaching out with my mounted archers and Lapot's routiers to the north and west, looking for Bernabò's army. I didn't want to be cut off, most especially as the Visconti had every reason to deal harshly with me if they caught me. The mountains rose to the south, beautiful when we could see them, but the weather kept coming from the north, and all of us were riding around with our new cloaks on and our hoods up. I promise you that a thick woollen hood over a basinet, even with the visor up, is not a good way to hear anything. We were scouting our bank of the Arda, by which I mean that Courtney and Grice and the Biriguccis were scouting the banks of the Arda, with Beppo pretending he wasn't in command, when they picked up a pair of German knights. The Germans were, apparently, just too miserable in the freezing rain to notice the four armed men on the road.

About the time this was happening near Casa Nuova, I was riding along a mud track in the foothills of the mountains, using a bad guide to try and find out whether the local castle had a garrison. I fully confess that I was riding along with my head down, the rain coming in torrents, and a rivulet of ice running down my back, when my riding horse, a four-year-old Arab mare named Giulia, started, bounced, and tossed her head.

I looked up to find that I was in the midst of several hundred soaking wet Milanese *provisionati*, a sort of superior paid militia.

I had ridden right in among them with Sam Bibbo and Janet and l'Angars. He was carrying our banner, which was, thanks be to God, in a leather case. With about a hundred years of making war among us, you'd think we'd have been awake to the threat, but we were not.

And neither were the Milanese.

'Hey!' bellowed a sergeant.

I had all but ridden him down, and Giulia, who really didn't like people, was moving under me and threatening every man within fifty paces with her hooves.

I knew them at a glance – good maille coats and textile armour, some pavises, and a lot of crossbows, expensive ones well cared for, trussed up in oiled leather.

'What in the name of Satan's fallen angels are you doing on this road!' I snapped.

The sergeant looked abashed. He looked over his shoulder for support, and there, under a broad kettle hat, was an officer – I could tell from the coat-of-arms on his surcoat. But the man was four files away, and not inclined to get involved.

'Aren't you supposed to be on the Via Emilia?' I asked.

'No, my lord!' said the sergeant. 'We're to garrison Castell'Arquato!'

I brushed my hood back so that they could all see my beautiful, expensive armet. I pointed towards distant Piacenza.

'Who in the name of Hell told you to garrison Castell'Arquato?' I asked.

It was a bold move, I confess, but I was surrounded, and cutting my way out was very unlikely. Italian militia are tough as nails.

A gout of rain fell, so heavy that it was as if we'd been thrown in the river. It passed.

By then the local knight had burrowed through his spearmen to my stirrup.

'My lord, we were ordered out by one of the German captains,' he said.

'Messire Bamgaudio,' said the sergeant.

'Hans Baumgarten?' I asked.

'The very man,' the captain said.

'He was wrong,' I replied. 'Castell'Arquato has a garrison. I have just seen to it.'

'Fuck me,' the sergeant said with real disgust.

'Amen,' the knight said. They clearly got along.

And like good soldiers, they turned about by files, quite correctly, and squelched off back down the road to Piacenza, just a few miles away.

Someone was going to be angry.

Behind me, Bibbo snorted.

I turned. 'We'll try for Castell'Arquato,' I said. 'Bibbo, find us a peasant to get us there. Janet ... No.' Suddenly I had the glimmerings of a plan. 'L'Angars, take your squire, ride for our camp, and get me the quarter guard. At least twenty men. We'll be holding the gatehouse, I hope.'

About an hour later, a noble Italian lady and her bedraggled escort demanded admission to the locked gates of Castell'Arquato. It's an old Roman military town perched on a rock above the river Arda, and it had a brand-new gatehouse just completed by the Visconti.

But no garrison.

The town probably had a militia, but they didn't love the Milanese despots enough to turn out in the rain, and so the gatekeeper, a man whose nose betrayed a love of the grape, opened the sally-door and let Janet in.

There's no story to tell. We took the gatehouse without loss to anyone. Best of all, in the pouring rain, we were dry, and no one in the town knew we had the gatehouse. When l'Angars came with twenty men, we held the gatehouse, and an hour later, without a single drop of blood being shed, we had the whole castle. The Comini family, the local stewards for the Visconti, were caught completely unprepared. I locked them in a tower and ordered them fed.

I now had one of the strongest castles in the region and the bridges over the Arda. I confess it, I felt like a hero, except for the part of me that felt like a fool for almost getting captured by the militia.

I sent for Sir John and moved my company south into the castle. It was a tight fit for two hundred men and a few dozen women, but it was dry and the granary was full. We filled the town with our horses. Four hundred horses eat a great deal of grain and take up a lot of room, but I negotiated with the podestà and the town's council and got them to feed our horses – and us – in lieu of ransoming the town.

It was like France. And I knew what to do once I had a strong place like this. I put my people back out onto the roads, despite the weather, and pushed my luck a little harder, trying to find bridges over the Chero and the Nure.

Unfortunately, we'd provoked Baumgarten. Someone had described me too well, from my encounter with the militia. After three days of patrolling the countryside below the mountains, Beppo and Lapot and Christopher all reported that there were a thousand men marching

28

along the edge of the mountains, and they were coming to take our castle.

'Artillery?' I asked. 'Big wagons?'

Beppo smiled. 'Many good knights,' he said. 'And very few working men.'

Baumgarten arrived before Castell'Arquato just before the end of the week. His siege, if I may call it that, lasted about three days and we were never close invested. Clario Birigucci rode out and jousted with a German knight on the Ponte d'Arda. The next day, it was Grice, of all men – a veteran routier playing knight errant, although I suppose the same could be said of me.

Baumgarten came in person the third day to summon me to surrender.

I didn't laugh. I'd served under him and fought him in a tournament. I thought highly of him as a commander and as a knight. I bowed.

'I must decline to surrender such a strong town,' I said.

He nodded. 'You are still wearing the Emperor's sword,' he said. 'May I see it?'

I handed it over, and he looked at it. 'You earned it,' he said, and smiled. 'This whole war is a piece of crap,' he added. 'My men are wet and cold and I haven't been paid in six months.'

'I'm with you on not getting paid,' I said.

He nodded. 'If my employer was worth a fart, I'd be here with an artillery train, or I'd bring a thousand ducats and buy you out,' he said. He shook his head. 'I'll summon you again tomorrow, and then we play for keeps. I don't think of you as a man who responds to threats, but I have to take this town.'

I understood. 'I hear you,' I said. 'But I think you'll find that Sir John Hawkwood is closer than you think.

Now, I said this as a piece of bluster, because I knew that when the town's food ran out, I was doomed. Two hundred men is too many in a castle that size. You feel impregnable right up until you eat your horses.

And he took it as the gasconade that I meant it to be, smiled, and nodded. 'Of course, Sir William,' he said.

Except that there were no jousts on the bridge the next day, because he was gone. And by mid-morning, I was pouring a cup of mulled wine for a very wet Sir John Thornbury.

He looked around. 'Damn me,' he said. 'Well done, Sir William. And you're dry, at least.' He shivered. 'It's colder than the Devil's teats out there.' He drank off half his steaming mug of wine and sat back. 'Sir John begs that you'll slow down,' he said, and laughed.

'Slow down?' I asked. 'If Baumgarten is in retreat, today's the day to grab the bridges over the Nure.'

Thornbury sat back, tilted his chair against the wall, and put his booted feet up on the table. 'Ahh,' he said as the weight of his breastplate came off his back. I knew the feeling. 'Sir William, I mean no disrespect, but you are taking this campaign a little too seriously. Piacenza will still be there in a week or two ...'

I took it ill, but I knew it wasn't Thornbury's fault.

'We have them now,' I said. 'Sir John can go right up to the gates of Piacenza! If we take it, we can change the war.'

Thornbury was a handsome man, older than me, with grey at his temples, a good harness and fine manners. He was a real knight – that is, well-born, and only a mercenary by profession, if you like.

'May I trouble you for another cup of this excellent wine?' he asked, and I sent one of the castles servants for more. I needed a new squire, since Marc-Antonio was now a knight, but I hadn't appointed one yet.

When we were alone, Thornbury smiled a cynical smile. 'I agree that we could swoop down on Piacenza,' he said. 'But I promise you on my hope of Heaven that we won't.'

I disliked this talk. 'You aren't saying that Sir John won't prosecute the campaign?' I asked.

Thornbury gave a sniff that reminded me of my grandmother, and of Sister Marie.

'Never,' he said. And that smile again. 'And yet,' he went on, 'let's be honest, shall we? Sir John hasn't been paid by the Pope, who ordered us out on a winter campaign without sending a florin.'

'Ah,' I said.

Thornbury nodded. 'I think you've set a good standard here, Sir William. I'll wager there are a dozen strategic castles around Piacenza, and every one of us can grab one. The Visconti will buy them back when the war is over—'

'When the war is over?' I asked.

Thornbury shrugged. 'That's what I hear. And there's a rumour that Lancaster is reopening the war in France.' He smiled ruefully. 'In which case, I've come to the wrong war.'

He finished his wine and I let him go.

As it proved, Piacenza did revolt. Clerics preached rebellion and the factions responded.

We didn't take the city. We did get a lot of support in the countryside, and John Thornbury took a pair of castles, and Ugolino da Savignano took another. Da Savignano was a local noble from a family of Guelphs, generations of supporters of the Pope. He knew the local farmers and the castles, and he and Hawkwood moved easily around Piacenza. Fontana complained constantly, mostly, I think, to cover his disappointment that we weren't seizing one of the biggest cities in the area, and he belittled our efforts every day.

From his point of view, our taking private castles and small Visconti holdings was a waste of time. From Sir John's point of view, taking Piacenza for the Pope while unpaid was a bad signal to give an employer.

I still had a great deal to learn about making war.

On the other hand, when we had secured a good base in the area, I was sent north and west to look at Pavia. Baumgarten had withdrawn from Piacenza, leaving a garrison, and I followed him up the Via Emilia. Piacenza to Pavia is no more than twenty miles, and I'd been there the year before. Beppo was handy, and so was da Savignano, but I knew the terrain well enough. And the savage rains of January had tailed off into a sort of pre-spring quagmire, unkind to horses but not so bad for scouting.

We didn't hold the Piacenza bridge over the Po, and the Po in winter is a torrent. Fording is out of the question, and wooden bridges wash away, so I roamed the south bank looking for options. At Speza, Marc-Antonio found a miracle – a stone span two horsemen wide, unguarded. He couldn't believe it, and when I rode up hours later I couldn't believe it either. There are perhaps six bridges over the Po all year round, and here was one sitting unguarded on a major road to Pavia.

In an afternoon, we were into the heartland of the Visconti. I took twenty lances right up to the suburbs and captured a Hungarian knight who was too slow leaving his mistress.

He had quite a tale to tell, but I didn't hear it right away. Instead, we spread out, grabbing a merchant's wagon full of gold, a dozen haywains for our horses, and so on. We were in the Visconti heartland – war had never come here. And we were within our 'rights' to take whatever we wanted.

I remember that I was sitting on a tired Percival, watching archers and pages methodically stripping a giant stone barn under Janet's watchful eye, and I was fiddling with my visor. My new helmet, not really so new any more but which was still the best helmet I'd ever owned, had a visor that usually stayed up when I raised it, but in the rain and cold, something had slipped. I invite you to try holding your visor open while your restless warhorse moves between your legs.

Regardless, I was thinking of how very rich these people were, and of the poor farmers east of Parma, who'd had years of our depredations.

Janet looked at me. 'Did the illustrious Fontana find you?' she asked.

I banished my dark thoughts. 'No,' I admitted.

She nodded. 'Good. He's fit to explode. He claims Sir John and Malatesta are deliberately letting his people die in Piacenza.'

'That's foolishness,' I snapped.

I heard it every time I went near the command tents – Este and Malatesta and Hawkwood refusing to take us against the walls of Piacenza, and Fontana claiming that his uprising had already begun, and we were missing our opportunity.

Janet raised an eyebrow, but didn't say anything.

'I need a good groom,' I said.

'I can probably find one for you,' she said with a smile. 'You need a squire who isn't a light horseman, too. Who helped you arm this morning?'

It was true – Christopher, a veteran cattle and horse thief, was much in demand for patrols and scouts, and was almost never by my side. He had quickly grown into an important man, and both Bibbo and Lapot liked to work with him.

'You should let Christopher go,' she said. 'Make him a master archer or something.'

'I'll speak to Bibbo,' I said. And I meant it. She was, as usual, correct.

For the first few days, I had kept my troops to seizing food. This wasn't the Via Emilia – no one here was going to starve. I'd never seen so many hams hanging in smokehouses in all my life.

Next day, south of me, Thornbury grabbed a castle in the hills south of the Po. Then, by luck – and skill – Lapot took an old fortified manse just north of the city by assault. I took my little command group, which by then was Marc-Antonio, l'Angars, Janet, and our armed squires and archers, and rose over to see 'our' new tower.

It was bigger than I'd imagined. And very defensible. I moved five lances into it, ate a good meal, and rode back south with Lapot's scouts, my own people, and Beppo. Darkness was falling over the deep mud of the fields, and it smelt like England – manure and fallen oak leaves and snow on the way.

Beppo pointed towards Pavia. 'There's not a soldier on the walls, but militia,' he said. 'No one was out in the fields today. Beppo thinks that Bernabò has stolen a march on you.'

I remember reining in and looking back, as if I could see through the walls of Pavia. I looked at Lapot.

As you may recall, he's not a man much given to speech. He shrugged. 'Sure,' he admitted after a moment. 'No one has opposed us for days,' he added – quite a long speech for Lapot.

'*Jesu Domini*,' I muttered, or maybe something more blasphemous. It's bad, when you are a commander, to learn something important after darkness falls, as there will follow hours of indecision.

And I was very tempted to say something bitter to Lapot, one of my best and most trusted officers. He'd had no opposition in days? That might have been nice to know.

And that put me in mind of my Hungarian prisoner, who'd never been questioned. So when we got back to camp, I sent for him, offered him wine, and asked him a dozen questions. And he freely admitted that Baumgarten was ... *gone.*

They were all gone, because Bernabò had pulled his forces together and marched on Bologna – just as Sir John had predicted.

I sent him to Sir John with my compliments and a précis of Lapot's scout. An hour later, Sir John sent a herald for me, and I rode over to their camp in my bad gown and worn hose. I really needed a new arming coat, new fighting hose, new shirts, braes ... No one is supposed to fight in the winter. I needed a city, or a big camp with women who sewed.

Hawkwood had Este and Malatesta and da Savignano and Fontana, all in his pavilion.

'William,' he said frostily.

I bowed.

'I think the Pope might have preferred if we'd known this yesterday,' Sir John said. 'Or the day before. How long have you known? You took this bastard two days ago!'

I hadn't expected to be chided, and my first reaction was anger, but I'd had several pilgrimages to work on my tendency to anger, although I flushed. I still remember Hawkwood's voice, and my annoyance as the blood heated my face. Despite that, I bowed.

'My apologies, my lords. I was not certain of the matter until this evening.'

Note to future commanders – it's worthless to blame Lapot. He can't defend himself, and anyway, most of these men didn't even know him. And I was his commander.

Malatesta threw his hands in the air. 'So Bernabò marched two, mayhap even three days ago!'

I thought Fontana was going to erupt like the ancient volcanoes. 'My people in Piacenza are dying!' he said. He hissed it more than shouted it, like a pot on the boil.

'Leave garrisons in your castles,' Hawkwood said, looking at Este, who nodded. 'We'll be back. But we need to head towards Bologna. Bernabò will have moved ... what, towards Reggio Emilia?'

I tried to hide my annoyance. 'I can send for my itineraries,' I said.

Sir John knew perfectly well I had four different northern Italian pilgrim itineraries, copied out myself. They described almost every decent road north of Bologna.

He shook his head, tapped his teeth with his bye knife, and fingered his beard. 'Gentlemen, leave me to think this over. William, you stay.'

Malatesta rose with a bad grace at the obvious dismissal. Sir John was not at his best.

Da Savignano caught his arm. 'Let's not stay and watch him kick the poor puppy,' he said. Da Savignano meant me, of course. I was the puppy to be kicked.

'If you *mercenaries* could bestir yourselves to seize Piacenza, the shoe would be firmly on our foot, and Bernabò would have to drag his fat carcass back here!' Fontana said.

I thought that he had a point, but it probably wasn't a good time to debate it.

Fontana gave me a long look, his eyes full of rage. I didn't think that I deserved his rage, so I raised my eyebrows.

'Bah, you are only here to loot out farms,' he said. 'Why did I ever hope for more?'

He stormed out.

Hawkwood smiled. 'That man has never been on a farm in his life,' he said. He met my eye. 'Well played,' he said. 'I would rather you'd told me, but I like that you kept it to yourself until you'd taken that nice little castle north of the city. That will be a burr under Galeazzo's saddle. I wager he offers us a thousand florins for it.' He pushed a wine cup across. 'I'm sorry to have bitten at you,' he said. 'You did right, of course.'

I felt that I was living in one of the more comic chansons. I had no idea what he was talking about.

For a moment. Then the light dawned. Sir John thought I'd kept the information back deliberately, until Lapot had taken the castle.

'This way, we've picked most of the farms clean. I have ten days' worth of food in my wagons,' Hawkwood said. He smiled at me again. 'You ain't usually so practical, young William.'

After a swig of wine, I took a breath to tell him that I hadn't known, and then decided against it. Instead, we were suddenly as intimates, and I leant back.

'And Piacenza?' I asked.

Hawkwood waved in its direction. 'Oh, pillage all you like,' he said. 'But Fontana's people can whistle for it, for all I care. We don't have the men or the siege train to take it, and if we took it, we'd be locked into a major siege all year.'

I didn't understand, and it must have showed on my face.

'Imagine us locked up inside Piacenza, facing Galeazzo and Bernabò,' Sir John said. 'Imagine how eager Galeazzo is to get his hands on you. Me, too, probably. And imagine that the Pope doesn't need to even *try* to pay us, because while we're safely locked up in Piacenza, we have no choice but to fight. And sieges are expensive, make no mistake. We buy food, we rent engineers, we pay peasants ...' He shook his head. 'If the Pope pays us, maybe then we'll take it.'

'You don't *want* to take Piacenza?' I asked, incredulous.

'Oh, William, you are such a kindly soul.' He smiled his devil's smile. 'I wish your chivalrous Count Amadeus of Savoy were here right now, because I'd make him tell you that *he* doesn't want us to take Piacenza either. Listen, my apprentice. We want a long war, fought as much as possible by manoeuvre, in untouched lands. And everyone but Bernabò and the Pope want a long war that exhausts the combatants but maintains the status quo ... including your precious Green Count.'

'So this whole expedition ...' I began.

'Is to get ourselves two months' worth of feed and fodder,' he said. 'And look, we snapped up a dozen castles – probably twenty thousand florins in ransoms.'

I sighed. 'Sir John, I was thinking that we were here to win the war for the Pope.'

'Oh, William,' he said, in mock despair.

The next morning, we were breaking camp and moving. Hawkwood's brigade was a mixture of Italian lances and 'English' soldiers – who were themselves a mixture of English, Bretons, Gascons, Germans, Hungarians, Greeks, Albanians, two Mamluks and an unbaptised Turk, but we were all 'English' in the eyes of the Italians. They might behave like brigands when they sacked a farm, but their discipline was excellent – we were moving in three columns before the last of the campfires was out. My breastplate was almost brown with rust because I didn't have a permanent squire, and the brown colour reflected my feelings in the present campaign.

I said something to Janet. I don't remember what I said, exactly – something bitter.

She furrowed her brow. It was an odd look on her. Listen, gentles, I don't praise Janet's beauty so much, because at some point she'd become a companion, a 'man-at-arms' in my mind, and I'd stopped looking at her as a woman. But when she furrowed her brow in concentration, the spell was somehow broken. I hope that I didn't laugh. She resented many things, my friend Janet.

'You are a prize,' she said fondly. 'What the hell did you think we were doing? Restoring Jerusalem to the Pope?'

'I thought that we were making war on the Visconti in the name of the Pope,' I said.

The sun was rising to the east, and it was going to be a beautiful day, marred only by the barns we'd set afire in every direction – one of Sir John's little stratagems to convince watchers we were still there.

She smiled at me, a brilliant, genuine smile. 'Guillaume, do you not love all this? The smell of smoke, the work, the scouting, the planning, the companionship?'

I suppose I shrugged. 'I could do without the smell of smoke,' I said. 'Otherwise, yes.'

'Then what difference does it make? A bad cause, a good cause ... no cause at all. It's all a game, and we're allowed to play. I wouldn't be anywhere else. I tried to go home ... You know that, right?'

I nodded. She'd gone home to France twice, once in '68 and again in '70, to look after her estates, or some such.

'One of my aunts asked me to visit, expressly to tell me that, as I had been raped, it was unlikely that I'd ever make a good marriage.' She kept her face blank, but I could see the anger. 'She told me that my only hope was to go into a convent.'

I probably looked as puzzled as I had when Hawkwood berated me for poor scouting.

'Oh, Guillaume, you have no fucking idea what it's like to be a woman. This is the *best* life I can imagine. A convent? A fucking convent?' She shook her head. 'You know that I'm rich, eh?'

I shook my head.

'I inherited from my father and both of his brothers. And now that the English are driven out, my lands pay.' She smiled, but the smile was bitter and false. 'Maybe I should marry someone and have some babies, eh?'

I shook my head again.

'You just don't understand. You think all this has to be *for something*.' She sat back in the saddle. 'We make war, Guillaume. It's what we do. If they're fools enough to pay us for it, why, it's on them to make it have purpose.'

'Just so,' Sir John said. He'd ridden up on my right hand, and the rising sun made him look like a ruddy picture of health, his bright armour lit salmon pink. He leant over and kissed Janet's cheek, the same kiss of peace he'd just given me. 'Lady Janet and I don't always see eye to eye, but in this, she is wisdom herself.'

'So we make war just to make war?' I asked.

'We make war to get paid,' Sir John said. 'And we leave anger and hate and all that trash to amateurs.'

'You see, Sir John, we already differ,' Janet said. 'I don't give a fart for getting paid. I just want to fight.'

John Hawkwood *crossed himself.* 'Now God preserve us,' he said with a laugh. 'I am your perfect opposite. I would be delighted to go the rest of my life without a single fight, as long as I got paid.'

I was pleased to see the two of them laughing together, and we rode across the sunlit morning, heading east towards Piacenza, with the produce of a hundred farms in our wagons and a line of fires throwing smoke into the cold winter air.

Sir John watched it all with satisfaction.

'Don't you think Milan can feel our warmth?' he asked me.

'Do we care?' I asked, probably pettishly. 'I thought we were only here for profit.'

Hawkwood smiled. 'William, you are so good at war that it is always a delight to find something I can still teach you.' He smiled. 'We desire to make ourselves rich. We need to survive to make ourselves rich. But we must have a puissant repute to evoke fear, and to invite the highest price. Fear saves us fighting – the price helps us get rich.'

'And the Pope?' I asked.

You might have thought Hawkwood would deliver something like 'Sod the Pope,' but he seldom used foul language. He was a parvenu as well as a Tard-Venu, and he worked hard to appear urbane, chivalrous and courteous. It made him a much better commander.

'The Pope's concerns are only our concerns when he pays regularly,' Hawkwood said. 'Even then, like most amateur commanders, he lives in a dream world of complex stratagems and manoeuvres. Even now, he imagines that Savoy will sweep down on Pavia from the north while we march in from the east.'

'Whereas my esteemed cousin Amadeus is actually sitting on his arse wondering how to avoid direct war with his brother-in-law,' Janet added.

'And we haven't been paid. Sometimes I wonder if these great monarchs are serious themselves. Perhaps they view it all as a game.' Hawkwood shrugged. He reached back to his squire. 'Gloves, if you please,' he said. 'I want to make sure all the wagons are rolling. William, please take the vanguard.'

38

'Of course, my lord,' I said, in French, the international language of war.

I gathered my 'household' and got out ahead of the main column. We might have been stopped at the narrow stone bridge over the Po, but we weren't – there really was no opposition.

László – or rather, Ser László – my Hungarian prisoner, was riding with Janet. I could tell that he wanted to talk to me, but I ignored him until all of my orders had been given. I left Tom Fenton in charge of our northern castle, with orders to surrender immediately if more than five hundred men appeared, on the terms that he be allowed to retreat to Castell'Arquato. I left La Motte to hold Castell'Arquato with ten men-at-arms and as many archers. After some discussion with Bibbo, Christopher was named master archer of the detachment, with extra pay. I hated to leave him – I enjoyed his conversation. But Janet was right, and Bibbo agreed – Christopher deserved to be his own man. He was a natural scout and raider, not a squire yearning for chivalry.

I told La Motte to hold that castle forever, if required. The place was victualled and virtually impregnable.

Then, shorn of twenty lances, I spread my remaining thirty across the countryside. Lapot stayed on the north side of the Po, moving cautiously across the frozen fields from wood to wood, covering our flank, gathering news. The rest were at the front of the column, heading for Piacenza. Because I'd dispersed so many of my lances to hold our precious castles, I was out with the screen myself, in high boots and a coat of maille, on a riding horse.

It was mid-morning before I had time for László, but our arrangements were made, and I'd sent Janet along the whole line of the screen to order a halt.

'You need a trumpeter,' László said. 'In Hungary, we use a trumpeter to control the light cavalry.'

I was sitting on my Giulia, watching the hill village to my right and the road to Piacenza.

'It would certainly help,' I agreed. 'I'm not sure where to find one in the rain.'

László laughed. 'Listen, Messire Vilmos, I wish to join your *compagnia*. If you will return my harness and forget my ransom, I will serve you for three months.'

I looked back at Marc-Antonio, who had dismounted and was

holding his squire's horse while both of them looked at her shoes. Marc-Antonio picked up a back foot, whistled, and pulled his rondel dagger, but he turned his head and looked at me. He made a face – a very Venetian face, that meant something like 'easy come, easy go.'

'If you want to be paid as a lance, you'll have to find an archer and an armed squire. Best if you also find a page.' I think I smiled. 'I'm sure they'll be standing around with the trumpeter.'

László laughed again. 'I accept. I'll find them somewhere. Perhaps when we face Baumgarten I can get my own squire and archer back, eh?'

'Or desert us for your friends,' I said.

László's face changed. 'You know why you captured me?' he asked.

'You were in an unsupported picket?' I asked.

László spat. 'I have been fighting since I was sixteen. The bastards left me to be taken – there was supposed to be a line of cavalry behind me. And why? Because I killed one of the fat Germans in a fair fight.' He spat on the ground.

I sighed. 'If you kill anyone in my company in a fight, fair or otherwise, you'll be hanged. Or at least sent away and your armour stripped. No duelling. No plunder unless I say. No rape. I'm paying fourteen ducats a month, all found.'

He whistled between his teeth. 'That's well below the market,' he said. 'I mean, you have my armour and my warhorse. But Florence is paying twenty.'

I smiled. 'Martin?' I called out to Marc-Antonio's Flemish archer. 'When were you last paid?'

Martin laughed. In broad Flemish French he said, 'Three weeks?', looking at the watery sun. 'Feast of Saint Crispin, give or take a day. We was west of Bologna.' After a significant pause, he remembered his manners. 'Er ... my lord.'

László raised an eyebrow.

'I pay,' I said. 'And I pray the Pope eventually pays me.'

László nodded. 'I see,' he agreed. 'Very well. I will take your miserable fourteen ducats, and find myself a page who knows horses, an armed squire, and an archer. Will you let me go on the archer until I can get my own back? He's very good.'

I smiled, and we shook hands.

László's French was accented but excellent, and he himself looked like an angel. He was as handsome as either of the Birigucci brothers, with long, straight blond hair and a pointed beard. He was big, and his laugh was booming.

'You've made a good bargain there,' Janet said. 'I like him.'

I thought he was lying about something, myself, but I liked him, too. I was just worried that he was planted by the Visconti, and I set Witkin to be his archer ... and to watch him.

Altogether, these things made it a good day. As we moved along the banks of the Po, we picked up outposts and followed our guides, and when the rain stopped, it was beautiful.

We made camp under the village I'd seen, which was called Stradella. We requisitioned food and got it, because the villagers, despite their lofty position, were terrified of us. We ate well, slept dry enough, and moved again at first light.

We were an army composed almost entirely of cavalry. That is, Sir John's forces usually fought on foot, but we all had mounts – most of us had two and some men had four. Our wagons were drawn by horses, not oxen, and they were small. In fact, on this march, we had a few heavy ox-drawn wains, full of fodder and grain, but as soon as we consumed the contents, we left the beasts and the wagons for the villagers behind us.

My point is that, unencumbered by a few thousand heavily armoured militiamen, we moved very fast. Fifteen English miles a day was our normal pace, and we could do twice that if required, although it was hard on the baggage animals. Some men, like Lapot's outriders or any archer in my lances, were riding twice that, out and back, but they didn't have to worry about the baggage, either.

So the next day, with no rain and a bright sun, we rolled fast, with half our force ready to deploy to the north, but nothing molested us or slowed us ...

Until we hit the tide of refugees pouring out of Piacenza. The road ahead of my scouts was packed with people. I could see them boiling out of the city like ants from a disturbed nest.

I was with Janet and her squire. We were spread so thin that our archers were off on their own to the north, and I cursed my foolishness for not holding a reserve on the road. War has a tendency to punish errors ruthlessly, and often.

I did have Marc-Antonio to hand, and I sent him for a dozen lances from Sir John with a warning of what lay ahead. And a request that Ser Dondazio Fontana be sent forward to me.

In a quarter of an hour, Janet and I had ridden in among the fleeing townspeople and heard something of their story. A Florentine merchant begged to move his cart in among our baggage, and in return he poured out a tale of atrocity, as apparently the Visconti garrison was massacring people.

'The town council wanted to open the gates to the exiles,' another man shouted. 'It's our right!'

At this, a few of the people on the road raised their voices, but most of them walked on, their faces set.

'The podestà set fire to the town hall,' the merchant said. 'I knew it was time to go.'

I sent him back to our baggage carts, and found László and Beppo had appeared.

Beppo was usually with Lapot. He pointed east, down our road.

'Beppo says, you never make it through all this.' He shrugged. 'Beppo found another bridge, south. Different road.'

A few paces down the road, a well-dressed woman caught sight of Beppo's face and crossed herself. Even in the midst of a rout.

Beppo grinned like Satan. 'Eh, you like what you see, *madonna*?' he called out. He smiled as she blanched and turned away. 'Always they find me so handsome,' he said.

'Where is this road south?' I asked.

'A mile back, more or less,' Beppo said. 'Beppo will guide.'

'László, go with him. Take ... both Birigucci boys.'

Janet laughed. 'All of our fallen angels together.'

I was looking north, at the distant city.

'What do we do?' asked Janet.

'We go back,' I said, but somewhere in the process of talking, I'd been surrounded by angry people. I think they'd seen my sword and half-armour and assumed I was one of the podestà's men. But they were frightened, and angry. Half of them were already running, or rather plodding, across the muddy fields, and the rest began to throw stones.

Beppo broke free of the crowd, leading 'his' knights. The crowd pushed in around us, and I got hit in the helmet by a clod of mud. My horse was hit. I reached for my sword – a bad answer, but the only one I had to hand.

Janet pulled off her basinet and shook out her hair. I've seen it before – the presence of a woman does a great deal to reassure people. In addition, it became obvious we weren't the podestà's men, and before a full riot could evolve, Fontana finally came up with a dozen of his own Piacenzan exiles. He was a superb horseman, I had to give him that, and he and his men were well mounted and well armed.

Some of the refugees cheered him. Some heckled, and many more crowded round, silently.

Fontana looked at me with narrowed eyes. 'Now what have you done?' he asked me in Italian.

'Nothing,' I said.

'Exactly,' he spat. 'Nothing.' He was, as usual, angry. He reminded me of someone, and I couldn't quite pin down who that was.

A young William Gold might have had to take him on about that, but mature, thirty-two-year-old William Gold just let him calm the exiles who crowded around him. More stories emerged. The garrison had killed and plundered a dozen houses, all belonging to the council of the town. Then someone had set fire to the town hall and the fire had spread, and with it, panic.

I could see the smoke rising.

Janet voiced my thoughts exactly. 'I wonder if the gates are open,' she said.

'Now you want to take the town?' Fontana snapped.

In truth, he was a difficult man to like. Perhaps exiles are always angry, but they make wearing companions. And of course, in a way, he was right.

I was watching a mass of grey, black and brown robes coming down the road. Monks and nuns. A bad sign for a town, as usually the religious orders stay put.

'Ser Dondazio Fontana,' I said, 'we need to get out of here.'

'These are my people, you worthless son of a whore mercenary.' He gestured.

I ignored him, because there was the flash of steel at the back of the religious crowd and a flash of gold at the front. This was going to get ugly. The religious houses were saving their relics, and the Germans . . .

'I'll leave you to them, then,' I said.

I gave him a polite wave, or at least that's how I'd like to remember it, but no one likes to be called the son of a whore. But before I could turn my horse, I heard my name being called, and there, once again, was Sister Marie. She was mounted on a good mule, on the saddle that Nerio had had made for her years before. I thought for a moment about my sister, and how alike they were, as Sister Marie was also a natural rider.

Behind her was her armoured bishop, whom I had no reason to like, and a flood tide of habits, brown, grey, black and white – monks, nuns and priests.

'William!' she shouted, and raised her hand.

She was holding a wooden cross, decorated with gold. It was some precious thing being taken to safety, no doubt, but she parted the refugees like Moses parting the Red Sea, and rode through. She had a brilliant courage, that woman. What a knight she would have made!

Regardless, she rode right up to us.

'William, the Visconti's bravos are killing innocents in the city,' she said, as if I could lower my lance – I didn't *have* a lance at that moment – and ride to their rescue.

'I can't—'

'There are fifty mounted crossbowmen coming after us,' Sister Marie said. 'They are looting the churches, William!'

I was tempted to say that they probably hadn't been paid, either, but I didn't. Instead, I looked back, past her bishop. There was a flash of steel, and screaming from the back of the mass of religious people.

I had Janet, and the uncertain assistance of Fontana and his half a dozen exiles, and my little force was trapped in the midst of a thousand refugees. But as the screams rose from the back of the column, the refugees scattered, running into the sodden fields on either side of the road, burrowing into hedgerows like rabbits running from dogs.

The mass of monks and nuns tried to break off towards me, but the men pursuing them were faster. Now I could see them, their swords rising and falling.

I was damned if I was going to sit and watch. Remember, though, that we were all in maille, without our warhorses or our good armour. I had a pair of Turkish javelins under my right knee, laced to my saddle. Janet had a light crossbow, a lady's toy for hunting birds.

I glanced over at Fontana. 'I intend to charge those men,' I said.

His lip curled. He was considering something nasty – a comment on my birth, or worse. But he never let it out. He wasn't an utter fool. Instead, he drew his sword.

'*Alora*,' he said in Italian.

I gave a last glance back up the road, on the off chance that Marc-Antonio and the legions of Heaven were riding to my rescue, but all I could see was that half a thousand muddy refugees were now between me and my retreat. And Beppo, pushing through them, alone. He was the right man to push a horse through a desperate crowd. In a moment, he came up.

'We're going to try to stop their soldiers from killing those nuns,' I said.

Beppo's face wore a strange, almost serene, expression. 'This will be a funny way to die,' he said. 'Beppo dies to save nuns. He likes it.' He smiled. 'So ... unexpected.'

'This way,' I called, and rode off to the right, where the hedgerow would screen us from the crossbowmen for about half the distance. I'd already seen a gap or a gate. There was a muddy lane – bad, but not as bad as trying to pass the fields. Giulia was none too pleased at the footing, but she put her head down and persevered, and we got to the gap. I looked back, and only Beppo and Janet had followed me.

'Fontana is trying to ride through the monks,' Janet said.

On the other side of the hedge, the muddy lane ran in more or less the correct direction back to the road from a small house surrounded by hedges. The yard was packed with people from the city – a woman on a horse, a man on a mule, a pedlar with his basket. They were watching me the way cattle will watch a wolf. I noticed them without really seeing them. My eyes were on the enemy, and I only looked into the yard to make sure it didn't hide more Germans.

I rode right past them, moving at a steady walk. I met the eye of the man on a mule, and then saw that the woman was my age, a matron well dressed in a wool gown and a veil that was pushed up under a man's bycoket. By her was a woman on foot with a basket, trying to defend the basket from a pair of ragamuffins.

I didn't have time to interfere.

Then I was past the corner of the hedge, looking at the mounted crossbowmen, a particularly Italian variety of soldiers, as they terrorised the monks and nuns. Now they were perhaps a hundred paces away. As I watched them, they, in turn, watched Fontana and his knights. A couple spanned their small crossbows without dismounting, and shot at the onrushing knights.

Onrushing is inaccurate, Master Froissart. The Italian knights were pushing through a tide of desperate clerics like a man swimming in gravy. The German or Italian mounted crossbowmen had no compunction about killing a few nuns or priests, and they began to snap their crossbows at the handful of Italian knights.

I was moving by then. The mounted crossbowmen were standing their ground, killing civilians. While I watched, they got one of the knights. It made no sense – they should have broken away immediately.

Instead, they were utterly focused on the exiles. And as I put my weight forward and got Giulia to a heavy, muddy canter, I heard a voice shouting in German. There was a big German knight in the road, wearing a monk's habit over his armour.

I was perhaps ten paces out when he noticed me. He was wearing a basinet with a brim instead of a visor – very popular with commanders, that style.

He roared something and turned his big warhorse to face me. He had a long, heavy sword in his hand, and he was an expert rider on an excellent horse. His horse pivoted like a dancer, his arm went back, and he cut precisely.

I cut, too. Luck, and training, put my cut and his in the same line. Our edges bit with a shock, and the Emperor's sword cut a chunk out of his blade that shattered away, burning like a star. His blade deflected mine, mostly because that's what I wanted. Now his horse was head to head with mine, but I was moving and he wasn't, so that I started to pass him, my hilt rotating.

I went for the throw, trying to get my arm across his throat. He snapped his helmeted head back, leaning in the saddle, and I missed my grapple. There was a tug, and I was past him and into the crossbowmen, who were on small horses like Giulia and who wore only light armour.

I saw Janet shoot one, her crossbow held in one hand. She passed the man she'd shot and slammed her pretty little birding bow into the second man. The steel prod caught on his helmet, and she dragged him from his saddle. I'd already knocked one of the crossbowmen unconscious with a heavy cut to his helmet.

Over to my left, the exile knights were into the front of the crossbowmen, and suddenly it was a rout, and they broke away like so many songbirds.

There was blood dripping from my quillons, which seemed odd, as I hadn't killed anyone.

The Monk of Hecz was no friend of mine, and I'd last seen him two years before. Apparently he was now holding Piacenza for the Visconti. Which was ironic, as he'd last been in the employ of the Prince of Achaea – against the Visconti.

On the other hand, almost everyone had jumped sides that winter. I didn't love him, though – he'd handed me over to the Bourc Camus, in clear violation of the laws of war. But that was all old news.

What wasn't old news was that Fontana, the leader of the exiles, was down. He had a crossbow bolt in his forearm, and he was down on the muddy road, pinned by the weight of a very expensive and very dead warhorse. The Monk of Hecz could be heard rallying his mounted crossbows. Bolts began to plough little furrows around me.

Of course they wanted Fontana. That's why they'd stuck around to fight. The reward for killing the leader of the opposition was always high in Italian cities.

Giulia was about done, and Janet, unwounded, was backing her horse – one of our Arabs, and capable of endless endurance with a light rider.

'Get help,' I said.

She just shook her head, dropped the wreck of her crossbow in the road, and drew her sword.

I dismounted. A bolt hit my shoulder and punched me from my feet to sprawl in the wet gravel.

'Fuck!' I spat, or some such, but the maille of my aventail and the maille of my haubergeon had combined to save me, although the bruise lasted for weeks. In fact, the bolt was stuck in my shoulder, which I didn't know immediately. The head had burst the rings on the aventail, but didn't get through the padding and the second layer of maille underneath.

Ha! Some things you remember clearly, like not being dead.

The pain focused me. And by good fortune, or the blessing of Saint Michael, it began to rain. I won't say it was out of a clear blue sky, but the weather changed suddenly. The temperature dropped, then there was rain. The accuracy and the range of the crossbows dropped.

The other exiles were shouting back and forth to one another. With Fontana down, it was clear that no one was in charge, and that they were shaken.

And I didn't think they'd follow me. It will sound ridiculous to you gentlemen, but because I wasn't dressed as a knight, in my good harness, I suspected they'd ignore anything I said, and I wasn't eager to try.

Instead, I got the butt of Fontana's broken lance under his saddle and used it as a crowbar. It took me three tries, but by then Beppo had got the idea. He leapt down and got his hands under the wounded knight's shoulders. I lifted, my new shoulder wound screaming, and Beppo, who was as strong as I, pulled. Fontana mostly just screamed.

And ... pop. Like a baby being born, we had him, armour and all. Beppo fell backwards, just as a crossbow bolt went 'slup' into the dead horse, as if to punctuate our efforts.

About this time, the Monk of Hecz had convinced his crossbowmen to charge us. He had quite a flock of them, but they weren't really up to facing knights. The exiles were still there, although wavering – ten fully armoured men on big horses.

I think the Monk assumed they'd run. To be fair, I was worried they'd run, but the nearest – a slim man in a beautiful great helm with a swan atop it – actually flicked me a salute with his lance, as yet unbroken. His horse gave a little rear, as if ready to joust.

The young man shouted, 'We need to cover our lord!' in good Italian. This very sensible injunction stopped the three men who'd been edging back. Honour was now at stake.

Thank God.

I got the wounded man across Janet's saddle.

'Go and get help,' I said, for the second time.

'You're making me miss all the fun,' she said, but she took the wounded man and rode away.

It took me two tries to get a leg over my horse, and this was a riding horse, not a destrier.

'Jesu, Capo! You have a crossbow bolt in your back,' Beppo said.

Before I could panic, he'd leant over and pushed it through the maille.

'Bah!' he said. 'Here's a little toy to keep for old age. If you ever get there.' He handed me the bolt. I still have it somewhere.

I turned my head and watched the crossbowmen change direction and race away. As soon as it was clear that our Italians were coming for them, they ran. Our exile knights almost got the Monk of Hecz, but his horse was marginally better. They chased him to the bridge, though.

I was gathering the monks and nuns as best I could, wishing for any of my various clerical friends. Eventually, I found Sister Marie, who was, naturally enough, in the yard of the house off the road, with most of the wounded civilians laid out in rows on improvised pallets of damp straw. Father Angelo came up shortly afterwards with Sir John Thornbury, who had orders for me to retreat immediately, but when he saw the situation, he relented. John Thornbury and I tangled a few times over the years, as you'll hear, but he was a good knight. The sight of twenty wounded people lying in the rain moved him, which, I'm sad to say, would not have moved Sir John Hawkwood by so much as an inch.

Father Angelo began to organise the clerics, and then suddenly Sister Marie's bishop was shouting at him.

I knew the tone before I knew who it was. It's a tone I've heard many times, perhaps used myself. When you are new to violence, it makes you afraid, but also angry – angry at the world that allows such things to happen.

The bishop was an aristocrat, a Roman, and he'd probably never seen a fight in his life. And now he was shouting at Father Angelo that he and his people needed to leave, right then.

I was resting Giulia, doing simple things for Sister Marie, like making a fire to heat water. I was a cook's boy. I can start a fire in the rain. And in some conditions, that's as heroic as winning a skirmish with the Monk of Hecz. I was just blowing on the sparks I had on my mostly dry charcloth, trying to coax them and a little dry tow into flame when the shouting started.

I could hear Sister Marie's voice – strong, calm, insistent. I could hear Father Angelo losing his temper. And I remained focused on my embers, which is both a failing and a skill I have. I shut things out and concentrate. Sometimes too hard.

Regardless, I got the top to burn, and suddenly I had a handful of fire. I tossed it into my little pile of shavings, bark and damp twigs.

'Get out my way, you useless hedge-priest!' roared Sister Marie's bishop, at Angelo Di Cavalli, born of the best blood of Verona, a cousin to the De La Scala.

The woman I'd seen earlier – middle-aged or a little younger, with a servant – was standing close by me.

I pointed at the young flames. 'Can you blow on them?' I snapped.

'You think I don't know how to make fire, eh?' she spat.

I suppose that counted as a formal introduction. Italian women are often touchy, but then, they have to deal with Italian men so often.

I darted away, if a man can 'dart' in chain maille, fatigue and pain. I came around the farmhouse from the firepit and found Father Angelo squared up to Sister Marie's bishop, who was in full armour.

Sister Marie had walked away. That will tell you how disgusted she was.

'Gentlemen,' I said. I can be very loud.

They both turned their heads.

'You are frightening people,' I said – very loudly.

It got through to Father Angelo. He stepped back, but the bishop stepped forward, his rings flashing on his gloved hands.

'Down in the mud and beg my forgiveness, you cur!' he shouted, spittle flying.

I have every reason to remember this incident, as you'll hear, but one of the things I remember best is that I asked myself how John Hawkwood would deal with this. And I knew the answer. He'd deal with it without anger, without fear.

I stepped between them. 'Your Grace is intemperate,' I said, using Sir John's tone of voice.

I looked past him, where I could see William Blood, one of Sir John Thornbury's best men-at-arms, coming round the barn on horseback, responding to the sound of voices.

'Intemperate!' the bishop tried to roar, but I stepped inside his space, so to speak, very close indeed, without touching him.

'Your Grace is needed giving people *comfort.*' Damn it, I was channelling Hawkwood pretty well.

'No one tells me what to do!' he said, but his voice was quieter.

I was very tempted to tell him what I thought of a shepherd of the Church in full armour who hadn't bothered to turn his horse and fight. But instead, I put a hand on his shoulder.

'These people are terrified,' I said quietly. 'It is our duty to help them.'

'Now I receive lessons from a routier,' he said, but his voice was calm. He was younger than I'd expected – closer to sixteen than twenty. But he didn't shake off my hand on his shoulder. Very quietly, he said, suddenly, 'I was terrified myself.'

I nodded. 'Everyone is, Your Grace. Go and help, now, please.'

Will Blood gave me a look that I treasured. As the bishop strode away, Blood shook his head.

'I were goin' to punch him, like,' he said.

'Very tempting,' I admitted.

'Sir John – by whom I mean Thornbury – he says we need to get gone.' Blood was watching towards the city gates through the curtain of rain.

'I can't see them coming for us here,' I said. 'We don't have Lord Fontana, for one thing.'

Blood shrugged, as I was no great shakes for him, and Thornbury was probably the only lord he knew.

But when I slipped back to my fire, it was burning merrily. The lady was kneeling on a wooden board to keep her heavy wool skirts out of the mud, blowing through a hollow reed.

'Do I know how to keep a fire, then?' she asked acidly.

'You are the very essence of fire, Siora,' I replied, with my best courtly bow, somewhat inhibited by aching hips and a wounded shoulder.

Her expression changed, her asperity replaced by what I hoped was a natural good humour. 'Did I just hear you mention the very noble lord Fontana?' she asked. Suddenly the termagant was gone, replaced by a courteous matron with a smile that was *almost* flirtatious.

'Lord Fontana is wounded,' I said. As a soldier, I have had to tell harsh truths to a number of people, and one of the things I've learnt is to be direct, even blunt. If this lady was his wife ...

She put a hand to her bosom. She didn't turn white. But she met my eyes directly for the first time. 'How badly?' she asked.

How round is a circle? You can die of a cut to your hand, or survive a stab in the guts.

'He took a bolt in his shoulder and had a fall from his horse,' I said, staying to my doctrine of bluntness.

She took a sharp breath. 'Do you have any idea where he was taken?' she asked.

I shook my head. 'I sent him with one of my knights,' I said. 'I would hope he is with the Sieur de Coucy and his doctor by now.'

She nodded.

I lost her in the next minutes, as my fire was crackling away, burning fast enough that suddenly it needed more fuel. Foraging firewood in the rain is a basic soldier skill that remains current, no matter what rank I hold. I was scrambling for wood with my old friend Michael des Roches, and heating water for Sister Marie. Then, to my surprise, I was handing a big iron kettle of hot water to Sister Marie's bishop, who carried it away, his steel sabatons squelching in the mud.

Later that evening, we were all in a barn. Beppo had found it at the end of a long march, and my company had gathered in the whole of Sister Marie's bishop's retinue, mostly to have Sister Marie. She had half a dozen nuns with her, and they had a corner of the barn and their own fire. Sister Marie's bishop, whose name was Matteo Orsini, had his armour off. He sat on my spare stool with Michael des Roches and Father Angelo, the three of them debating the permanent return of the papacy to Rome. There was no sign whatsoever now that Orsini had called Father Angelo a 'hedge priest'. He sounded quite human – if very, very young.

'Men,' said Sister Marie. She shook her head, but took a swig from my wine flask. 'Here, I have a man I want you to meet. I think you'll be surprised.'

I shrugged. I was so happy to have her around that I was willing to put up with her less than effusive views on men, knighthood, chivalry ... and her friends. She left our little fire and fetched a man from the bishop's conversation – which, to be fair, was quickly turning into Michael des Roches's conversation, as he, a theological scholar of note, was holding forth.

John de Capell, when introduced, looked more like a knight than a priest. He was in the young bishop's retinue. He was English. He was a priest, and best of all, he knew my sister, and we heard a tale of her prowess during the plague that made my heart glow.

If you have sat at this table long enough, you know that I am as proud as Lucifer of my sister. She is a religious, vowed to the sisters of the Order of Saint John, and I expect that in time she'll be a prioress. During the last plague year, she gained some good fame visiting victims in London and elsewhere.

So you can guess that I was very willing to like John de Capell.

Sister Marie leant over and whispered very softly in my ear, 'He was the Duke of Clarence's chaplain.'

I think I may have jumped a handspan in the air, like a horse stung by a bee.

Sister Marie grinned. 'It is nice to surprise you from time to time.'

Michael, apparently done with his defence, or polemic, or what have you, came over. He looked at Sister Marie.

'You told him?'

'He jumped like a cat faced with a dog,' Sister Marie said.

John de Capell leant back against the slightly damp wall of the barn. He had on a cloak and a hood, so the damp wouldn't both him much. 'Are you three plotting?' he asked.

'I told William your secret,' Sister Marie said quietly.

Capell smiled. 'It's not so secret, now that my lord's will is published. I have written out a testament and left it with the Pope's secular secretary. He knows what's in it.'

'You know the duke was murdered,' I said.

'I *believe* the duke was murdered,' Capell said. He nodded to des Roches. 'As Michael will no doubt explain, belief and knowledge are seldom the same thing.'

'Sir William can read and write. In Latin,' Sister Marie said, before I could be further patronised.

Capell looked at me with real interest, peering through the smoke of the closed barn like a man buying a cow at a fair. 'Was you brought up to be a clerk, then?' he asked.

I smiled. 'No,' I said. 'The good sister here taught me Latin so that I could read Vegetius.'

'Vegetius?' Capell smiled. 'I copied Vegetius out for the duke. And Richard Musard.'

'Why do you believe the duke was murdered?' I asked.

He shrugged. 'Because, despite the rumours I now hear everywhere that he was a glutton and a lecher, he was neither – or at least, no more a glutton than any other rich man, no more a lecher than any

Plantagenet, and not at all once wed to the lady.' He nodded at Sister Marie. 'Sister Marie has heard all this before.'

I wanted to ask 'How are you alive?' but that seemed rude. However, Beppo and I had created layers of distractions to keep the duke's former cook alive. Visconti assassins were hunting her. Or so we *believed*.

Janet came back from fetching wine. I pointed to her.

'Anything I know, Janet knows,' I said.

Janet made a pretty courtesy, which looked a little odd as she was still wearing parts of her leg armour.

'You are a woman,' Capell said.

Janet raised an eyebrow, ready to fight. 'Yes,' she drawled.

'You are Musard's leman!' de Capell said, as if solving a difficult logic problem.

'I am Dame Janet de Sauveterre,' she said. 'I am no man's leman.'

Father de Capell flushed. 'My apologies, madame,' he said hurriedly. 'It's only that I have heard you praised so often.'

Janet managed a smile. 'That seems unlikely,' she said. 'As I am a woman in armour.'

Capell shrugged. 'Madame, I beg you to excuse me. And life as a chaplain to a Plantagenet prince does not incline me to make ... ahem ... *judgements* about the lives of others.'

'Father de Capell was Prince Lionel's chaplain,' I said.

Janet whistled. 'How are you alive?' she asked.

I probably laughed out loud.

Capell nodded at Sister Marie. 'This good sister of Christ gave me a warning two years ago, and I am living as a working scholar in a small monastery in Rome.'

'With me,' Michael des Roches said. He smiled. 'If I was an astrologer, William, I would guess that it was in my stars to be linked to you and your plots.'

'But you don't believe in astrology,' I said.

Michael frowned.

Capell shook his head. 'Michael is a deep well of unintended heresy.'

Des Roches smiled. 'I won't say that I don't believe,' he said. 'I'll merely say that I see the whole artifice of the new Platonism as ... resting on delicate foundations.'

Janet laughed. 'I like them,' she said. 'This is delightful. We need some educated men to travel with us all the time.' She smiled at Sister Marie, who smiled back. 'And women,' she added.

She and Sister Marie were each other's chaperones. Neither, strictly speaking, approved of the other, but they'd shared enough to be something like friends, and after the struggles of the day, everyone was very much at their ease.

Marc-Antonio was beside himself at having missed all the fighting. He'd gone for help and then been ordered away, leaving Sir John Thornbury to rescue us as best he could. He brought me my spare saddle to sit on, as if he was still my squire, and then settled by Janet.

'Did you see what happened to Lord Fontana's wife?' I asked Sister Marie. Des Roches and Capell were hard at it about the heavens and predestination, or that's how I remember it. Sister Marie looked bored.

She shook her head. 'I noted her,' she said. 'She did a nice job with the fire.'

Beppo appeared with my best camp chair, which he sat in. I was sitting on a saddle. Ah, the life of arms. Beppo ignored the two scholars.

'Beppo took her to Lord de Coucy,' he said, 'after Beppo saved the nuns and found the safe bridge. Beppo had a busy day.'

'Doubtless why Beppo gets the best chair,' I said, with what I hoped was humour.

'Yes,' Beppo said. 'Doubtless.'

'She was quite pretty, wasn't she?' Janet asked.

I shrugged. 'She could start a fire,' I said.

Sister Marie laughed. 'And she didn't like being told how, did she, William?'

I shook my head ruefully. Sister Marie laughed, and so did Janet.

'I don't think she's his wife,' Sister Marie went on. 'She's a volunteer with the lay Dominicans.' Her laugh vanished. 'She ought to be here with us. An army camp is not a good place to be as a woman, William.'

'If Beppo took her to Coucy, she's as safe as houses,' I said.

Sister Marie gave me a look I knew well, that suggested that women are never 'as safe as houses' in an army. But she relented.

I leant in. 'Is Capell really one of us?' I asked. *And does he know anything useful?* I wondered.

Sister Marie nodded. 'His role with the Duke of Clarence is public since the will was published, but *certes*, William, it was published in

England, not Rome or Milan. He's got his own money, and he's living quietly in Rome and I have Michael with him.'

I nodded. 'As usual, you are ahead of me.'

She made a face, mumbled something about the bar being low, and took another swig of my wine. Beppo was trying not to laugh, but he was leaning in.

'But does he know anything?' I asked.

'He knows that a man with a black beard came into the household the day that the duke got sick. He served one meal and the duke died.'

'Christ on the cross,' I blasphemed.

I remember it well, friends, because I did a little penance later. But I had had that very man, the poisoner assassin, as a prisoner, perhaps a week after the murder. We took him in the Bourc Camus's 'House of Madmen'. And somehow he escaped, and was still out there.

Sister Marie, who knew it all, shook her head. 'Blasphemy has no excuse,' she said. 'Christ died for your sins, not for your exclamation of surprise.'

'Yes, Sister,' I said.

We all drank a little too much. But it was a good night – the kind you remember later, when everything goes to shit. Sister Marie mocked Marc-Antonio's pretensions to manhood, and Janet joined her until we almost had blood on the floor. Suddenly Beppo was playing a pipe and we were dancing, including some of the younger nuns, one of whom danced with the bishop, who was laughing as if he'd never laughed before.

Later I found myself sitting by him. I had to ride my posts out in the darkness, so it was time to stop drinking, and I wasn't too far gone. Des Roches was already in his blankets, and so was Capell. Sister Marie was looking a little fuzzy, but she was sitting with Janet – hearing her confession, or so it appeared.

'Where are you headed, Your Grace?' I asked.

He smiled. 'Bed,' he said. 'Sweet Jesu, I don't have a bed.'

I pointed out Sam Bibbo. 'That man will get you a bale of straw, and perhaps even a cloak if you lack one, Your Grace,' I said.

'I'd never expected routiers to be so friendly. So courtly!' He laughed. 'But, as my father never hesitates to remind me, I know nothing.' He was suddenly grim. 'I was a fucking coward today. I hate it.'

'Ah, Your Grace,' I said. 'Look at me.'

He did.

'Are you a veteran knight? A hardened commander?' I stared him down. 'Not knowing what to do is not the same as cowardice. Fear is not cowardice.' I shrugged. 'I have to go and look at my pickets. Where are you bound after tonight?'

'You and Sister Marie are lovers?' he blurted.

He was, what ...? Sixteen? I suppose that at his age, both of us were so horribly old that we might be any kind of sinner, and Rome is a cesspool.

Sister Marie was watching her nuns with a proprietary eye – the eye of a commander who wants to make sure the troops have some fun, but not too much fun. Janet was weeping. I looked at Sister Marie, who gave me a shake of the head. *Look away.*

I definitely loved Sister Marie, but had never felt the slightest attraction. Isn't that odd? I'm a lovesome man, as I've said, but Sister Marie ... it was a joy to see her. I'd learnt a great deal from her. And I'd seen her be a woman – cursing the cow turds in Spain, hoisting her skirts to run, laughing ...

And yet, of that attraction, nothing. Or not much. I had to smile inwardly. I'd seen her naked, once, and been struck by how ... athletic her body was. I just hadn't expected her to have a body, I suppose.

I smiled. 'No. Never.' Mostly true, anyway.

The young bishop slumped. 'There ... Put my foot in it again, haven't I?'

I shrugged. 'It's not really a nice thing to say of a devout nun,' I said. 'But we are old friends. She was my wife's confessor.'

'Christ,' he swore. 'In Rome, we assume any girl in a convent ...' He looked up. 'I'm a fool as well as a coward.'

My smile probably got a little frosty. 'If I were you, Your Grace, I'd avoid making such an assumption about Sister Marie.' I could hear Father Pierre Thomas in my mind. 'Or any other woman,' I added.'

He shook his head.

Well. I remember being sixteen, and I hadn't been burdened with an amethyst ring and a tonsure.

And later that night, after I'd visited all my pickets and bedded down my horse, I thought about what it would do to you, to be a bishop at sixteen, full of sex and foolishness. But a bishop ... So that every time you kissed a pretty nun or even fancied one, you were committing a whole variety of sins.

It could drive you to being a very bad person indeed, very quickly, eh?

Maybe I was lucky, being just a cook's boy in France. I saw evil from the bottom, so to speak.

In the morning I collected my company, such as it was, and found that I'd inherited Fontana's knights. They'd followed the Birigucci brothers home like stray kittens. In fact, they needed fodder for their horses and they needed help untacking. They were drawn to us because we suddenly had a tail of Piacenzan refugees, most of them farmers and local merchants. I put Lapot and l'Angars out in the rain as soon as it was light and then spent the morning, fully armed as a proper knight, with Janet beside me, cap-à-pie, enlisting a dozen new pages for my sudden wealth in Piacenzan refugees. I didn't have archers to give to the exile knights, but I assumed they'd be gone as soon as their lord recovered from his wound.

They were very young men, all seventeen to twenty, and it proved that the skirmish had been their first action.

The young knight who'd rallied them was a young member of the mighty Pallavicini family, Andrea Carlo-Maria Pallavicino, to give you the full mouthful. He looked at me in my fine Brescian armour and shook his head. 'Yesterday I thought you were some sort of routier,' he said.

And today you are some sort of routier. His words grated on me. Once again, I kept my mouth shut, and signed him on.

I lent Sam Bibbo to Sister Marie. They were old comrades, and he got her nuns mounted on 'borrowed' donkeys and mules and sorted them out. There were a dozen monks and priests with the bishop, including John de Capell, and he didn't seem to care much what happened to them, but Sam shamed him into paying for horses. It proved that he was very rich.

Sam is very good at this sort of thing.

That all happened miles behind me, however, because as soon as we'd straightened out our personnel issues, I was ahorse, moving back into the vanguard.

In late afternoon, a young shepherd rode in on a pony, with a sealed scroll from Lapot. It said that Bernabò was ahead of us, already in the fields around Bologna by the northern route. I left l'Angars in command and rode to Hawkwood.

'Quite an adventure yesterday, young William,' he said curtly.

I smiled. 'The Monk of Hecz is commanding the sallies from Piacenza,' I said.

Of course, Hawkwood had been elsewhere when I was dealing with the Monk, but I explained.

He nodded, as if my personal rancour for the man made sense of the whole thing.

'If I thought you'd almost lost my advance guard for a bevy of nuns, I'd have to admonish you,' he added. Then he read the note from Lapot and cursed. 'Bernabò is a *week* ahead of us.'

'Yes, sir,' I said.

He shook his head. 'No more knight errantry, William. Please.'

I wanted to explain that it had developed faster than I could ride out of it, but there was no point.

'And next time, please leave Ser Dondazio to die,' he said, with a little savagery. 'I'm that tired of listening to him.'

I couldn't tell whether he was serious.

'Did his wife find you?' I asked.

'Oh, the lady?' Hawkwood shook his head. 'I have men buzzing around her like flies. She's in his tent, which is to say he's in my tent.' He looked at me. 'I would be very pleased if you'd take them all, as I hear you've absconded with his men-at-arms.'

Sir John was not in a good mood.

I ignored his mood. 'One of my rescues is an Orsini bishop,' I said. 'In his train is a man named John de Capell. An Oxford graduate.'

Hawkwood looked at me. 'I am not particularly interested in theology,' he said.

'The Duke of Clarence's chaplain,' I said.

Hawkwood turned his head very slowly to look at me. 'Ahh,' he said.

'He has information that confirms—'

'Yes,' said Hawkwood. 'Write it all down and then bury it. That's an order.'

I nodded. 'Yes, Sir John.'

'And take Fontana,' Hawkwood snapped. 'He's all yours.'

59

The rain had stopped, and our camps were all together on a long ridge south of the river. I wasn't going to tell Sir John that I had fifteen nuns in my own pavilion, and I was sharing a couple of blankets with Marc-Antonio and my new pages. I had two, both local farmers' boys, both sixteen, and both in love with horses.

So, with Sam Bibbo and Ewan and a couple of my veteran archers, I moved the wounded knight into l'Angars's pavilion. I got them half a dozen servants from the refugees, and the lady moved into my pavilion with the nuns.

All in a day's work.

When my horses were all tacked down, and as clean as damp straw and fatigue could make them, with Tommaso and Marco, my eager grooms, hard at work, I found Sister Marie sharing my wine store with the women in my pavilion.

I called her outside, drank my wine out of her wooden cup, and waved over the hills towards the south.

'We're going to move fast the next few days,' I said. 'Bernabò is currently between us and Rome, so I think you need to stay with us.'

Sister Marie snatched her cup back with a smile, finished the wine, and tucked her arm through mine.

'Nothing would suit me better,' she said. 'Honestly. I have a heaven-sent opportunity to whip these ladies into something like discipline, surrounded by men and war. I'd never get this done in a scriptorium in Rome. Who knows? Maddalena may yet join us and take the veil.'

'Maddalena?'

'Your Lord Fontana's sister. Half-sister?' She shrugged. 'She's very pious. And she really doesn't have anywhere else to go just now. They burnt her house because of her brother, or so I hear.'

'We'll cover ten miles or more tomorrow,' I said.

She nodded. 'I'm sure we'll be fine,' she said, in a tone that was meant to remind me that I'd seen her *walk* farther than that in a day.

I had my pickets move out before the sun broke above the rim of the world, and the next day I was with them. We left the river at Piacenza, where it swings east. We didn't follow it. Instead, we raced down the Via Emilia for Parma and Reggio Emilia. We held all the bridges now, and the only limiting factor was our big wains of fodder, which we wouldn't give up because they saved us money. Looked at another way, they saved us from plundering the poor peasants again.

On the day we passed south of Parma, I launched a little expedition of my own. I got together half a dozen of my best veterans – Lapot, with Grice and Beppo, Ewan and Gospel Mark – and a pair of guides I'd kidnapped from the market. We gave them the pick of our still excellent horse herd and sent them off north.

I wanted to know where the hell Bernabò was. I could tell that Coucy felt defeated and Hawkwood was bored.

The next morning I told Hawkwood what I'd done and he slapped my back. 'Well done,' he said. 'Keep me informed.'

In fact, we were west of Modena when I got word from Lapot that he had Bernabò's camp under observation.

'He's had days to loot the suburbs of Bologna,' he wrote, along with some details of the force and camp. Bernabò had three thousand horses and some foot, according to Lapot.

I went straight to Hawkwood, and reported. It was bitingly cold in his pavilion, despite two braziers burning fiercely. The whole tent smelt of charcoal, and the roof was starting to turn red-brown from the smoke. Everyone in the camp had a cough.

Hawkwood slapped my back as if I was his oldest friend. Whatever had been eating him two days before was gone.

'Well done,' he said.

He called in Thornbury and the other officers, who included Richard Romney, John Brice and William Tilly, as I remember, and together we went over the pilgrim itineraries between Modena and Bologna. It didn't take us long to determine that Bernabò must be on the other road from Pavia to Bologna – the northern way.

'He's camped at Bargellino,' I said, from Lapot's note.

On a wax tablet, Thornbury, a literate man, made a picture of the suburbs of Bologna. We all knew them. Bargellino is a village to the north-west of the city, outside the walls.

'Fortified camp?' asked Thomas Biston. He'd been with Hawkwood since the old days of the White Company, and he didn't mince words.

'If Lapot didn't say fortified, I'm going to assume it's open.' I shrugged.

Hawkwood waved at the pitcher of very cold red wine. 'Pour yourself another,' he said. 'I'm going to go and report all this to Coucy.'

Richard Romney made a face. 'You're the real commander,' he said. Which was, to all intents, true.

Hawkwood shook his head. 'Coucy is competent. He's just not very interested. And Este is also competent. In fact, Romney, this army probably has the best commanders you'll see in this war. Which will not stop us from accomplishing very little.'

He ducked out, and Romney was sullen. There'd been a time when we got along very well, but something had come between us.

Regardless, we drank a second cup of wine, freezing our teeth and talking about swords, I think, or maybe songs. Who knows? And then Hawkwood returned with Coucy and Este and Malatesta.

'Gentlemen,' he said. Of course we all stood.

We went over it all again. But this time, it was decisive.

Coucy had more life in his face than I'd seen in a week. He winked at me.

'Perhaps, thanks to Sir William, we'll have some fun,' he said. To Hawkwood, he said, 'Good knight, my inclination is to cut across country, threaten Bernabò's retreat, and see where the old beast runs.'

It was play-acting. The two of them had already decided it. Still, it was an excellent plan, and I was happy to see it adopted. Coucy invited me to dine with him at the end of the day. Outside, archers were taking the pavilion down around our ears.

In less time than it takes to say a paternoster, we'd decided on a route. Coucy smiled at me and took his leave. 'This will change everything,' he said cheerfully.

Romney looked at me. 'Thanks to Sir William,' he said in a high falsetto, parroting Coucy's words.

I looked at him.

'Have a problem?' he asked.

'I think you have a problem with me,' I said.

'Fuck, it's like having a priest around. Why do you get the credit for everything?'

'Why don't you send out scouts?' I said.

'Because this war is fucking play-acting! We ain't facing the French, or the Scots.' Romney sounded as angry as I felt. It *did* feel like play-acting.

It's odd, that when you fully understand the bug biting another man, it's difficult to be angry.

'I like to keep busy,' I said. 'Even if it's play-acting.'

Romney looked around at the other officers and nodded. 'You must be paying your lances under the table,' he said. 'I can't get mine to do much more than ride and eat.'

I nodded. I liked him. I wanted his regard, not his anger.

'Yes,' I said. 'I'm paying them out of my own purse.'

'And fucking the rest of us,' Romney said. And then, with sudden heat, 'We can't all marry a rich bitch who conveniently dies.'

Suddenly my sword was in my hand, and all my good intentions were gone.

Hawkwood reappeared as if by magic.

'Are you two insane?' he said. He hit Romney fairly hard with his baton of command.

Romney stumbled back, drawing his sword. 'I'm sick of being second fiddle to the cook's boy,' he said.

John Thornbury had my right arm in a friendly lock. 'Calm, William,' he said.

'This gentleman just insinuated that I killed my wife,' I said.

Hawkwood looked at Romney. 'Richard?' he said in his emotionless, and thus very dangerous, voice.

Romney made a face and sheathed his sword. 'That was anger,' he said. 'I apologise. But holier-than-thou here is paying his lances out of his pocket. It makes us look bad with our men.'

Hawkwood looked at me. 'Yes,' he said. 'It makes us all look bad, William.'

I was trembling with indignation. 'You're happy enough with my scouting reports,' I said. 'Which you get because my men do work and take risks ...'

'If I needed a lecture on the art of war from a man half my age,' Hawkwood said, his voice icy, 'I'd be sure and ask you, William. In the meantime, no more paydays until we pay everyone.'

I stood there, full of rage.

'Dismissed, William,' he said. 'Master Romney, stay.'

Thornbury spun me around and pushed me gently out of the tent.

'That's us told,' he said without adornment. 'I paid mine a week ago.'

I was getting myself under control. I felt the guilt I now feel when I lose my temper, combined with a terrible anger. It was unfair, and stupid. And yet, we hadn't been paid. And we were in the field, in winter, unpaid. Whose decision was that?

And now we were moving to a battle. Up until that minute, I'd never doubted that our polyglot English, Breton, Hungarian and Italian company could defeat all comers. Now I had to wonder if unpaid men would fight.

We'd picked the names off one of our itineraries – Castelfranco, Sant'Agata, Crevalcore, Camposanto, It was a dangerous game. We were assuming that Bernabò would retreat when we were threatening his route home, but he was living off the country – raiding our peasants, as it proved – and he might move in any direction. Scouting became vital, and I combined forces with Thornbury. We put most of our men out in pairs of lances, well spaced out, trying to cover all the ground between us and a line from Modena to Bologna – a wide front with slow communications. For a few hours in the morning it was very complicated, and then it suddenly got much simpler, because Lapot met up with one of Thornbury's patrols. By Nones we knew where Bernabò was, and that he was retreating in haste.

I was riding Giulia, with one of my warhorses close to hand, led by Marco, the bigger of my two new grooms. My dozen Italian lances were all fully armed, standing by their mounts – my ready reserve. The Turks had taught me to keep a few men in hand in case of a sudden raid or a new opportunity.

Janet was out somewhere to the east, towards Modena. I hoped that she was in contact with the main column, under Coucy and Hawkwood.

I made a map in the dirt – just pebbles placed to remind me of places. Then, when I had it clear, I left l'Angars in command and rode to the column, where I found Malatesta and Hawkwood riding along like old friends.

'Bernabò is moving,' I said as a greeting. 'He's retreating north from Bologna, towards …' I paused to read a note. 'Towards San Giovanni something.'

Malatesta pounded one gauntleted hand with the other. 'I know that town. He's going for the Brescello road to Milan.'

Hawkwood looked at Malatesta. 'You are sure?'

Malatesta shrugged. 'Sure?' he asked, in a very Italian way. 'No. But sure enough to wager on.'

It was late January, and night was already close. Ahead of us, perhaps two English miles, we could see Sant'Agata and a fine brick campanile rising over the very flat plain.

'Right,' Hawkwood said. 'William, Coucy likes you. Ride to him, he's in the middle of the column. Tell him what you told me and tell him, from me, that I intend to camp at Sant'Agata, if he is agreeable. We will camp on the north side, and we will march at dawn.'

I touched the visor of my helmet and rode away, almost due south, even as I heard Hawkwood deliver a volley of orders behind me.

I found Coucy, delivered my message, and then swept back west, collecting my far-flung patrols as I went. I finally found Lapot after I'd changed horses. It was the edge of dark, and an icy wind was blowing.

'Has Bernabò spotted you?' I asked.

Lapot made a derisive gesture. 'I don't know whether it's Bernabò or Ambrogio,' he said. 'I didn't ride over to ask.' He smiled, looked east, and then shrugged. 'But they're not much for guarding themselves, if that's what you mean. Not so much as a harsh word exchanged.'

I smiled. 'Hawkwood intends to surprise the Milanese in the morning.'

'Perfect,' Lapot said.

He gathered in all my best people, and we rode east until we passed through Thornbury's pickets and found our camp set, our fires lit, and food being prepared. I left my horses with my grooms and, still muddy, went to Coucy's magnificent pavilions.

Janet was already there, as was Fontana's sister, and several of Coucy's knights. I was given hot hippocras that tasted divine and ran right down to my frozen toes. Sabatons are not useful cold weather gear, I assure you. Oh, I know it was hippocras, Monsieur Froissart, because here is the recipe written into the leaf of my breviary.

We were served a remarkable repast for being in the field – pork sausage and little meat cutlets pounded flat and rolled around strips of marrow, with pepper. Hawkwood came in, ate one of my cutlets, drank off my wine, and said that we should all be abed. He was suddenly in tearing good spirits.

If I haven't said this before, Hawkwood was a very controlled man. When I say 'he was angry' or 'he was in tearing good spirits', I'm not sure a person who had not known him for ten years would even have noticed a change. But when he was angry he was, if anything, even more reserved. When he was in high spirits, he put a hand on your shoulder and drank your wine. That was about all there was to tell of his emotions. It's a good practice in a commander, and one I still strive to emulate.

I took his admonition as an order and rose. Coucy toasted the ladies and we all simpered a bit. I happened to meet the eye of Lady Maddalena Fontana, and there was an expression there that suggested that she found such compliments more amusing than worthy. I may have winced.

But I had a mission as well, and after she'd been seen out, I approached Coucy.

'My lord,' I said.

'Ah, Sir William,' he said. 'How may I be of service?'

His people were talking to Janet. I think they'd never seen a woman in armour before, and there was some posturing. I left them to it – it gave me a little cover.

'My lord is aware that I have ... looked in to some ... affairs ... for his lady wife?' I asked this carefully, and with several pauses.

He smiled. I'd seen the smile before. It said 'I'm really not a fool.'

'Yes,' he said. 'The matter of vipers, and her brother.'

'Yes, my lord. I don't know if you care to be involved ...'

'I am here, Sir William, from which you might guess ...'

'Just so, my lord. That being the case, I wanted to tell you that the Duke of Clarence's confessor, a man named John de Capell, is here in this camp.'

Coucy looked at me for a moment, and then nodded. 'I should like to meet him. Perhaps after the battle, if we have a battle. Sir William, may I tell you a secret?'

Great lords do not ordinarily favour upstart knights with secrets, but then, they don't usually feed them, either.

'Of course, my lord.'

Coucy took a drink. 'I long to capture one of the Viper's brood. I would feel this whole pointless campaign was worth our time if we could take one. If I could lay hands on Gian Galeazzo, I might even try him for Clarence's murder.' His face had taken on an angry, almost feral, look, but in a sip of wine it was gone, and he was again a pleasant, empty-headed rich noble.

After I left Coucy's tent, I decided that I needed to know more of the surrounding countryside, and I made my way to the church.

I could hear voices above me, so I climbed the town's campanile by candlelight, with a very hesitant priest who probably thought I was the Devil incarnate, only to find Thornbury, Hawkwood and Malatesta already braving the vicious wind.

'There he is,' Malatesta said.

Indeed, the ring of campfires could only be an army. Nor were they all campfires. The Visconti were bringing fire and sword to the Pope's people.

'They are already at Crevalcore,' Malatesta said. 'They are ahead of us.'

Hawkwood smiled his fox's smile. 'We'll have them about midday,' he said. 'William, in the morning, I want you to find them. And perhaps, put the fear of God into them.' He winced at the wind. 'Or perhaps the fear of the English, eh?'

Tommaso awakened me with a cup of hot wine. It was still dark. My clean linen shirt was as cold as the frozen Thames, and my armour was the same temperature as the darkness around me. I promise you, the life of arms has many adventures which neither Master Chaucer nor Master Froissart mention in their tales, and arming on a winter morning without a pavilion is one of them. The two farm boys weren't really squires, and they didn't really understand how all of the armour worked. Marc-Antonio had to come and help them. We'd slept in a sort of byre, because, of course, the nuns had my pavilion.

Chivalry was stretched thin, that morning.

Cold is unkind to horses, too, but thanks to God, my two farm boys, bad squires that they might be, were miracle workers with horses. My little herd had none of the afflictions of a cold night. It was still dark when I mounted, with Lapot, our pair of guides, and the Birigucci brothers, as well as our new Hungarian knight and Beppo.

I was going to do my own scouting. Now if you've been listening, you know that I almost lost us the Battle of Cascina, riding blind into a wilderness of small trees and irrigation ditches. I wasn't doing that again. I wanted to see for myself.

I was fully armed, but I had a big dun cloak over me, as much for hiding the glitter of my armour as for warmth. I had a hood buttoned over my helmet, and my visor up.

We passed through Sant'Agata before a cold cock could crow, and headed north over very flat ground. I knew the direction of the enemy camp, but I wanted to see it.

Their fires were burning low, but they were only a few miles away, and we smelt their smoke before the sky was grey. Bernabò knew he was in trouble. His wagons full of loot were already moving, north and east. I could see his infantry, mostly Milanese militia, just breaking camp. They would probably be the rearguard.

I remember thinking that he had made a mistake there, unless he really didn't care how many infantrymen he lost.

I watched the wagons plod off and then saw the chaos as Bernabò – or Ambrogio, or whoever was in charge over there – tried to get his men-at-arms mounted and on the road. They hadn't been paid either. I could all but hear the German curses. But what I couldn't do was see. North of Modena, Lombardy is as flat as the surface of a good table.

I turned to my guides. One was a Jewish pedlar, the other a local farmer from Sant'Agata. Both of them had been with us for two days, picked up at the market in Modena, both apparently content with their rewards.

'Is there a hill anywhere around here?' I asked.

They both shook their heads, *no*, and contrived to look sad.

I was trying to imagine the pilgrim itinerary from Bologna to Milan.

'Does the road cross a river?' I asked.

'What road?' the farmer asked. 'There are roads everywhere.'

That was true, too. There were the big old Roman roads like the Via Emilia, but there were smaller roads that were still better than most roads in France. We were on one.

I could feel the press of time. The sun was rising, and I hadn't a notion of what to do.

The Jew looked at the retreating column, and then looked at me, as if speculating on my worth.

'They will have to cross the Panaro,' he said. Then, an emphatic shrug, as if to disown his own words. 'I mean, if they are going to Milan.'

'It's true,' the farmer said. 'It's not a big river, but the wagons will never cross it.' He paused, and added, 'I mean, my gracious lord, not without a bridge.'

I tried not to betray impatience. 'And if you were taking a wagon to

Milan from Crevalcore, where would you cross the Panaro?' I asked.

'Ain't got a wagon,' the farmer said.

This is where it's very useful to really know the local language, because the way he phrased it, I knew he meant that he had an answer, but hoped for a bigger bribe. To buy a wagon.

'If I gave you a wagon?' I asked. 'A good one. One of our fodder wains.'

The Jew smiled and shook his head, as if the iniquity of the world never ceased to amaze him. 'Solara,' he said.

The farmer looked as if he'd been bitten. 'Now, damn you to Hell, you sodomite Hebrew.'

This is what comes of questioning your guides together, which Hawkwood had often told me not to do.

'There, there,' I said. 'I will provide the wagon if the information is accurate. And six soldi for you, master pedlar.'

The farmer shrugged. 'Well, then. Solara is right.'

The Jew, who was an older man, rolled his eyes.

I immediately wished for my Turks, or Syr Giannis's stradiotes, or almost any light cavalry. What I had were pages, a few of whom had been to Jerusalem and faced the Turks and been taught by John the Turk, who I missed.

'Lapot, stay in contact,' I said.

He made a gesture as if to suggest that he was perfectly capable of doing so without instruction. I was reminded of the annoyance Fontana's sister had shown at being asked to maintain the fire.

I rode back, wondering if I had developed a patronising tone.

An hour later, thirty pages and as many archers, all mounted on Arabs, blew through the camp's pickets and showered the forming infantry with arrows. It was a flea bite, but it did its work. Chaos reigned for a bit, and then the Milanese began to move all the faster.

I didn't see any of it, because I was already riding almost due west. At Ravarino, I saw the Milanese vanguard turning north to take the road to Solara, and I sent Marc-Antonio back to confirm my report to Sir John and Coucy.

And then I rode like the Wild Hunt, with the Jewish pedlar as my guide, riding the web of farm roads that was his monthly round. He knew them well, and he earned a gold ducat of Venice for his trouble, because he got us to the bridge at Solara ahead of the Milanese van-guard.

It was perhaps Terce, three hours after sunrise, when we came to the bridge – a short, high arch wide enough for a single wagon or two good riders to pass. It wasn't very wide. There was room to swing an axe. The bridge didn't have any side rails worth the name – just a low kerb of stone to keep a wagon from sliding off.

I put Tommaso, the smaller farm boy, up on Giulia and sent him back to Hawkwood to say we had the bridge.

'Gentleman,' I said to my knights and squires, 'we are about to do a deed of arms, because I believe the Visconti are counting on crossing this bridge, and we are going to get very rich, stopping them.'

'Or maybe very dead,' someone said.

We rode over the bridge and gave our horses to the youngest pages, those too young or too ill-armed to have participated in the raid on the Milanese camp. Then we posted two men on the bridge and the rest of us had a brief drill on how we'd fight. I had more than thirty fully armoured men – and one woman, of course – and we had a variety of weapons, but, for the most part, spears. A few men used axes on foot, and I had one of the new Italian poleaxes, as did Janet.

I looked them over. I was missing a few of my best, off holding our castles around Pavia, but I had Lapot, l'Angars, Grice and Marc-Antonio. I missed Fiore. He would have held the bridge by himself. He would have taught us all a lesson on holding a bridge.

While I was looking them over, I noticed a man-at-arms I didn't know, or rather, one who shouldn't have been there. Young Giancarlo Orsini, Bishop of Marino, stood in his harness with my Piacenzan knights.

'Your Grace,' I said, 'you have no business here.'

He looked away, and then looked back. 'I *humbly* request that you not send me away.'

He had fine armour, if a little old-fashioned, with more maille than I liked, and boiled leather where my knights wore steel. Still ...

'Your Grace, what do I tell your father if you fall here?' I asked.

He shrugged. 'Tell him I was a fool. It's what he always says, anyway.'

I ordered them to fall in, and began to set what man would stand where.

There was some grumbling. One of the Italians opined loudly that we would all be killed or captured in this foolish *geste.*

I smiled and put a hand on his shoulder. 'We are all afraid,' I said. 'Every one of us. But this is not foolish. We will win, and we will be rich. And Piacenza will be that much closer to liberation.'

He was Ser Antonio – I don't remember his surname. But he gave me a sidelong glance. 'I am *not* afraid,' he said.

'Excellent,' I said. 'You can stand with me in the front rank.'

Waiting is one of the very worst parts of warfare, and that morning was the worst waiting I think I have endured, at least until the Chioggia War. If you remember my tales of Poitiers, for example ... We were always moving, riding, relaying orders, and then suddenly, the French were on us. But at Solara, we just stood on the frozen ground, without even our horses to warm us, waiting. The wind blew, finding every crack and crevice in our armour, every patch in our gambesons and our hose. Wind blows right through your maille, and if you have sewn eyelets into your fighting doublet to allow your body to breathe in summer ... well. The icy fingers of Lady Wind reach right through and touch you to your marrow.

And there was nothing to see. It was winter – soggy ground frozen solid. No dust. No sign of the Milanese army at all.

Had I got it wrong?

As the morning wore on, it was increasingly likely that I had. Men began to fret. When l'Angars held a second drill to sort out how exactly we'd fit on the bridge, there was a great deal of grumbling. Several men took a long time to come over from the warmth of the big fire our pages had started.

I chose to ignore their passive mutiny, because you have to know when to push and when to pull, as Hawkwood says. The Italians weren't really integrated into my company yet – that is, the Piacenzans. The Birigucci brothers were steel-clad pillars of my little company.

Beppo stood to one side with a very elegant arbalest.

'You want Beppo to ride out and find these vipers?' he asked.

I shook my head. 'No.'

It was just a feeling I had, that anything that warned the Milanese we were there would ruin the day. But as the weak sun climbed higher and we got a brief shower of light snow, I cursed inwardly, tried to pray, and paced too much. A better commander might have just stood and been cold, but I was not that man.

After two of the longest hours of my life, the sentries on the bridge reported a horseman coming, and then more horsemen, and we formed up. We could only really fit three men abreast on the bridge, and we had two 'teams', with l'Angars leading one and me leading the other. I was first.

The lone rider was one of Thornbury's men-at-arms.

'My lord,' he said to me.

I'm not really anyone's lord, but when Hawkwood wants to bait me he calls me 'Baron', as I am, technically, a baron. Not what you want to hear right now, I take it? *Eh bien ...*

So the man explained that the Milanese rearguard hadn't held together. Our cavalry was all over their column, and they were abandoning carts and loot and prisoners in all directions. The main body was coming straight at me, perhaps three miles away.

A few minutes later, Ewan the Scot rode up with all my archers and senior pages. They looked very pleased with themselves.

Ewan grinned. 'I took me a five-hundred florin ransom afore the sun was a finger abo' the horizon,' he said.

Gospel Mark pointed east. 'Every man 'ere just made a few silver, eh, lads?'

And the pages all had very expensive military crossbows – the kind that required a belt and windlass to load.

'Och, aye,' Ewan said, dismounting. 'They were just lying in a ditch.'

The excellent spirits of the archers and the reports of ransoms did everything to put heart into my men-at-arms. When the lead elements of the Milanese army came into sight on the flat plain, their armour twinkling in the sun, which was finally coming out strong, we were standing at the crest of the bridge, ready to receive them.

It was perhaps seven hours into the day when the first men attacked us. There were sixty or so, all well mounted and well armoured. They dismounted after some discussion and an argument whose sound carried on the wind. We jeered at them. And no one jeers like the English.

They formed up in a solid body and came at us. They weren't well disciplined, and they were four wide, or perhaps five – they couldn't decide. Men fell off the bridge as soon as they started up it, and then there was a little shoving. A man fell from well up the arch, and the whole mass hesitated.

A volley of newly liberated crossbow bolts struck them. The pages were standing on our side of the stream, shooting up into the enemy men-at-arms at point-blank range. It was a devastating volley.

Ewan and the archers shot from the left side of the bridge, with the wind at their backs. Aside from one awkward sod who managed to pink one of the Biriguccis in the front rank of our block, the rest of the arrows went home with a rattle and some cries of pain.

They never reached us. They backed down, and I ordered the archers and pages to cease fire.

They began to search for a ford.

Ewan mounted the archers and shadowed them.

More and more men came up. A brave man charged us on horse-back. He came on at a gallop, without warning, and he surprised the pages, who were, for the most part, warming their hands at a fire someone had started. His horse wouldn't charge home against our wall of steel, but it half-reared at the top of the arch. One of its hooves struck Ser Antonio atop the shoulder, breaking it. I put the butt-spear of my poleaxe into the horse's chest and Janet stabbed it in the head. The spike on a poleaxe can penetrate a horse's skull. The horse died in front of us and I took the rider as a ransom. He was pinned under his horse with a broken leg.

We'd also scooped all four of the knights who fell off the bridge. They were wet and cold, but alive.

After a few minutes, someone arrived who had authority. He organised another attack. A dozen men tried to cross the stream under the bridge and found that it was deeper than it looked.

Another group of men-at-arms came at us. This time they were all beautifully armed in the best and most recent armour, and they came at a run – Bernabò's own knights, I suspected.

I don't remember much of the fighting, to be honest. It was brutally unfair. We were 'uphill' at the top of the bridge, and we had a dead horse to break up their rush just below us. They made five tries, and by the fifth, we'd become expert in sending the wounded – their wounded, left lying around the horse – back through our ranks.

After the fifth assault, we backed down the bridge as fast as we could and let l'Angars up. My poleaxe was broken, and I'd been fighting with my dagger because the press of the last two attacks was too close to get my sword out. I don't remember any particular encounter, but I do remember wishing that I had a spear instead of an axe.

I stood and panted. The pages shot into the next attack, and then ...

And then it was chaos. Men drove their horses into the river and drowned. Men managed to swim across, but instead of fighting us, they just rode away. Men stripped their armour in full view of our people and swam in the icy river. Some swam only to gasp and drown. Others swam and came straight to our fire to surrender. A few ran off into the country.

The attacks on our bridge stopped. And after another hour, we had only the wreckage of an army in front of us. The rest of them had gone away north. Ewan told me later that they found a ford, and he contested it until they ran out of shafts, and then they gave up and rode away.

Bernabò escaped, and so did Ambrogio. But they lost six hundred knights as prisoners from the best families in Lombardy. They lost *all* of their infantry, captured – and all their loot and most of their baggage.

I know, because someone abandoned Bernabò's baggage about half a mile from the bridge. As soon as we had no opponents, I mounted my men-at-arms and we rode out into the wreckage of an army. There weren't many dead. The Milanese had got most of the way to the bridge, realised that they were trapped, and their army disintegrated.

My private irony is that I found Ser Antonio Visconti's baggage. Ser Antonio and I go way back – he had been in Bulgaria with the Green Count. And after that debacle I'd sold him two good horses, for which he'd never really paid me. And lo! Standing by a baggage cart, two beautiful Asian horses.

And Bernabò's portable collection of pornography. It was with a double dozen religious texts, which I took on the spot, climbing off my warhorse into a wagon ...

I just barely warded the dagger blow. I was half in, half out of the wagon, my hand on a breviary that was incredibly, beautifully well-decorated by some Pavia master, and trying to keep my left foot in my stirrup ... I leave you to imagine ... Regardless, I caught at the dagger right-handed, and found myself looking at one of Bernabò's mistresses. You may doubt me, but the moment I saw her perfect complexion – blond hair and pale face – I knew her provenance.

'*Madonna*,' I said, still holding her small wrist pinned against the side of the wagon. 'I am not here to kill you or ravish you.'

She gave me a flat look of hate.

I put two archers and one of the Biriguccis on the wagon, and moved on through the rout. In many cases the Milanese had left animals in their traces. All our people had to do was lead them away.

The sun was setting when I found Hawkwood, Malatesta and Coucy all sitting on warhorses back towards Crevalcore, where there had been some fighting while the Milanese were still holding together.

'Well, well, Sir William,' Hawkwood called out. 'Nicely done, sir. The cork in the proverbial bottle.'

'We missed Bernabò and Ambrogio,' I said as I rode up. I met Coucy's eye. 'I think I saw Bernabò ordering the last attack on my bridge, but he was already slipping away north. I lacked the men to cover a ford ...'

'Bah,' said Hawkwood. 'Never mind. We took a fortune in baggage and ...'

'And there was scarcely a fight!' Coucy said. He was more puzzled than angry.

Hawkwood looked at him, and I think his look was fondness. In Coucy, Hawkwood had an able commander of impeccable nobility, who wasn't touched with the ... corruption, if you will, of the Italian commanders. Most of them were every bit as grasping and venal as we were ourselves.

Coucy glanced at me. 'You, at least, had some fighting,' he said.

'We did, too,' I admitted. 'Seven or eight assaults on our bridge.'

'On foot?' Coucy asked.

'On foot.'

Coucy sighed. 'That is where I should have been.'

Hawkwood looked away and smiled.

I bowed in the saddle. 'My lord, if you had been there, perhaps we might have had Lord Bernabò.'

We got our tents up, and since we now had all of the Milanese baggage, I had the pages put up Ambrogio's pavilion for the nuns, and my own for me. I was getting my armour off when Greg Fox came in.

'I, uh ...' He looked around. 'Gospel Mark says you left John Taylor with a wagon full of books and a woman,' he said, after a pause.

'Blessed Virgin,' I swore, or something stronger. 'Where are they?'

Gospel Mark pushed past Greg , who, when not sewing or fighting, was a very quiet, almost shy man. 'They's right here in camp, Sir William, an' if I might say, that's not a woman to leave in a baggage cart.'

I probably growled. I was out of my tent in my ragged fighting hose and my second-best arming doublet, stalking across my part of the camp. I wanted to blame someone else, but I'd lost track of the day. Anyone who has had to organise a camp after a fight knows that the time flows away in a hundred decisions. I needed a lieutenant, and while Janet was the obvious choice, many of the men wouldn't have taken her orders.

I found László and John Taylor standing by the high-wheeled wagon with Witkin, who had a long staff in his hand.

'Witkin?' I asked.

He spat. 'People had ideas,' he said.

Right.

'Master Fox, if you would be so kind to get me ...' I stopped. Where could I keep one of Bernabò's mistresses? Was she a prisoner? By the risen Christ, was she even with Bernabò of her own free will?

'Get Sister Marie, if you would be so kind,' I snapped.

Greg set off at a run. I had a moment to realise that he had all-new arming clothes. Beautiful arming clothes, probably as good as Coucy's. Doubtless made them himself. And a fine long cloak, too.

'*Madonna?*' I called out. 'May I speak to you?'

A long stream of northern Italian profanity was my only answer.

After a few minutes, Lord Fontana's sister Maddalena emerged from the women's pavilion. She wore a big houppelande buttoned to the neck – enough wool to dress a dozen archers, and she was a small woman. She said something to Greg Fox, who bowed, and the two of them crossed the frozen ground to the wagon.

'Sister Marie is seeing to injured men,' she said with some asperity. 'I can be spared.'

I nodded. 'Siora, there is a young woman in this wagon who ...'

As soon as she heard a woman's voice, the wagon's occupant poked her head out, the way a cat will emerge from a warm blanket when food is on offer. In fact, she looked a little like a kitten – a small nose, widely spaced eyes, a small, full-lipped mouth.

Lady Fontana raised an eyebrow. At me.

'How can I be of service?' she asked. Her tone suggested that she was doing me a great favour.

'I think this woman is justifiably afraid of emerging from the wagon without knowing there are women to protect her,' I said.

Lady Fontana smiled at the creature in the wagon. It was a real smile, and fairly made her glow. Then back to me.

'She has been raped?' she said.

'Not here, and not by my people,' I said.

She raised her chin. 'Ah,' she said, and looked back at me. 'She is ... yours?'

'She is her own. That is, I have no claim on her. We ...'

How did I get into these situations?

'We found her, like,' Gospel Mark put in. 'On the battlefield.'

Lady Fontana was clearly nobody's fool, so I said, quietly, 'We found her in this wagon. Full of Lord Bernabò's ... possessions.'

'Ah,' the lady said. She nodded, three times, very rapidly, a habit I would get to know. 'Yes, I understand perfectly. I will take her, then.' She raised an arm trailing a long hanging sleeve, took the woman's hand, and helped her down from the wagon. The young woman was dressed in a shift and a very light kirtle.

Greg Fox, who really was a gentleman born, threw his cloak over the woman. Lady Fontana took her away, watched by half a hundred enraptured archers and men-at-arms.

I went back to getting disarmed. When Greg came back to tell me that the woman was sitting with the nuns and getting warmed, I nodded.

'Master Fox, is it still your intention to become a man-at-arms?'

'Yes, Sir William. I mean, after today ...' He shrugged and pointed towards the trophies we'd taken.

It's true – we had a literal pile of armour, most of it highly polished, brand-new Milanese stuff.

'I have almost everything but legs, Sir William,' he added.

Greg Fox was, as I have said, tall and almost cadaverously thin. He might find plate legs difficult to find. I waved that aside.

'Could I interest you in being my squire?' I asked him. 'My armed squire. I'll see you have your own lance in a year's time.'

Greg Fox was not an effusive man. 'May I consider, Sir William?' he asked.

'Of course. In the meantime, before you become a great noble, I wonder if I could pay you to make me a new set of arming hose?' I smiled.

Welcome to the world of the English companies, where tailors became knights but were still expected to sew.

'Of course, Sir William. I have a few projects ahead of yours ...'

Really, he sounded like a great noble already. Or a famous tailor.

I dined with Coucy and all of the commanders that evening. While I have no idea what we ate, I know it was delicious, and included some wonderful sweets that I contributed from Bernabò's wagon. John Thornbury outlined the whole battle, of which I had been a very small part, and I'll lay it out here for you, Master Froissart.

The Milanese marched very early, from their camp around Creval-core, heading north and west on the main road for Milan. But before they cleared their camp, we hit them, first with a few small bands of raiders, and a little later, with Malatesta's Italian light horse. That forced their rearguard to form and stand instead of moving. By the time I was at the bridge, the enemy rearguard had mostly been bypassed. They had some crossbowmen who might have done good work, but they were badly led and there was dissension in their ranks. The upshot was that by late in the morning, the whole rearguard surrendered to Niccolò d'Este, leaving the column, now several miles up the road, virtually naked.

As soon as Malatesta and Hawkwood came in sight, the Milanese column disintegrated, aware of the level of disaster they were caught up in. Many fled north, across country, or simply sat down and surrendered. The mounted men-at-arms headed for the bridge, found it defended, tried to burst through, and then went north again, to the ford their pages had found downstream on the Panaro. Some of them made it across. Some drowned.

As Coucy said, it was never a battle. What it was, was an abject lesson in how not to conduct a retreat in the face of an aggressive enemy.

Coucy was not satisfied by it, we could tell. Some of the knights there present were listing their ransoms – counting the florins, as it were. That was rude at any time, and ruder because a few of the captured nobles were sitting with us, quietly playing with their borrowed wine cups.

Coucy cleared his throat and men fell silent, and he looked around.

'The lords of Milan had a disaster,' he said, and shrugged. 'But given our relative positions, what could they have done?'

Hawkwood looked away.

Coucy caught his movement. 'Ah, Sir John, you are the very man. An expert on war. What could have been done?'

Sir John could be very mild. He looked down the table at the captives.

'It can only be painful ...' he began.

'Ah, never mind them, Sir John.' Coucy was genuinely curious.

Hawkwood bowed.

'If you were in command,' Coucy asked, straight at Hawkwood, 'what would you have done?'

Hawkwood swirled the wine in his silver cup for a moment, and then nodded as if he'd decided.

'A thousand things, my lord. For starters, I might have rid myself of all my baggage yesterday and been long gone.'

'Fair,' said Malatesta, now professionally interested. 'But let's say we have to keep the baggage.'

Sir John made a wry face, almost a smile. 'Well, then,' he began. He looked apologetically at the prisoners. 'At dawn, I send all my heavy cavalry to attack your camp.'

There was silence.

'They have orders to break off at a trumpet call,' he said.

Coucy smiled. 'As if your knights would leave a fight at the sound of a trumpet!' he said

'If they ever wanted to be employed again, they would,' Sir John said. 'My infantry and baggage marches an hour before dawn, because the road is good and wide. So no matter how the cavalry fight comes out, my baggage is safe.'

'Unless your cavalry is overthrown,' Este said.

Sir John nodded polite agreement. 'Of course. There is always bad fortune.'

Malatesta shook his head. 'But honestly, when the sides are equal, who has ever seen one side utterly overthrown?' He leant forward. 'They outnumbered us!'

Well, that wasn't quite true. We had two thousand Bolognese militia who had come up about the time I left camp. They brought the numbers up in our favour, although their only role was guarding the prisoners.

'Or,' Sir John said, with the bit in his teeth, 'I do what the prince did at Poitiers. I slip the wagons off early and dig in for a fight with my whole force. If you offer battle, battle it is. If you don't, we march away.'

At the word Poitiers, Coucy frowned. I winced. Coucy had been taken at Poitiers. He'd been an English prisoner for six or seven years.

'Very instructive, Sir John,' he said smoothly.

I have one coda to offer. Years later – quite recently, actually, when I met with Sir John to ask him a hard question at his castle in Romagna – we talked of old times and he said that Crevalcore was his greatest battle.

'Almost no fighting. I lost a dozen men. We recovered almost all our wounded – we didn't even get our horses knocked up. We did everything by manoeuvre, and we made a fortune.' He shrugged when he said it. And then he turned to me and said, 'Most of these so-called "great captains" think that fighting and blood are what makes war, William. But you and I know it's money and manoeuvre.'

It was a pity that his masterpiece was wasted.

PART II

THROUGH VIOLENT BLOWS

Montichiari and Northern Italy

1373

By the grace of God who dispenses his councils otherwise,
we came to battle in a long and broad field above Montichiari.
Through violent blows we succeeded in bitter fighting.

Sir John Hawkwood's own words, 1373

Sister Marie left us two days later, taking with her all of the women, Bishop Orsini and his retinue of priests, and Michael des Roches.

Des Roches clasped my hand before leaving. 'Do you ever think of Greece?' he asked me out of a clear blue sky.

'Often,' I admitted.

'I want to go,' he said with enthusiasm. 'There are collections of books there in Greek that people say are staggering. Ancient texts no one here has ever read. I'm tired of debating Plato based on a few books. I met a Greek monk in Piacenza who said that Plato wrote fifty dialogues! Fifty!' He grinned.

'I could write you a letter of introduction to Nerio Acciaioli,' I said.

'That would be very useful,' he agreed. 'And I believe you know the Emperor of Constantinople?'

I did, too. It made me think of another world, and a time when I had all my friends by me.

'It was interesting,' des Roches said, 'seeing you in your natural place, as it were. In command.'

'Interesting?' I asked.

He was mounting the mule that Gospel Mark had 'found' for him.

He smiled. 'I don't mean to annoy you, William, but I liked you better in Spain.'

I thought about that for a long time, too.

I scandalised the younger nuns by embracing Sister Marie. Lady Fontana scandalised me by walking up to me and asking if she could stay.

'I need to take care of my brother,' she said. 'I have the ... woman ... you found,' she smiled winningly, 'as a companion, and Lady Janet has offered to host me.'

'Lady Janet.' That made me smile.

'Siora, we will be delighted to have you, and you know perfectly well that a military camp is no place for a woman.'

She raised both eyebrows and gave her three little nods. 'And you, Ser Guglielmo, know equally well that there are sixty women within the sound of my voice.'

There were, too.

I was too busy over the next weeks to worry much about her, or anyone else. The Pope asked us to go back to Piacenza immediately. Word was that my liege, the Green Count, was coming out of the mountains of the north to meet us, and we were to crush Milan between us. Certainly, Bernabò was suing for peace. We passed his ambassadors through our lines with heralds, bound for Coucy, and other men were reported going north over the passes to Avignon.

Hawkwood just spat in the mud and moved us back to Piacenza as fast as we could go. For me, that meant organising the advance guard, choosing camp sites, and at the same time, sometimes while in the saddle, negotiating with bankers about ransoms and sales of loot – all in a day's work. I had never been so happy to be friends with a banker. Nerio was very much in my mind in those days, as I shamelessly used his name to various Florentines who followed us like carrion crows. But, with Janet's help, we sent all of our prisoners off to be ransomed, and the money began to flow in. Most of it went straight to individuals, but some came to the company or to me. Miracle of miracles, Malatesta, who'd taken several good ransoms, used them to pay Hawkwood, who paid me – making a profit, of course. I didn't care. We used the loot to pay a month's wage to every man. All the companies did, including Coucy's three hundred French lances. Morale improved, and so did everyone's willingness to work and fight.

That was good, because Bernabò, who was lacking almost everything, burnt the fields around Piacenza, burnt the barns, and left us a desert. And we lacked the men to mount a proper siege of so prosperous a city, and we lacked the heavy siege machines to put the walls to the test.

In other words, we were back where we'd started the campaign. It was still cold. It was now very wet, with the frozen fields turning to mud, and there was no one to fight. Food was running short, and Bernabò was building a new army. With money.

And Count Amadeus of Savoy had moved to within twenty miles of Milan and stopped.

On a positive note, we controlled most of the south side of the Po, which meant that our castles were safe. I relieved my boredom by taking a column to relieve the outposts around Pavia, and we managed to fill a dozen wagons with fodder on our little raid, which Richard Romney repeated two weeks later with the same success. Bernabò really was beaten – so badly beaten that we had all of Lombardy to ourselves. As one very small example, László, my Hungarian capture turned man-at-arms, got his page, his squire and his two mounted archers back. They came to us like stray dogs and were, at least apparently, delighted to find that their master had changed sides. I put Witkin back in his proper lance. László had had every opportunity to desert and had never done anything of the kind.

I could have added fifty lances to my already bloated squadron, as there were Germans looking for work every day, but we were past our limits. Despite the recent pay day, we all knew the Pope was having money troubles.

In fact, he was unhappy, to say the least.

'I have written to His Holiness half a dozen times,' Hawkwood said one afternoon. 'Without money and a siege train, this is pointless. If he's out of money, and I'm afraid that I think that they're *all* out of money ...' He looked off to the west. 'Damn it, William, I've made a bad bargain, and I thought I was so canny. I thought the Pope could pay for this war. In fact, they're both making war on credit, and now their credit is gone.'

It was a sunny day. We were sitting outside and getting warmer. All of my clothes smelt of horse sweat and smoke. Janet was delighted to have a female friend and didn't need to sit in my tent drinking wine. Coucy was obviously too full of melancholy. I was spending my time with young Greg Fox and with Hawkwood. They were both good companions, although Hawkwood tended to treat me as a very young man, and I suppose I passed that straight on to Greg.

'I wonder ...' Hawkwood said.

I knew immediately he wanted a favour, because he hated to ask.

'How can I help you, Sir John?'

'Am I that transparent, William? So be it. I wonder if you'd ride to Count Amadeus and see if you can get him to move forward. I have no idea what he's doing, and I'd like to know. I didn't want to give Bernabò this much time to rest. We could have been riding a chevauchée around Milan by now.'

Sir John Hawkwood was not usually given to speaking his mind, much less exposing his unease. And I was Count Amadeus's liege man – I might almost say, friend.

'I'll go,' I said.

Sir John took my hand. 'I won't forget, William. And I promise you, absolutely nothing will happen here.'

It might have been a very dangerous mission, as I didn't know exactly where to find the Green Count, and I had sixty miles and more to cover, at least, in early spring, with all the roads full of mud.

But there were advantages to fighting for the Pope, and one of them was that most of the Church, regardless of local loyalties, put their faith in His Holiness. That meant that I could move from monastery to monastery virtually unnoticed, and that monks and nuns would be happy to share information with me.

I'd learnt a surprising amount about the inner workings of the Church from going on pilgrimage. I knew that most religious houses had rooms for pilgrims, for example. And my own order, the Knights of Saint John, would always host me.

The Green Count was supposed to have moved to Varese in the mountains north of Milan, by the big lakes. That meant I would have to pass Milan.

I won't bore you. It was a six-day journey, there was an incredible amount of mud, most of it on my horse and me, and absolutely no patrols. The Milanese heartland, the plain of Lombardy, was so empty that we could have marched in and emptied their barns. I took detailed notes.

I slept, for the most part, in pilgrim hostels. No one asked me anything. I didn't wear a sword, and I rode Giulia with a spare named Fero, a heavy plug with a good gait, and I rescued no maidens, and drank some decent wine with monks.

I was at the Benedictine house west of Milan, near the city gates, when a friar informed me that the Green Count was north and east of the city with 'a mighty army', coming down the passes from Lake Como. I remember how afraid I was, riding around Milan, waiting to be stopped and arrested by a Milanese patrol, but the countryside was empty. The roads themselves were also relatively empty – no one likes mud.

On the eighth day out of Piacenza, I rode up to the vedettes around the Green Count's camp and was escorted to a magnificent green silk pavilion through a silent camp that made me feel uneasy. Where men should have been working, or lying in the shade, or flirting; where camp followers should have been cooking, instead, there was a heavy silence.

The first man I saw inside the tent was Richard Musard.

'William!' he said, and threw his arms around me. 'What are you doing here?' he asked, his tone *almost* accusatory.

'Looking for you, brother,' I said. 'Hawkwood sent me to find out what the count is up to. We're stalled in front of Piacenza.'

'We have a lot of sick men and half our horse herd is dead,' Richard said bitterly. 'Poisoned.'

I probably swore.

'Albin is sure as of this morning. He's doing tests. But someone—'

'Sir Richard, do I hear that famous knight, Sir Guillaume d'Oro, in attendance?'

That was the count's voice, coming from the closed room inside the pavilion. Richard took me in and there he was – still debonair, still wearing his fine green kaftan with the wolf skin lining. I had the very same one, but it was far away – not the kind of garment that you wear to be inconspicuous.

'Is Sir Richard telling you all our troubles?' he asked.

'I gather you have Albin looking into the possibility of poison,' I said.

Peter Albin was a doctor, the nephew of the count's former doctor. He was better on horses than people, and had a degree in theology from Oxford, and was married to a woman who'd nursed him through the plague. And he been one of my spies on the Visconti. A very old friend. And, at least technically, a member of my company.

'Tell Enguerrand de Coucy and Sir John Hawkwood and any of your other officers ...'

He was working up to something really biting, I could tell. My eye caught Richard's, because we'd both been this man's minders at various times. He was a good lord, a fine leader, but tended to vent

87

his anger on any available target. And there was an empty wine flagon on the table and it was not yet midday.

'Damn it to Hell,' he finished. 'We're fifteen miles from Milan and I'm done. No horses. I'll have to retreat, and I've lost so many mounts that I'll be paying for them for years.'

What could I say? I stood silent.

'I thought that if we could get this war over quickly, we could move on to more important things. The Union of Churches. Peace in Italy.' He glanced at me. 'Do you know, Sir Guglielmo, you and Richard and I are probably the last men in the world who care about the Union.'

'I'm sure Francesco Gatelussi supports the Union, too,' I said. 'And Nerio Acciaioli.'

Gatelussi was the Prince of Lesvos, a pirate who had made a brilliant marriage and now owned the western Mediterranean. I liked him, and held my barony from him. And Nerio, whom I hope you remember, is one of my best friends.

Count Amadeus smiled. 'Ah, the good Nerio, now master of Corinth. I had a letter from him. Yes, I believe that he espouses the Union.' He winced. 'And Gatelussi, as you say.'

'And the Emperor John,' I put in.

The Green Count raised his wine cup. 'The real emperor. In Constantinople.' He smiled wryly. And shook his head. 'I'm not at my best, monsieur. I'll prepare a civil answer for Coucy, but the short of it is, we're done.'

I gathered that. Richard led me from the presence of the count, shaking his head.

'I'd like to see Albin,' I said. 'Any chance I can have him back?'

'Not right now,' Richard said. 'He's vital.'

When I saw the young doctor we embraced, and he thumped my back – all the usual greetings.

'I thought you were going back to England?' I said.

He shrugged. 'Ah, Sir William, you know how it is. The count was godfather to our daughter. I have more *interest* here than I'd ever have in London. And I'm on the count's staff, now – in his household.'

'And Caterina?' I asked.

He grinned. 'Working on becoming a great lady of the court.'

For a woman who'd started her career as a prostitute in Venice, Caterina had done well.

'I could use you if you were at leisure,' I said.

He nodded. 'If the count will release me, I'll follow you for a season. For a price, of course.'

'Tell me about the poisons?' I asked.

Albin gestured, and we went into a big stone barn, where he had a magnificent warhorse partially dissected on a table. Three tables, really.

'God and all his angels,' I spat.

Albin shrugged. 'Dissection is illegal in many places, but army camps are their own law. I dissect all I can.'

Richard turned his head away. I avoided the obvious question – 'Do you cut up people, or just animals?' – and tried to imagine what that magnificent horse had cost.

'One of the count's?' I asked.

'His favourite,' Richard spat.

'How many dead?' I asked.

'More than two hundred. Not just warhorses, either – hacks, rouncys, carthorses. Probably five hundred all told. Enough carthorses that we can't march away.'

'Christ risen.'

'Yes, it's not pretty. It has to be in the feed. I can't find anything in the bodies that looks wrong ...'

'The men are saying witchcraft.' Richard shrugged.

Albin washed his bloody hands. 'I want to look at the feed,' he said.

I was appalled when we got to the horse lines – it looked worse than the aftermath of a battle. Dozens of animals ... big, expensive German warhorses, smaller rouncys, working horses ... They just lay where they'd fallen. By the hundreds.

Albin described his life at court and his place in the count's household, and he and Richard had obviously become close. It might have passed for a pleasant afternoon, except that I was following them through the results of what looked like an equine plague.

Albin sent a pair of squires to find where the feed store was. We were knights. We didn't necessarily know where the fodder was stored, although in my own camp I'd have known. Albin summoned the grooms – clearly not the first time, as they came grumbling and resentful, and in their Savoyard French they complained of the unfairness of being summoned.

Albin wouldn't be swayed. 'What's different about the horses that survived?' he asked.

'They're alive,' called out a wag.

But after some sullenness, one young boy allowed as how his master's horses were fine, and he'd been on patrol every day. And then some very young pages – pages for archers – said the same.

'So it was fodder in camp,' Albin said. 'Where is the fodder stored?'

And then we all walked to the fodder store, another 'borrowed' Milanese barn. The Green Count had appropriated six of them, probably tax barns.

The barn was full of fodder – mostly hay. It would have to be months old. There was no fresh hay in early spring, although, when I thought about it, there was enough new grass on the verges to give patrols some fodder.

Albin took a pitchfork and turned it over. 'A lot of this is damp,' he mused. 'I wonder if damp fodder affects a horse's humours.'

I looked back. 'Winter hay shouldn't be damp,' I said. 'It should be dry.'

Richard agreed. We'd been grooms. And we'd been poor enough to care for our own mounts, winter and summer.

'No fresh stuff this time of year,' he said.

'And where'd you get fodder anyway?' I asked the grooms. 'Down by Piacenza, Bernabò's burnt the fields.'

'Oh, here, too,' said a mouthy page. 'But these two farmers rode in wi' wagons and sol' us the whole lot.'

Albin swore, a long, multilingual, blasphemous profanity. And then ripped something out of the fodder pile.

'First,' he said, 'the middle of these piles is hot as Hell. Wet hay will do that. And it's wet because it was cut in a marsh. And hemlock grows in marshland.' He threw a mass of tubers down at our feet. 'Hemlock. In with the fodder.'

'Some bastard thought he'd turn a quick profit—' I said.

'No,' Albin interrupted. 'Hemlock plants might gripe a horse, but it takes the tubers to kill them. Someone went to a lot of trouble.'

'Sons of Satan,' Richard muttered.

'Who purchased the fodder?' I asked the grooms, and they all agreed that would have been 'Karl'. Karl was apparently the count's steward on campaign.

He'd bought the fodder two evenings before, from two farmers.

My red hair sparked his memory, because one of the farmers had a red beard and didn't seem to speak. The other man was taller, very well-spoken, almost like a knight. And he'd had jet-black hair and a black beard.

I looked at Richard. 'Sound familiar?'

Richard looked as if he'd seen an unclean spirit. 'Christ and his angels,' he swore. 'Not the bastard who was Camus's hired killer?'

'Makes you think,' I said.

Before I left, the count summoned me again, and gave me a letter for Coucy. He gave me a long look, one that I had seen before, when he wanted to share a confidence. I waited with my 'bluff, honest soldier' expression pasted on, while he prevaricated. Then, at last, he came out with it.

'I said I had a letter from your friend Nerio,' he said. 'He's proposing to support the Emperor John. I may help him.' He was actually looking down his nose at me, but Count Amadeus did that, and you couldn't take offence.

I had no idea where this was going, so I just stood there.

'Nerio says he has paid you a retainer,' the count said.

I assumed I was about to be charged with disloyalty, as I was the count's liege man.

'My lord,' I began, but he waved his hand.

'No, no, I approve. In fact, in this case ...' he smiled. 'Well. We'll see. I understand you want to take my medico away.'

'I would like him,' I said. I wanted to say 'back', but hedge knights don't say such things to sovereign counts.

Amadeus nodded. 'Perhaps I'll send him as a messenger,' he said.

I left with no understanding of what was going through his head. I'd served him for several years, and I was used to the feeling. But I knew he was planning something, and it involved Nerio. And me.

If I was on my guard riding north to visit the count, I was twice as cautious riding south, knowing that the Bourc Camus's special assassin was loose somewhere in the Milanese domains. That is to say, I didn't *know* he was the same man. But I'd had a few brushes with him – I'd even captured him once. And, most importantly, I believed that he was the actual assassin of Prince Lionel, the Duke of Clarence. In fact, I'd recently had confirmation of my theory from John de Capell. And Richard and I knew he'd tried to murder Count Amadeus.

But the ride back to Piacenza was shorter, as I didn't have to ride around Milan the wrong way, and easier, as I had five days of sun. Spring was bursting across the fields of Lombardy, and the roads were suddenly full of men going to plough, women with baskets on their heads, and real pilgrims.

I alternated Fero and Giulia and made it to Piacenza in five days. I tried not to think about what the Visconti might do to me if they took me, because they were not as powerful as they thought they were.

Or so I told myself.

I returned to my company on the Sabbath, and after I'd reported to Sir John, I had the pleasure of finding Father Angelo saying Mass in my own part of the camp, on an altar made of two wine barrels with the company standard draped across them. I had plenty for which I was thankful, and I listened with pleasure to a sermon on brotherly love. As if the good Father Angelo was a conjuror, his sermon, which put me very much in mind of Nerio and Fiore and Miles Stapleton, seemed to have an immediate outcome, because no sooner had I taken communion and knelt by my prie-dieu (which had once been Bernabò's) than Greg Fox announced ... Fiore!

'By God!' I said, thumping his back.

'Yes, yes, I'm back,' Fiore said. 'Although not for too long, I hope.'

'Not for long?'

'Nerio wants your whole company in Greece. No later than the first week of Advent, or so he told me.' He smiled. 'A great deal sooner than that, if it can be done. I'm not going about this correctly, am I?' He patted his pockets. 'I have a letter from Nerio.'

At the words 'in Greece', my heart rose. Listen ... I am sometimes given to reflection, and even self-examination. And you may recall that Sister Marie taxed me with being a mercenary just a season before, and suggested to me that I needed to find a cause in which I believed. I suspect she meant the Order of Saint John, or some worthy fighting order, but at the words 'in Greece', I realised that I would be perfectly satisfied fighting for Nerio. I believed in him. That is to say, if the world must have bankers and aristocrats, I prefer that they act like Nerio, with casual justice.

All that in a glance at Nerio's perfect *bastarda* hand. He could write beautifully – he came from a banking family, and clarity mattered.

'Advent is a long way off,' I said, scanning the letter. Nerio was offering excellent rates, and transport from Venice or Ancona for a year's service. He apologised that I would not have the overall command, but promised me some independence.

And he offered for one hundred lances. I had to blink.

'But I have a contract here!' I said.

Fiore brushed a crumb off one glove, and realised that he'd just eaten the apple tart that young Marco had put out for my breakfast after Mass. He looked at me.

'Greece!' he said. 'Nerio!'

'I remember when you hated Nerio. Also, that was my breakfast.' I may have sounded pettish, but inside, I was elated. A hundred lances! Greece!

Suddenly the Pope's mostly phoney war with the Visconti seemed even more of a waste of time.

'When does your contract end?' Fiore asked.

I sent for Marco, who was waiting outside.

'Where did the apple tart come from?' I asked.

Marco smiled at the ground. 'The lady,' he said. 'She is making them.'

Probably not a time to ask too many questions.

'Would you go and buy me four more?' I asked.

'Hmmf,' Marco said. I had noticed that my two Italian grooms were not much on the courtesies. They were very good with horses, though. '*Alora*, Maestro, I will need money.'

Marco was off with several silver soldi in his hand. I went back to Fiore.

'The difficulty is that we are under contract to Hawkwood, and Hawkwood hasn't been paid since the *condotta* was signed.'

Fiore threw his hands in the air. He did it with an air of artificiality, because all of his mannerisms were learnt.

'I am not a lawyer,' he said. 'But if you haven't been paid, there is no contract.'

'I would not be unfaithful to Sir John,' I said.

Fiore shrugged. 'That's another thing entirely.'

Marco returned, produced three apple tarts like a conjuror, and allowed as how that was all there was to be had as the 'lady' wasn't making more, but sent them with her compliments.

'And Messire Acudo would like a moment of your time, *Illustrio*,' Marco said with a little bow. A complete change of deportment from half an hour earlier.

Knowing Fiore as I did, and still do, I ate one and a half apple tarts before attending on Hawkwood – Acudo, as the Italians called him.

He was looking at the city. Need I say we'd accomplished no more in terms of taking the city during my two-week absence than when I'd been there?

He was standing with Sir John Thornbury and John Brice, both of whom smiled at me – grim smiles, but smiles.

'We have a problem,' Thornbury said.

'Well …' Sir John Hawkwood managed a smile of his own. 'William, we have an opportunity, but only at a risk. And you have just taken a rather sizeable risk on our behalf, so I'm loath to ask.'

As I say, we were outside, on a beautiful spring day in April. The sun was out, birds were singing, and we had no siege train. Oh, what I mean is that our camp did not have the ugly sounds of war – neither the reek of the new powder nor the deadly whirr-thump of a trebuchet. I had just been to Mass and Fiore was waiting for me. I was in as good a mood as I'd found possible since Emile's death.

Hawkwood turned to me. 'The Pope believes that the abbot of the city's premier monastery is so loyal a churchman that he'll open a gate for us.'

Thornbury bit his lip. He didn't like it, whatever it was.

'I need certain assurances from the abbot before I risk my soldiers, and the abbot apparently requires certain assurances before he lets us in.' Hawkwood looked at me.

'And I speak Italian,' I said. Hawkwood spoke Italian like a native. Brice and Thornbury spoke a little, but only the kind we used in camp. 'Where are we to meet?' I asked.

'We don't know,' Hawkwood said. 'The Pope is probably a very good man, but he's neither a captain nor a spymaster. He gave us the name of the man and assertions about his loyalty and his concerns, but no plan to meet.'

'God's blood,' I muttered. 'You want me to go into Piacenza.'

Thornbury frowned. 'Honestly, William? I think it's a fucking trap, and you should steer clear.'

He looked grimly at Hawkwood. Hawkwood never engaged in contests. He didn't glare back. He looked at me. 'I agree that there's an element of risk. But if the abbot were to open a gate, and we took Piacenza ...' He made a face. 'It would change the war.'

'It would change the profit we made out of the war,' I said, but I smiled.

'Ah, William, sometimes I think you really are a proper routier. Yes. If we take Piacenza, we will all be very rich indeed.'

'Tell Will the rest of it,' Brice said.

He looked at me and gave a very small negative head shake. Brice had been around for years, while I came and went – Venice, the Holy Land, Count Amadeus – but Brice was always there. We weren't 'good comrades', but we'd always done well together and Brice had been one of Andy Belmont's favourite men.

Hawkwood shrugged. 'I've already revealed my hesitations to Sir William,' he said. 'If we *don't* take Piacenza, I believe that the Visconti peace proposals will end the war this month or next. Everyone is out of money. And that leaves us in Lombardy with no friends, unpaid.'

Brice made a *tsking* sound.

Hawkwood laughed. 'If they knew what was best for them, they'd never leave us unpaid,' he said.

Well, that was an interesting comment to discuss another time.

'So,' I said, 'in short, you want me to go into Piacenza, find the abbot and make some sort of deal.'

'Yes,' Hawkwood said. 'And you'll need a guide, as I doubt you've ever been in the city.'

'A guide,' I agreed. 'Perhaps a description, street by street. And how do you propose that I get in?'

We were both dressed as women, me and my guide. Because, as it proved, I had to find my own way in, and my own guide. It's another story entirely, but my guide was a native of the city, and also a woman – Fontana's sister, Donna Maddalena. And we were dressed as women because we saw women go out to work in the fields just under the walls, and Maddalena swore she could get us in. In fact, I guessed that she was eager for the work, and while we sat in an abandoned hut close to the tilled fields, she admitted that she wanted to get her money and silver out of her house.

'I have nothing,' she said. 'I have the clothes that I wear and a change your friend Janet gave me, and that's all. I'm too small to be a man-at-arms like Janet, and too old to be a whore.'

That wasn't a statement that seemed to call for gallantry. Also, soldiers really aren't that choosy. However, neither comment really seemed appropriate.

I didn't really like her much, but her courage and practicality were very appealing. So I just grinned.

'Well,' I said, 'we'll fetch your silver, then.'

So, when the women who'd worked all day under the walls started across the fields at the tolling of a bell, we just walked out of the hut, across two ploughed fields, and fell into the queue of women waiting to go through a sally port. We went in one at a time, and my heart was beating so loudly I assumed the guards could hear it. All these farming women had to know one another ... and the Monk of Hecz certainly knew me.

Maddalena went through and there was a pause. I heard her say something harshly, and I put my head at the sally port gate.

A soldier had grabbed one of her breasts and was trying to raise her skirt. She kept the skirt pinned down with one hand and was pulling a dagger with the other.

Well ... I'm a big man, and I was a giant of a woman, and my somewhat craggy face made me appear older than I was, so I went through the sally port like a ship under sail.

'Maddalena!' I shrieked. 'Stop annoying the soldiers.'

I grabbed her wrist and pulled. The soldier let go of her breast and pushed her away, and the other two, German men-at-arms, both laughed.

Twenty steps later, she stopped and was sick.

'I hate them all,' she said.

'I understand,' I said. 'But your killing one wasn't going to get you your silver, nor me my meeting.'

'I forget ...' She spat. 'Christ, I'm sorry. Christ. I hate them. I hate them all.'

I had to suspect that perhaps I came in under the 'hate them all' and I didn't want to guess why, so instead I steered us up into the town. Piacenza sits on a hill. I went up. Several of the other women looked at us, and I suspected they guessed we were strangers, but no one said anything.

'We need to vanish,' I said.

Maddalena made a very quick recovery. 'Hellish brutes.' She spat again, rubbing at her left breast. 'Come. Follow me.'

We walked along one broad street and then we were in a warren of alleys and overhung side streets. We emerged on a small piazza, and my guide lifted her skirts high and all but ran into a narrow alley that smelt of cats and men both. The brown slosh under our feet was too vile for me to think about much, but I followed Maddalena until she put a key into a lock, shot back a bolt and pulled me inside.

She fell on her knees before a very fine icon of the Blessed Virgin painted on the wall by the door and prayed. I admit that I crossed myself and prayed as well, while reminding myself why I loved Venice. Venice didn't have an alley that smelt like that. My camp didn't have an alley that smelt like that. I was afraid my shoes were ruined. On the other hand, they were borrowed from Long Mag, a lady of somewhat catholic virtue who shared her loyalties between my people and Thornbury's.

Maddalena rose from her devotions. 'I want to fetch some things,' she said, and walked off into the house.

It was a good house – a lord's city house. It had a small central courtyard, beautiful high ceilings, and frescoes on every wall – nice geometric patterns in cheerful and expensive colours. It had also been stripped. The looters hadn't left much except the refuse of someone's life – a receipt book with pages torn out, a lot of filthy rags that proved to be clothes that had been discarded, some rotten vegetables, a table too big to be carried out easily.

Maddalena muttered about 'animals' and went up the stone steps to the first floor. I didn't follow her, but instead went to the narrow windows on the small piazza and looked out carefully. There was no one on the streets, not even beggars. The garrison had probably instituted a curfew of some sort.

My guide was gone for perhaps half an hour, and then she re-appeared with a leather bag.

'They've taken or ruined all my clothes,' she said in a matter-of-fact voice. 'But they didn't find my brother's hideaway. Or mine. Come, sir, I'll take you to the abbot.'

I pointed out of the windows. 'I believe there's a curfew,' I said.

And even as I pointed, there was movement in the piazza, which proved to be three soldiers and a man in good woollen clothes, a long gown like a merchant.

He pointed at the house.

'I think . . .' I began.

'Follow me,' she said, and walked down a long hall to the kitchen, which was ransacked. There was rotting flour all over the floor and all the herbs had been cut down, leaving dangling linen threads like empty nooses hanging from the rafters.

She stopped for a moment, and when she turned, her eyes were narrowed and her anger was visible.

'My brother was always a good lord. We gave to every church. Our *neighbours* did this.'

Behind us, we could hear a rattle at the front doors.

'Come,' she said.

I followed her, wishing that I had a sword.

We went out of the kitchen into the central courtyard. Something stank.

'Oh, the bastards.' She spat.

Three hounds lay dead, rotting.

Three fast little nods. She'd promised herself something – revenge, I suspected.

We went into what might once have been a stable, and then a storage house. It had also been looted. And to a small wicket gate. Maddalena opened it carefully, and I followed her out into a narrow street paved in mud. It opened on to a little park full of apple trees just coming into bloom, and there were voices somewhere close, and the sound of a smith's hammer working a horseshoe.

And chickens. First the smell of them, and then twenty of the birds all pecking away in a little yard, which we crossed, our hems lifted fastidiously, and we were going down some steps and out into another street.

My guide knew her town very well. If there were pursuers, they were far behind.

Two more turns and we were in an area that, had it been London,

98

would have been the stews, or perhaps Southwark. And it was getting dark. There were no lanterns anywhere, and it was not a good place to be a woman. Now there were people on the street, all men – a rag-picker, a man selling sausages, a few louts gathered around an outside fire.

'Don't stop,' Maddalena said.

I hadn't planned to stop. Someone made a comment and we kept walking.

'Hey, sweet! Have anything to sell a man?'

'Let's see your purse, honeypot!' called another.

We kept going, and no one followed us.

We went up a long flight of steps and we were suddenly in a different world – a paved piazza, a fountain, the black side wall of a big church, and then a narrow street, clean, with a lit lamp at the end and two long blank walls. We hurried along, going slightly uphill.

'I don't suppose you'd like to tell me where we are?' I asked.

She glanced back at me. 'If I said we were close to the Benedictine church, would it mean anything to you?'

'No,' I confessed.

'Then shut up and follow me,' she snapped. And then, relenting, she pointed at the brick wall. 'San Raimondo,' she said. 'We will see.'

We turned at the corner, under a fine stone crucifix, and she rapped at the gate. A shutter opened.

'Yes, *madonna*?' a smooth voice asked.

'I would like an audience with the abbot,' she said. She held up something from her leather bag.

The shutter closed, and the gate opened. Just like that.

Before the bells rang for Vespers, we were through the abbey gate and in a comfortable room in one of the monastery buildings. A monk offered us wine. Maddalena accepted gratefully, sat and put her bag on the floor. After a minute, the monk returned with a tray and a stone bottle of wine.

He spilled a little of it while pouring, and handed the first cup to Maddalena. I watched him pour mine and my suspicion was confirmed. His hands were trembling. Your head moves very quickly sometimes. I remember thinking that he wasn't old, that he had strong hands, and then noting that he wore shoes, not sandals, under his robe. His hood was up, which was not so odd as it was cold, but I pulled it down. He wasn't tonsured.

'Don't drink that,' I spat, and threw him and his tray to the ground. The tray fell with a smash – a great deal of noise.

So much for being clever. He had a dagger, a big baselard, which he drew as he tried to rise, but he used a hand to push himself off the stone floor. By pure ill luck for him, he put his hand on glass, swore, and I kicked him in the head and took the dagger. His greatest error was his assumption that I was a woman. He was still deceived as he rolled back, cursing, from my kick.

Maddalena stooped, plucked the stone bottle off the floor, and slammed it on his head. He went down as if his sinews had been cut.

I paused to listen at the door. Running footsteps, the clatter and jingle of sword belts and swords.

'A trap,' I said.

Maddalena's eyes narrowed. But she had the presence of mind to pick up her leather bag.

'Through the church,' she said.

We were out of the door to the room and running down the corridor. We were a floor too high for the church, which I guessed was the next building. We'd come up out of the central court, but a glance back said that way was closed. There were soldiers running across the courtyard, and at least two on the broad stone steps we'd taken ten minutes before.

'There!' shouted a man.

Damn.

We ran down the corridor, but we'd come the wrong way for anything. We were on a corridor of offices and cells. On the other hand, the doors were mostly open.

I pulled us into one, about halfway down, and proceeded to strip off Long Mag's kirtle and overgown. If I was going to die here, I was going down fighting.

Maddalena looked at me.

Very quietly, I said, 'They'll have to search the corridor. As soon as they start, we run for the stairs. People make mistakes. It's our only hope.'

She smiled, and rose far in my estimation. 'You've been trapped in a monastery before?' she asked, in her sarcastic way.

She still had the stone bottle in her hand.

The voices were close, an officer ordering every room searched. I risked a look into the corridor – half a dozen armed men. Armed, but most hadn't drawn their swords, because ... Because they thought they were looking for two women, I suppose.

I nodded at my guide, and she nodded back and we went for it.

When I burst into the corridor, the officer was the only one still standing in the hall. All of his men were in various rooms. When I saw him, he saw me, and our mutual recognition cost both of us a heartbeat.

He was Blackbeard. Camus's assassin. Perhaps Robert of Geneva's assassin. And the murderer of Prince Lionel, the Duke of Clarence.

And he knew me, too. He said, 'You!'

It is difficult, in retrospect, to break down how you make complex decisions. Had I been alone, perhaps I would have killed him, or tried. But I had a responsibility to Maddalena, and I wasn't particularly interested in a heroic death, and I knew that if I was taken, it would be terrible. All that, in the blink of an eye.

My left hand covered his right arm, so that he couldn't draw, and I kneed him hard between the legs and he fell. I supposed I might have killed him, but it would have cost me a step or two, and people are harder to kill than you think.

As he fell, I was pushing past, and my hand found his sword hilt, the way you sometimes find a man's dagger hilt in a close press, in armour. I drew it as I passed him and he fell away, so that I had it in my hand by the time I was three steps on. That meant I had a baselard in my right hand and a sword in my left, which made what followed memorable.

There were two men at the head of the stairs and, worse luck, they'd seen the whole encounter. Both had time to draw as we ran at them. The closest cut at me as I entered his distance. I made a sloppy parry with the dagger, damn it, because it was in my right hand. His blow fell on the baselard's broad backbone, but momentum carried it through and he pinked me in the shoulder. His heavy blow turned him and I kicked, hard, as much from pain and fear as training, and he went down the stairs and didn't rise.

The other man thrust. I used the sword on his sword and he backed away, the way many people do when countered.

'Run,' I said to Maddalena.

I had five or six men running after me now, and I turned, flipped the dagger, and threw it at my nearest opponent. He tried to parry it. The hilt clipped his hand, and then he was dead, my left-handed sword in his throat. It wouldn't come out, either, so I took his and went down the steps as fast as I could. The men above me were shouting various alarms, and the courtyard was suddenly *full* of men – angry men, in brown robes. Monks. And off to the right, coming through an arch, men-at-arms in heavy armour. And at their head, *another* man I knew.

The Monk of Hecz.

But it was my good fortune that the monks didn't like him any better than I did, and his men-at-arms weren't like the dogs Camus had trained. They slowed at the sight of all the brown robes, and hesitated.

The monks let Maddalena go right through them. So I followed. The monks were angry at the soldiers, I know now. At the time it was like a miracle, and it gave us quite a head start. We didn't waste it. Maddalena, despite her skirts, was fast, and she led us back through the gate, down the long alley, down the steps, into the stews. It was fully dark by then, and by the time we were passing the sausage seller, we could hear the alarm being raised behind us – shouts, the telltale clatter of men in armour, running.

The louts on the wellhead in the dirty piazza didn't call out any trash as we passed, either. A sword in your hand is a sovereign remedy against insults, I find.

The moment we were away from people, we ran again. We had some luck. It began to rain, a cold, stinging rain that may have had some ice in it, but it was too dark to see it. But I think that it discouraged pursuit.

Maddalena looked back at me, her face a flash of paleness in the dark.

'How do you propose to get out?' she asked.

'Straight out the sally port, the same way we got in.' I tried to sound confident.

In fact, it was a desperate idea, but the only one I had. The little sally port was set into a pair of towers. It was unassailable from the outside of the town, hidden behind a low bastion of earth, but from the inside, it didn't have a good sight line to any of the major gates.

Most gates have complex keys. In Italian cities, where no one trusts anyone else, there are often multi-part keys to require several men, like the podestà and the captain of the garrison, to both work together to open a gate. But sally ports need to be used quickly to be effective. I hoped that it would be unguarded, defended by just a heavy bolt or bar.

Like many plans, I got some of what I wanted, but not all. There were three men crouched under the arch of the gate, their kettle helms tilted down against the rain. Maddalena and I were both soaking wet. I had a naked sword in my hand, and I was very cold in a light doublet and hose and no shoes. My feet sloshed in the stretched-out feet of my hose every step, which made walking clumsy.

And once we rounded the last corner in a narrow street, they could see us as soon as we saw them. And everything about us was suspicious. Odds of three to one are terrible odds in a close fight, and worse in the dark and rain, and ten paces before we reached them, they had drawn their swords.

And I didn't even know if I could get the gate open.

Any hesitation I might have felt was dispelled when the largest of the three blew a horn. On the other hand, wet and hurry caused him to sound more like a dying cow than a desperate sentry.

I had no choice. I ran at them, my footed hose like sodden hands slowing my feet. I threw a simple cut to try and draw a response from the closest man as I slowed and went to his right, so that I put the three men in a line.

The nearest man had a blue-painted kettle helm, and he bought my provocation and made a hasty parry even though I was not quite in distance. I stepped in with my left foot, rotating my sword from his heavy parry. He'd only caught the tip, and I kept moving, passed the blade over his shoulder, stepped through, caught it in my bare hand and put my sword across his throat as I passed. I threw him into his companions, already dead or dying as my blade went deep into his neck. Unfortunately, having caught the blade in my left hand to make the throw, it cut into my left palm, too.

The man in the middle was caught by the weight of my victim, his sword pinned against him as he tried not to stab his friend in the back. I thrust with my hand high, over the corpse. I didn't kill him. I was too sloppy and he was slightly too far away, but my point slashed across his nose and he screamed, and the third man was pushed into the arch against the gate. I went at them both because there is nothing

but *ardentsia* in these things. My wrist cut hit steel – a helmet, a
sword ... it didn't matter. No sword was coming back at me. The
first man was bleeding out on the cobblestones, so I cut again, left
to right, trying to get under the flash of wet steel that might be a
helmet. I knew from the feel of the blow that the man was wearing
a brigantine. I was virtually naked, and this wasn't going to go well,
so I went in close. I gave the screaming man a shove that threw him
into his companion again, and tried to get my pommel into the third
man's nose. He cut at me from too close and his quillons went into
my left shoulder. You can kill a man with your cross guard in the right
place, but luckily, all he did was blow all the cold out of me in a burst
of combat spirit and fear. His sword was caught in my shoulder, or
my doublet, and I slammed my pommel into his face, spinning him
against the stone arch with my superior size.

He dropped. I kicked at his blade and got it out of his hand at the
cost of cutting my foot. I'd forgotten I had no shoes. Three wounds,
and two of them basically self-inflicted. That's fighting in the dark,
when you are desperate.

I could now hear horns, and men calling out, and the rush of
armoured men and their clanking progress from the main gate, just a
tower and a stretch of curtain wall away.

I cursed.

Maddalena was trying to move the bar. It was a sliding bar, maybe
eight feet long, solid oak, across the whole gate and the sally port
door, and it moved freely – about a handspan. And bounced back.

'There's a key!' she said. 'There must be a key.'

We had no light. There were three dead or desperately wounded
men, and one of them probably had the key.

Purse? Around his neck? It had to be easy – sally ports need to be
used in a hurry.

Remember, we had virtually no light.

We could run into the darkness and live a little longer. I could
search the bodies.

If they caught me, this was going to be very bad, and possibly worse
for the woman with me.

Blackbeard and the Monk.

I won't lie. They scared me.

And I was bleeding. Really bleeding. Three shallow wounds are like one bad wound, I guess. But I could feel the cold, suddenly, and I also felt the drowsy feeling blood loss creates. Just the start, but I'm quite experienced at losing blood.

I knelt by the man who had had the horn. I felt his neck – felt his pulse. He was alive, unconscious. I left him alive. No key around his neck, just a cord with a medal. No purse on his belt. I'd have missed the damn thing entirely if I hadn't lost my balance a little and put a hand down on his wrist. The key, which was just a bronze pin with a little device at the end, was on a cord attached to his wrist.

'Here they come,' Maddalena said. For the first time, her voice was a trifle unsteady. 'Kill me, please.'

There spoke a realist.

'I have the key,' I said. 'Get the gate open.' I put it in her hand by touch and stepped away from the gate into the rain.

Maddalena was praying. I may have muttered a prayer to Saint Michael.

They had torches, which spat and sputtered and gave away their advance, while casting so little light that they couldn't see us. Torches are like that. And they only had two.

I moved as silently as I could to the corner from which we'd started our attack, an eye on the glimmer of torches up the street. They weren't coming fast, which was good. They were cautious.

'Is it an attack?' called out one man. 'Roberto! Say something, man.'

'I don't like this,' another said.

I heard a snap, an exclamation that was not pious, and the bar shot back. Then the creak and grind behind me. Maddalena had the gate open.

'Fuck! The sally port is open!' shouted a man. 'Sound the alarm!'

The whole body of them stopped and a half a dozen horns rang out. The first blasts weren't very good, but in a few heartbeats they sounded like the horns of the Wild Hunt.

By then, I was out of the sally port in the pouring rain. Maddalena caught my hand and I whimpered a little – it was my left hand. I was hobbling, but fear and whatever power it is that comes on a person in a desperate fight kept me on my feet through a ditch now half-full of water, then around the little outwork and across the muddy fields.

We were well across the second field when I just stopped going. I paused for a moment, trying to figure out what was happening, and then I was lying in the freezing mud. It was too bad that my leg wouldn't support me, because I could hear a lot of armoured men splashing along in the dark, shouting.

Maddalena stopped, looked down and said, 'Damn it, I can't carry you.'

And then she was gone.

I returned to life about six hours later, bandaged and warm, in my own bed. Marc-Antonio whooped and got me soup.

I went to sleep after the soup, and awoke to John Hawkwood standing by my bed. It was quite cold, despite two braziers. I was cold, under several counterpanes and a heavy blanket from England.

'What happened?' he asked.

'They were waiting for us,' I said.

'That's what the lady said. I just wanted to be sure.' He smiled grimly. 'When the alarm bells rang in the town, your friends Fiore insisted on taking the whole of my night guard up to the walls. Probably the only reason you're alive. They sent some sort of sortie after you. Fiore captured a few of them.' He shrugged. 'We're done here.'

I wriggled. 'Sir John ...' I said, or something to get his attention. 'I saw him. The man who killed Prince Lionel. He was there, waiting for me. I think he works for Bernabò now, or he always worked for Bernabò, or Galeazzo.'

Hawkwood shrugged. 'Interesting,' he said. 'But it doesn't change anything. We can't take Piacenza, and we're wasting men and horses here.'

And so it proved. While I was still wounded, we moved back towards Bologna. I know now that Coucy and Hawkwood were in agreement, but the Pope was outraged, bombarding them from Avignon with demands to continue the 'siege'. Except that it was no siege – and without a siege train, food or money, we had no chance of taking a powerful city.

I lost a week there. I managed to get on a horse for a few hours a day. I vaguely remember a long conversation with l'Angars where I thought I made sense, explaining to him how I wanted the outposts run. I know I asked Janet to help l'Angars run the company.

But mostly, it's gone. I think they celebrated Easter in there, somewhere, and I missed it. Mostly I lay on my camp bed, with

Pilgrim sometimes taking up more than I did, and I slept a great deal.

And then it was May, and we were close under the walls of Bologna. No one particularly wanted us there, which matched up with the sad truth that none of us particularly wanted to be there. The Pope made Hawkwood some promises. I know he got a fine benefice for his bastard son, which was worth something to Sir John and nothing to the rest of us. At Bologna we had to pay for every blade of grass for our horses and every mouthful we ate, and that made war very expensive – for us.

We had desertions. That is, I didn't, not immediately, but Brice and Romney did. Our spirit was virtually non-existent, and discipline was poor.

My foot was fevered. It got thicker and redder instead of healing, and the cut wept pus, and then, after another week, there were black lines spreading from it. I'd seen enough wounds to know that this was bad.

Bologna was one of the great centres of learning for all of Europe, and it had a medical school. I sent Beppo to find me a physician, and he persuaded not one but two of them to attend me. By this time, I was sharing my pavilion with Lord Fontana, who was healing but still bed-bound, and his sister, who had taken on the role of our nurse.

The two eminent men had a long conversation in Latin, which they assumed in their arrogance that none of the rest of us understood. The conversation ranged from how much they hated foreign mercenaries to how much money they could charge me, based on what they knew of my career.

The shorter of the two men came and sat on my camp bed, put on gloves, and unwrapped the bandages on my foot.

'I will have your horoscope cast,' the shorter of the two worthy masters said, 'but it is clear to me from your profession and your complexion that you are a man of sanguine temperament. It's equally clear from the condition of your foot that you suffer from an excess of yellow bile.' He suddenly squeezed my wound and foul yellow pus came out. I may have screamed. 'This indicates that the season is acting on your wound to produce a choleric response.' He wiped his gloved hands on a towel. 'I will recommend that the wound be bound again, but after repeated washing in cold water to counter the effects of the excess of bile.'

The taller man made a face. 'I suppose,' he said. In Latin, he said, 'Galen would insist on preserving the yellow pus.'

'Oh,' said the first master. 'Of course. Let us cleave unto Galen in all things.'

To Greg Fox, whom he took for a servant, the shorter man said, 'Carefully extract the pus, however painful. Wash the foot in cold water, paint the linens with the extracted pus and replace them.'

'I'll need the date and hour of your birth,' said the taller man, to me, in Italian. And then, in Latin, '*Quantum possumus accipere ei?*' That, my friends, means, 'How much can we get him for?'

'*Quinquaginta quisque,*' the shorter said. In other words, 'Fifty each.'

They had hurt me cruelly, and I hated both of them by that time. I sent Greg for Sam Bibbo.

'Now about our fees,' the shorter man said. 'We will need an astrologer. Luckily the university provides such. Each of us will expect our normal fees ...'

Bibbo came in. 'Sir William?' he asked.

'Put these two gentlemen somewhere for a little while. And get me a horse leech.'

The taller man was appalled when Bibbo put a hand under his elbow. 'Release me this instant, barbarian, or—'

'Best come along, sir,' Bibbo said in his Anglo-Italian. 'You have annoyed Sir William.' He steered the two men out of the tent.

Maddalena stepped forward from the partition that separated her part of the tent with her brother from mine.

'Charlatans,' she said. 'Quacks. Listen, any monastery or nunnery can do better. I can do better myself. Warm wine painted on the wound, constant cleaning, strips of boiled linen. Any convent knows these things. And prayer, Ser Guglielmo. When did you last pray?'

I couldn't tell whether she despised them as secular men of learning or as bad doctors, but the horse leech, when brought, proved to be a middle-aged Hungarian man. I knew him immediately – László's mounted archer.

He looked at the wound, sniffed it, and then shrugged. 'It's fucking bad,' he said. 'Keep it clean. Works on horses.'

'And no one asks horses for their dates of birth,' I said. 'Right, give each of the learned gentlemen five florins and escort them out of camp. Have Bibbo mention that I read Vegetius every night before bed, so they get the message clearly.' I looked at Maddalena. 'You and János here are now my doctors.'

She looked at the Hungarian. 'Hmmf,' she said.

Every day, while her brother got better and returned my hospitality by telling me repeatedly that all mercenaries were cowards and fools, Maddalena came in, unwrapped my foot, let in 'air' for a while because László's archer said that was good for horses, and then cleaned it – a very painful process – before ladling hot wine over it and rewrapping it with clean linen. It was a lengthy process. She didn't sniff, or complain, or make jokes. She was as quick as she could be, using the small scissors from her sewing kit which I assumed she'd reclaimed from her house, and tying the bandage off neatly.

The black lines around the wound grew worse, and then better. They grew paler.

I couldn't walk on the foot. It was swollen, and I felt listless. L'Angars and Bibbo came and went, and mostly I remember being cold, and miserable.

After some days of this, Fontana demanded his own pavilion. Bibbo found him one captured at the fight by the river, and he and his sister moved to it.

The next morning, Maddalena was back, with clean linen and her little scissors and a local woman she had engaged as a maid, I suppose. She came in while Fiore was examining a sword he'd bought. He was in raptures. She glanced at him once, rolled her eyes, and started on my foot. Fiore didn't even notice when I cried out – Maddalena was very thorough. When she was done, she asked, 'Do you have a breviary?'

I handed her this one. It was beside the bed, because I had accepted her direction and returned to prayer. I couldn't manage a meditation, as the fever still had me strongly.

'Would it help if I read to you?' she asked.

'I wouldn't mind,' I began, and then realised how rude that sounded. '*Madonna*, I would be most pleased and honoured if you would read to me.'

Fiore looked at me over his sword blade and raised an eyebrow.

'*Alora*,' she said.

She sent Greg Fox for a chair, and she sat and began to read psalms. Some I'd copied out myself, and some Sister Marie had copied – here, you can flip through yourself. But even with my private prayers, reading the whole of it only took a few hours.

'You have little marks,' she said, when she'd come to the end.

'Yes,' I said. I think I realised then that I wanted her approval, because I didn't tell her what they were for.

She raised an eyebrow. 'And ...?' she asked.

'The crosses are for men I killed, sometimes with a date.' I shrugged. 'It's not because I am so very proud of killing, Siora.'

Fiore peered over her shoulder. 'A fine notion,' he said. 'Do you mark which way you killed them? What technique you use?'

'I usually remember,' I told him, which is sometimes true.

'I always remember,' Fiore allowed, and went back to his sword.

'You pray for them?' she asked.

I thought about that. 'Some of them,' I said. I *had* prayed for Camus, more than once. And my uncle. But I thought more of the boy I'd killed in Hungary, and the poor innocents in Alexandria, and so on.

She put the breviary down. 'Is this the only book you own?' she asked.

I smiled, as I assumed she wanted to read more. 'I have Vegetius, and ...' I suddenly remembered. 'And another breviary.'

I had to ask Greg Fox to find it – it was Bernabò's, from his wagon.

Maddalena leafed through it. 'This is magnificent,' she said.

'I believe it was made for the Visconti,' I said.

She read through it, snorting at the prayers. 'Asking God to slay his enemies,' she said after one. 'Does he think that God is some sort of malevolent sorcerer?'

When she was done, she handed it to Greg. 'A beautiful book with horror inside the covers.' She shrugged. 'Perhaps I will read you this Vegetius, instead.'

I felt better that day, and better yet the next. Fiore made his daily visit, as did Bibbo and l'Angars with reports, and then Maddalena worked on my foot.

'I think you enjoy my pain,' I muttered.

She raised an eyebrow. 'Of course I do,' she said.

I was beginning to wonder if I had missed a very dry sense of humour. But I didn't pursue it. She began to read Vegetius in Latin, and I discovered that her Latin was much better than mine.

'You must have heard what the two medical men said,' I asked her.

Maddalena smiled. 'I felt you dealt with them justly.' She paused in her reading. 'We will be moving into the city in a day or two,' she said. 'My brother has quarrelled with the lord of Coucy.'

I should have watched my tongue, but I didn't.

'Your brother quarrels easily,' I said. 'He is a difficult man.'

She frowned. 'My brother and I do not always see eye to eye,' she said. 'But he is a good man, and he has endured many hardships as an exile. And he is truly loyal to the people of his city. His reward for that loyalty was to have his house pillaged.' Her face was suddenly blotched with anger. She stood up to leave.

'I'm sorry, Siora,' I said. 'I apologise.'

She looked at me. 'Don't you think I sit here writhing when he calls you a coward?' she said. 'I know his temper, none better. But his anger is the anger of frustration.'

'I am sorry, Siora. Truly. And I have never taken offence.'

She nodded. 'No, you have not,' she agreed. She settled down with the book.

I was thinking that it was at least something that she writhed when he called me a coward.

'Do you think ...?' I began, when Peter Albin came into the tent.

'I was sent with messages,' he explained, as he sat on my bed. 'Some for Coucy, some for Sir John Hawkwood, one for you. But Sir John said you were wounded. May I see?'

Maddalena put the book away and looked at her maid.

'Please, stay,' I said. 'Siora Maddalena, this is Peter Albin. He is a doctor.'

'Of theology,' Albin said with a smile. 'But my uncle was a most able physician and surgeon.' He unwrapped my foot. 'Warm wine?' he asked, sniffing it.

'Yes,' I said.

'Nicely done. I don't like those black lines.'

'They were worse,' I said.

Maddalena stood up, but instead of leaving, she came over by Albin. 'They ran all the way to here, on the ankle, a week ago,' she said.

'Christ,' Albin said. He looked at her, and then at me. 'You might have died.'

'Died?' I asked.

'Did the cut run all the way to the bone?' he asked.

'I don't think so,' I answered. Maddalena shook her head.

'That's a mercy, anyway,' Albin said. 'It looks as if it's healing – the edges are closing and the ends are not red.' He looked at Maddalena. 'Your work?'

She shrugged. One of the things I found that I liked in Maddalena was that she was not very womanly, by which I mean that she didn't hide her eyes and her thoughts, like many women. Nor did she flirt. She was always serious. Like Sister Marie.

'I did the bandages. I have read a book or two.' She shrugged. 'There is a man in this company who advised me. A horse doctor.'

Albin smiled. 'That's what some of the count's people call me,' he said. 'Well ... I'll look at it again tomorrow.'

'You are here for a few days?' I asked.

He looked at Maddalena, and I understood his look. I really was feeling better – I could read people again.

'Her brother is the illustrious Lord Fontana of Piacenza,' I said.

'Ah,' he said. Albin knew his Italian politics. 'Then I won't hesitate to tell you that Galeazzo and Bernabò have raised a fresh army and it's coming your way.'

Maddalena nodded, picked up her basket, and made a slight courtesy. 'I will leave you two gentlemen to talk,' she said.

We both said something suitable and she was gone.

Albin sat in the chair she'd vacated.

'Amadeus wants you to win, but he needs the war to end,' he said. 'Not immediately, but soon.'

'Hell's gates,' I cursed, or something worse. 'Damn it to Hell. I thought better of him.'

Albin took a deep breath and then let it out. 'If I may be so bold, Sir William, what did you expect? The count no more wants the destruction of Milan than he wants the defeat of the Pope. Galeazzo is his brother-in-law. He's happy to see Bernabò chastened, but he doesn't want to see Hawkwood laying siege to Pavia.'

'As to that,' I said, 'we couldn't even manage a proper siege of Piacenza.'

Albin sat back. He was wearing tall boots and spurs, and the spurs caught in my tent floor and there was some cursing. Then he had to pull the spurs off and wash his hands.

'That's part of it,' he said from my washbasin. 'It's pretty clear that even when you win on the battlefield, you don't have the money to win. Amadeus wants the war over. He's still paying for his crusade, you know?'

'I know,' I admitted.

And if the Pope hadn't paid Amadeus of Savoy any more than he'd paid Coucy or Hawkwood, then the count owed the Pope nothing in return.

'Which reminds me,' Albin said, and handed over a letter. I noted immediately that it was unsigned, and in my friend Richard's handwriting. I think I'm a better scribe, but I could read it.

I read it over twice. It was in English, easy to read. I looked at Albin.

'But the Visconti have come up with enough money to pay another army?' I asked.

Albin nodded. 'Two thousand lances, or so I've heard. That again in good infantry.'

'And you've told all this to Sir John?' I asked.

'I have,' he said.

'I'd better heal up.' I said promptly. 'Where is this army? Who commands it?'

'Up north, moving along the road to Verona. They say Gian Galeazzo, the young Count of Virtu, commands.'

'The Count of Vertu,' I snarled. I didn't like him at all. I went back to my letter. 'The count wants me to take service with Nerio,' I said. 'What's he up to?'

Albin's eyes sparkled. For a man of learning, he enjoyed the game of politics a little too much.

'I can tell you two things,' he said. 'One is that this is something about the Union of Churches. The other is that your friend Nicolas Sabraham visited the count about a month ago.'

'Sabraham!' I exclaimed.

Sabraham was another volunteer for the Order of Saint John, but he'd made something of a career of it. He was also often the messenger of the Order to various western princes, as well as a spy. He spoke

Arabic and Turkish. He'd taught me a great deal in one summer, back in '65 when we took Alexandria.

The Green Count was up to something that required me to go to Greece and serve Nerio. It made me grin, I can tell you. If you don't understand why, well, you hadn't spent a winter fighting a non-war for no pay.

The next day, Lord Fontana and his sister moved to a house in Bologna. My foot continued to mend, which was good, because Coucy was determined to meet the Visconti army in the field.

To do so, we had to cross the territory of our esteemed neighbour the lord of Mantua, the illustrious Ludovico Gonzaga. You may recall from last night's tale that Gonzaga had not been very careful with his neutrality, and I had been sent to punish him for it. There was very little love lost between Gonzaga and Sir John Hawkwood. So we sent Gonzaga a well-written request to pass his lands, and then we marched. Mantua didn't have the men or money to stop us, and by stealing a march through Mantua we could gain several days on the Visconti.

I got my foot wrapped in a leather bag and got on a horse for the first time in weeks. I'd lost weight, and I still got light-headed easily, but I managed to stay in the saddle as we went north. It was finally warm, or I was leaving my fever behind – or both – and I suddenly had a great appetite and ate every time we stopped.

I noticed that Janet was distant. She had previously attended officers' meetings, but no more, and I saw her seldom, but didn't particularly remark on it. She and l'Angars had held the company together, but we had, in the end, had desertions. Several lances had left us for Venice, who paid regularly, and several of our archers had simply taken their horses and ridden away. As they were in arrears on pay, they hadn't really broken any law, and there was little enough we could do. And, of course, all of Fontana's fellow exiles left us when he did.

Bibbo was taciturn, and I could tell that he took the desertions of the archers personally.

And there was still no money. The Roman road ran straight to Mantua, and the lord thereof had arranged markets. Gonzaga didn't do this for any love of us – rather, he did it to protect his peasants and his taxes. We were careful to preserve his benevolence by allowing no pillage or thievery as we passed, although Beppo kept up a running commentary on the richness of the place.

As we camped outside Mantua, Coucy held a command meeting in his beautiful pavilion, which now showed some signs of wear after a winter and spring in the field. The Lord of Coucy himself showed some signs of wear. His clothes were still beautifully maintained, but there were stains and marks from belts and maille and armour. He was frustrated, that much I could see.

'Bernabò's army is at Brescia, as best we can guess,' he said. 'I am told he intends to march on Modena or Bologna.'

'So we're going to stop him before he begins,' Hawkwood said.

Coucy gave the older man a glance that suggested that he might have liked to do the explaining himself, but was too polite to say, and Hawkwood went on.

'Thanks to Mantua's pliable conscience and sense of neutrality, we are well suited. We have food and fodder.' He glanced at Coucy.

'I mean to force Bernabò's army to battle,' Coucy said. 'And I mean to do it before he moves the war to the Pope's lands.'

That made sense. I nodded.

'Does the Pope plan to pay us?' Brice asked. He was a blunt man. 'Or are we expected to risk death because we're chivalrous gentlemen?' His tone conveyed what he thought of chivalrous gentlemen.

Coucy looked away.

Hawkwood narrowed his eyes. 'We will fight,' he said, 'and we will discuss payment after we win.'

Brice glared right back, and Romney shook his head. 'Rumour is that the commanders are getting land grants,' he said. 'Church lands. But we haven't got shit.'

Thornbury looked pained, but I noticed that he was standing with Brice.

Niccolò d'Este, whose cousin Francesco was one of the commanders of the enemy army, crossed his arms.

'Perhaps I don't like the expression,' he said, 'but the sentiment is accurate. My little devils do not usually couch their lances for nothing.'

Hawkwood's glance didn't waver. 'We will fight,' he said. 'And we will discuss our payments afterwards.'

There was grumbling, but no open revolt. But after I left, Hawkwood sent one of his men for me, and I went back. I remember that evening best because the mosquitoes were terrible, like a pestilence, and we were all covered in bites. Mantua is surrounded by wetlands.

Hawkwood had me sit. Thornbury was there, and Brice, and Romney, and most of the other corporals.

'Gentlemen,' Hawkwood said, after we all had wine, 'it's bad, and I know it's bad. I'm doing my best to squeeze the Pope for money. If we fight and win, there might be some. If we lose, or don't fight, there will be none. There, now you know.'

'And if there's no money after we win?' Brice asked.

Hawkwood shrugged. 'Then we disband,' he said.

'Disband!' Brice said. 'Christ, John, when you sent me to the Pope after Christmas there was no talk of this.'

It was the first I'd heard that Hawkwood had sent Brice to the Pope.

After they were all gone, it was just Thornbury and me. Hawkwood refilled my wine cup himself. It was dark, and there was just one candle burning on the table, which gave him a disembodied air.

'Sometimes it is difficult to believe how stupid they are,' he said. 'With money, I could win this war in a summer. Piacenza and Bergamo and even Pavia are ripe to revolt. The Visconti are bastards, as we have reason to know, eh, William?'

I nodded.

'Their own people hate them for the most part. But no. The Pope is sending money to the King of France, not to us. I chose badly this time.'

'I'll stay and fight,' Thornbury said. 'But I don't trust this army much.'

'Nor do I,' Hawkwood said. 'And I fear a defeat. I'm too old to build a new reputation.' He looked at Thornbury, and then at me. 'You'll stand by me, then?'

We nodded. I owed Sir John. I would stand by him.

Back in my corner of the camp, I informed my officers of what they could expect.

'I will pay for this month, whatever comes,' I said.

'Lads will like that,' Bibbo said.

L'Angars nodded. 'I think, with this news, I can keep them together.'

Janet was silent, but after the men left, she poured herself a cup of

116

my wine. I was quite conscious of how much I imitated Hawkwood, right down to the meetings, but Hawkwood was always very good at passing information down and I liked that.

'What's next?' she asked. 'Since this is all going to hell?'

I sat back and motioned her to sit. I noted that she didn't sit on my bed, which was closest to her, but moved to a stool. Pilgrim went and curled at her feet.

'I have an offer for a year in Greece. Outremer. A good offer from an old friend.'

Janet blinked. 'You'll just leave Sir John?' she asked.

I shrugged. 'He's already talking about breaking us up, Janet. In Greece we'll be paid regularly and have definite goals for an employer I trust.'

'You don't trust Hawkwood?' she asked, incredulous.

'I don't trust the Pope,' I said. 'Hawkwood has been fairly open about telling us that the Pope has no more money.'

Janet nodded. 'I like it here,' she said. 'But I can't be with you any more.'

I paused, as that was a line women used when they were leaving you.

'Janet?' I asked.

'I probably said that badly,' she said. In French, she went on, 'I can't be with your little company, Guillaume. I want to be a knight, and not a knight's mistress.'

I raised my hands. 'I haven't ...'

She shook her head. 'Of course you haven't,' she said. She got up. I had a pair of lanterns hanging from the spokes of my pavilion, and she was very beautiful by candlelight. 'I'll stay with you until you leave for Greece ...'

'You are a vital part of this company,' I said. I summoned my courage, because I wanted to save something from this, and I was confused as to what she wanted. 'Whatever is between us, you are part of what makes us ... better.'

She delivered a straight-backed courtesy.

'That is ... very ... nice ... to hear,' she said.

She was standing close to me. Was I supposed to take her in my arms? Kiss her?

Obviously not. I took one of her hands and clasped it, knight to knight.

'I wish you'd stay.'

She looked at me for a long time, and then withdrew her hand.

'Oh, Guillaume,' she said, and left.

The next morning, we rode west, leaving the city of Mantua behind. By the end of a day's hard marching, we arrived near the Mantuan border with the Visconti. With Hawkwood's blessing, I sent Lapot and my best archers across the river Mincio before last light and into the Visconti lands, looking for an enemy army, or any sign of activity.

My foot was better – I could almost get it into a shoe. Fiore kept reminding me of the fight at Corinth, where one of my shoes was burned away and I fought the last part of the action barefoot.

'An astrologer would no doubt have something to say,' he added.

'And would doubtless try to charge me a hundred gold florins for saying it,' I said.

The next day was the first of May. We were woefully short of women or time to dance, so May Day celebrations were limited, but all of the English and most of the French and Breton soldiers wore sprigs of green or flowers, and there was a May pole in Thornbury's camp. I went and watched the dancing. Otherwise, the only event of the day was the arrival of twenty lances under Lord Fontana. He camped with the Bolognese levies. We had about a thousand lances, all told, and perhaps twice that in infantry. They were good infantry, for the most part, and better motivated than many of our lances, as they, at least, had been paid.

The Green Count was coming out of the north, despite whatever hesitation he'd felt. A cynic might suspect that Galeazzo was throwing Bernabò to the wolves, and we were the wolves, but it wasn't that simple. Galeazzo's son – and Count Amadeus's nephew – Gian Galeazzo was one of the three commanders of the Visconti force that was rumoured to be at Brescia.

Coucy thought that we had the Visconti at their last throw – their one army facing two of ours.

Sir John was less sanguine, and we moved slowly, with our archers and pages well spread. We were in Lombardy now, and columns of smoke from burning farms announced our arrival. I didn't like it, but I understood that Sir John was taunting the Visconti to come and defend their own land.

'I think they'll just sit in Brescia and thumb their noses at us,' Thornbury said to me.

Three days from Mantua, an entire command of fifty lances was gone in the night, and we had reason to believe they'd gone over to the Visconti. They were a mixed bag of Germans and Italians under a Gascon, and, like the rest of us, hadn't been paid since the beginning of the campaign.

'They weren't worth much,' Coucy said with contempt.

They weren't, at that. But other men would now be thinking about what the first fifty had done, and I didn't like it. I hobbled around my campfires that night and the next, trying to see every man. I sat with Witkin, listened to Ewan, played Briscola with Marc-Antonio. Dick Thorald was still out east with our outposts south of Pavia, but I made extra time to visit the men I'd brought from England and Calais. I made sure that everyone knew I'd be paying for this month, even if the Pope never paid.

Mostly, the men sounded like soldiers. There was a lot of complaining, but for the most part they were fed and clothed. They laughed at my jokes and gave Pilgrim a pat and looked forward to looting the Milanese camp.

The fifth day of May dawned clean and bright, the way a good spring day should be, and it promised to be hot. We were on a stretch of road that ran from San Giorgio to Madonnina, both small towns with rich religious establishments. Coucy met with the abbots, promised them they'd be safe, and then moved the army up the road in three divisions. I was moved out of the vanguard and into the rearguard with Thornbury and Hawkwood. The Bolognese lances took over the vanguard with some papal troops.

I sent Greg Fox to retrieve Lapot and his pickets. I was a little annoyed, to be honest. I thought highly of my abilities in running the chain of outposts of the advance guard, something that neither Italians nor Englishmen are particularly good at.

'Bide,' Sir John said. 'I want you two,' he jutted his chin at Thornbury, 'close at hand.'

Sir John's three hundred lances looked splendid – armour well polished, and plenty of it. Their horses looked good, too. If my fifty looked a mite better, that might be my own bias, or might be our large horse herd. Regardless, we looked good, and Thornbury's looked good, and all told we were almost five hundred lances and as many English archers, all well mounted. To be fair, the 'English' archers included Scots, Italians, Picards, Hungarians, and at least one Greek and one Turk, but we were 'the English' as far as our employers were concerned.

By midday we knew that the Visconti's army had marched out of Brescia, and that they were headed straight for us. The Bolognese seemed to know their business, and used some mounted crossbowmen as scouts, but in the late afternoon, Hawkwood stared at the horizon for a long time, which was his version of gnawing his knuckles, and then asked for Lapot by name. Lapot went out with Ewan and a dozen archers.

I sat by a fire with anyone who cared to join me, polishing my harness. Greg Fox had a good harness of his own, a little like mine when I'd been an ill-made knight, a collection of pieces, but they were, for the most part, good armour. He took excellent care of them, as he did of most things.

We had a good fire. I admit it had been someone's woodpile, but they had gone away, and it was a cool night. Men came and joined us at the fire and we threw more wood on and widened the circle, polishing, sharpening. I didn't make a speech or anything foolish, but I knew it was good that I was there, working.

Father Angelo came to the fire and sang Compline, and a surprising number of hard men knelt and sang responses. When we were done, Sir John was there.

'Anything from Lapot?' he asked.

'Sir John, he would report to you first,' I said.

He nodded. He was very obviously on edge, which was very rare for him.

Greg was sitting on the ground, sewing a ripped seam in another man's arming coat. Both of my grooms were seated by him, learning to work on the tack from an expert with needle and thread. I went into my pavilion and fetched Sir John a cup of wine.

He drank it slowly, watching the stars and the campfires.

With almost inhuman calm, he handed me back the cup half an hour later and nodded, his face bright in the firelight.

'If Lapot appears,' he said, 'send him to me and Coucy. We'll be awake for a bit.'

I went back to polishing, and my next visitor was even more of a surprise than John Hawkwood – Lord Fontana. He had a servant, a page, and the boy put a stool down and Lord Fontana sat by me while I polished a spot out of my helmet. You know why armourers hate polishing? So do soldiers. It takes forever.

I wander from my road, as ever. I haven't really described Fontana, which is unfair of me. He was small and finely boned like his sister, and quite personable when not angry. His hair was dark, with a lot of grey at the temples. His pointed black beard shared the grey. His eyes were green, where hers are a sort of grey-blue, but now that I'd spent time with both I thought myself a fool for missing their obvious shared parentage.

'Listen, Ser Guglielmo,' he began. 'I have come to apologise, and as a hot-tempered man, I am not good at this.'

I was at a bit of a social disadvantage, sitting on the ground by the fire with my back against my spare saddle and my legs stretched to the warmth. I couldn't rise and clasp his hand, or do any of the things that good courtesy might have required.

He leant forward. 'I believe that I have used many expressions towards you and your people, and I regret them, the more so that my ... sister ... has brought me to mind of the many favours you did both of us, in providing shelter, food and taking care of my ... men.'

I leant back so that my head was almost against his knees, looking up at him. He was earnest – very earnest. It suddenly struck me how much he was like Fiore. That very earnestness was also the embers of the fire that caused him to erupt at injustice, or what he perceived as injustice.

As if summoned, Fiore appeared out of the darkness. He plopped down with the grace of a dancer.

'I love the care you take with your equipment,' he said. It was just the sort of thing he said.

'Lord Fontana, the most noble Fiore dei Liberi of Udine, a knight of the Emperor,' I said.

'And Spatharios of the Emperor of Rome,' Fiore added. He liked to hear his titles repeated. By the Virgin, so do I. Vanity, thy name is knighthood.

Again, I wander. Fontana was at the point of drawing back, and I didn't want that to happen.

'Messire, Fiore is my closest friend. Please feel welcome to stay.' I smiled. 'I have not taken offence at anything you have said. I believe that I understand your frustration.'

'Do you?' he said, the choler rising, but then he pasted a smile on his face. 'My sister says you saved her life in Piacenza.'

'I regret to say, messire, that it was the other way round. She most definitely saved my life after I was fool enough to step on a sword blade.'

I made him smile. 'That sounds like my sister,' he said, ruefully. 'Listen, Ser Guglielmo. I wonder if you would consider . . .' He paused.

I wanted to fill in for him, but I had no idea what he might ask.

'My knights would like to ride with you tomorrow,' he said. And then, as if he had to force it past his lips, 'As would I.'

Well, there are times when you keep polishing your harness and times when you put it all aside and rise to your feet. I'm English, but I've lived with Italians more than half my life. I put my helmet on the damp ground and rose to my feet, brushing my hose with my hands, and then I embraced the Italian lord.

'I would welcome them and you with both hands,' I said.

He flashed a rare smile. Rare for him, I mean. 'You are a good man, as Maddalena says,' he said quietly.

Well, I'm not, but I try to be a chivalrous man, and as I said, I knew where his insults came from. I was too careful to say that, to some extent, I agreed with his criticisms. But here and now I'll say . . . we could have had Piacenza. Twice. If I'd been an exile, I'd have said a few choice words, I promise you.

It was no surprise to me that Lord Fontana, with a cup of my wine in him, engaged immediately with Fiore. Neither had any small talk – another thing they had in common. But Fiore had a new sword, a long, narrow sword, and he'd been playing with it for days. Now Lord Fontana asked to see it, and they were off. I had seen Fontana fight. He was no Fiore, but he was a good jouster and an adequate blade. What he was, that I had seen, was a superb horseman. When I mentioned this to Fiore, because he can dominate a conversation without meaning to be rude, he began to ask Fontana a hundred questions.

I wasn't sure either of them was listening to the other, but they were both talking, and the other men-at-arms at my fire smiled and continued making and mending. I remember that Greg Fox was by then sewing a pair of quilted hose that made me regret my awful arming hose all the more. Young Giorgio Cavalli was more interested in patting my dog Pilgrim than in polishing his breastplate.

Clario Birigucci had the pickets. He appeared at my fire on horseback.

'Sir John is asking for you,' he said. 'Lapot is back.'

I found them standing in the darkness under the stars, staring north.

'William,' Hawkwood said. 'Monsieur Lapot has found the Visconti.'

'Just upriver,' Lapot said. He gave me the slight smile he used when he knew something, had it dead to rights. 'I saw Gian Galeazzo's banner and Francesco d'Este's.'

Coucy materialised out of his pavilion, as did Niccolò d'Este.

'Did I hear my faithless cousin's name?' Lord Niccolò asked. He nodded. 'Ah, Monsieur Lapot. The eyes of the army.'

It pleased me that they knew Lapot – knew his skills. I wondered if he also needed to be promoted, like Christopher. In truth, scouting and guiding had become a very important skill for us. As I have said, too many times, that was something we'd learnt in the Holy Land.

Regardless, we withdrew under Sir John's pavilion. A page I didn't know put boards on trestles, and we sat at his table. Lapot drew a picture.

'This is Montichiari – next town north of the monastery at Madonnina. There's a bridge at Montichiari, over the river Chiese. I have a dozen archers holding it and, begging Sir William's pardon, I asked Marc-Antonio to take the night guard there.'

I nodded. Lapot was in his element. He knew his business.

'Their advance guard is here, at a village whose name I don't know. It's three buildings and a church. They didn't keep a good watch. Their camp is another Roman mile up the road at Macina. My guide swears it's called Macina.'

'Not on my pilgrim itinerary,' I said.

'But I saw their camp,' Lapot said. 'I counted tents and banners. I had all the time in the world, because they only had one night patrol and it kept regular rounds.' He grinned at me. 'If I'd had Ewan and Black Christopher, I'd have lifted their horse herd.'

Well ... I missed Christopher, too. In fact, I missed being on night patrols myself.

123

Or so I tell myself, eh?

'So ...' Hawkwood looked at Coucy.

'Speak your mind, Sir John,' our noble commander said.

'He'll come at us in the morning,' Hawkwood said. 'Let's find a good piece of ground and invite him to cross the river.'

Coucy smiled. 'Ah, *bien*. I assumed we would hold the line of the river.'

Perhaps I'm a poor Englishman, but I had also assumed we would hold the river line. The Chiese was just wide enough and deep enough to be a major obstacle to cavalry without being impassable. It was, in all respects, a perfect river for holding a larger army at bay.

'We want a fight,' Sir John said. 'We want to force the lads into action before they all decide to go home.'

Coucy winced.

'Crossing will disorder the Visconti people and they won't re-form well, because that's who they are. We take a good position and let them attack, and then ...' Hawkwood shrugged. 'I'll send William to work around the flank if I can, as that has worked before.'

Now it was Este's turn to wince, and Malatesta's. It's what we'd done to them, the year before.

'And if we just hold the river line?' Coucy asked, his voice polite, urbane, courteous. I couldn't tell if he was annoyed or simply curious.

Hawkwood made a face. 'If the Visconti have found a reserve of money, they start buying our people,' he said. 'That's what I'd do.'

Malatesta nodded, and Este sighed. Coucy looked disgusted.

'Such an odd form of war,' he said. 'But when I am building a palace, I don't interfere with the architect. Very well, Sir John. Pick your battlefield.'

Sir John actually made a full reverencia, bending his knee to Coucy. I think Hawkwood really liked Coucy. I also think he loved being under the command of a famous knight, so that our companies had the air of a real *empris*.

The stage of chivalry. Never discount it. Even as we talked of money and bribery and treachery, we also wished to appear brave, loyal and *preux*.

As it proved, Malatesta, Sir John and I rode off into the darkness with Lapot and a dozen of Hawkwood's lances, to pick a battlefield in the dark.

We were up again before dawn. My day began brilliantly, because young Greg Fox had made me a beautiful pair of new, bright scarlet arming hose, quilted and fitting perfectly, and they were laid over my armour. I was still grinning when I mounted.

Janet and l'Angars had the lances formed, and true to his word, Fontana brought me almost twenty lances. Of course, I'd left men in the castles south of Pavia, but with some spare archers and Fontana's men, I had fifty-eight lances complete that morning. Most of them were complete with a man-at-arms, an armed squire, a page with a crossbow, and a proper archer wearing a fair amount of armour, carrying a big, heavy bow and twenty-four war arrows, all mounted. We marched off to the right in four files, a Byzantine trick that we'd practised in the East, and by the time the sun was a finger above the horizon, we stood on the back side of a low ridge north of the town of Montichiari. We were invisible from the west. My lances were at the extreme left of our position. John Thornbury and I sat on our horses at the top of the little ridge, if a long low hill only three times the height of a man can be called a ridge, but on the plains of Lombardy, it was a major feature. A road ran along the top – I can only guess that it was the old riverbank. The road was lined with hedges, almost like France or England. To my left was the tiny church of Santa Margherita. I'd already made an offering, and then sent the priest to the rear with Father Angelo. The church's sanctuary wall was reinforced with brush bundles at the speed of fear by archers. Ewan led another group of archers in thinning the hedge to our right to make a shooting position. Gospel Mark smiled at me.

'Better 'an Poitiers,' he said.

Off to my left, Lapot and Marc-Antonio and a dozen of Hawkwood's lances held the bridge of the town of Montichiari. The river was deep in the bend around the town – there was no need to hold the banks. To my right were Sir John Thornbury and his hundred lances, the archers working with mine. To their right was Hawkwood, with his three hundred lances, including Brice and Romney. Beyond them, in the centre, was Coucy and his three hundred lances, and then on the left, our Italians – Este and Malatesta. Malatesta's right rested on a small wood, and he had the Bolognese militia driving stakes into the riverbank. The Bolognese were steady men in good armour, backed by some of the best *balistieri* I'd seen in Italy. They were guild militia, yes, but masters of their craft, with good weapons, well maintained. Unlike our lances, they'd all been paid. I thought that the far right was absolutely secure.

The river in front of the church was an easy swim, a cold, wet plod, but fordable the whole length of our position. The little ridge ran most of the way from the churchyard to Este's woods. It was a good battlefield. All it needed was a battle.

Like many battles, it was a long time starting. The morning wore on, and because our noble opponents rose late and didn't do a great deal of scouting, their advance guard blundered into our bridge guard. My pages shot their new crossbows, Lapot put someone down with his axe, and some of Hawkwood's archers shot into the enemy advance guard, and they rode away. Only then did they see our army north of the town.

With the usual tunnel vision of commanders, each portion of their army, as it arrived, lined up against us. They might have marched south and crossed with no opposition, and we'd have had to retreat. But because their captains were all in the middle, there was no one at the front to give – or even consider – such an order.

I know this for reasons I will explain later.

They'd taken so long to come that Hawkwood had moved our camp. He did it just in case our opponent decided to swing south of the town, so now we had the whole camp set up behind us – lines of tents, and our wagons. I really only mention this because I was watching the teams being taken off the big military wagons, and I saw a hawk rise into the air. Someone was practising their falconry with a good little bird who took a songbird out of the air like a scythe cutting wheat. Suddenly I knew I was looking at Maddalena. I was absurdly pleased. And then afraid.

Be that as it may, I was eating a sound winter apple and some very good Lombardy ham, sitting in the shade because the noontide sun was already hot on armour on the seventh day of May, when Fiore waved from the low wall we'd built around the churchyard.

'Here they come,' he said.

I tossed half an apple into the woods to my left. Greg Fox put my helmet on my head and buckled the aventail before and behind before closing the cheek plates. My favourite helmet is what you might call an 'armet', and has hinged cheek plates — a Venetian or Brescian invention, or so I'm told.

I locked the visor up and mounted, again with some help from Greg, who then mounted his own horse unaided. Such is the privilege of rank. At thirty-two or so, my back hurt when I mounted in full harness, and my foot hurt, and I generally felt my age.

From the back of my ugly but serviceable Percival, I could see right down into the enemy advance. They had Francesco d'Este facing me, with Gian Galeazzo in the centre and Hans Baumgarten on the right — I knew all the banners immediately. After a quick look, I guessed they had perhaps three hundred more lances than we had, and about the same number of infantry.

Baumgarten's Germans crossed first, on horseback. They did it in an organised way, in columns, and some of the Bolognese *balistieri* pelted them with bolts as they crossed and formed. They did damage, and then, like the well-trained militia I had taken them for, they fell back to their waiting spearmen. It was all like something from Vegetius — the professional cavalry crossing a river in the face of determined light infantry. Baumgarten then pushed some Milanese *provisionati* infantry across to face the Bolognese. There was a sparkle of fire from the hand gonnes, and the smell of sulphur, like demons released from Hell. Percival didn't like it, and he was restless.

The Viper of Milan moved forward from the centre, across the belly of the river. He had the easiest crossing and the widest. He moved a block of Milanese knights across all together, facing Coucy, but the Vipers overlapped the end of Hawkwood's line because their army was bigger. On the other hand, they were crossing at a reverse bend, so that as they crossed their forces bunched up on our side.

When the Milanese were across, infantry began to cross behind them, which appeared to me to be a foolish move. I looked to the centre to see if Hawkwood or Coucy would attack into the apparent chaos, and discovered the flaw in our position. Due to a clump of trees and a very slight bend in the road that ran along the ridge, I couldn't really see the centre of our array, or the banners of our commanders.

While I was contemplating that, Francesco d'Este came for me. He crossed with infantry first, which seemed to me the better choice than the one Gian Galeazzo — if that young monster was really in command — had made in the centre. He could outflank my position to the south, but the town, the woods and the hedges made it very difficult ground. And I had the churchyard built up as a little fortress. Nonetheless, his disposition made it clear he intended to try and outflank me to the left. His advance was slow and cautious and very professional.

Thornbury, at my suggestion, sent twenty lances to Lapot in the town, outflanking their advance.

Francesco d'Este was just crossing with his men-at-arms when the Viper banners dipped and the whole line of Milanese men-at-arms in the centre went forward. I suspect they were only meant to ride forward to give the infantry room to deploy, but they went forward far enough to enter the range of Sir John's archers.

I have said many times that it is stunning, awesome and frightening how many arrows a few longbowmen can throw in the time it takes to say a prayer. Robert Gall, one of Hawkwood's master archers, told me later they only loosed five shafts a man from two hundred archers.

The arrows fell like a continuous hail on the far right of the Visconti line. Because the gentlemen of Lombardy generally have maille where we would wear plate, and very few of them armour their horses, the plunging fire did more harm than Sir John had a right to expect. Perhaps thirty or forty men-at-arms were unhorsed, wounded, or slain outright, but that was a serious proportion of Visconti's mounted strength – perhaps one man in ten or fifteen.

Stung, they charged.

Now, if this was Crécy, I'd tell you that our archers ate them alive, and the survivors crashed back over their poor infantry, but it wasn't Crécy, and the Italian knights were better armoured than the French used to be, and better trained, too. They came on over dry fields.

It still should not have been a contest, as we had hedges and a hill.

Coucy's line began to unravel from his right to left. I saw it happen even through the trees. I heard Thornbury curse and saw Fiore shake his head in disgust.

It wasn't Coucy's fault. He sat in the centre under his banner some-where, even though we couldn't see him. But someone on the right of his lances, some French hothead decided to abandon military prudence and return the Italian charge with a counter-charge. Even then, even at that moment, the French charge might have been devastating, as they reckon themselves the best knights in the world, and I have reason to think that true.

But they went a few at a time, from right to left, as I say.

Most battles are a compound of errors. Hawkwood's victory at Panaro was a rare demonstration of a brilliant plan well executed, but most battles, in my experience, are a contest of which side makes the fewest errors.

An hour into the Battle of Montichiari, our two armies seemed to be hurling errors at each other like two angry cooks hurling gobs of dough in a kitchen fight. As soon as Francesco d'Este saw Gian Galeazzo throw his knights at our centre, he attacked me, and my eagle's eye view of the battle vanished. I was too busy to watch, so I missed the disaster.

From the church towards Thornbury, my front was covered in places by hedge and low brush along the road. To my left, it was all woods and hedges and small farms up to the edge of the town.

I'd told all my people that if we held the churchyard, we'd hold the whole line. They knew what to do. I rode down the back of my line, and sat in the centre, halfway to Thornbury.

Este came up the low ridge under archery all the way. We didn't have any French knights to burst out of our position. Our longbows and crossbows flayed his unbarded horses, and the whole Visconti right wing – the part facing me and Thornbury – flinched back without contact, leaving a hundred men dead or wounded or pinned under dying horses.

On my left, five hundred Milanese *pavisieri* tried to push their way through the hedges and farmyards. But when they were halfway to our position, broken into clumps of twenty or thirty men, most of whom had abandoned their heavy pavises, they saw their cavalry repulsed, and they just ... stopped advancing.

I hadn't fought anyone. This was a new world for me, in many ways. I'd had a small command at Rubiera, but this was different. Thornbury and I were sharing the command of a third of an army, and the opportunity to make errors was enormous.

As soon as Francesco d'Este's banner retreated, I rode to my left, looked down at the pavisiers, and then back along my line about two hundred paces to where Thornbury sat on his charger with his banner and a dozen lances he held in reserve. I didn't have any reserve. Oh, I knew a reserve was a fine idea – I just didn't have anyone left over except me, and Fiore, and our squires.

'No troubles,' I said, or something equally full of relief at having failed to fail, if you take my meaning.

Thornbury glanced behind him and his horse shied. He looked at me. 'We're fucked,' he said.

Thornbury was a clean-spoken man who never swore.

'What?' I asked.

Thornbury pointed back at our camp. I could see Viper banners, three of them, *in our camp*. I think perhaps my heart stopped. People say that, but it was as if the moment just froze. Enemy cavalry in our camp meant …

… meant …

It meant that our centre was broken and we'd lost the battle. Hawkwood and Coucy were … dead? Taken?

And somewhere in the back of my head was the memory that Maddalena was in the camp.

Doubtless, I let forth a stream of blasphemy.

It may seem odd to you, but to see our centre, because of the wooded ridge, I had to ride *forward* – that is, down the slope towards the camp and the enemy, which I did. What I saw was what I most feared. Our centre was, for the most part, gone – Coucy and Hawkwood, too.

Hawkwood, too.

I spent a moment looking hard at the far right, but it was easy to see that our Este, Niccolò, and Malatesta still held.

But our centre was gone.

I trotted Percival up the short slope. Greg Fox was right there with Gabriel, and I changed horses.

Thornbury was calm, which raised him still further in my estimation. 'We still hold the town and the bridge?' he asked.

'Yes,' I said.

'So we have a clear line of retreat.'

He looked down into the maelstrom of our camp, and I kept thinking with a sick feeling that Maddalena was down there, and a camp taken by storm was no different from a city.

Sweet Jesu.

Thornbury looked at me. 'You think we can save this?' he asked.

I nodded. 'Yes,' I said. I was proud of my voice – steady, almost cheerful. 'Have to try, right?'

He nodded back. 'Good. I'm of your mind exactly.'

He shouted for all his men-at-arms to form on him. He rode to his master archer and told him to hold the line.

I assumed he knew his business and rode to talk to my people. I found Bibbo in the churchyard.

'Sir John's in trouble,' I said. 'I'm taking all the spears to help him. I need you and the archers and pages to hold here. If it all goes to shit, we're retreating down the road, through the churchyard, and out past Lapot, so you *have to hold*. If you can't hold the hedge, hold the churchyard.'

Bibbo nodded. 'We'll hold,' he said.

'Tell Lapot what's happening,' I said.

He nodded. 'Right.'

I stood in my stirrups. 'LISTEN UP!' I roared in my battlefield voice. Big lungs help.

Every head turned.

'Spears, mount, form line on me. Archers and pages, stand your ground.' I looked at them all. My whole company only filled about three hundred paces of ground. 'MOVE.'

The pages ran forward with the horses, and the armoured men – the knights, the unknighted men-at-arms, and the armoured squires – all grabbed their horses and mounted, and their pages handed them up their spears. Archers and 'spears' – that's how I divided my lances when I had to.

This is where we were better than other companies – our pages were paid, and we trained. The horses came forward, the 'spears' mounted, and we were formed. It took perhaps a minute.

Gabriel's nostrils flared, scenting something he didn't like, or maybe he did. His head came up, and I turned him. I had about a hundred and twenty spears with Fontana's exiles. A fair-sized block of knights in a battle on this scale.

Fontana had his visor up, and he looked stricken. 'My sister,' he said. 'I must ...'

'Ride with me and we'll find her,' I said, or something like. I reached out and slapped his armoured shoulder.

He nodded. 'She'll probably save herself,' he said.

I didn't know what he meant, but I could guess. Maddalena was a very competent woman.

Then I dismissed the whole thing and became the 'commander'.

I ordered the squadron to wheel by sections, which the Italians made a hash of, but I'd put them on the far left, where their manoeuvres – or lack thereof – couldn't foul the rest, and we were off, moving to the right. Sir John Thornbury had almost two hundred armoured men together, although they were still a bit of a mob, with horse holders and armoured men in all directions.

I wanted to send someone to scout. I wanted to get down there and rescue Maddalena. I wanted to find Sir John Hawkwood. I wanted to turn the battle.

It struck me that here, in my first major battle as a commander, I'd neatly rid myself of every man I trusted to bring a reliable report. Christopher, Ewan, Lapot ... I'll observe now that this was a major error.

'L'Angars!' I shouted. 'Hold here. Form a line to the right. Understand?'

I used my lance as a pointer and then held it sideways to indicate the exact line I wanted.

L'Angars nodded. 'I was thinking more of a wedge,' he said.

He was right. For a confused fight down in the camp, we'd want to form a smaller force.

'Yes, do it,' I said. Then I thought about what I was seeing. 'Keep to the hedge and keep the banners down until I signal,' I said.

I would use the lines of sight to my advantage. With our banners down, our little cavalry force would be invisible to the looters in the camp.

He nodded and wheeled his horse, and I rode down the back of our position to be my own scout. It was foolish, but I needed to see the centre.

Almost immediately I saw Hawkwood. His black and white banner was still up. It had just been hidden from me by the trees and the curve in the line of our ridge. Coucy's banner was nowhere to be seen. Off to my right, on the main street of our camp, was Gian Galeazzo's personal banner, surrounded by his beautifully armoured bodyguard knights.

I rode to Hawkwood. I needed him to know we were coming. If he gave up the ridge, I thought we were done. But I realised in a glance that Niccolò d'Este – our Este – could see Sir John's banner. It was all sight lines and guesswork, but it seemed to me ...

At some point, you just have to say 'sod it' and act. Alone, I rode across the back of the Milanese chivalry. Gabriel was magnificent, and we flowed like Pegasus, and then we were up the back of the ridge and I was in with Brice and Romney.

There were a lot of gaps.

'Fuckers ran,' Romney said.

I could see that almost a third of Hawkwood's force were gone – men-at-arms, for the most part. The archers were still there.

'Sir John,' I called.

He didn't have a helmet on, just a big hat. He looked at me and nodded coolly.

'You and Thornbury?' he asked.

'We're about to throw our spears at Gian Galeazzo,' I said. I pointed with my lance at the Viper banner and the Milanese bodyguard.

His cool look turned into a smile – a fox's smile. 'Hold hard,' he said, and he began to issue orders.

'Coucy is down!' came a cry, and suddenly everyone around me was calling it. I couldn't see, but there it was – the uttermost disaster, in more ways than one.

Hawkwood cursed, looked north once, and made a decision.

'Very well, William,' he said. 'You and John get Gian Galeazzo and I'll try and save Coucy.' He smiled, though. 'We're not done yet, young William.'

I turned Gabriel and rode back to Sir John Thornbury, this time along the 'front' of our position, the side facing the river, which, due to the remarkable way the battle had gone, was the safer side.

I heard Sir John Hawkwood's war cry behind me, and the rumble as his household charged. Then Gabriel was slowing and I was in among Thornbury's archers.

Gabriel was done after two long runs across the battlefield. He was the best warhorse I'd ever had, but I wasn't staying on him to fight that day. I changed back to Percival while I told Thornbury what was happening.

He nodded. 'I'm charging,' he said. 'Hawkwood isn't getting any-where. I'm going to take the pressure off him.'

We were both smiling.

'You wait for a paternoster and then sweep my flank.' Thornbury waved.

I nodded, because I agreed.

Almost at our feet, we could see the Milanese pages pillaging our camp. And some of their infantry had kept up. There were *pavisieri* in among our tents, and Hawkwood's pavilion went down, the ropes cut, even as I watched.

But there were men forming on horseback under Gian Galeazzo's banner. These were his bodyguard knights – the very best in Italy. I suspected they would be under one of the family bastards – Ambrogio, who wanted me dead, or Antonio, who owed me his life.

But they formed well, and quickly, and they clearly saw Hawkwood trying to rescue Coucy, even though I couldn't because of the trees and the curve in our line.

Thornbury started forward. He had to ride diagonally down the back of our low slope, which cost him some organisation. Then he threw his lances straight at the mob trying to get at Sir John Hawkwood, who was trying to rescue Coucy, who was lost somewhere beyond the clump of trees, out of my sight but just to Thornbury's left. It was a maelstrom, and he crashed in with impetus, scattering the first lines of Milanese and sending men to the ground to his right and left.

But the commander of Gian Galeazzo's guard was watching, and he pointed his lance into the flank of Thornbury's charge. The Milanese chivalry drew in close, put their visors down or their great helms up, and started forward. Of course, only then did I let Greg Fox raise my own banner, which I'd had down behind the hedge.

I pointed my own lance at Gian Galeazzo's banner.

'Take that young viper and we're all rich,' I said.

L'Angars had formed us into a deep column, almost a wedge, with the best armoured men on the best horses at the front. Again, this was something we practised.

We were charging into our own camp, and that was going to be bad. We were fighting in the wrong direction, and that was not good.

But we weren't beaten yet.

It was Antonio Visconti, commanding the enemy bodyguard – one of Bernabò's bastards, and my friend. I saw him as he saw my banner, and shouted an order. His well-trained Milanese wheeled at a trot to face us, which no one else on earth except perhaps the Emperor's bodyguard and the Knights of Saint John might have managed, but the Milanese did it. They lost their close order, and they weren't at a gallop when we hit them, but they were good. Very good. And remember, my English usually fought on foot. On the other hand, I had Janet, Fiore, Marc-Antonio, and me at the front, and we were all very good jousters.

A cavalry fight – a real one, not an open horse race for prisoners like the latter end of Rubiera – is mostly about the size and quality of your horses. We had excellent horses. So did our opponents. But we were packed tighter, and we had a little hill behind us and we were moving faster. The result was that we blew through the Milanese front despite their best efforts. I didn't cross spears with Antonio, worse luck. If I'd encountered him, he might still be alive. I unhorsed someone with a sable pennon on his great-helm – a lady's favour, no doubt. My lance tangled in his fall. I let go and drew the Emperor's sword, but Percival was still at a heavy gallop. By the time I had the sword in my fist, we were through the back of the Milanese, and I reined to the right, looking for Thornbury, Hawkwood, Coucy … Looking for Gian Galeazzo or Antonio Visconti, or anyone who might be important.

Instead, I saw Gian Galeazzo's personal banner go down. I know now that it was Clario Birigucci who unhorsed the banner bearer, and Janet, fittingly enough, who unhorsed young Gian Galeazzo. But it was almost a separate fight. I have said that a cavalry charge in a camp, with its mess of ropes and lines and canvas, is a nightmare for riders. Our entire melee was split by a line of tents, and Janet was as far from me as Hawkwood was in the other direction.

I'll note that I still knew her instantly, just from her size, helmet and her perfect seat.

Worse luck, most of the Milanese bodyguard were on her side of the line of tents.

On my side of the tent line, l'Angars burst through the back of the Milanese with his squire close at his heels. He did exactly as I'd done, except he was looking to the left, his whole body and helmet looking that way. And he saw something I didn't, but he didn't tell me what it was, either. He recouched his unbroken lance and went like an arrow towards what had once been our centre, and the chaotic maelstrom where Thornbury and Hawkwood were.

Fiore emerged behind me, and his squire was towing two captured horses as if we were in a tournament melee.

I'd never lowered my visor. I pointed back at the melee.

'Gian Galeazzo,' I said.

Fiore frowned. 'Not today!' he shouted.

In fact, his bodyguard had him on a horse, looking more like a sack of turnips than a great captain. Janet and both Biriguccis were locked up in a close cavalry fight, but they had most of my company.

Somewhere behind me in the camp, a woman screamed.

Let me be clear. It wasn't Maddalena. It wasn't, as far as I know, anyone I knew. She was probably some camp follower, although every camp follower is someone's daughter, someone's sister.

It didn't matter. It was like a sign from the Virgin about where my duty lay. Call me a fool, but it was clear we would win the cavalry fight, at least in the camp. And that we were too late to get Gian Galeazzo, much as that might have pleased me. He was sacrificing his bodyguard to run through the gap in the centre.

'Fiore,' I said.

He had his visor up. He smiled a half-smile. 'Perhaps we should clear the looters out of our things,' he said.

We'd never stopped moving, although my gallop to the right had become a slow canter back towards the tents.

What followed was messy. And it reminded me too much of the hour after Brignais, except in reverse.

The Milanese infantry and some of their men-at-arms had settled into looting. Once men set to looting, they generally become animals. I promise you, I have experienced this from both sides.

Fiore and I each picked a street. Our squires and a few other men-at-arms joined us. Giorgio Cavalli was right by me.

We rode down the street of tents, and killed anyone in Visconti colours. At the end of the street, we came up behind a mob of Milanese *provisionati* and some dismounted men-at-arms. They were trying to break into our wagon park.

Father Angelo stood on a wagon with Peter Albin and a pair of wagoners. They all had spears. And down on the wagon's cross tree stood a small woman with a *ghiavarina*, a heavy spear that I favoured myself, and behind her a dozen other women, including Big Mag, with spears and polearms and swords and axes.

Fiore and I went into the back of the mob like avenging military angels. I lost the Emperor's sword in a man and had to use my Turkish axe, but the Milanese broke the moment that they heard our hoof beats, and it was just slaughter.

I rode back along the path of my charge to find my sword, and there was Father Angelo, already kneeling by a fallen man. And Maddalena, with the heavy spear in her hand.

She reached up and handed me the Emperor's sword.

'You lost this,' she said.

'So I did,' I said, or something equally dull. I'm just not that good at wordplay.

She was untouched, unhurt, her wool gown buttoned to her throat, and she still had a hawking glove on her right hand. How had I ever seen her as a 'matron'? She was beautiful in her calm and courage.

I saluted her with the sword in time to find her brother was at my back. He waved at her, and then I began to rally my own people. Fiore had followed someone and came back out of a side street of tents.

We turned and rode back up two more streets, but by that time the looters had the message and were running. Most were encumbered with stolen blankets and pewter plates and other things not worth dying for.

Again, I wished for a trumpeter. I had found Ser László and his squire, but Ser Giorgio had disappeared. I stood in my stirrups and roared, and men came in. As I collected them, I moved back up the camp towards the cavalry melee in the centre.

I think we were back at the edge of the main street before Sir John's squire Robert found me.

'Sir John Hawkwood requests that you join him in the centre,' he said.

'Right,' I said. We'd cleared the camp, for the most part.

Percival was done. Just trotting back over the ground of the cavalry fight was work for him. I sent Fiore's squire to fetch me Gabriel, and I was at a heavy walk by the time I reached Sir John. It was perhaps one hour since I'd last seen him. Time passes oddly in battles.

'What in the name of Hell have you been doing, Gold?' he snapped.

That was the last greeting I expected. I didn't answer. It wasn't my new-found attempt to struggle with my temper. I was stunned. Hawkwood had never bitten at me, and here I was, in front of all of them, including a somewhat bedraggled looking Coucy. And l'Angars, who was fairly glowing with pride.

I bowed. 'Clearing our camp,' I said.

'You might have had Gian Galeazzo, you fool,' he spat.

I owed, and continue to owe, Sir John Hawkwood a number of debts, but in that moment, I was ready to put my sword in him. Rage, my usual foe, sprang on to my back, fully formed.

Luckily, Brice and Coucy had the same impulse, and stepped between us. Coucy put his arm around my neck, his steel arms sliding on my silk surcoat.

'Sir John is ungenerous,' he said. 'Your man l'Angars just saved my life.'

That explained what l'Angars had seen.

I was still eye to eye with Hawkwood. I saw the moment in which he realised that he had allowed a rare slip of temper – I saw it in his eyes. But he could not, and did not, back down.

This is the problem with displays of temper in commanders. Their reputations depend on their authority. It's almost impossible to back down.

'Never mind,' he snapped, as if he hadn't just called me a fool in front of the whole army. 'The fortunes of war.'

I changed horses, still in that spirit where I might have cut him if he'd come too close, and then, when l'Angars tugged at my bridle, we rode away to our own lines.

It probably sounds impossible, but Francesco d'Este and Baumgarten didn't attack us during the whole hour we were fighting the big cavalry melee in the centre. I was told afterwards that they were sure our army was breaking up and, like any of us would have done, they were just letting us go.

But as our banners came back to the ridge and Gian Galeazzo slipped through the gap in our lines that Sir John Hawkwood and Coucy had left, Baumgarten learnt from the chastened young viper that we were restoring our line. Too late, he threw his mailed fist at our right, and Este went for the left.

I said that Francesco d'Este – their Este – had sent infantry to work their way around our position. They stopped when they saw their cavalry retreat. Now they ploughed forward again, pushing through vines, stepping over walls. They weren't a line, or even a mass. From the slight eminence of the churchyard I could see them quite clearly.

I could also see Lapot manoeuvre his borrowed lances and archers like a chess player, so that before the *pavisieri* could charge at the flanks of our churchyard, he took them from the flank and rear. His people were outnumbered, but the *pavisieri* broke and ran at contact.

Francesco d'Este was a brave man and a good captain. He threw his knights at my archers. Most of my armoured men were still down in the camp or simply too tired to rise and fight again, although l'Angars had the best with us – Courtney, Grice and Cavalli and their squires – around me. We stood with Bibbo in one of the hedge gaps and prepared to fight on foot.

They charged us on horseback. Only a dozen of them made it to our lines, but they struck hard. I think Giorgio Cavalli went down then, and some archers, although I didn't see it. A mailed horseman burst through our lines and came around the back, and he went for Greg Fox with my banner. Greg was on foot. He stood his ground, stepped off line, and unhorsed the knight with our flagstaff, a simple thrust to the throat.

The rest of their mounted knights milled around on the other side of the hedges, unable to break in.

It lasted forever, although it really didn't take long. Then the Italians withdrew a few spear lengths and dismounted.

Gospel Mark was just down the line.

'For what we are about to receive ...' he said. And around him, a dozen Englishmen said, 'Let us be truly thankful.'

'This is going to suck,' spat Witkin. I noticed he had his maille on for once. And a big, lead-headed sledgehammer in his hand.

Francesco d'Este was still mounted. He gave a speech, his visor open, which was safe enough, because my archers had shot away their shafts, and because our camp was taken, and in chaos, we had no more arrows. Usually, we'd have had some young pages, or just boys, to run sheaves of arrows to our people. Not today.

It suddenly occurred to me that we could *still* lose this thing.

The Milanese plodded forward. They were fresher than we were – but they'd seen Gian Galeazzo retreat, and few victories begin with watching your commander leave the field.

Francesco d'Este was right in front of me. His banner looked enough like his cousin's that I had no trouble recognising it. About twenty paces from our line, he leant back to say something, and Bibbo shot his horse. He put a quarter-pound war arrow into the horse's neck as Este turned its head. It was dead in ten beats of its mighty equine heart, and Este went down.

I had time to say 'Nice shot,' or words to that effect, and slam my visor shut, and then their dismounted knights hit our line.

I'd love to tell you of all my feats of arms, but here's what I remember. I remember the fatigue, the feeling of taking a wound, the grisly triumph of my point going in under an opponent's arm in a close press, half-sword to half-sword, and the awareness in the man's visored eyes as he went down. The moment when I was pushed back, and there was a shoulder behind my shoulder holding me steady. I had my dagger in my fist, and Greg Fox at my shoulder and Fiore beside me, and we began to push them down the hill. First it was a step or a stumble, but in a few seconds I went forward twice. My immediate foe tripped over Este's dead horse and went down, and their line just seemed to blow away like smoke as they stumbled away. I can't say they ran. They were, by then, too tired to run.

Archers run much faster than knights, most of the time. Especially when they are winning, and there's money in it.

My people took fifty rich ransoms in less time than it takes to tell it. I wasn't pursuing. Because I was standing over the prone form of Francesco d'Este. He was alive and awake, trapped under the warhorse that Bibbo had shot.

As soon as it was safe, I popped my visor and stepped past him so he didn't have to look up at my new red arming hose and stained braes.

'I know your cousin Niccolò,' I said.

He had some *sprezzatura*, that Francesco.

'Then I know the wine will be good,' he said, despite two broken legs and a lost battle.

Bibbo found some boys to get the warhorse off our capture.

'I'll split him with you,' I said. 'After all, you dropped him.'

Bibbo grinned. He wasn't a man much given to grinning, but he smiled like the sun was rising.

'Damn,' he said. 'I can retire.'

That wasn't necessarily what I had in mind, but the moment of victory was not the moment to tell him so.

*

By nightfall, we had some order in our camp. Hawkwood had a new pavilion, and Coucy's pavilion was the centre of a victory feast. I heard a dozen stories there – how the camp's noncombatants, mostly women, had retreated to the wagons and held them, for example.

'My sister never needs rescuing,' Lord Fontana said. 'She is a better knight than I am.'

Maddalena was in Janet's tent, I knew. Janet said that she was badly shaken. Yet she had apparently stood, spear in hand, with a hundred wagoners and monks and camp women, laundresses and prostitutes, and faced down a rabble of looters. I remembered her standing there with the *ghiavarina* in her hands.

Well. I generally shake afterwards, too. And Janet, of all people, would know how to reassure her.

But the climax of the evening was when Coucy summoned l'Angars by name. There was my best man-at-arms, often my 'first spear', in his rusty maille and mismatched arm harnesses and his ragged coat of plates.

Coucy smiled at us, very much the victorious general in his moment of greatness. Coucy was an actor, but a damned good one.

'I was lying in the dust behind the ridge,' Coucy said. 'My horse was dead, and I had an armoured man across my legs, and I watched as the tide of battle rolled across me. And one of Sir John's men all but stood on me, but the Vipers pushed him off again.' Coucy looked around. 'And then, before the men standing over me could realise that the richest ransom on the battlefield was under their hands, *this* man rode out of the battle dust like Saint George and Saint Maurice together. I swear to you, gentles, he glowed with valour!'

Men cheered. Hell, I cheered. Coucy told a good story.

'Alone, he broke the Milanese!'

L'Angars was shaking his head – no, no, it was not true. In fact, I knew from camp stories already told that he had had a dozen men-at-arms at his heels, but Coucy would not be stopped.

'Set me on my feet and gave me his horse!' Coucy finished. 'And so I can do nothing for this good man but to give him a good warhorse in return for his chivalry.'

He nodded, and a groom brought a fine chestnut stallion, a magnificent warhorse, seventeen hands, yet elegant, into the tent.

Coucy was on a stool by then. 'And then it came to my attention

141

that this paragon was not yet a knight, but merely a humble Gascon squire—'

'Never met a humble Gascon!' shouted someone.

There was a lot of laughter. Victory begets laughter.

'So with the horse, I think I must give the Sieur l'Angars something else.'

And he bade him kneel, and knighted him.

In front of the whole army.

Honestly? I thought l'Angars might expire on the spot.

It wasn't all good. My long-time friend and occasional foe, Antonio Visconti, died on that field. Fiore found him, with a lance point right through his side, like Christ. God rest his soul.

John Courtney died at Montichiari. He'd been with me since Cyprus and before. He died in the close fighting on top of the ridge at the very end – a dagger through his visor. Giorgio Cavalli, who was Father Angelo's cousin, took a wound there and died the next day. We lost four archers, dead, and we had a dozen wounded. We were lucky that Peter Albin was in our camp and had escaped to the wagons before the looting began. We took the worst casualties at Montichiari that we'd had in years, and that was in victory.

The Milanese lost about three hundred men-at-arms, dead, and as many again taken, and all their infantry. We didn't massacre them. In fact, Coucy let most of them go the next day. I kept a hand gonne from the battlefield to play with. A memento of the victory.

We won, but our victory was worth no more than the value of the ransoms we took and anything we collected in their camp. Lapot and Ewan had a jump on that. They crossed the bridge the moment they were sure of victory and snapped up a lot of very good warhorses, and they did that for the whole company, improving our horse herd. Almost every man on our ridge had a ransom, or at least a piece of one. The bankers came around quickly to settle up. I knew that I was in for a dangerous time when the ransoms were paid. I had the best ransom of all – Francesco d'Este was worth a lot.

I was thinking these professional thoughts while sitting in one of our captured pavilions, watching Maddalena Fontana read prayers to Ser Giorgio Cavalli as he lay dying. He was holding her hand.

Sometimes he would murmur responses. His cousin had already heard his confession and given him the last rites.

I just sat there. I hate the waste of war, and I hated losing Courtney, but young Giorgio had spirit. And he believed. It was sometimes good for *my* spirit just to be around him. Because the day after Montichiari, I didn't believe any more. I wanted out. But Cavalli had believed – in the Pope … in the cause.

And now his chest was a mess. Bloody froth blew out of his mouth at every breath.

Maddalena held his hand, and read to him. And then she leant over and asked him if he wanted to say the paternoster with her. A bubble formed on his mouth.

She leant closer, like a lover. She had on a wimple of linen. It was absolutely shining white, except that a corner fell on his chest and she bent over him, and the fabric began to drink up the blood. That's what I remember best – Giorgio's blood gradually wicking up her wimple.

'*Pater noster qui est in caelus,*' she said clearly.

I remembered sitting on a horse with a hemp rope around my neck, waiting to die. I always do, when I say the Lord's Prayer. Instead of frightening me, it has the power to steady me. To remind me who I was, who I am, who I want to be.

My eyes were suddenly hot, and wet.

'*Santificetur nomen tuum,*' she said.

I fell to my knees.

'Snnnn … n … … tmn …' Giorgio repeated. His body gave a convulsion, and his hand reached up – I don't think it was with any volition.

Maddalena stumbled back, and bright blood came out of his mouth, and his eyes glazed, and he was gone.

She finished the prayer. '*Adveniat regnum tuum. Fiat voluntas tua. Sicut in caleo et in terra.*'

I joined her, as did Father Angelo and Janet, who were in the tent with us.

'*Panem Nostrum quotidianum da nobis hodie, et dimmitte nobis, debita nostra sicut at nos dimittimus debitoribus nostris. Et ne nos inducas in tentationem, sed libera nos a malo.*'

Maddalena looked up, and realised that her fine linen veil was all blood. She flinched away, and Janet got an arm around her and helped her to a chair.

And that's how we were when Sir John Hawkwood came into the tent.

'There you are, Sir William,' he said, as if there wasn't a new corpse cooling on the camp bed.

I was on my knees. I hadn't really intended to kneel – it just happened as I prayed.

'Did I interrupt a prayer circle?' Sir John asked.

'One of my knights just died,' I said. I suspect my voice was colder than a January night on the Thames.

Sir John had no time for God. I knew that.

'Ah,' he said. 'Walk with me, William.'

'I think this is a bad time, Sir John,' I said, as carefully as I could. I wasn't sure why I was angry, but the kind of rage that I tell my people never to use in battle was creeping over my limbs like a plague of anger.

'I must insist,' Sir John said, his coldness echoing mine.

I rose from my knees, and took a deep breath.

Janet put Maddalena in a chair and stood up.

'It's really not a good time, John,' Janet said. She was good at reading men.

Sir John ignored her as if she didn't exist. He was angry, I could tell.

And so was I.

I suppose I knew what was coming, and almost welcomed it. I followed him out of the pavilion, stooping to go under the low door. It was a beautiful May day, and the smell of the dead permeated the air, which was fitting.

'I'd like you to sell me Este,' he said.

That was reasonable – I'd sold him Malatesta after Rubiera.

'I think that can be arranged,' I said cautiously.

'I'll give you a thousand florins,' he said.

Este had already offered me far more than that, and I shook my head.

'Twenty-five hundred,' I said.

Hawkwood's head snapped around. 'I said a thousand, William,' he said carefully.

'You are always telling me to be a better mercenary,' I snapped. 'He's already offered me more than twenty-five hundred. So that's my price.'

'Really?' he asked, his voice hard. 'If you really want to be a better mercenary, William, you can stop playing knight errant and get on with business. You had Gian Galeazzo under your sword yesterday and you let him go. So that you could rescue some whores.'

I thought of explaining – Lord Fontana, his sister, the camp. Perhaps I'd made the wrong decision, although Janet and I have refought it a dozen times and Janet, who unhorsed Gian Galeazzo, said we never had enough spears on the spot to get him. It happened on one of our flanks, as I have said.

I also thought of a lot of hot rejoinders. But this was *John Hawkwood*. It wrecked me that he was angry at me. Probably something left over from my childhood.

'In addition,' he said coldly, 'it has come to my attention that you are considering another contract.'

I wondered how he knew, but it didn't interest me much.

'You said you were breaking up the army,' I said. 'I need other options.'

'Your commitment to this contract pre-dates that,' he said. 'I trusted you, William Gold. I thought you were one of my own.'

He wanted me to quail. In fact, I knew in my heart that I was being manipulated. He wanted a declaration of loyalty.

I wasn't in the mood, even for John Hawkwood.

I had no trouble meeting his eye. 'My contract with Nerio Acciaioli pre-dates any contract with you,' I said. 'And let me add, sir, that as I haven't ever been paid a farthing of my wages or my company's—'

Hawkwood interrupted me. 'You do not have a company, William Gold. You have a contract to raise men for me.'

I was more hurt by that than angry. 'That's foolish talk, Sir John. I have had—'

But he cut me off again. 'You are not an independent commander, William Gold. If you ride away, you can have your squire.' His face was red.

I thought about it all. I wanted to smile, to play the great man, but I was angry and hurt and sad, and maybe even afraid.

'Very well,' I said. I was breathing hard, as if I'd just fought three bouts on foot with a poleaxe. 'Very well, sir. I will take my leave.'

But after I'd taken three steps, I looked back. His expression hadn't changed.

'I will take anyone who wants to come with me,' I said. 'And, Sir John, since I can pay them and you probably can't, I wouldn't expect many of *my* lances to stay with you.'

'To hell with you, William Gold,' Hawkwood spat.

It was like the end of a romance, and other men, like Coucy and Thornbury, did their best to patch it up, but for my part, something was broken. I didn't want to go back. The worst of it was that Hawkwood's denial that I was an independent commander, a corporal, cut me deepest.

Fiore just shrugged. 'I prefer Nerio to Hawkwood,' he said. 'And Greece to Italy. So let's be gone.'

That was more difficult than either of us imagined. I had a castle south of Pavia to dispose of, and the garrisons to retrieve, and Este's ransom to arrange. Then I needed to move men and horses to Corinth, which was best done at Venice.

And then, not everyone was coming. Janet was the first. She hugged me. Her eyes filled with tears.

'I'm not coming,' she said.

I already knew, but I had hoped.

'I'll go with Thornbury,' she said. 'I have a few years' fighting left.'

'I'll probably be back next year,' I said.

'Sure,' she said.

But the next two hurt me just as much. Sam Bibbo took his half of Este's ransom ... and retired, just as he'd threatened to do.

'Too fuckin' old,' he said. 'I don't need to wait around in Italy for someone to put an axe in my head.'

I couldn't really argue with him. He'd been with me for a long time. He was like my right hand, but I was not going to stop him from having the life he chose. In fact, it was only talking to Sam, saying goodbye, that I realised that Hawkwood didn't know how to *ask* me to stay, so he just tried to *force* me to stay.

Interesting. I still owed Sir John, but not in the immediate future.

Last was l'Angars. He came to my pavilion looking ten years younger, and wearing a very pretty haubergeon of bright maille edged in bronze links over a new arming coat. We were just about to march for Venice. I'd heard him out on our small parade ground, ordering pages to change the loads until the pack animals were all balanced.

'You look fine,' I said.

'I'm a knight now,' l'Angars said, his voice serious. And then, without taking a breath, he said, 'I'm leaving you, William.'

'Coucy?' I asked.

L'Angars smiled. 'Yes, Sir William. I will be one of his bodyguard. And he will give me a piece of land, and I will eventually retire, a landed man and not ...' He stopped himself.

Not a brigand in Italy, I thought.

I embraced him and we promised each other to write letters, to visit when I was in Savoy, and so on.

Janet, Sam, l'Angars.

No one battle could have killed them all, but they were gone.

My convoy was big – ten wagons, forty pack animals, a horse herd of three hundred unridden animals, and then thirty lances. And somewhere south and west of Modena, a second convoy under La Motte and Tom Fenton, with another fifteen lances.

I was doing everything myself, because I didn't have a master archer or a first spear, and Greg Fox now had enough cash from his ransoms to pay for a lance. He was about to be lost to me as a squire. A busy morning. I was not in the best of moods, either. In fact, I wasn't angry about l'Angars or Janet or Sam. It was more like I was wondering why I wasn't retiring to Savoy to raise my children, instead of haring off to Outremer to fight.

Lord Fontana was sitting in my pavilion. I saw him a way off because Gospel Mark was directing pages in pulling my pavilion down and packing it, and the side walls were already gone.

I hadn't seen Fontana since my quarrel with Sir John. Now, he rose as I entered.

'Ser Guglielmo,' he said.

I assumed he was there to say goodbye. It was definitely a day for saying goodbye.

Fontana bowed. 'I need a favour,' he said, like a man expecting to be killed.

I made myself smile. I assumed he wanted to borrow money, which was all right, as I had money, and also, I had an employer who was going to pay me.

'I'd like to come with you to Greece,' he said. 'With my exiles.' He looked at me, and I swear his beard bristled. 'And my sister. At least for the present.'

That was all so unexpected that perhaps I just looked stunned.

He shrugged. He was nicely dressed, in a long wool coat over riding clothes. A beautiful sword. He looked like the great noble he was.

'Coucy is leaving,' he said.

I knew that, from l'Angars.

'This army will now break up. Hawkwood is pretending the Pope will pay a victory bonus for the battles, but I have reason to know ...' He paused and looked at me. 'There is no money. A French cardinal has taken all the money and sent it to the King of France.'

'Robert of Geneva?' I asked.

'Ah, you already know,' he said.

'Only guessed,' I admitted.

'So, no chance of poor Piacenza. The Visconti will kill all my friends and destroy my house.' He looked at me. 'I have a little money and a house in Bologna. I know no profession but war. I hear you have a contract for money – for actual money.'

I nodded. 'But Greece is poor,' I said. 'No rich ransoms, and no rich looting.'

'A year in which I don't get poorer might save me,' he said.

I was, of course, delighted to have him. Twenty more lances? All the difference in the world.

'Some men would say that an army camp is no place for a gentlewoman,' I said. 'In fact, I'm not one of those men. But your sister will not have Lady Janet for company. She's made other choices.'

Fontana looked at me, a curious, angry look. I had no idea what it meant or why he was suddenly annoyed.

'My sister does not need your "Lady Janet" to remain modest and chaste,' he snapped. 'Regardless, I will be placing her in a convent in Venice until I return.'

I had seldom heard a woman more completely described as useless baggage. Definitely something there, and probably none of my business.

'Well, then,' I said. 'Welcome to the *compagnia*, my lord.'

PART III

THE EUXINE VOYAGE

Greece and Outremer

1373

Son, in the place where you would go,
Twisted and tortuous will the roads be;
Swamps there will be, where the horsemen will sink and never
emerge; Forests there will be, where the red serpent can find no
path; Fortresses there will be, that rub shoulders with the sky ...
Your destination is a frightful place. Turn back!

Anon, *The Book of Dede Korkut, Ballad 6*

We marched across an exhausted Lombardy and into the Veneto, where war had not come recently. Verona looked prosperous, although we didn't linger, and Padua looked both rich and militant. You didn't have to be paying very close attention to hear a lot of anger directed at Venice. We ignored the anger, and took boats down the Brenta to Chioggia, with the pages and grooms bringing the horse herd along by stages.

Nerio Acciaioli, one of the richest men in Italy or Greece, and one of my oldest friends and sword-comrades, met us at Chioggia, the port town at the southern end of the Lido where the main channel of the Brenta flows into the lagoon. Chioggia has not one but two entrances to the Venetian Lagoon, and although, back before the war, it was not a direct part of the Venetian Republic, it nonetheless was full of people whose cousins were Venetians, like my friends the Corners. Marc-Antonio was born and bred in Chioggia, which, as you will see, was important.

Regardless, we met Nerio at Chioggia, and we went straight to the Lido by barge. If you don't know, the Lido is the long sandbar that closes the Venetian Lagoon from the east against the Adriatic, rendering the Lagoon itself a sort of natural nautical fortress. The Lagoon has only four real entrances, and two of them are at Chioggia, as I have said. I'll just keep saying it, because Chioggia turned out to be a very important place indeed, as you will hear.

Nerio, by mean of the sorcery of riches, had billets on the Lido for all of my company, and stabling for our horses.

'I am very glad to see you,' he said after our third, or perhaps fourth, embrace.

Indeed, with Nerio sandwiched between me and Fiore, it seemed very much like old times, except that Nerio was dressed in the very height of Venetian fashion. He had beautiful white elk-hide gloves decorated with pearls, and a hat like a Turk's hat, also completely edged in pearls.

He was grinning, which was nice to see.

'Damn it, I've missed you two,' he said. 'And not just for your lances, although I'm damned glad to have them.' He smiled at Fiore.

I knew that the two of them had arrived at some sort of real friendship after years of internecine spats, but it was still surprising to me to see them together, as easy as ... Well, as easy as either was with me.

Nerio was asking after people he knew. When he got to l'Angars, I said, 'He's gone to serve Enguerrand de Coucy,' and Nerio winced.

'If he was looking for a rich lord, I'd rather he'd chosen me,' he muttered.

'I might prefer it as well,' I said.

I was working long hours trying to be l'Angars and Janet, and I'd snapped at Tom Fenton just that morning over ... nothing.

'And who is that lovely woman you have in your train?' Nerio asked.

I looked at him. 'Long Mag?' I asked.

Even Fiore snorted. Mag is tough as an old boot, knows a fair amount of physic, and has the ability to get a shirt really white no matter how much blood you've left in it, but lovely she is not.

Nerio raised an eyebrow. I followed his eyes to where Maddalena Fontana sat on her palfrey. She wore a linen veil, carefully pinned, a houppelande buttoned to the chin, a Northern style seldom seen in Italy, and her hair in long braids on either side of her face. She was, as I have said, a small woman, and a very good horsewoman, so she looked utterly competent when mounted.

Nerio was clearly smitten. He's always fancied women who could ride well.

Or not. Nerio's tastes run pretty wide.

'She's the sister of one of my officers,' I said. 'Lord Fontana of Piacenza.'

'Ah.' Nerio smiled. 'Married?'

I knew that smile. 'Not, I think, available in any way.'

Nerio grinned at me. 'Yours, then?' he asked.

I rolled my eyes. 'She's very religious ...' I began.

'They often are, I find,' Nerio said. He smiled, perhaps at some salacious memory. 'She's very short,' he added.

Fiore glanced at him. 'Sometimes,' he said, 'I feel that I understand you perfectly – when you are plotting, for example. And then, suddenly, you are this odd creature. She is short! Of course she is. She is as God made her, and you are no more likely to bed her than lightning from the heavens is likely to strike me. Can we please discuss something interesting?'

Most of the men riding in my vanguard heard every word of this diatribe, and some looked fit to explode. I prayed – really prayed – to the Virgin that Lord Fontana would never hear a word of this.

'Nerio,' I said quietly, 'this is a lady. You are playing with fire.'

'I like playing with fire,' Nerio said. And then he deflated. 'Oh, fine. You two will tame me yet.'

'I thought you were marrying someone ...' I said.

'Hmm,' Nerio said. 'It's rather like Fiore's marriage.'

'Fiore's marriage?' I asked, and then wished that I hadn't, because of course I knew the lady he loved. I had met her, and the courtship had been furthered by my own lady, who was now ... dead.

And I'd promised to help him make contact again.

I'm a poor friend.

'My lady,' Fiore said. 'In Genoa. You are going to find her for me.' He said it with the complete trust he showed most of the time.

'And I ...' Nerio smiled. 'Well ... Everything did not go as I'd wished, let's say. I don't suppose I'll be King of Cilician Armenia any time soon.'

As soon as we encountered Nerio he began paying, which was accounted a miracle by most of my lances. The first night on the Lido we had a pay day. I divided most of my half of Francesco d'Este's ransom to provide the double-pay bonus that men had a right to expect for a battle. Nerio paid them two months in advance, something virtually unheard of in Italy, although, as he pointed out to them in a good little speech, they were getting on ships for Corinth and not likely to desert.

Naturally, by the next morning, we had archers as far away as Padua and Treviso. Soldiers with money are mostly harmless, but incredibly capable of crossing vast distances. Men spent small fortunes to be rowed or paddled or poled across the lagoon to Venice or Mestre, so that they could gamble or fornicate away the rest.

'You are not making money,' Nerio said that night.

We were staying in a private house he'd rented on the Lido. It was for the officers, but we'd found beds for the night.

I winced. 'This campaign, I've done a little better than break even,' I said. 'The Pope never paid Hawkwood, so I'm the one paying.'

Nerio made a face. 'Foolishness. You condotierri are the only merchants in the world who provide your services up front and then wait, hoping to be paid. Imagine a whore who provided her services and waited patiently for the customer to pay?'

Fiore's eyes became slits.

'Brother, I don't think Messire Fiore wishes to be characterised as a whore,' I said.

Nerio laughed. 'And yet, the two professions have so many things in common.'

Fiore went out and slammed the door.

'I see that not everything has changed between you,' I said.

'I have a big mouth,' Nerio said. 'And I'm now sufficiently powerful that almost no one tells me when I'm an arse.' He looked at me. 'You were supposed to receive three hundred ducats above your pay, as an incentive, correct?'

'Yes,' I said, already bored. Money has never been my strong suit.

Nerio, on the other hand, was making notes in a neat little bound book.

'Fifty-eight lances, two double pay victories?' he asked. 'December, January, February, March, April, May, June. Seven months, sixteen ducats a month per lance, your incentive double pay for two victories.' He looked at the air in front of his face. 'Twice sixteen is thirty-two, times fifty-eight, added to the base ...' He looked at me. 'The Pope owes you eight thousand, six hundred and fifty-two ducats, payable immediately.' He wrote the figure in his book. 'At the moment, as I haven't received your estate money from Lesvos or Savoy, you owe me more than half of that. I will collect this debt for you, or rather, my agents will. But you really need to stop fighting for free.'

I owed Nerio's bank almost five thousand ducats. The money had flowed out because I was Nerio's friend and had his deep pockets to back me, but just then I had to struggle with the full amount – an amount that would have strained Emile's finances. I was owed almost nine thousand ducats. A staggering sum for a jumped-up hedge knight like me to have fronted to my men.

'I owe you four thousand ducats?' I asked.

'Closer to five,' Nerio said. 'But look you, the Pope owes you almost nine, and your estates haven't paid yet, so really, you are in funds. Don't let it concern you. I will collect from the Pope.'

'Hawkwood didn't think he could collect,' I said.

'Ah, Messire Acudo is a fox and a brilliant commander, but he is not a bank. I am a bank. My bank and its solvency are connected to other banks. The Pope cannot default to me. He can ignore Messire Acudo, but not Florence.' Nerio shrugged. 'Still, I recommend that you stop working for the Pope. He's edging towards some very dangerous waters.'

'Tell me what we're doing in Greece,' I said.

Nerio sat back. Fiore came back in, carrying a pilgrim flask that proved to be full of wine. He poured for the three of us as if he had not just stomped out, mortified. I began to see how Fiore handled Nerio.

'I want to take Megara,' he said. 'It's the next city to the east of Corinth. A good little town that produces silk and mutton. It has a garrison of Catalans. I think that the King of Sicily might put more men in the field if I am not careful. It really needs to be taken by *coup de main.*'

I nodded. 'Most of the old storming party experts are gone,' I said. 'I suppose Lapot and I might get it done together.'

Fiore spread his hands. 'I'm sure I can help,' he said.

'But first,' Nerio said, 'I need you two to join me on an embassy to Constantinople, and perhaps a visit to the Gatelussi.'

Venice was like a dream. I had friends there, and I had Fiore and Nerio with me. We went to the street of the sword makers, and we went to the armourers, and we drank wine with various patricians, soldiers and old comrades. We stayed at the commanderie of the Knights of Saint John in Castello, and we brought both Lord Fontana and his sister, who could not, of course, stay with the knights.

I had ways of dealing with that. Nerio and Fiore and I landed a day before the lord Fontana and we found Vettor Pisani visiting the knights. He was kind enough to invite Lord Fontana and his sister to stay at his palazzo while a suitable convent was found. The bailie of the knights knew everyone in Venice, and was inclined to help us, but for all that I was nettled by Fontana's lack of interest in his sister's welfare. He was mostly interested that she be in a place with 'honour', which seemed for the most part to mean a guarantee that she could have no contact with men.

We'd been in the great city for perhaps three days, and I was still delighted by the sights and smells, the cleanliness, the food, the music, the glass, the rows of ships tied at the end of every street, the canals, the secret orchards ...

It's true. I love Venice.

I had just come home from the purchase of a new breastplate from my usual armourer, a lovely thing, lighter than my much abused old breastplate. I had new shoes, new boots and I'd ordered shirts. What Fiore is to gloves, I am to shirts. I love having them, clean, neat, ready to wear ...

I digress. I arrived at Pisani's by boat and had Marco, my groom, carrying various bundles. I had the breastplate. I went up the steps into the damp 'ground' floor, then up a stone staircase to the living area and found Maddalena sitting alone, sewing.

'I'm sorry to interrupt,' I said. My hands were full, and I was fairly sure I'd been very loud in my blasphemy coming up the stairs.

'Yes,' she said, with a trace of a smile and unaccustomed bitterness. 'Yes, you are most definitely interrupting. I was just enjoying the absolute solitude of sewing. So essential.'

I don't think that, through mud, blood and danger, she'd ever used that tone. In fact, she had seldom used any tone at all. It confused me, and I couldn't think of anything to say, so I bowed.

'Marco, take all this up to my room, please,' I said.

Marco, who was wearing brand-new livery and was proud as a peacock, leapt to obey. I admit I couldn't help but think of the last two boys for whom I'd bought livery, right here in Venice. Both were dead.

I bowed again. 'You are bored?' I asked.

Her eyes met mine. 'How could I be bored?' she said. 'I'm in a beautiful house and I have sewing to do. I'm in the world's most famous city and I'm not allowed to go out, but I'm sure that in the journey from here to my convent I'll get to see all that is good for me.'

'You are angry,' I said.

'Oh, how could you think so?' she said. 'How could I be angry? Nothing pleases me more than knowing that I won't be a burden to my brother.'

She turned her head away with a snap.

I thought of women I'd known – my favourite women, that is. Emile had been free by virtue of power and riches. Sister Marie was free by virtue of a licence from the Pope, and Janet was free because she'd survived rape and horror to become a woman who fought in armour, and she defied any convention.

Maddalena Fontana had none of these freedoms. I thought I understood, and yet I couldn't think of a thing to say.

'I wish you were coming with us,' I said. I don't know where it came from. I'm not even sure that I meant it.

She snapped her eyes back to mine as fast as she'd jerked them away. She leant back slightly, as if I smelt bad, and her face flushed.

Fiore appeared at the head of the loggia stairs.

'Ah, Siora Fontana, the blessing of the day to you,' he said. 'Your colour is high. Has Nerio said something offensive?'

Nerio coughed. He was, in fact, behind Fiore.

Maddalena picked up her sewing and made a very, very small courtesy.

'Gentlemen,' she said, her voice harsh, and she went out through the door that Marco happened to be holding as he came down the stairs.

Nerio glanced at me, and then at Fiore, and said ... nothing.

But the next day, I found her on the grand balcony, looking out over the canal and watching the boats. Her hair was down, which I had never seen before. It was a reddish brown, which surprised me utterly. And it seemed to have a life of its own – every hair seemed to want to go its own way.

'Siora!' I said. I hadn't expected to find her on the balcony.

She smiled, so I bowed.

'Let me apologise for yesterday,' I began.

'You, apologise?' she asked. 'I was rude. I was impudent. Indeed, it's apparently one of the features of my character.' She laughed, but it was rueful, not bitter.

'You were unhappy,' I said.

She shrugged. 'In truth, I was mostly annoyed by being treated like baggage. In fact, a nice convent with some intelligent women and a library full of books will suit me very well. Perhaps I'll take the veil this time.'

She smiled again. It was quite a nice smile, and I wondered suddenly how Nerio had seen this woman's beauty so quickly and I hadn't. She was, in fact, quite lovely, just as Nerio had said. And not just with a spear in her hand, like Athena.

'This time?' I asked, trying to match her tone.

She frowned. 'I should not have said that,' she said. 'Please forget it.'

I nodded.

She smiled. 'And, messire, although you prove to be excellent company, I must ask you to find me someone to join us here. I cannot be alone on this balcony with you.'

I understood that, and went back inside, but I couldn't find anyone but Nerio, who was hardly anyone's chaperone. Still, he amused her, and the three of us sat watching the world of Venice go by. I remember it as a very pleasant afternoon. Nerio flattered her, and she resisted him, but I got the feeling that she enjoyed his flattery and hadn't experienced very much of it.

We were discussing the possibility of attending church when her brother stepped out of the piano nobile and onto the balcony.

'Maddalena,' he said, and his voice was full of suppressed anger.

She rose, and smiled at Nerio, and then me. And then, between beats of my heart, she gave Fontana an absolutely poisonous look. In a carefully controlled voice, she said, 'I have had a very pleasant afternoon with these two gentlemen.'

Fontana all but spat. 'Of course you did,' he said. 'But I think you would be happier in your own room.'

She swept out and he followed her. We could hear their voices in quiet combat as they walked towards the stairs – she hissing with rage, he icy in his condemnation – but no words carried.

Nerio smiled. 'Ah, I want her,' he said. 'But I suppose you'll think less of me if I bed her.'

Now it was my turn to look angry. 'Nerio …' I said.

He raised a hand. 'Listen, brother,' he said. Then he shook his head. 'No, never mind. But she likes you, not me, and an hour of my charm didn't change her mind. Her brother is a fool – worse than a jealous husband.'

'Nerio,' I hissed. 'Please do not end up fighting a duel with one of my officers. One of your own officers ...'

He smiled and poured himself a glass of wine, and then held the flagon over my glass.

'Wine?' he asked.

The next day Maddalena went to her convent on one of the islands. Lord Fontana was nowhere to be found. Our transports arrived and began loading on the Lido, and Nerio informed me that we'd have an armed escort down the Adriatic to the Gulf of Corinth. In fact, it proved that we were to travel with the Venetian *muda*, the yearly convoy to Constantinople and the Black Sea (or Euxine, depending on who you asked). There were great galleys for Constantinople, but also for Trebizond, a name that sparked my imagination.

All this while I recruited every out-of-work lance available in Venice or the mainland. There were a fair number, to be sure – the effective bankruptcy of both Milan and the Papacy had left a lot of men on the market.

'I'm more an ally of Venice than of Genoa,' Nerio said. In fact, he purred it, while we sat in a little tavern and ate seafood. 'And Genoa and Venice are getting ready for the big fight, you know? Which the Green Count and I are trying to prevent.' He was cracking open clams and sucking them out of the shell as he went. His squire, Achille, was standing behind him with a towel. 'That's why there are so many mercenaries here. Venice will take them all, soon enough.'

'Don't tell me that Genoa would attack you – by which I mean me?' I said. I was eating noodles with squid's ink and cuttlefish, my very favourite Venetian dish.

Nerio shrugged. 'The Signory has allowed us to sail with the *muda*,' he said. 'I'll take it. Besides, it's Carlo Zeno commanding, and he knows everything that's happening in the East. I want to hear his gossip.'

I looked at Nerio. I knew him well – there were few men I knew better. And he was hiding something. Venice didn't provide armed ships to escort merchant princes and their private armies, usually. Or allow foreign merchants to join their convoys.

I supposed I looked at him for too long.

'What?' he asked, around his clam.

Fiore was looking away. Fiore was the worst liar imaginable.

'Nerio,' I said, putting a hand on his arm. 'What are you doing in Venice?'

He finished his clam and took a sip of wine. 'Ah,' he said. 'Well, I was waiting for you.'

'Yes,' I said, 'I understand that you had nothing better to do with your summer than wait for me.' I smiled.

He smiled back, and there was the wolf within him. 'I admit that your arrival was ... fortuitous.'

Fiore said, 'I told you I'd bring him before you left.'

I leant back.

Nerio nodded. 'I needed soldiers. In a hurry.' He shrugged. 'Venice always has some, if you know the right people. But I didn't have to roll those dice, because you ... came.'

I leant forward. 'You wanted my company for next season. But you started paying them as soon as we met you. So I assume you have something in mind for this season.'

Nerio nodded. 'I did mention that I wanted you to go to Constantinople,' he said.

When we'd been an hour at sea, and I was leaning over the side, still going through the lists of things I'd purchased in Venice and wondering what I'd forgotten – I'd found a farrier, a German, and bought him a small wagon and a stock of horseshoes and nails ... Never mind. Pilgrim sat beside me, watching the sea as if he might jump in at any moment. And we had a dozen ships with us – four great galleys, the kind the Venetians use for trade, and some enormous round ships, as well as a few galleys under Zeno.

Nerio came up next to me at the rail amidships. We were on a cog, a big one, and just off our port side was an ordinary galley – a *galea sotil* – running under sail, her long low hull predatory under her big lateen.

'I admit I have been duplicitous,' he said.

'The very first time, no doubt,' I replied.

He shrugged. 'Listen, Guglielmo. Things in Constantinople have been very ... bad ... since we were there. The Pope did nothing for the Emperor. Indeed, if anything, he set the cause of the Union of Churches back.'

'I remember.'

'Hmm. So the new Pope sees the Emperor as just another schismatic. A heretic, to be tamed. And the Emperor ... has begun looking elsewhere for allies.'

'Genoa?' I asked.

Nerio raised an eyebrow. 'Genoa, of course. But no. The Turks. And ... farther east, too.'

'The Turks?' I asked. 'Aren't the Turks the problem?'

Nerio looked out to sea for a bit. 'Yes and no. In the long run, yes. In the short run, he trusts them more than he trusts most Latins.'

'I see,' I said. And I thought that I did.

'Prince Francesco Gatelussi and I ...'

I had to smile. 'Of course, you and the old pirate are allies.'

'Hmm,' he said again. 'Yes. For the most part, we are allies. Listen ... The immediate problem remains Andronicus, the Emperor's son. He is trying to take the city from his father – it is all too possible that he's already taken it. He and Manuel, the emperor's other son, hate each other, and the Emperor is caught between them, just as he is caught between Latins and Turks, Venetians and Genoese, the Roman Church and his own Patriarch. He is a man being ground down by a dozen millstones.'

Well ... I had been to Constantinople and I'd played a small role in keeping the Emperor on his throne, which is why I was 'Spatharios,' a sword bearer and protector of the throne. A nice title, as I've said elsewhere.

'So Gatelussi and I and a few friends are going to pay you and your company to spend the winter in Constantinople,' he said. 'To give the Emperor options. Or rather, to keep him from choosing the wrong option.'

'I'm not sure my seventy-odd lances are going to keep the Emperor on the throne,' I said.

I was going to take three hundred men into a city of eighty thousand souls. We'd vanish.

'All we need is for you to keep the peace over the winter, and maybe take a short sea voyage. In the spring, I'll come and fetch you and we'll take Megara.' He sounded very earnest, but then, he usually did when he wanted something.

I noted the words 'short sea voyage'.

We had a good trip. It was early July, and the sun beat down unmercifully, and the tar in the deck planks ran so that there were black smears all over the deck, no matter how hard the lubbers worked to scrub it. Off Ancona we ran in with two Genoese galleys, and they edged down on us and then stood away, having decided that two cogs and two galleys were more than they wanted to try.

When we dined with Carlo Zeno at Corfu, with all our ships at anchor and the men allowed a run ashore, I asked him. Zeno and I had served together before Alexandria, and we'd met several times in the intervening years, and now it turned out that he was commanding our escort. He had much the same piratical reputation as Gatelussi, but he was much younger. In fact, he turned forty as we entered the harbour, and we drank to his health that night. He was also a hardened realist, who had once explained to me in no uncertain terms why the Pope didn't really care whether our crusade took Jerusalem.

'Would the Genoese just attack you?' I asked.

When he looked away, I said, 'I'm no seaman, but those two came down at us until they saw your galleys.'

He smiled mirthlessly. 'Any time they can catch one of ours without witnesses,' he said. 'We are *almost* at war.' He looked out to sea and then back at me. 'This is our convoy to Constantinople and the Euxine. The Genoese claim we are not allowed to trade in the Euxine, so all of this will be rather delicate. And may lead to war.'

'A war I'm trying to avoid,' Nerio put in. 'If Venice and Genoa fight, it will be catastrophic for trade, for the Union of Churches ... for the whole Latin community in the East.'

Zeno smiled into his wine cup. 'Messire, I have the deepest respect and honour for you, but I promise you, we will fight. Lines have been crossed. Crimes have been committed. And Genoa cannot decide where Venice is allowed to trade.'

Zeno was a veteran mercenary, and usually quite cynical. I was unused to this sort of talk from him.

'You believe such a war is necessary?' I asked.

He frowned. 'I believe that the old men in Genoa, and enough old

162

men in Venice, now believe this war is necessary. But I agree with Nerio. It will be terrible, and the effects will linger for a generation.' He shrugged, and then looked at Nerio, like two men in on a secret. 'I want to see Genoa's possessions in the East, and I fully admit I'm here to make sure that our ships are allowed to trade at Trebizond, at least.' His look became harder. 'By any means necessary – quiet if possible, military if required.'

Nerio winced.

I noted that, as well.

Anyway, do you remember young Aldo, the Venetian oarsman who became Fiore's squire back in '67? He chose to stay in Venice when the company went south. Five years later he was still alive, and Zeno's second in command. He was happy to see us. It is always a pleasure for me, as a man who came up from nothing, to see another such man make his way. Aldo, now 'Aldo di Mytilene', looked like a gentleman of Venice in a fine doublet and hose, and he showed us around Zeno's fighting galley with pride.

He told us a dozen amusing tales, some far-fetched. One was about rescuing a drowning man, and how he was revived from death. It sounded a bit like a pious miracle, but Aldo insisted that it was true, and I still remember it with good cause, as you will hear.

But he let slip that Zeno had been waiting impatiently for Nerio. Well, then. I knew Nerio was plotting. And I was being paid. I didn't worry about it unduly.

A day out of Corfu, we could see the Genoese galleys on the horizon, their sails deep white cuts in the smooth line where the sea met the sky, like nicks in a sword blade. The master of our cog cursed and set his sailors to getting a little more speed out of his big round ship.

'Not that the bastards can do us much harm,' he said. 'My planks are as thick as castle walls, and we're thirty feet higher than they.' He grinned, a predator like Zeno. 'And my hold is full of your soldiers. By Saint Thomas, I wish they'd make a run at us, I truly do.'

But they didn't. They stayed just there, hulls down on the horizon at dawn and dusk, when the sun made their sails visible.

We passed the entrance to the Gulf of Corinth, and I knew that whatever Nerio had said, we were going straight to Constantinople, which he had the good grace to admit to me later that evening.

'I'll be with you,' he said. 'I want to make damned sure that the

Emperor John knows who is holding his hand this winter. Also, I need a favour.' He smiled, as he did when he thought that he was much smarter than other men. 'Also, I need to be sure that Zeno doesn't get overzealous.'

Our arrival at Negroponte was heralded by a boy with a trumpet sounded from the sea bastion. We rested our rowers after a three-day calm, drank some good wine and exercised our horses. Nerio told me that we were waiting for more men, and when he told me that they would include John the Turk and more than a dozen other men who'd stayed in Romania with Nerio, I was delighted.

I had decided that it was time to organise my company again, after the loss of Janet and Sam Bibbo and l'Angars. I thought to try Lapot as my senior lance, the position that l'Angars had held. I confess that I hesitated for an unworthy reason – Lapot was a good friend. We'd made the Camino together. L'Angars, a man I had valued extremely, had also been a good subordinate, whereas Lapot and I knew each other a different way. I wasn't sure it would work.

But then, Janet was a good friend and *almost* a lover, and she and I had worked well together. I wondered again at her staying with Sir John. I wondered about it a great deal.

I also took advantage of a Roman monk on his way back to the Holy City, and I sent him off richer by a few ducats and with a letter for Michael des Roches. If the man of learning wanted to come to Greece, this was certainly promising to be an interesting time for a visit. And I imagined that Nerio could, if he wanted, open a great many monastery libraries for Des Roches. I knew that he'd come to an understanding with the Greek Church, and that spoke well for whatever he was plotting.

I divided my company into two and placed Lord Fontana in charge of one half and La Motte in charge of the other. I divided the lances evenly between the two, kept Tom Fenton as my banner bearer, and, after a consultation with Gospel Mark, I made Ewan the Scot my master archer with extra pay. Christopher the Aethiopian got to be master archer to Lord Fontana.

And I wandered out to the sea bastion and hired the teenage boy who'd blown the trumpet. His name was Giorgios, and he's still with me – right over there, Master Chaucer. You can ask him about the truth of all my tall tales. Ha!

Regardless, I provided him with livery and a pair of horses, and a very nice trumpet that had, I suspect, been Turkish.

Two small ships arrived less than a week later, and I watched John the Turk leap his horse off the ship and swim her ashore. He dismounted with a flourish in a spray of seawater, and immediately looked over our horses.

'That's one ugly horse,' he said of Percival.

'Good fighter,' I said.

I suppose this is what passes for small talk among the steppe nomads.

John smiled, and all the hundred creases in his face deepened, so that he looked a little like the 'Green Man' faces you see in England.

I embraced him, and Hector Lachlan and a dozen other men I'd left behind. I didn't embrace John's Kipchak Mongols, who looked very much like your worst nightmare of Eastern bandits, scarred and covered in weapons.

There were only eight, where there had been ten.

Kerchus, the man who had opened for our team in the tournament at Didymoteichon, gave me a hard smile.

'Turks,' he said.

John nodded. 'Fucking hard times,' he said. And spat.

That was all he had to say about three years of fighting for Nerio.

Sir Hector had more to say, though.

'The Catalans are a cruel race,' he said.

This from a Highland Scot who viewed cattle raiding as a form of social interaction.

He nodded at John. 'They took one o' our'n, and they cut him up. An' that was just for scoutin', like.'

John shrugged. His shrug was tremendously expressive, suggesting a deep-seated hatred for Catalans ... and something like contempt for a man who allowed himself to be caught while 'scouting'.

Hector looked at me with a bushy eyebrow raised. 'Now that the whole company is here,' he said, 'mayhap we'll pay 'em back, eh?'

I remember looking around at all these men with whom I'd journeyed to Jerusalem. It gave me heart to have them back, especially John and Hector.

'I expect we'll engage the Catalans in the spring,' I said. 'And for now, an easy winter doing garrison duty in Constantinople. Maybe a short sea voyage.'

John spat. 'Nothing easy there,' he said. 'Remember?'

I remembered those words. *Short sea voyage.*

Our next stop was the small island of Tenedos.

It was mid-July in the eastern Mediterranean. Carlo Zeno told me that Tenedos was beautiful in springtime, and that's possible, but when we landed it was like a desert set in an ocean, with little patches of briars and thorns to indicate there was life here, and it was harsh.

We landed under the castle, on the customs wharf. All traffic – which is to say, all legitimate traffic in and out of the Dardanelles – had to pass this point and pay tolls.

I went ashore with Nerio, Dondazio Fontana, Fiore and John the Turk. Lapot had taken all of our credentials and gone with Carlo Zeno and Achille Orsini, Nerio's squire, to pay our respects.

I was looking up at the Venetian flag flying from the fortress.

'I could have sworn this was part of the Empire,' I said.

Nerio was eyeing a waterfront taverna. There was an attractive woman standing inside with a big pitcher nestled on her hip. Years of experience with Nerio told me that we were going to go in and sit down, so I led the way.

Nerio smiled, first at her, then at me.

'It's as if you can read my mind, brother,' he said. He motioned for wine, very much the lord, and then leant back. 'Where the hell have you been, Guglielmo?' he asked.

I assumed he meant this as an endearment. I grinned and probably said something foolish, like 'I missed you too, Nerio,' and his mouth set in a hard line.

'You know the Emperor has been in Venice, virtually in prison, since ...' He counted back. 'Three years.'

'Of course,' I said.

After all, the best captain of light cavalry in Italy was Giannis Lascaris Calophernes, and he'd been commanding the Emperor's bodyguards in Venice. And not serving with me. The Byzantine Emperor had arrived in '69, while I was climbing mountains in Spain.

'And the Venetians only let him go last year,' Nerio said bitterly. 'And the Pope is a fucking idiot.'

'There, you would have the wholehearted agreement of Amadeus of Savoy,' I said.

The young woman proved even more attractive close up, with the long, straight nose of the ancient Greeks, dark eyes, and a certain air that suggested that she didn't tolerate fools but she might be open to entertainment.

She had a pitcher of wine, and we all put our cups on the table. Mine was glass, which I kept in a little case in my purse. Nerio's was solid silver. John's was wooden, turned from a burl. Fiore's was pewter, and so was Fontana's. We all had a laugh. It's something I remember – those cups on the table.

She poured the wine, and exchanged a long glance with Nerio. I'd like to say that I don't know how he does it, but I do. I know exactly how he does it.

But you want to hear about battles, so let's get on with it.

'So you know that the new Pope, the idiot, did nothing but abuse the Roman Emperor and demand his unquestioning submission?' Nerio said, tearing his eyes away from the young woman.

I hadn't known that.

'Oh,' I said.

'And he refused to lend the Emperor any money. In fact, he reneged on everything Amadeus had promised.'

'Christ,' I muttered. 'What's this to do with Tenedos?'

'It's an open secret,' Nerio said, glancing at his wine cup, which was already empty. 'The Emperor John sold Tenedos to the Venetians for thirty thousand ducats and the return of his crown jewels.'

'That's the thirty thousand ducats he paid Amadeus of Savoy,' I said.

Nerio sneered. 'Perhaps,' he said. 'And the crown jewels he pawned to win the civil war. Before our time.'

Fiore was uninterested, and begun to watch two boys fighting ineptly with their fists.

Fontana's eyes narrowed. 'I do not like to hear the Holy Father described as an idiot,' he said. 'And why is this rock worth so much?'

Nerio had the young woman's attention again. Perhaps he'd never lost it, and she came back smiling, with the pitcher of wine. It was excellent wine, and while Nerio considered Fontana's words she served us a pretty bowl of pickled fish, a loaf of good bread and a little bowl of oil.

The pickled fish were superb.

Nerio ate some bread, wiped his beard, and looked at Fontana.

'All of the trade from the Black Sea comes through this point,' he said. 'All of the trade from the East. Do you know the phrase "Silk Road"?'

Fontana was toying with his cup. 'I can't say that I do,' he admitted. 'It sounds like something for merchants.'

Nerio chuckled, but there was malice in his chuckle. 'It's not actually a road, mind you. It's a hundred tracks, or so I'm told.' He leant back. 'It's the main route by which the wonders of the East reach us in the West. Silks and spices. Sometimes called the Road of Gold.'

John smiled his devil's smile. 'Going to shit, now,' he said.

Nerio looked at John. They'd been together for three years. Nerio had finally accepted that John the Turk truly viewed himself as any man's equal.

'Why?' I asked.

John made a face. 'While Mongol people held the steppes with one great khan, a woman with a bag of gold could ride from Samarkand to Trebizond.' John's Italian was almost as good as mine, now, except when he was angry or excited. And his Greek was fluent, if pithy. He waved. 'But now the empire of the khan is falling. All the grandsons of Chingiz Khan fight among themselves. The bandit tribes, the little men, each want their cut.' He made a motion across his throat. 'They will kill the golden road.'

Nerio pointed at John with his thumb. 'I sent him east two years ago.'

John nodded. 'I went all the way to Saray and Samarkand. To where the Chagatay are lords, and beyond.'

I probably looked blank. Nerio drank off the rest of his wine.

'Mongol capitals out on the steppe,' he said, and picked up my wineglass. 'Venice,' he said. Then he put his silver cup next to it. 'Constantinople,' he said. Then he put a pewter cup next to that. 'Trebizond,' he said.

I nodded, as if I knew the ground, which of course, I did not.

'Since Baghdad was destroyed, Trebizond is the terminus,' Nerio put in. 'Baghdad was destroyed by the Mongols.'

Fontana was trying to be interested. 'Yeesss,' he drawled.

While Nerio was laying out cups, Carlo Zeno joined us, and Lapot.

Lapot gave me a nod that told me our dues were paid and all was in order. He was a very quiet man, Lapot. But so far, a very efficient one.

Zeno looked at the cups.

'All of these are sea stages in the trade,' Nerio said. 'Venice or Genoa to Constantinople to Trebizond. After that, it's all by land. Across the western steppe – Trebizond to Samarkand.' Then he put down John's wooden cup of Mongol manufacture. 'And even then, you are not quite halfway to China.'

He put the pretty dish with olive oil in it at the end, far across the table.

'Every piece of silk comes this whole distance,' he said, 'and all of it comes through the Black Sea, past Constantinople, and through here. A squadron of warships here can – and does – close the Dardanelles. The Turks want it, the Genoese want it, I want it. Tenedos is the most valuable rock in the Mediterranean.'

Zeno nodded. 'Except?'

John the Turk spread his hands, a remarkably Italian gesture. 'Except that the trade coming across the steppes is a trickle of what it was before.'

Fontana shrugged. 'In Italy we have our own silk and our own spices. What do we care?'

Nerio sighed. 'My beautiful Florence leads Italy's silk trade,' he said. 'And we still buy mountains of the Chinese stuff. And spices, and a dozen other commodities. But that's not the essential issue. The issue is that the Emperor John needs that trade to flow. It's his primary source of income.'

Fontana shrugged dismissively.

'You think the Turks are trying to take the trade?' I asked.

Nerio made a face. 'No. The Turks are barbarians.' He held up his hands. 'I don't mean they are bad men – you and I both know they are honest fellows, for the most part. But they have no more idea of taking the silk trade than of disrupting the gold trade with Africa.'

'Gold trade?' Lapot asked.

Zeno nodded. 'Africa,' he said, the way a man might say his lover's name.

'So, Tenedos ...' I said. 'The tax gate on the silk trade from China.'

'Exactly,' Nerio said. 'You are quick, I find.'

'And now it belongs to Venice,' Zeno said.

'Until Genoa comes to take it from you,' Nerio said.

'They can try,' Zeno snapped. 'And then we will have the war.'

Nerio shook his head, but he changed the subject. We drank a fair amount, and Nerio didn't come back to the ship with me, which was no surprise to me or Fiore.

Fiore and I were fighting on the deck the next morning – no harness, just gloves and an arming coat and our fighting helmets. Fiore was giving the watchers a demonstration of all my failings, and I was trying to take it in good part. I remember Marc-Antonio standing by the stern rail trying desperately not to laugh as Fiore stepped into my cut, took the pommel of my sword and almost made me eat it.

And I'm reckoned a good blade.

I got my visor open.

'Damn it, you are better!' I said.

Fiore shrugged. 'Better than you, anyway. I think I see room for us to work on these things. You have developed a number of tells, my friend.'

Ah, Fiore. How soon I forget what it's like to have him instruct you.

At any rate, Nerio came up the gangplank, looking clean and neat and like a great merchant prince, not like a man who had spent the night in fornication and debauchery. It didn't seem fair that he could look so good.

And honestly, I was beginning to think of fornication and debauchery myself. Emile had been dead for three years. I missed her. Almost every day I thought of something to tell her, to write to her ...

And she was still dead. I could forget that for an hour, and then it would come back.

Anyway ...

Nerio came up behind me and watched. I took a few breaths, rid myself of anger at Fiore, who was, in fact, merely being himself, closed my visor and stepped in. Fiore had his sword in a forward garde, taunting me. I held my sword low and to the left of my body, as he had taught me. That is, Fiore had taught me that this garde was the appropriate response to his own. When he took no action, I did what he'd taught me to do. I snapped the point up at his sword and, at the same time, let go of the hilt with my left hand and seized the blade of my own sword at mid-sword. To my astonishment, I made the cross, possessed his sword, and put the tip in under his arm – a killing blow.

He stepped back and laughed.

'Beautiful,' he said. 'Absolutely perfect. You have not forgotten me altogether!'

Nerio slapped my back, and Marc-Antonio looked as if stability had been restored to his world. But I knew better. Fiore had fed me that play, to make sure I remembered my basics. Fiore never worried about being hit. His confidence was such that he never hesitated to let a student hit him, although I remember him being puzzled by Sister Marie once. Regardless, that ended my day, and I stripped my sweat-soaked arming coat off and watched Marco hang it on a sail rack to dry.

I leant against the rail as Marc-Antonio took his turn.

Nerio turned to me. 'I didn't say this in front of Zeno,' he whispered. 'But the Genoese won't come with a fleet. They'll come with assassins and gold. Even now, I think they're trying to kill the Emperor John. Or lock him away and replace him with Andronicus, his son.'

'Which is why you are spending a fortune to put my company in the city for the winter.'

'No one ever called you a slow learner,' Nerio said.

'I'd like to propose a plan of action,' I said.

Nerio nodded. 'You are a famous captain,' he said. 'Also, I saw you storm Corinth. Tell me.'

'We should land at Gallipoli and ride to the land walls of the city,' I said.

Nerio smiled his annoying smile. 'We'll ask Prince Francesco when he arrives.'

'He's coming here?' I asked.

'Of course,' Nerio said.

In fact, it was Francesco Orsini, my former corporal, who joined us. The natural son of Francesco Gatelussi, the prince of Lesvos, he was another old friend, and another reminder of the happy days I spent in Emile's arms on Lesvos. And less happy times, when I served Count Amadeus.

Ah, well.

Francesco brought me ten lances, all fully outfitted. He was going to serve with me, but he was there to watch over the Emperor and any deal that was made. He was older now, and seemed taller. Very much his own man, and used to command.

'Why do you want to land at Gallipoli?' he asked. 'Reliving old glories?'

Francesco had been with me when we took Gallipoli, back in '67.

We were in our taverna, watching the five Gatelussi galleys as they were beached and turned over to dry their hulls and scrape the worms off. This time we had the whole taverna. At the table were all of my officers, and all of Nerio's people, too.

I looked at Nerio. 'Is there any chance that Andronicus has already seized power in the city?' I asked.

Nerio whistled. 'Yes,' he said. 'By the cross of Christ, Guglielmo! You think ...'

I smiled, because I'm rarely thought to be clever, and I value those moments. 'I think that if we arrive, and Andronicus holds the port, we'll either be denied permission to land or arrested coming off the boats. And can you imagine lading us in Genoese Galata?'

'Whereas, in full kit at the Blacharnae gate ...' Francesco smiled. I had missed him, and I think he missed me. He was two years older, he'd filled out, as I say, and he had ... dignity. Something usually lacking in men his age.

'Unless the gate guards are suborned, we can ride in and do ... anything ... that needs to be done.' I made a vague motion.

Young Francesco looked at Nerio. 'We are very late, according to the timetable you laid down last autumn. We thought you might have changed your mind.'

Nerio looked at me. 'I was waiting for Guglielmo,' he said with a smile.

Fiore looked at him. 'That's not really true,' he said, in his Fiore way. 'You only sent me for Guglielmo after you found that there was no one left at Mestre to hire.'

I laughed aloud.

Nerio frowned.

At Gallipoli we had no trouble landing. We'd retaken the place from the Turks, the Ottomanids, back in '67 with the Green Count. It still had a Savoyard governor, with a mercenary garrison who were not friends with the Greek garrison. The mercenaries were well paid and looked capable, and the Greeks looked like peasants dressed as soldiers. Since I knew just how tough the *stradioti*, the Greek light horse, could be, I assumed that the garrison wasn't considered important. But I sent my Greek archer to listen to them and learnt that Constantinople was in an uproar. The commander of the garrison didn't speak Greek and didn't seem to know much about what was happening outside his walls – the fate of the Franks in the Holy Land.

We landed all of our horses and men, and spent a day exercising the horses and resting. Then we marched. It is a little over one hundred and sixty miles, on horseback, from the port of Gallipoli to the walls of Constantinople. I've done it several times, and I know the roads. More importantly, it meant that my horses and my people would arrive in condition, and that we'd get a long look at the most valuable part of the empire. That is, the most valuable part that was still left after the Venetians, the Franks, the Genoese, and the Turks all took a piece or two.

We moved quickly, with our Kipchaks out front, gathering news and arranging a market and a camp site every night. I still had my small silk Imperial flag, which Tom Fenton carried instead of the company standard, and we made good time through excellent weather. The horses recovered from a sea voyage and their hooves dried out. The sea is never good for your horse herd.

Just north of Lefki we encountered a band of Turks pillaging a village, or rather, the Kipchaks found them and slipped away unseen. Turks are the most dangerous opponents I've ever faced, and I was cautious, but I had numbers and time. In the end I closed an open-air trap as if I was hunting stags on horseback, with my lances closing in on them from two sides, and my Kipchaks appearing with a dozen mounted archers when the Turks thought they could ride away to freedom.

Their captain protested that he was in the service of the Emperor, and that he had orders.

'This village, and all these, they stay loyal to the old Emperor,' he said. 'Andronicus now claims he is emperor and pays us to punish them.'

There were thirty of them, all hard men. We'd killed a few in the skirmish, and I hated executing men in cold blood, but they were rebels against my emperor. When Father Angelo brought me the Greek priest from the village and I heard his tale of horror, I determined to punish them.

Young Francesco was a magistrate in the Greek empire. We had a brief trial, and three witnesses from the village identified individuals. We executed those who were identified, and took the rest under escort to the city.

Lapot rode up next to me the next day.

'We've done the same,' he said.

'Killing children?' I asked. 'Raping?'

Lapot shrugged. 'You know who I was before Jerusalem,' he said.

I nodded. 'As I was before I met Father Pierre Thomas.' I didn't like executions. But I turned to him. 'But should we just let them go to do it again?'

Lapot nodded. 'No,' he said. 'I just don't like it. Probably because I know I deserve it.'

John rode up next to me later. 'There are fucking Turks everywhere,' he said. 'A thousand, maybe.'

Nerio looked at me. 'You're the one who wanted to come across country,' he said.

'I don't think we have anything to fear,' I said with a confidence that wasn't quite real.

The Turks are the best mounted warriors I've ever faced. They set ambushes, they make false retreats, they always leave themselves a line of retreat. They play the game of war very well.

A thousand Turks were a real threat to my command of eighty lances, but we had almost four hundred men and much better armour. I didn't think the Turks could take us in a straight fight, but I doubled the guard on my horse herd at night and took some elaborate precautions with my camp and night patrols.

'Shadowing us,' John reported the next day. 'Maybe three hundred.'

I looked at John. 'Can we take them?'

Nerio put a hand on my reins. 'This is no part of our contract,' he said.

I shook my head. 'Nerio, I love you like a brother, and I know you are twice the great lord I'll ever be, but trust me ... Andronicus has paid for these bastards. They're not even real Turks – just steppe bandits.'

John nodded agreement. 'Bad men,' he said.

Young Francesco Orsini reined in. 'If we die here—'

'We won't,' I said.

And then I prayed. I knew Nerio was unhappy with my decision. I knew he was in a hurry. Against that, I was already convinced that Andronicus was on the throne in the city.

So I did something I'd never done before – I called a council of war and allowed a discussion. After all, these were my friends and comrades, and every one of them had a slightly different interest in our operations.

I laid out my point of view as simply as I could. In effect, I said that we had to behave as if Andronicus was emperor.

Nerio threw his hands in the air. 'Jesus wept!' he cried. 'If what you say is true, we're done already, and I'm out a great deal of money.'

Francesco Orsini shook his head silently. 'I agree. If this is true, we're too late.'

Fiore raised an eyebrow. 'You think otherwise, Guglielmo?'

I looked straight at Nerio. 'Would Andronicus murder his father?' I asked.

Nerio shook his head. 'No. The Church would never allow him to be emperor in that case.'

'And Giannis Lascaris?' I asked. 'Still commanding the Emperor's bodyguards?'

Francesco and Nerio exchanged looks.

'I don't know,' Nerio admitted. 'You know as well as I do how hidebound this court is. Arrangements made in Venice probably ended there.'

I nodded. 'I think it's worth trying to make contact. I have a Greek archer in my company. You, Francesco, can no doubt walk in one of the gates of Constantinople and pass for a native.'

'As can I,' Nerio said. He shrugged. 'I can already see what you plan. Make contact with Giannis and the Emperor John, and then a *coup de main* and we restore him.'

I shrugged.

Fiore smiled. 'It sounds just a trifle grandiose,' he allowed.

We were sitting at a fire. It was summer, and we didn't bother with tents. All of us were sitting on our saddles. Nerio was lying down, raising himself on an elbow to speak and then subsiding back.

'I might say that the four of us have never been beaten,' I said. 'But instead I'll stick to the cold facts. Wars in this empire are decided by hundreds of men, not thousands. Clearly, Andronicus has brought in the Turks. But he can't bring Turks into the City of God. I propose that we risk a fight with the force shadowing us. We want a crushing victory, and then we ride for the city to be our own harbingers. Francesco, you take my Greek and head for the city now. On horseback. Get to Giannis. Get to Emperor John – or his wife.'

Francesco made a face. 'If I'm captured ...'

'I'll buy you back,' Nerio said. 'It sounds insane, Guglielmo. Your plan depends on the total defeat of a Turkish force that last night you claimed was very dangerous.'

I shrugged. 'I'm offering you my professional advice. The other option is to ride away, rejoin your ships, and abandon Constantinople to Andronicus.'

We actually discussed a third plan, where we worked a little more cautiously to raise the Greek militias outside the city and strangle the Turkish bandits before moving on Andronicus, but we all agreed that was a year-long campaign and might fail anyway.

'My father needs John on the throne,' Francesco said. 'I'm willing to risk it.'

Nerio lay looking at the stars for perhaps as long as I might say the Credo. Then he sat up.

'No one ever built an empire on caution,' he said. 'If Francesco and your archer are game, I'm in, both my right arm and my bank.'

'I'll pack,' Francesco said.

Morning. A dull grey, lit with a rose pink in the farthest east. The very first signs of the rising sun brought colour and birdsong to what had seemed a sterile desert.

We were set up across a narrow valley that held a dirt track that ran west, towards Adrianopolis – Edirne, as the Turks call it – and Didymoteichon. It wasn't the old Roman road by any means – just a dirt track through a stony pass between two high volcanic hills. The oak woods on either side of the road might have been in England or France. It didn't feel like Greece or Outremer at all.

We were in the woods.

With the birdsong and the first glimpse of the glorious colours of a Thracian morning came the distant sound of hooves, and some keening screams. The sound of Kipchaks stealing horses.

Quite a few horses, as we saw when they galloped past us, driven by John and Kerchus. They went by like centaurs, long whips in their hands, and unleashing demonic screams.

When the horse herd had passed us, the whole valley was full of dust. Half a dozen horses had come adrift from the herd and now wandered back and forth across the open ground around the road. One was a pregnant mare whose cries were pitiful.

The Turks were about a minute behind them. The dust was just settling. The wandering horses slowed them, and I led my men-at-arms out onto the road. We filled the open space in a tight mass.

These were Turks. I've called them bandits and worse, but the leaders, at least, were as good as my friend Timurtash. They never charged our line. The moment their commander saw the rising sun on our armour through the dust, he turned his men.

Our archers began to shower them with shafts. Most Turks are effectively unarmoured. A few have maille shirts, but more just a good aventail or a thick leather coat. Against quarter-pound war bow arrows, they and their ponies were effectively naked.

On the other hand, they were superb riders and my archers were shooting into a dust cloud. In the time it takes to get a candle lit, they were gone, raising more dust in the still morning air.

But John and I had some notion of facing Turks, and we needed a flat victory, not a successful skirmish. So the fleeing Turks found that about five hundred paces to the east, a wagon had rolled across the road, and crossbow-armed pages began a steady stream of bolts.

The best men – the Turkish captain and his officers – made one gallant rush at the wagon, lost men, and then turned and dashed back. The captain, or so I guessed later, judging from his Chinese silk sash and beautiful helmet, died about fifty paces from me as my wall of armoured men walked down the road, closing the trap.

Maybe two dozen of them made it into the woods and rode up the steep ridges. Even then, some discovered that Ewan the Scot and Gospel Mark were also very dangerous men in deep woods.

Nerio had commanded my mounted reserve, and when it was clear that there was no secret double-trap from the Turks, I let him charge in and finish the enemy trapped on the road. That was red slaughter, not battle – armoured men on big horses against nomads with no armour. We lost one man to a well-placed arrow, and then it was over, and the column of road dust rose into the air as if we'd burned a pyre to the old gods.

I took the commander's silk sash and also the parchment in his quiver. It was a sort of 'letter of marque' from the so-called 'Emperor' Andronicus, very like one of our Italian condottas, offering wages for military operations in a given area. I think it says everything you will ever need to know about Andronicus that he was paying Turks to raid his 'own' subjects. But I took it, and put it into my purse.

We had about forty prisoners. I tied their hands, stripped them of weapons, took their horses, and let them go. It wasn't particularly kind, as the Greek peasants hated them, but I wasn't going to hang them all. There's room for a lot of muddy morality right here. By some lights, I was responsible for any of them who lived to rape and kill again. By another argument, I should have ransomed them. But I wasn't sure they served anything like a government, and yet the idea of slaughtering them stuck in my throat, and Lapot's. It would be easier to see them as evil Saracens, except that I didn't, which always complicates matters.

Regardless, the first part of our plan had mostly worked. As it proved, only about half the Turkish force had pursued the Mongols, and so half remained. They'd lost their leaders and most of their horses, and they'd had the sense to run for it before we could reach their camp, but we hadn't wiped them out.

I'd never really expected much better. In fact, I was a little surprised that the double ambush had worked at all.

But we now had three hundred horses, mostly small, hardy steppe ponies, as well as our own excellent herd. We could move very fast, and we did. We had about seventy miles to go, through the heartland of the empire, and our entire force was mounted.

We did it in two days. They were long days, and they weren't free from delays. We were blocked by a sheep herd for an hour in the closed country south of Syrallo, and we got lost trying to go around a washed-out bridge – lost in a web of farm lanes and old roads and hedges and walls higher than a man's head when mounted on a horse. Through it all, I had the awful feeling of command – the endless stress of things undone and enemies unseen, and the nameless horrors of unguessed failures. And despite these stresses, my role was to act like John Hawkwood, being stern, fair and apparently unmoved by ... well, by anything.

I was about as good as a commander as I am as a Christian, by which I mean that I probably snapped a dozen times when people were trying to be helpful. I definitely lost my temper when we couldn't get across a stream a little wider than an English road. I allowed the press of time to fall on me like the weight of sin. I think I managed to frighten my Piacenzan boys into thinking I'd leave them for the Turks, because they didn't heat me some wine to break my fast.

I think you get the picture, Master Chaucer. And well might you smile.

It was the first day of August, and we came over the ridges west of the city to see the gilded domes and the vast walls, and smell the smoke of fifty thousand breakfast fires with a trace of the incense of ten thousand churches. Constantinople – 'the 'City' – lay before us. The walls towered in an orderly profusion of stone and brick, vast and impregnable. My plan seemed insane. I had three hundred men.

'Well,' Nerio said. 'That went well enough. Next time I'll trust you better, Guglielmo.'

I hope I laughed. 'You think we're done with the hard part?' I asked.

Nerio made a face. 'Listen, brother,' he said. 'For my money, either Francesco has made contact and got us an open gate, or he hasn't. If the former, it's all easy. If the latter, we ride home.'

Well, that certainly made breathing easier. And the truth is that while I was learning to be a commander, I had the support of my best friends, who did a great deal to moderate my flights of fancy, my anger and my fear.

Yes, fear. I'd much rather fight a maddened bear than lie awake all night waiting to be ambushed. I can imagine more failings that any mortal man can commit. I have a notion that the ideal military commander is somewhat unimaginative, and just doesn't worry the way I do. I am not ideal.

Nevertheless, we rode straight for the Blacharnae Gate. The flow of traffic into the city was such that there was no point in waiting. We could only have surprise by staying on the crest of the wave. It only took one farmer going through the gate to give us away.

I had given John the official parchment from Andronicus, and he wore the Turkish officer's sash and played the part to the hilt. John loves almost any form of deception that is not theological in nature, which is odd, as in personal matters he is absolutely, even painfully, honest.

He rode ahead of us about half a mile, so that we could just see the sun on his gilded skull cap as he turned in towards the walls. In fact, I knew almost immediately that he hadn't entered by the Blacharnae Gate, where we foreign mercenaries had entered in '67. It sent a bolt of ice into my heart – John had gone through the wrong gate.

On the other hand, I knew that John was both trustworthy and extremely capable. And I was too far away to do anything. So I held my tongue and kept riding, one of the longest and hardest performances of calm of my whole life. Fiore spoke at length about some aspect of jousting, and Nerio chatted with Francesco about various aspects of lechery, and I ... fumed.

John vanished through the gate with a dozen of our light horsemen. I know now that he'd seen something he didn't like, and turned. He showed the letter, overawed the outer gate guards, and waited there until we were all through the Gyrolimne Gate in the Blacharnae Wall, with its double lines and towers. It was not the gate I'd come through in '67, but John had chosen it and it was too late to change. We rode in under the massive arches, past the handful of garrison soldiers, and went straight into the grounds and gardens between the palace of Blacharnae and the Palace of the Porphyrogenitus, where I had stayed briefly in '67.

And there was Francesco Orsini, dressed as an Orthodox monk.

'Straight for the palace,' he said.

Marco brought him a horse and he stripped off the habit, dropped it in the dust with some disgust, and waved.

'Twenty men to follow me and guard the Emperor John,' he said.

'Where is he?' Fiore asked.

'In the Tower of Anemas. The prison.'

'Now by the Virgin and all that's holy,' I spat.

Imagine, putting your own father in prison.

I sent all the Italians, with Lord Fontana and Nerio, and kept Lapot and Fiore and Grice and the rest of my spears, and we went for the palace.

It is vital, when reviewing this little action, to understand that Constantinople, like Venice, has very few troops in it. There are urban militias like an Italian city, except that they are more for controlling rioters than for fighting. There are a handful of regular military units, mostly guards like the English Guard and the Vardariotes, all foreigners who are very difficult to bribe, and there are some garrisons on the massive, incredible wall. Other than that, nothing. None of the emperors trust soldiers. So many of them are former soldiers themselves, who've used the army to take the city, you see. And, like Venice, Constantinople is a city of law. The citizens obey the law, and they don't live like Englishmen, I can tell you. Murder is virtually unheard of, and Byzantine gentlemen do not attack each other's castles.

Rather, they do, but only when offered the excuse of civil unrest.

Andronicus, the would-be Emperor, had perhaps three hundred real soldiers to face us, or about what I had. The Varangians, or Axe-Bearing Guard, or English Guard, had never supported him and had simply stayed in their barracks or their homes. The Vardariotes, or Christianised Turkish Guards, were with the field army. Andronicus had a hundred of so mercenaries, mostly Catalans and Neapolitans and Sicilians from various companies paid by his Genoese masters, and he hadn't even thought to quarter them in the palace. He was very sure of himself. And he had every reason to be sure, as he had his Turkish mercenaries patrolling the countryside and the only armed men inside the walls.

All we had was surprise. And John the Kipchak, and a thorough knowledge of the ground.

The leader of Andronicus's mercenaries was a Genoese, Matteo Socato, and he was well-dressed in a silk jupon and a hat covered in pearls. As I leapt from my horse in the yard of the palace hall, he grabbed the pretender, Andronicus, and bolted with a dozen of his men, running across the gardens and fruit trees that surrounded the palace. They were heading for the little port at Tekla, or Teukla – really, nothing but an escape hatch for the Blacharnae palace, behind the complex of the chapel and St. Mary's.

I saw the pretender's red robe, and the bejewelled hat, and guessed that my quarry was on the run. If they could make Galata, the Genoese suburb across the channel, we were in for trouble. Or a siege.

We rode them down. We were fresh, on good horses, and apple orchards are not much of a hindrance for riding. John and his Kipchaks reminded me what good riding was really like, and when one of the Genoese climbed into a pear tree, Kerchus, John's lieutenant, tipped him back out with the butt of a javelin.

Messer Socato did not bluster. He and half a dozen of his men surrounded Andronicus, about three hundred paces from the gate to the port of Tekla, facing outwards in a ring of sword against my thirty lances and my Kipchaks.

I rode up, moving John's drawn arrow aside to make my views plain.

'Please surrender the person of the pretender, Andronicus,' I said.

'Pretender!' Andronicus spat. 'I am the true emperor. My father is deposed. And useless. But I do not expect a barbarian mercenary to understand.'

Andronicus was a very handsome man, and in that moment, he was unbowed – angry, but not beaten.

'Majesty,' I said, bowing my head. But I was, after all, mounted on a tall horse, and he was covered in dust, unarmed, and at my mercy.

'If I may,' came the soft voice of Matteo Socolo. 'I am the emperor's *protospatharios*.'

'Are you, now?' asked Fiore. His Italian was contemptuous, and the Genoese man flushed, but his voice remained calm.

'Everyone's interests may be fulfilled here,' Socolo said. 'Please allow the emperor to reach that little gate over there, and I will be sure that all of you are well rewarded.' He smiled. 'And you, sir, will not be thanked by the emperor's father for handing him over. John is too indecisive to know what to do with his own son as a prisoner.' He smiled again.

'Your sword, sir,' I said.

Again, I was sitting on Percival in a hundred pounds of plate armour, and he was wearing a nice jupon and a fancy hat. It was a good sword he held – I suspected he knew how to use it. But only a fool takes a sword against an armoured man when he has no armour himself.

'You are making a great mistake, sir knight,' he said. 'And none of you can bear the weight of the enmity of Genoa.'

'Your sword, sir,' I said. 'I will count down from three. On the last count, you will have an arrow in your gut.'

I gave Percival a very light leg pressure and he stepped neatly to the side, so that John had a clear lane to the Genoese captain.

'Three,' I said.

'You are making a terrible mistake.'

'Two,' I said.

'Christ Pantokrator,' snapped Andronicus. 'Give over your sword, Matteo. These barbarians are too stupid to know what's best for them.'

I took Socolo's sword and put it under my knee and we rode back to the palace. Socolo had the last word. As I passed him to Lapot, he smiled at me.

'I'll know you again, Judas-head.'

I nodded. 'William Gold, at your service. Spatharios to the Emperor John. Baron of Methymna.'

And his smile died. 'You!' he said.

That was satisfying.

Lapot took Andronicus off my hands as well, while I rounded up the rest of his immediate garrison of bravos and replaced them with our people. In fact, by the time I went to the throne room, the Emperor John was seated on the throne exactly where I'd last seen him. Georgios Demetrios Angelus, one of the Emperor's most loyal officers, an adherent of the Union of Churches and a friend of Father Pierre Thomas's, was setting a watch and sending for the Axe-Bearing Guard to return to their posts.

Just like that, the government of an empire was changed.

About six hours of hard but entirely bureaucratic work later, I was stripping out of my armour in a fine room in the palace. Marco was getting the stuff off, and Tommaso was packing it all away in straw, and Pilgrim was 'helping' by rolling in the straw. Achille was disarming Nerio. Fiore was already in his arming clothes. He had a text, a scroll, and he was devouring it with his eyes. Francesco, the youngest of us, was still in full harness, looking out over the gardens. His squire, Roberto, was on a diplomatic errand, and I could tell that Francesco was deeply troubled by the Genoese involvement in toppling the Emperor John, as his family were themselves Genoese.

'Isn't it about time that Achille was knighted?' I asked softly. It just shot into my head – nothing to do with the politics of Constantinople.

Nerio's head snapped around, as if I'd slapped him. 'Christ,' he muttered. 'How will I ever find anyone to replace him?'

I grinned at Greg Fox, who was managing the two boys as if he'd been born a great noble.

'It's not impossible. And he's been your squire for, what . . . ten years?'

'Bah,' he said. His eyes narrowed. 'I'm ashamed. When you and Fiore aren't around, I suspect I'm blind.' He glanced at Achille, who was just coming back with a trio of young Greek men and some wicker baskets. 'Achille.'

'*Illustrio?*'

'I wonder if you'd like to be made a knight?' Nerio asked.

Achille fell on his knees. 'Of all things, my lord.'

Nerio's eyes met mine and he shook his head.

'I'm a tyrant,' he mouthed. 'I'll see to it,' he said aloud. 'Achille, you have served me with perfect loyalty for ten years. I will see to it you are well rewarded. But please help me find a new squire.'

Achille, a very sober man whom I remembered as a very sober youth, had a grin big enough to split his face. 'Yes, *Illustrio*. Immediately.'

Greg Fox got my new breastplate off. Nerio admired it. Fiore came and looked at it, and then said, 'Does anyone but me think that was too easy?'

His hand waved in the vague direction of the palace, and I followed the chain of his thoughts – the scroll, the palace, the coup. Fiore's mind was always exciting to follow.

'It was as if Andronicus was just waiting to be toppled,' I agreed. 'No precautions, no plans.'

'He unleashed the Turks on his own richest farmers,' Nerio said. 'That argues a level of incompetence that is truly staggering.'

'Do you know that this document claims that there are no fewer than thirty-one treatises on the art of war in Greek in the Emperor's library?' Fiore asked. 'The Emperor Maurice actually wrote one!' He glanced at me. 'And not one of them is a sword training manual.' He was very disappointed.

Nerio looked fondly at Fiore. 'What do you have there?'

'This?' Fiore tried to conceal it, but too late. 'Ah ... It's a scroll of all the manuscripts in the Imperial Library that have to do with secular matters,' he said.

'And I thought we'd wasted our time coming here,' Nerio said.

And then, with less sarcasm, he said to me, 'You were right, by the way – and in case you think I didn't notice.'

I must have looked puzzled. Look, Fiore is brilliant and his mind is a little like a magpie's nest, but I can follow along, whereas Nerio is brilliant and I am never quite sure what he's thinking unless perhaps there is a beautiful woman.

'The Blacharnae Gate. The overland path. We did it. Venice could have paid five thousand men for six months and not have accomplished as much, and we did it in a few weeks with three hundred men.'

I shrugged. 'I could very easily have been wrong.'

In fact, I didn't feel any of the triumph I'd have felt if we'd won a battle or I'd done well in a tournament. I couldn't stop thinking about all the things that could still go wrong.

Nerio shrugged. 'Well, my investment in the Emperor is now worth something again. And the Green Count's.'

'And my father's,' young Francesco Orsini said.

But what I was thinking was that Nerio had just said *Venice. Venice could have paid five thousand men* ...

In that moment, I realised that Nerio and Amadeus of Savoy and Francesco Gatelussi may have planned all this, but it was *Venice* who was paying. Venice provided the transport. Venice was sending her *muda* into the Euxine. Venice who needed her ally John on the throne at Blacharnae.

I was a deniable captain for Venice.

The very next day we had an audience. The Emperor John appeared a little thinner and a little more like an ascetic saint than he had six years before. On the other hand, he wore actual jewels and a magnificent crown that I hadn't seen before. Christopher the Aethiopian had seen them. He'd searched the usurper's apartments ruthlessly and found all of the regalia that John had bought back from Venice.

And handed them over, instead of pocketing them. A rare man.

But I digress. We had an audience. The four of us waited patiently with sixty or so other courtiers and lawyers, and the Venetian and Genoese bailies, or mayors of their communities,

We were not the first summoned. That was the Genoese bailie, who'd crossed from Galata to congratulate the Emperor on his restoration and insist on the continuance of some privileges.

Nerio listened unashamedly. Francesco Orsini watched with a look of profound cynicism – eyes narrowed, and one eyebrow slightly raised. It's not an easy expression to hold for a quarter of an hour, but he did. The man took his time, hectoring the Emperor in a low voice, and John sat on his throne with a heavy gold crown on his head and listened with a stunning impassivity. Indeed, he endured the Genoese bailie the way I endure arrow fire. Eventually the man was done, and he bowed, although not very low, and swept towards the exit. But his eyes caught Francesco's magnificent tabard with his coat of arms, the scales of the Gatelussi. He stopped, turned, and walked to the four of us.

'Boy, you and your infernal father have made a great deal of trouble,' he said to Francesco, as if the rest of us weren't there.

Francesco cocked his head to one side. 'Do I know you, sir?' he asked, a little too sweetly.

The Genoese bailie was a big man with a neatly waxed moustache and beard in the Italian style, and a long robe of heavy black silk. He wore a narrow plaque belt at his waist above a bulge of fat. The belt was solid gold, and from it, suspended by a golden chain, was a very businesslike dagger, a baselard with ivory grips and gilt furniture. On his head was a small cap of the sort scholars wore, except that his was of squirrel fur, or 'vere'. He reeked of money.

Nerio bowed. 'Prince Francesco Orsini of Lesvos and Chios, this is the most illustrious lord Filippo De Merude of Genoa.'

De Merude glanced at Nerio. 'And you know me? Some mercenary bravo, and you claim my acquaintance?'

Nerio's smile vanished and was replaced by his killing smile. 'I am Renerio Acciaioli of Florence,' he said.

'I have nothing to say to you,' De Merude said with calculated rudeness. 'I do not count foreign adventurers as acquaintances.'

Young Prince Francesco – and that morning he was every inch a prince – nodded. 'Ah, illustrious De Merude, I think that someone should tell you that courtesy is better suited to diplomacy than arrogance.'

'I save courtesy for my peers,' he snapped. 'You and your father have meddled in something that should not have been touched, and cost important people money. If your father wishes to have any further co-operation from Genoa – if that miserable pirate remembers the land of his birth – he will arrange to reverse this betrayal of his fatherland.' De Merude spoke low, but with a powerful voice.

Francesco bowed his head, but only to hide the fire in his eyes.

I deliberately poked the Genoese bailie in the arm. I had taken an instant dislike to him – something he apparently cultivated – and I was happy to distract him.

'Take your hands off me!' he spat. 'Ah, the Judas-haired captain. Socolo mentioned you. You have a great many enemies for a man so utterly unimportant.'

'Did you bring a company of men-at-arms, by any chance, *illustrio*?' I asked. 'Because if not ... Well ... The tone you are taking ...' I was doing my best to *be* Sir John Hawkwood.

'No, no,' Fiore put in.

Nerio's face was a thunderstorm of rage and injured pride, and Francesco was preparing to say something irrevocable. Of all people, Fiore stepped in, with the same air he'd have worn stepping between two duellists if he thought they needed instruction.

'Messire De Merude is afraid,' he said, 'and because he is afraid, he launches into all of these gasconades. Look at his face! Look at the set of his brow, the sweat. Use his fear against him, certainly, but take no offence at it. Scared men posture.'

'Who the fuck are you?' De Merude spat. In that one reaction, I realised that Fiore was exactly correct. This was a powerful man, an intelligent man, and he was terrified.

'No one of consequence to you,' Fiore said. 'But you are scared, and you are angry, and it is making you vulnerable. I offer you this for nothing.'

De Merude favoured us with what was obviously supposed to be a withering glance. He really should have met Emile. She could kill plants with a glance, or freeze men in place. De Merude simply looked ... looked what Fiore claimed. He looked scared.

And then, in a slightly less dangerous tone, he said, 'Gatelussi, whatever plan you and your infamous father have hatched, Genoa will not tolerate intrusion into the Black Sea. Do you understand? That is our stated policy, and we have the tools to make sure it is obeyed.'

Nerio was over his rage. He smiled thinly – a very dangerous look indeed.

'Do you, really? Do you have the "tools" to face us? Here? Now?'
Nerio laughed in his face, a calculated insult.

De Merude turned on his heel. A few paces clear of us, he turned
and said, 'I have access to legions of heathen Turks. Your handful of
sell-swords won't last a minute.'

Francesco raised his voice. 'Do you imagine you are so powerful as
to task us for restoring the rightful Emperor in his own throne room?'

De Merude set his jaw. 'You will all be dealt with. This is far more
important than you children seem to think.' His voice carried. 'And
this city, and everything in it, and everything in this flea-bitten empire,
belongs to Genoa.'

Across the room, the Bailie of Venice turned his head.

De Merude paced away, watched by every man in the throne room.

Francesco turned to us. 'And Genoa is Father's closest ally,' he said.

Fiore smiled. 'Gentlemen, at least now we know who provided the
money that unseated our emperor.'

Nerio was still watching the arc of light where the great double doors
of the throne room were open to the long steps of the palace below.
'No, it's worse than that. Fiore, you really are brilliant, aren't you?'

'Only now you notice?' Fiore asked.

Nerio rolled his eyes. '*He was afraid.* What do you think he's afraid
of? He must be one of the richest and most powerful men in the East.'

Ahead of us, the Venetian bailie was making his final bows. He
was several degrees less arrogant than his Genoese peer, although he
was not in any way an example of humility. He was also aware of the
four of us. And he made a beeline for us when he was dismissed by
the Emperor.

'You are the men who are friends with Messire Zeno?' he asked in a
voice not much less haughty than De Merude's had been.

Nerio spoke up. 'We have that pleasure.'

'Tell Messire Zeno that I wish to speak to him, and that matters
like this cannot be handled without consultation.'

Nerio smiled, and it wasn't a good smile. '*Illustrio*, Messire Zeno
had nothing to do with this event.'

Ha! I didn't think that was true at all.

'You are the Florentine banker, Acciaioli, are you not?' The Venetian
smiled. 'And you expect me to believe that this wasn't planned by
Carlo Zeno?'

Nerio shrugged as if the topic held little interest for him. And in this one case, I do not think he intended to be insulting.

The Venetian turned red with rage, and turned away.

'I am so glad that we give equal offence to all,' Fiore said.

The Emperor smiled on us and motioned for us to approach at last. We were about halfway through the list, and we had caught a great deal of courtly attention by then, as both of the foreign bailies had spoken to us.

First, our ranks as 'Spatharioi' were confirmed. My Greek wasn't up to the other honorifics, but there were a few. The Emperor was kind enough to make a few remarks about our loyalty and skill, and then we were dismissed.

The eunuch who acted as chamberlain gave me a note, which proved to be an invitation to a private audience.

Francesco frowned. 'Are we having fun yet?' he asked the sky.

We were on the steps outside the throne room, from which we'd been ceremoniously dismissed after an audience lasting perhaps two minutes.

Nerio glanced at Francesco. Nerio was older, but in this adventure, I think Francesco and Nerio were partners, and Fiore and I were merely advisors.

'Did Carlo Zeno have anything to do with this little plan?' I asked Nerio.

He glanced at me and raised an eyebrow. 'Of course he did. Zeno is his own man, as I am, and Gatelussi of Lesvos is, and Amadeus of Savoy. And yet we are all in this together, Guglielmo, and now you are, too.'

'I don't understand,' I said, because I didn't.

We stopped halfway down the steps, which are long and broad and very beautiful, in veined marble, polished by thousands of feet passing up and down. We were all dressed as soldiers – if wealthy soldiers – because overland travel isn't kind to court clothes. Nerio wore a chain worth a fortune, and the rest of us had swords and sword belts that proclaimed some status, but we really didn't look like anyone else at Blacharnae. I had a somewhat rueful notion that the Genoese bailie had taken us for wealthy bravos, and that's what we looked like.

I only offer this because courtiers and functionaries were passing us on the steps and every one of them, Greek or Frankish, gave us long looks and walked around us.

Nerio raised an eyebrow. 'This isn't an empire any more,' he said, his voice low. 'Now it's just a battleground. This city, and the trade it controls, is worth ... a thousand fortunes. Nothing will save it now, for the Greeks. They don't have the population to support the army it would require to hold the ground.' He shrugged. 'You just took this city with three hundred men.'

'Not exactly ...' I began.

Nerio made an Italian gesture – 'a little of this, a little of that' – with his hand.

'I'm working on saving what can be saved,' he said, 'and avoiding this war that Zeno is so certain is coming. I do so for personal and very selfish reasons, because if Constantinople falls, it will all go, all the way to Italy and perhaps beyond. I have wagered my fortune on Greece, and I can't afford to let the Emperor John go down.'

Coming from Nerio, this was an immense revelation.

'For what it is worth,' he continued, 'your esteemed liege lord Count Amadeus is of the same mind. Only by preserving his cousin the Emperor can he have any chance of his Union of Churches. Which, let me add, I also favour as the only way to save this place. Because Andronicus is directly in league with the Turks. Indeed, he was far closer to one of the Turkish princes than to his own brother. Andronicus hates the Franks and the Union.'

'But not the Genoese,' I muttered.

'The enemy of my enemy is my friend,' Nerio said.

Francesco spoke up. 'My father feels the same way,' he said. 'We must prop up the Greeks for as long as we can. And war between Venice and Genoa will destroy everything. The Emperor requires to have enough tax money to pay soldiers so that he has enough authority to collect taxes ... It's a terrible circle.'

Nerio was looking out over the city. Blacharnae is higher than many parts of Constantinople, and has a beautiful view.

'And the Union ...' He made a face. 'You know that I don't ... care ... deeply about the religion, yes?'

I probably managed a smile. Nerio was a sort of praying atheist. He cared for God when he needed something.

'But here in Constantinople, and the old Roman Empire,' and as he spoke, there was real anger on his face, 'there are men so self-serving as to make me look like an altruist. Men who will sacrifice their own people so that they can remain comfortable and in power. Every society has these leeches, but here, they are ingrained deeply in the Church and the bureaucracy.'

'The Patriarch,' I said quietly.

'And our Pope, of course.' Nerio almost spat. 'And your friend Robert of Geneva – the cardinal. He had fingers in pies here. He has most of his own fortune in Genoa. You know why the two Churches can't be unified? Because these petty tyrants of the spirit can't imagine sharing their fake power.' Nerio's voice ran with anger – Nerio, the cynic, who took nothing seriously.

'I think we should go somewhere and drink some wine,' Fiore said, 'before Nerio gets us burnt at the stake.'

'The waste makes me angry,' Nerio said.

It was interesting, seeing him so ... involved – passionate, even – about something that wasn't just about him.

He took one step down, and suddenly turned back to me.

'Of course it's the Turks,' he said.

I had no idea what he was talking about, and neither, from his expression, did Francesco. But Fiore did.

'Ah!' he said. 'Of course. De Merude is afraid of the Turks. Because the Genoese have already made some deal or other, and now ...'

'And now the Turks will come to collect,' Nerio said. 'I'd give a pile of gold to know what was offered and what is now missing.'

Fiore shrugged. 'And you say swordplay is complicated,' he quipped.

We didn't drink much wine, as I remember. Instead, in our rooms at the Palace of the Porphyrogenitus, we listened to Nerio and Francesco outline the stakes with the island of Tenedos and the trade in spices, silks and other goods from the East. Only this time Marc-Antonio was there, listening and contributing. As a scion of the Corner clan, he knew a great deal about trade.

And then it was time for our private audience.

I'll spare you the ceremony, although the Emperor of Constantinople, even if he rules fewer people and less ground than the King of England or France, keeps a level of ceremonial that would stagger the most eager herald or the most punctilious courtier in Italy or England. But we'd seen it before, and besides, the Court of Constantinople always provides barbarians like us with an equerry or a palace eunuch to guide you through the ceremony.

Besides, the Emperor John was a good ruler. He knew us, and he knew that he owed us. We were led through the corridors of Blacharnae, an honour all by itself, and then up two flights of stairs to a solar which was, I think, the Emperor's actual 'sitting room'.

'Gentlemen,' he said. Actually, what he said in Greek was '*Hetairoi*', or 'companions'. It was a nice compliment, if you like.

We all made our obeisance. He was, after all, the Emperor – the embodiment of an empire that stretched back in history to before the time of our Saviour.

'*Alora*,' he said, in good Italian. 'You gentlemen have saved us again.'

Nerio was still kneeling. 'Our pleasure, Majesty.'

The Emperor shook his head. I think he was tired. Certainly, his handsome face showed something like world-weariness, or some darkness of spirit.

'We detest being made a plaything,' he said slowly.

Nerio nodded. I stayed silent.

The Emperor looked at Nerio, and then at Francesco.

'So this little cabal of Franks has come together to save our throne,' he said. 'So that you may more efficiently strip our realm?'

'My father has always been loyal to you, and to your father,' Francesco said.

John nodded. 'We know. But we're at a point where we begin to wonder what, exactly, loyalty is. So many people tell us they are loyal. Our son, the usurper, claims that he, not we, is loyal to the empire. Our cousins, the Kantakouzenoi, claim that they are loyal to their people.' His weary gaze rested first on Nerio and then on Francesco. 'We have begun to wonder what role we actually have. What is God's will for us? Are our people better off with us or without us?'

'These are councils of despair,' Francesco said.

'We have no money, no army, and no good councillors, and despite years of neglect and failure, we have a million subjects and a great nation to protect.' John looked at me. 'And, despite your best efforts, Ser Guglielmo, your three hundred cannot save our empire.'

I thought Nerio would speak, but it was young Francesco who

spoke up. 'Majesty ...' he began, and paused. There was something like despair on the Emperor's face. It was not easy to speak to him.

But Francesco tried. 'Majesty,' he said a second time. 'It was my father's thought, and your cousin of Savoy's, that with a company of reliable soldiers and a few ships, you could see to the collection of taxes owed on the Marmara. And with that money, you can pay your own soldiers, and with a little help, restore ...'

Francesco stopped, because the Emperor had tears in his eyes. None rolled down his cheeks, but his eyes shone, and his face worked – he, who was an absolute mastery of impassivity, a sort of living icon of his ancient empire.

'You mean it, do you not?' he asked. 'Your father means to work our actual restoration.'

Nerio nodded eagerly. 'Yes, Majesty. None of us seek to control you. We believe ...' He paused, but then went on boldly. 'We believe that only you can prevent disaster. War between Venice and Genoa.'

'Yes,' John said. The despair was back. 'We very much doubt that we can stop it. The war over our corpse, like Achilles and Hector fighting over Patrokles.'

'You can prevent it being over Tenedos,' Nerio growled.

John shrugged. 'Perhaps.' He glanced at me. 'Sir Guglielmo, I remember a certain tower in Bulgaria. Will you save me again, and collect my taxes?'

'Of course,' I muttered.

The Emperor rose and motioned for his chamberlain, the *koubikoularios*, to come in.

'These men have the right of entering the Imperial presence whenever they ask,' he said. 'We command it.' He motioned at me. 'Please write out a commission for Prince Francesco of Lesvos as our admiral '*Droungarios*' of the Black Sea, and ask the *Kanikleios* to assign two secretaries from the chancery to him. Someone will also need to hold a civil rank in the Deme. Call for my *Logothetes tou Genikou*. I think that we can make Sir Guglielmo the *Praktor* for both Cherson and Chaldia. And perhaps he can carry the title *Protospatharios* as well. Perhaps *Dometikos ton Thematon*.'

He may have been at the brink of despair, and he may have become extremely cynical about foreign interference in his empire, but the

Emperor John could issue a string of orders with authority. He expected to be obeyed, and he was.

'I will send you the relevant documents and personnel,' he said. 'And I'll see to it you are thoroughly briefed on the problems facing ... ahem ... the collection of back taxes, most especially at Cherson. Until then, you are my guests.'

Nerio cleared his throat. 'Ah ...' he said.

The Emperor looked at him. 'You needed a title?' he asked.

'Majesty, I had hoped for your favour, I will not deny it. I would like to build a pair of warships here, in your Imperial harbour.'

'That is a very expensive favour.'

'Majesty, I'm happy to pay the entire expense, but I do not have access to a port that can build me a war galley, and I need a small fleet. And it would make clear to my neighbours that I have your approval.'

'Even though you occupy our great city of Corinth.'

'Even so, Majesty.'

'You are a bare-faced, impudent barbarian adventurer,' the Emperor said. 'But I owe you a great deal, and I've given more, and worse, to the Genoese. So yes. If you will pay the wages and materials, you may use the Imperial shipyard to build a pair of dromons.'

'And one more thing,' Nerio said cautiously.

'There is always one more thing, with Franks.'

'Majesty. Your son Andronicus ...' Nerio kept his head bowed.

The Emperor showed his first signs of impatience. 'Even after rescuing me from a dungeon, you do not get to ask me what I will do with my son,' he said frostily.

Francesco nodded. 'Majesty,' he said.

'My brave companions, you have my thanks.' The Emperor smiled. 'Please, go now, and enjoy a meal or two at my expense. It is almost all I can do for you these days.'

The Emperor rose, and we all bowed deeply.

And that was all.

Not everyone was really pleased that Francesco and I had been offered high office. I mention it because I love Fiore, but he was mortified that I, not he, had been named *Protospatharios* – which, of course, means 'First Sword'.

'It's not about his ability to wield a sword,' Francesco told an angry Fiore.

'If it is not, why not change the title? It's quite clear that "First Sword" means he is the first sword of the realm, and I challenge him to prove it.'

'Oh my God,' Nerio spat. 'You are like a beautiful woman who must always prove to herself how beautiful she is!'

Fiore whirled, and there it all was – ten years' worth of antagonism.

I stepped between them fast enough that Fiore's blow caught me in the back of the head.

'Nerio, apologise,' I said.

His eyes were like fire, and his face was a storm of anger. Smoke might have curled out of his nostrils.

He had a hand on his dagger.

Francesco had also placed his not inconsiderable bulk between Fiore and Nerio.

Nerio's face cleared, the way a storm blows off a mountain. I'd seen it happen, in Spain.

'I'm sorry,' he said past me. 'Fiore, I'm sorry. I spoke in anger.'

'Yes, yes,' Fiore said, as if he was already done with the whole matter. 'But I wish to be *protospatharios*,' he added, in case none of us had got the message.

Eventually we calmed him. In fact, it was not so much that he was angry, as that he thought it made no sense. I loved him for it.

Regardless, Fiore's objections weren't the strongest that we faced. In three days, it had become clear that the chancery and some officials were dead-set against any of us having formal titles within the empire. Giannis Lascaris Calophernes and Giorgios Demetrios Angelus, after a warm welcome, became our advisors on court etiquette and on the local politics. And it was clear they were coming with us. Or were, perhaps, in command of us.

Greece, land of ambiguity.

Sir Giannis was drinking wine with us in our rooms in the Palace of the Porphyrogenitus. We had an enclosed fireplace with a fine chimney piece, as good or better than anything in Venice. Have you seen one, Master Chaucer? The Greeks and Venetians have them ... Regardless ... Unnecessary in August but a boon in winter. We were sitting around a very small fire. We'd just visited the convent and church of Saint Mary of Blacharnae, the Imperial church, and been allowed to venerate a number of incredible relics. Even Nerio had been impressed by the relics. All of us were, except Fiore, whose expressions of doubt had shocked the Greeks.

'The thing that I don't understand,' he said, 'is the riches.'

Nerio nodded. That was odd – Fiore and Nerio in agreement.

'I saw that as well,' Nerio said.

'We hear all these tales of pawned crown jewels and the Emperor's poverty,' Fiore said. 'And yet, today, in one church, we saw ... how many vessels of solid gold?'

'More than fifty,' I agreed.

'Relics themselves worth a fortune in the West, whatever I might think,' Nerio said. 'And the crystal swan that held the blood of Christ?' he asked.

'The *supposed* blood of Christ,' Fiore shot back. 'Have you ever seen blood that colour?'

'Christ's blood! The blood of God! Perhaps ... his immortal blood has different properties?' That was Lord Fontana, who, with several of his knights, as well as the Biriguccis and Grice, had accompanied us on our visit to the closest holy places. Grice was far more religious than his friend La Motte, and very pleased to be invited.

Fiore was dismissive, even patronising. 'Rank heresy, my friend. Our Saviour was born into a mortal body in every way. Otherwise the Gospel is a lie.'

I thought Fontana might go for Fiore right there.

Nerio was smiling his cynical smile, but he stepped into the breach.

'Gentlemen,' he said. 'We are none of us theologians. But we can reckon the value of all we saw today.'

'More treasure than all of Venice,' Marc-Antonio said. 'I mean it, *signore*! I have seen fabulous things at San Marco, but these two churches, Saint John and Saint Mary, they beggar what Venice has.'

Fiore nodded at Nerio, his comments on theology forgotten. Or perhaps he thought he'd won the argument. Regardless, his eyes narrowed.

'This place is still incredibly rich. Why does it behave as if it is on its last legs? That one church could buy an Italian army for five years.'

'Perhaps ...' I thought we were on dangerous ground, even in private. 'Perhaps Andronicus, who has the friendship of the Church because he is against the Union, can pay the Genoese.'

Our old Greek friend Giannis shook his head.

'The Genoese paid for Andronicus to take power from his father,' Giorgios said sadly. 'And there were many pairs of hands that helped shape that conspiracy, and some of them are Greek.'

'You mean that there are people in government who want John off the throne?' Nerio asked. I thought his tone sarcastic.

Giannis ignored the sarcasm and answered honestly enough. 'Many.' He ticked them off on his fingers. 'The clerics who hate the Union of Churches. The bureaucrats who fear any sort of change. The landowners in the countryside who fear an emperor with the power to levy and collect taxes. Most of all, the Genoese, who refuse to be taxed at all, the Venetians, who are not much better, and the Turks, who want the empire to continue as a state too poor to own an army.'

Francesco made a face. 'I *am* Genoese,' he said. 'We have always been loyal to Genoa.'

Giorgios shrugged, and Giannis looked away, and then back.

'There is not much difference between the Venetians and the Genoese,' he said. 'And I suspect that if the Venetians ever held the whip hand, they would be as bad masters as the Genoese, but at the moment, they are the Emperor's allies.'

'And,' Nerio put in, 'we agree that we need to prevent this foolish war. Any conflict between Venice and Genoa will only lead to the Turks dominating everything.'

Francesco was still dissatisfied. 'If I use my father's ships to collect the Emperor's taxes in the Black Sea, Genoa will disown us. Much less support the Venetian *muda* to Trebizond.'

Nerio shook his head. 'Your father is as powerful, by himself, as Genoa.'

Francesco shook his head. 'Genoa can raise a hundred galleys. We might field forty.'

I had little to contribute in these discussions, but this time I had something to say.

'Francesco, as long as I have known your father, he has been faithful to the Emperor, and that loyalty has always been rewarded. Surely the Doge of Genoa understands ...'

Francesco shook his head. 'My immediate concern is this De Merude. He is powerful, and he will write reports against which I have no defence.'

'So we do nothing?' I asked.

'You can do nothing until the Emperor either does or does not convince the chancery to write out your commissions. Without them, you haven't the power to collect the taxes.' Giannis spread his hands, a very Greek gesture. 'I agree that what you saw today shows the Church to be very rich. But I promise you that those relics and that gold is not at the service of the empire. The Church would never give it up.'

'It's as if the Church is allied with the Genoese and the Turks,' Nerio said. I didn't think he was serious. 'Fine, we're back to the taxation scheme.'

I nodded, although, if you are following, I suspected that the 'taxation' scheme was really about escorting the Venetian *muda* to Trebizond. So many wheels within wheels.

Nerio looked at me. 'Unless you just took the ships and forced the collections without commissions. And cleared the path of the Venetian trade ships, just by chance.'

Aha, I thought.

'Piracy,' Giorgios said. But he *smiled*.

'A bureaucratic error,' Nerio answered with a half-smile.

'Not with my father's ships,' Francesco said adamantly. And then, more slowly, 'But otherwise, a very neat solution.'

Nerio looked at me, and I could see the daring writ on his face like a prayer in a breviary. He had an idea.

'What if I could find the ships?' he said. 'Francesco, would you crew them?'

Francesco looked at Nerio. 'I could find crews,' he admitted. 'And so could Zeno, I'll wager.'

I looked around. 'Perhaps I'm no sailor,' I said, 'but isn't one ordinary galley very like another?'

Francesco looked at me with something approaching pity. 'No,' he said. 'I can tell one of our ships a league off. Venetians are narrower and lower. Genoese have more elegant sterns. The Emperor's ships still have something of antiquity about them.'

'Ah,' I allowed. 'How many ships does the Emperor have?'

'Five,' Nerio said. 'Only three of them seaworthy. You saw two of them back in '67.'

'So I did. They are here?' I asked.

'In the Imperial yard.' Nerio was nodding with me.

'So,' I said, 'we have the Emperor write out an order in his own hand. We take the ships, which are clearly the Emperor's ships, flying the Emperor's flag, and we crew them with my *compagnia* and Francesco's oarsmen and some Venetians. We sail into this Black Sea and the *muda*, if that's your pleasure, can follow us by a week or so.'

'And Carlo Zeno,' Nerio said. He sounded ... smug. 'I'm sure he will help. Especially if we are making the sea road smooth for the *muda*.'

It was a secretive operation, or rather, two or three all nested together, as I have mentioned.

A short sea voyage.

In fact, it took almost four weeks to get the ships and get to sea. By then, many things had happened. We still didn't have formal commissions from the chancery – every day, new excuses were made. Nerio very cleverly got the three best ships in the Imperial yard refitted while apparently inspecting them and discussing the building of his own ships. He paid for everything and made no demur, and the workers in the Imperial yard became very fond of him and his gold. But the ships were in worse shape than we expected. Even after some new rigging and a rebuilt bow, they all suffered from 'worm' and poor storage, and one had to be sunk in the harbour and then completely recalked.

Giannis undertook to care for our horses. We only took a few – enough to mount a dozen men-at-arms, including Percival and Artemis, but leaving Gabriel behind. We took twenty horses for the Kipchaks.

Late in the process, Nerio received a letter from Corinth and decided that he had to go there.

'I have no choice,' he said. 'I'm facing a local revolt.' He embraced each of us. 'See you in the spring. Get the Emperor's taxes in and we'll all be healthier for it.'

We seriously considered cancelling the whole daft enterprise, but in the end, Nerio took none of our people. He boarded a Venetian ship heading west and was gone, and our rooms were quieter. But the Venetian *muda* wasn't ready to travel east yet – two great galleys and two round ships. The rest of the convoy had done its trading and turned for home, carrying Nerio.

A few days later, Michael des Roches stepped off a Genoese

merchant out of Ancona with a bag of books and not much else. In less than a day, he was an intimate of the Imperial library.

'Half these scrolls are missing,' he said. He had Fiore's list of secular books. 'Just the titles are so exciting I can barely sleep. Thucydides! Plato! An early copy of the *Suda*!' He grinned like a boy having a name-day party. 'But someone has taken many of them or they are stored elsewhere.'

'I suspect they've been sold,' Francesco said. 'The Emperor is very poor.'

'They haven't been sold in the West,' Michael said, 'or I'd have heard.' He looked around. 'Or perhaps not. But it is very exciting.'

Despite his excitement, I enlisted him for the cruise of the Black Sea. He was eager to see new places, and he could read anywhere, or so he said.

'Scythians!' he said. 'The Golden Fleece.'

And so, just before the middle of September of 1373, we set off up the Dardanelles from the Golden Horn in three antiquated Imperial warships. Carlo Zeno commanded one, Francesco took one himself, and his father's personal pirate, Andrea Carne, took the third. I knew Carne from of old – a deadly man, and not one with overmuch scruple.

We raised the Imperial double eagle and headed north, for the Euxine. The Black Sea.

We had three major ports of call. First was Kerasous, or Giresun, as the Turks call it, an Imperial city that had been seized by Genoa in the fifties, chosen by the Emperor as a reasonable target to tax. Then nearby Trebizond, the almost independent rump of the old empire in Asia, capital of the Deme of Chaldia. Finally Kaffa, and the Genoese coast in the Crimea. We had been provided with sailing directions for all of these areas by the office of the Logothete of Skythika, if I remember that correctly. An ancient office from Roman times.

The problem was ...

No one seemed to agree that the Emperor had the right to tax anyone in the Euxine. The Genoese claimed that they had the exclusive right to trade in the Black Sea. The 'Empire of Trebizond' had, in fact, renounced its Imperial titles almost a century before. Their 'Autocrat' was a close relative of the Emperor, but they collected their own taxes, engaged in sporadic warfare with the Turks and the Genoese, and remitted nothing to Constantinople.

In fact – mostly thanks to careful reading by Michael des Roches – we learnt that we were, in effect, pirates. We were going to prey on Genoese shipping, and to force payments by unwilling towns along the coast in the best tradition of the English chevauchée and John Hawkwood's 'Free Companies'.

I suppose we might have asked why we didn't take my company out into the countryside west of Constantinople and collect from the landowners there, but Giannis had given me a strong sense of the political repercussions of such a move.

Des Roches looked at me one afternoon, and tapped the scroll he'd been reading against his beard. It was a list of court offices from the last reign.

'I think they're after something else,' he said. 'The taxes are just a cover.'

A sea voyage, I remembered.

'That matches something that Nerio said,' I agreed.

Later, Zeno, amused at my hesitations, simply shrugged.

'No doubt the Emperor will apologise to the Genoese and disclaim any responsibility for us,' he said. 'And you are naive if you think he ever intended to give you official status.'

And yet, Nerio, the Green Count, and Prince Francesco all saw this as the best way to save the Emperor. And behind them stood the Lion of Saint Mark – Venice.

I was put in mind of the winter campaign of the year before, wherein we were not trying particularly hard to take Piacenza (because we hadn't been paid) while our opponents didn't try very hard to stop us because they hadn't been paid, and yet, a lot of innocent people died or were exiled. When you fight for money, the people who pay you do not feel required to tell you what they are actually doing. It's worse when they have little or no idea themselves.

I didn't like it. And I thought again about Sister Marie's words. I needed to fight for something I believed in.

To be fair, I preferred Nerio and the Emperor of Constantinople to the current Pope or the Visconti. And I rather like Venice.

But when you are a tool, it's difficult to feel any loyalty.

As an *empris*, we had a very promising start. When you come to the northern limit of the Dardanelles, where they enter the Black Sea or

Euxine, there are two towers, one on each shore. Both used to belong to the Greek emperor, but now the one on the right-hand side, the Asian shore, is in the hands of the Turks. We landed under the Tower of Greece and took on fresh water and bought some good barley, and all the while we could see signals from the Tower of Turkey across the strait. The Greek Tower burns a signal all day and all night to help navigation. It's a genuine lighthouse, one of the signs that the old empire is not dead.

I was right there back in '67 with the Green Count, and it was in familiar waters just off the lighthouse that we were challenged by a Genoese galley. The captain, with the same arrogance we'd seen from De Merude, closed with us. He pulled in close and bellowed at us to leave the Black Sea, or the Euxine as the Greeks called it. He told us that the Euxine was a Genoese lake, and we had no business there.

He threatened us, especially when Zeno laughed at him. I confess to a certain admiration for a captain who, with one galley, threatens three. Perhaps he thought our crews were as old-fashioned as our ships, but we soon disabused him, taking his ship in a boarding action that lasted for less time than it takes a priest in a hurry to perform the Eucharist. Grice was lightly wounded, and so was the Genoese captain.

And we had a fourth galley. It was an excellent start. We crewed our capture from the Genoese slave rowers, leavened with a few of Zeno's Venetians and a few of Gatelussi's Chians. Zeno put Aldo in command of her, which pleased the young man inordinately. And we needed the space. I'd left half my company at Blacharnae, but a hundred and fifty men fill every nook and cranny on three galleys. I was sleeping on the deck, with Marco on one side and Fiore on the other. Pilgrim usually fitted between us, which would have been comfortable if he was not a very active sleeper, given to chasing imaginary rabbits in his dreams.

And in the hold we found a gonne. It was cast of bronze, threw a ball about the size of my two hands clasped, and beautifully decorated. The gonne had been cast in Genoa and was bound for Kaffa – for the walls, I assume. That reminded me that I had a hand gonne from Italy in my baggage.

The next day, as we cruised east along the southern shore of the Euxine, one of the somewhat antiquated Greek ships lost its lateen yard, which snapped in the wind, which beat back and forth off the mouth of the Dardanelles like a mad thing. We had to take her in tow – it was Zeno's ship, the *Holy Anne, Mother of Mary*. We landed on the rocky beach and the Venetians and Chians had the sail down and a new yard swayed up in three hours, but it was a foretaste of all the problems we would have in the Euxine with the old Greek ships. We got off the beach before the Turks came beyond some shepherds, who sold us live goats.

In the night, we passed Finogia, a Genoese-held port. We could see a few fires burning on shore and that was all, but Zeno, whose ship I was on at the time, assured me that it was a major Genoese station.

After another stop to get fresh water and fish another cracked yard, I returned to Francesco's galley and we headed for Kerasous. We took turns to spar with Fiore on the catwalk. Our rowers were free men, and thus we were jeered, cheered, and wagers were placed. The oarsmen learnt very quickly not to bother betting on whether we could hit Fiore, but on more reasonable things – how long we lasted, how many times we were thrown or stabbed, or how long before Fiore snapped his irritated '*Alora*' and began to make us practise the most basic cuts or stances or postures or steps. I thought Lord Fontana was going to explode when Fiore made him walk around the deck, a little more like a crab than was quite right, making exacting comments about weight changes and muscles until, as Giannis quipped, it looked as if Fontana had forgotten how to walk altogether.

Francesco came forward from the helm. Peter Albin was on the aft deck, rewrapping Grice's bandages and watching. We were all packed like salt fish, as I say – four galleys and a hundred and fifty fighting men. If we hadn't picked up the Genoese, we would have been sore-pressed to stay at sea at all.

We were taking turns fighting in our arming clothes. Giannis and I had taken our turns and were now joining the fun of commenting on others. Michael des Roches was with us, and Giorgios Demetrios Angelus, the latter covered in sweat as he, too, had been on the main grating, swinging a sword.

'Won't we make quite a lot of enemies sailing into a Genoese harbour with a Genoese capture?' I asked.

I was still not sure of our actual role in the Black Sea. Or rather, I understood it all too well, and wasn't sure that I liked it.

Giorgios nodded. 'They will not like it, but we are here to send a message. And Genoa can afford to pay.'

Giannis's expression suggested that he knew more than Giorgios was saying.

'This was all Nerio's idea, was it not?' I asked Francesco.

Grice took a toothpick out of the purse his squire was holding for him and began to pick his teeth.

'Salt pork,' he complained. 'It's just a job, *Capitano*. Let it go.'

Francesco was looking out to sea as if his role as captain made it impossible to answer my question.

I knew when Francesco was prevaricating.

'You are clipping the ears of the Genoese,' I said.

Francesco smiled, and suddenly looked very much like his father. It wasn't the nice smile he kept for women, or the beaming smile when he was truly pleased, but the somewhat reptilian smile he kept for when he was being very, very Italian and a little Greek at the same time.

'As Giorgios says, they can pay.'

Michael, of all people, came to Francesco's rescue.

'You are carrying on a great tradition,' he said. 'I have with me a copy of Thucydides. This is how the Athenian navy took "taxes" for Athens. This is how Macedon "taxed" the Euxine. With a fleet.'

'This is hardly a fleet,' I said. 'What if Kerasous just closes its harbour and fires on us? And how many ships does Genoa have in these waters?'

Francesco looked at the helm, looked up at his mainsail, and then back at the coast.

'Not many,' he said, 'and very few warships, because this has been their very own lake, as you heard the man say. That galley at our tail may be the only military galley in this sea.'

'Most of the trade goes in round ships now,' Giannis said. 'The new carracks and cogs.'

'One of the reasons we have to be so ... precipitate ... in our methods of taxation,' Giorgios said. 'In the old days, the galleys could not help but stop at Constantinople or Tenedos, or both, so that we could tax them. Now the big round ships wait for a good wind and sail the whole strait and out into the Aegean without touching on shore. Or being taxed.'

'There is no such thing as an easy *condotta*,' I said to Grice.

Giannis was right, as he often was. It was a job. I should do it.

But I could imagine a dozen ways this could go wrong.

'I admire the way Nerio got us into this and then sailed away,' I said.

Francesco's smile slipped, and I could see that he carried the same weight I did myself.

'Yes,' he said simply.

The Genoese ship had come with some gunpowder. After remixing it to Zeno's specification – he seemed to know a lot about gonnes – we entertained ourselves shooting my hand gonne off the galley. The little gonne was provided with a sort of rest which fitted nicely against a ship's bulwarks, and we shot at targets. I only mention this because I became more used to the smell, and reasonably proficient at loading the hellish thing with its small iron balls. We shot them all, save three – I saved those against some future need.

We knew that Sinope and the coast beyond it was in Turkish hands. A well-known pirate emir held the city, not an Ottomanid prince. In fact, according to Giannis and Michael, there wasn't an Ottomanid Turk on the whole coast after the 'Tower of Turkey'. Instead, there were twenty independent emirs, the way Cilicia had been ten years before.

We kept a sharp watch, standing well out to sea to avoid detection. That evening, we beached on an open headland well past the town to get water and eat some mutton, and slept with our swords in our hands, but the pirates of Sinope must have had other prey that day. The next day, our fourth in the Euxine, or Black Sea, we stayed well out to sea, so that the coast was just a smudge on the horizon, and not even that at times. The ground beyond the coastal beach was rising into the high plateaus and mountains of Anatolia. There were deep woods on the high ridges. Valleys full of water seemed to rush down to the sea, and a few held hamlets or fishing villages. It was a wild coast, not a settled one. But as afternoon passed towards evening, and we turned towards land, we saw three galleys. They had been hidden against the trees, but as we turned landward, we saw a flash of their oars. They ran west, right against the beach.

We never got close enough to see whether they were Genoese or Turkish, or some other player in this dangerous sea. As soon as we turned to chase them, our galley lost half of her forward oars in a few heartbeats. The *telaro*, the box-like outrigger that supported the heavy oars, had broken away from the main hull, the cleats having rotted through. A few oarsmen were injured, and again we had to beach to make repairs. This time we had to cut trees and unload tools to get at the rot and replace the tree nails that held the cleats and braces, all made of bent wood. We made a camp, and slept very little. The thing I remember best is that Pilgrim ran off into the deep woods while I was hunting for standing dead trees that might have good wood for the carpenters, and didn't come back for hours. I thought him gone. When he returned, he smelt like carrion, and had the look of a very sorry dog who promised never to do anything bad again.

See? Fiore even drew him in the margin of my breviary.

Kerasous, and the smell of slaves and spices. A tall hill dominated a series of lower ridges against an iron-grey sky. The castle on the hill isn't imposing and lacked anything that could reach our ships, and the headland has two open beaches and no deep port. We came out of the rising sun like the veteran pirates our captains were, and trapped the shipping against the beach. I led my company ashore, or at least, fifty lances of my company. The rest were mounting guard at Blacharnae and keeping the supporters of Andronicus at a healthy distance from Emperor John. But we made a fine sight in our white armour, with the company standard and a fine banner of the emperor flying with it. Grice was the banner bearer. The men formed faster than I could have imagined as my new trumpeter played the new signals.

We were impressive as long as you ignored our busy carpenters, who were replacing yet more rot in the bow of the *Holy Anne*.

There was a thriving market on the western beach and they were not happy to see us. The podestà came down from the castle with a dozen mounted men and tried to abuse Grice, with little result.

When I came up, Lord Fontana had dumped the man from his saddle and disarmed his escort.

'You'll be hanged – every one of you!' he spat. 'This is sovereign territory of the Doge of Genoa.'

Giorgios stepped forward, wearing the red padded gambeson embroidered with the Imperial double eagle. He pointed at the same symbol on the banner Grice was carrying.

'It was sovereign as long as we could not take it back,' he said smoothly. 'You stole the city. It was never yours.'

'There were agreements! Signed treaties!' The podestà wasn't even afraid. Merely enraged. He was sputtering.

'Made under duress,' Giorgios said. I could tell that he was relishing his role. 'You Genoese take things and then later insist on "your rights". This is a city in the empire, and you will now pay taxes to the empire.'

The podestà glowered, but I could see that he was changing from anger and bluster to calculation. He was no fool – an older man in a good cote, who had survived out here for many years.

'You cannot hold this town,' he said. But he was unsure. I had fifty lances of the most modern, best armoured Europeans in the whole of the East, and for all he knew, we were the Emperor's new garrison. 'How much tax?' he asked, after a pause.

There were some negotiations.

He paid. It didn't take us a day, although, in my professional capacity, I pointed out to Giorgios and Giannis that I could probably take the citadel and return the town to Imperial authority.

Giorgios smiled a Greek smile. 'Yes,' he said. 'But no.'

Giannis explained. 'It's over a hundred years since this town was under the authority of the Emperor in Constantinople,' he said. He shrugged. 'The Grand Komnenos, or Autocrat, in Trebizond is usually lord here.'

'So we really are just raiders,' I said.

Giannis made a particularly Byzantine gesture, something that combined a head-shake of negation and a shrug of dismissal. 'The Genoese have not paid an asper of tax in fifty years,' he said. 'Where should we force them to pay? Genoa?'

We all laughed.

'They tried to make their own emperor,' Giorgios said. 'We are making them hurt a little, in exchange.'

My other experience on that beach was not as amusing. Most of the merchants quailed, or were obsequious, but not one slave trader, probably the richest merchant on the beach. He was perhaps fifty years old, and his face looked like a desert landscape that had been eroded by long forgotten rains – a hundred wrinkles around one working eye. I thought he was a Turcoman, one of the nomads who roamed Anatolia and the steppe.

I saw his eye on me, and I walked over to him, or rather trudged. Sand and armour are not friends.

'You could get yourself into real trouble here,' he said to me, by way of greeting. 'I'll tell you that for nothing.'

He had fifty slaves or thereabouts. They were almost all steppe peoples – a few Eastern Mongols, some Khazaks, a few Kipchak boys and two Georgian girls. The girls were stony-faced. So were the Kipchak boys. The Mongols looked ready to kill everyone, except for one who had managed to get drunk. The Khazaks just sat listlessly. There were a few Greeks, too, most of them working.

John the Turk came rolling up the beach. John on horseback looked like a god. On foot, on sand, he looked like a lame old man.

I was still considering whether to bother answering the old slave trader when John stomped up and looked at the merchandise. His eyes caught the Kipchak boys, and he spat something in his own language.

The old man spat right back.

'I want the Kipchak boys,' John said to me. 'I will kill him if he doesn't give them to me.'

I dislike slavery. I'm aware that it occurs in the Bible and I've heard all of the excuses, but I would note that Our Lord never kept a slave. Maybe the New Covenant was meant to end slavery. Maybe I just dread being a slave myself – the worst possible nightmare. And we all know what happens to young boys and pubescent girls, do we not? Terrible.

So I just nodded to John. I was in a position of power, with my fifty lances on that beach. To the slaver, I said, 'I recommend that you do as he says.'

'Like fuck,' the slaver said. 'Do you fools know who I am?'

'No,' I said.

The man put his hand to his beard. 'Infidels,' he said, shaking his head. 'You think it's justice to rob me of my goods?'

John spoke in his Mongol-Turkish, his voice low and gravelly with rage.

'Keep your dog on a leash,' the slaver said. 'Or I will tell my friends to muzzle him.'

I probably frowned. 'I think you should look at your situation,' I said, or something cautious and reasonable, or at least, that's how I remember it.

He barked a laugh. He was afraid, but fear made him angry. I have seen this all too often in men used to absolute command. He had half a dozen bravos with whips and knives – very unimpressive to a man sweating in his Brescian plate armour.

'You are trying to steal my fortune,' he said. 'These Kipchak boys are worth their weight in gold in Egypt. Ask your Frankish friends, eh? The emir of the town will tell you that I trade with all the Genoese. I have powerful friends. I know the Genoese bailie. Do you? In your Infidel tongue he is Filippo De Merude, eh? See, you know that name. So fuck off.'

John was looking at me, which had the effect of making me think very carefully about what I said. Perhaps I'd have said less, or done less, or perhaps I wouldn't have, but with John watching me, I felt that I had to act to support him. Our friendship required it. I could tell.

I could also tell that our slaver had made a classic error. Just as crusaders almost always assumed that all Moslems were allies and friends of one another, so the slaver assumed that all Franks were the same – united in the same interests, afraid of the same men. You may think that's a great deal to pull out of a few words, but then, I'd heard this sort of thing before.

'We are not here representing the Frankish merchants,' I said. 'We are here for the Emperor in Constantinople. And he really doesn't like slave traders. Consider the Kipchak boys your tax.'

I wasn't at all sure that was true, but I wanted my slaver to know that he should back off.

He moved his left hand, wiped the seat of his braes, and flipped his fingers at me.

'My shit for your tax and your "emperor",' he said.

It is remarkable that some people cannot understand when you are reasoning from strength, not weakness.

'I have to doubt that your five bullies can face my two hundred men-at-arms,' I said.

John spoke about ten words, in Turkish.

The slaver frowned. 'I can give you the two Georgian girls,' he said. 'My gift to you. As beautiful as angels. Take them with my ...'

He'd given some signal to his bravos. I saw it – his right hand opened and closed. The talk of the girls was to freeze me in place.

God only knows what his plan was. I had fifty lances of armoured men at my back, many within twenty paces.

Stupid, powerful people are very dangerous. I think it is a form of possession, or perhaps insanity.

His bravos certainly were loyal. A whip snapped, and I felt it as a blow to my arm, like a light punch. The end of the whip curled around my left vambrace. I got a hand on it and pulled. There were other whips, and other sounds – a war cry.

I pulled the man with the whip to me and kneed him, my steel kneecap into his genitals. And then dropped him. He was too hurt even to scream, just making facial expressions like a fish hauled out of water.

'Infidels,' the slaver spat. 'I ...'

He never finished his sentence, because as John made a sound of contempt behind me, for whatever reason, the slave owner then attacked me. Why he didn't attack John is probably best explained by his thorough knowledge of the fighting skills of an adult Kipchak – or possibly he'd just lost his temper. Perhaps he thought the whip would hold me for a moment.

He wore a heavy sabre, which he drew straight into an overhand cut. He did it well, and had probably used this move to effect in the past, but he'd never met Fiore. I drew my arming sword *sotano* into his overhand cut and nicked his thumb. I flicked a stab at his face, and cut down. It was never a fight – a little more like murder than I would have liked.

My cut, with just the tip of my sword, went across his throat. There was a lot of blood, but I'd stepped back, sword in a low garde, watching him die. His blood – and people hold a great deal of blood – soaked into the beach sand very quickly.

Two more of the bravos were on the ground, dead, with John's arrows in them. John had drawn his bow, nocked and shot twice in the time it had taken me to drop two men.

Behind me, on the sand of the beach, Fiore called, 'Ah, nicely done. Almost perfect. A little more effort on the thrust and you might have ...' He waved an arm. 'Never mind. It was very good.'

Everyone else was silent. The three remaining bravos had knives and whips. They looked at one another and at us. Then one of them gave a scream, a long undulating yell, and John dropped him with an arrow, and then the other, who stood frozen with indecision. The third fell on his knees.

Five men dead. I cleaned my sword tip on the slaver's robe. Kerchus was already searching the bodies.

'What do we do with this one?' he asked, pointing at the kneeling man.

'Let him go,' I said. It was an act of mercy I would eventually regret.

Life and death in the Euxine. I'll never understand why the old Turcoman attacked us.

'That was a very important man, in the trade,' the podestà said a few minutes later. No one had touched the corpses after Kerchus and flies were gathering. 'Men will come looking for you.'

'They can find us at sea,' Francesco said, 'if they want to discuss our views on the slave trade.'

We also handed over the Genoese captain we'd taken in the straits, as well as any of his crew who wanted to go with him – about thirty men. The rest, all slaves, were quite happy to be free, and willing to row for pay. I fancied that Nerio would buy the ship and the men to crew it, and so I offered my own guarantee.

Zeno smiled his predatory smile. 'Fucking Genoese,' he said. 'This is why you don't use slaves on your galleys. Look how happy those men would be to kill their former captain.'

The Genoese podestà just shook his head. 'You can't imagine you will get away with this?' he asked. But there was very little heat to his assertion.

Our next port was the fabled Trebizond. Our sleeping arrangements were complicated by two blonde Georgian girls and a several dozen steppe nomads, all former slaves. The Tartars were laconic to a wonderful degree, as unmoved by their new freedom as by their slavery. The Kipchak boys followed John and Kerchus everywhere, which, on a close packed galley, was not useful. When John went to the side, the ship would lean a little. The rest of the slaves were willing enough to row, for a small wage. They were all looking to work their various ways home. But if we'd been packed like cord wood before, we were now salted anchovies. Pilgrim was the least popular passenger on board, given to a night-time frolic on the carpet of bodies. The two

Georgians loved him, though, and considering what the two of them had probably endured, it was worth his antics to see them smile.

Trebizond was remarkable. It may even be worth a fable or two. The gilt domes of churches, the superb outer wall. The town itself runs back from the sea, up a ridge towards the palaces, and then into the mountains behind. The town isn't so big – perhaps eight thousand souls all told, and it had been hit very hard by the plague back in '46, but the backdrop of wooded mountains and sparkling streams is magnificent. The red-tiled roofs and gold-domed churches are set off by the verdant wilderness like an icon hanging against a green velvet brocade.

'Here,' Giorgios said, 'we will proceed differently.'

'Differently' meant that he and Giannis went ashore with a small military bodyguard and a writ from the Emperor in Constantinople that I had not yet seen. I might have given the task of bodyguard to any of my more reliable knights, but I chose to go myself, accompanied by Fiore and Michael des Roches. As it was clear that Nerio, and perhaps Venice, had sold my services for someone else's operation, I was curious as to exactly what we were doing here. Des Roches merely insisted on going as a scholar.

As it proved, we were still gathering taxes, but in a very different way.

Giorgios and Giannis were received with court ceremonial on the docks, almost as if they were expected, and then we all proceeded high up the ridge to the palace. There, we heard a Mass said in the Greek rite, and I had a chance to look at the population, or at least the courtiers. It appeared that there were as many Turcomans as Greeks present. The Mass was, as far as I could observe, completely correct and exactly as it would have been in Constantinople. Of course, my Greek was, and is, mediocre, and I'm not a regular practitioner of the Greek rite.

After Mass, we went into the palace, where Giorgios and Giannis were elaborately received by the Autocrat. He had, as far as I under-stand, until recently claimed the purple for himself, despite ruling only a small fraction of the empire. I thought that I understood that we were nigh on enemies, but what followed demonstrated how little I understood. Over the next hour, Giorgios offered various sums taken from Kerasous as tribute, and left with a writ from the Autocrat empowering us to collect on his behalf, as well as the Emperor's, from other 'factories' and Genoese outposts.

I understood little of the negotiations until later, but I was fascinated by the court and the court etiquette. First, the lord, the 'Grand Komnenos' as he was known, was Alexios, the third of that name, handsome as all the Komnenoi are, and obviously a soldier. If it is possible to like a man from thirty feet away, then I liked him. Second, I was fascinated by the titles of the court. The first I noticed was that I was announced as *protospatharios* but also as *Emir-i-Candar*, a Turcoman term that I recognised from Syria which means something like 'captain of the guard'. At this announcement, the Grand Komnenos nodded to me. A big blond man at his side, in a long maille hauberk, looked at me, and then smiled. He proved, some time later that evening, to be a German from Nuremberg, a mercenary who'd come out with the Genoese and stayed because the pay was good.

I think I've left my road. My point here is that Trebizond was a small empire, but a real one. The Grand Komnenos could actually field an army in the old Roman style, as I saw the next day when they paraded one of the cavalry units with horses and bows – a little like Christian Tartars, but well armed and well trained. Every man had matching horse furniture. Every man had a uniform gambeson and matching armour, a tuft of red horsehair in his helmet and on his horse's head. They were very impressive when they drilled, as good as the Emperor's Vardariotes in Constantinople.

His farmers were well protected and only lightly taxed. The plain fact was that the 'empire' of Trebizond was a tenth the size of the 'empire' of Constantinople – but on a much more secure footing. Business was conducted in both Greek and a local Turkish dialect. Men who were obviously Moslems attended a Greek Orthodox Mass and took their law cases to the courts of Trebizond.

As to the agreement reached between my Greek friends and the Grand Komnenos, I no longer knew whether this was part of Nerio's original plan or not. I suspected we were now in the Emperor John's hands. And that evening, as I sat with Fiore and Michael des Roches, Francesco Orsini and Carlo Zeno, as well as some new companions, it was made clear to me how little I understood.

I don't know if I have clearly described Carlo Zeno, although he is vital to this tale. Zeno was a small, broad, heavily muscled man, a little older than me, with a long beard and a fearsome military reputation. He'd killed a famous French knight in a duel, in Patras down in the Morea, and it was almost impossible to believe that he'd been intended for a career in the Church, but that's his story. His unscarred face and shining eyes were the only thing that distinguished him from the purer form of a pirate found in my old companion, Andrea Carne, who sat with us, drinking steadily.

We'd been joined in a very good stone taverna run by the prince for travellers, set in the lower town near the sea. We were sharing the common room with a pair of local Turkish emirs – a court officer who knew Giorgios Angelus from of old, and the German *Emir-i-Candar*, who sat with Fiore almost all evening talking about fighting with an axe.

Zeno smiled at me, and the smile was genuine. 'You remain a curiously chivalrous and gentlemanly fellow,' he said. 'For a man who has killed his way up from the bottom,' he added.

'Not all of us who have come up from cook's boys like to be reminded of it,' I said.

He shrugged. 'Perhaps on land, men think that birth matters, but at sea, we all know that's just so much wind. All that matters is what you do.'

I thought of Charny's words. *He who does most is worth most.*

'Men on land often believe the same,' I said.

'Eh,' he said, indicating that he didn't believe me but didn't mean to debate the matter. 'Listen, Guglielmo. We are on a mission for the Council of Ten in Venice, to destabilise the trade of Genoa in the Black Sea and undermine their certainty of control. We are *also* on a mission for the Gatelussi of Lesvos, to ensure that the Emperor John has the means to stay in power for another decade, which protects their family monopolies on trade. We are *also* on a mission for the Emperor John, to collect money and to project his waning power in the Euxine while he has some forces he can rent or borrow, but really to punish the Genoese for supporting an attack on his throne.' He spread his hands. 'And your busy, busy friend Nerio has made all of their separate plots into one ball.' He mimed this, patting the pieces together with his hands. 'And why? So that all of them can make more money.'

Andrea Carne wasn't as drunk as he looked. 'They're all a pack of fools,' he said.

Francesco looked as if he might resent that comment, but Zeno raised a hand. He had the age and the dignity to command us all.

'Why, brother?' he asked.

Carne raised both eyebrows, surprised to be taken seriously. He took a sip of wine, and put his cup down with a click.

'The Euxine trade is ending,' he said. 'The slave trade ... it's the rump. When everything else is gone, there are always slaves, and as long as the Mamluks will pay in gold for Mongol boys, well ... there's still that trade, I suppose.' He looked at Zeno. 'I can remember when Trebizond and Kerasous and Kaffa all had silk and spices and lapis to trade. And they wanted ivory and ebony and gold and silver. Eh? Where is it now?'

Fiore looked up from his sword conversation. I knew he was perfectly capable of listening to two people at once, if he listened at all. That was his way.

'Aside from the moral scruples,' he said, 'why is the trade in men any different from the trade in silk?'

'The trade in men runs on war,' Carne said. His slight smile suggested that he knew a great deal about the origins of slaves. And how they were taken. 'Silk and spices come from weavers and farmers.' He shrugged, as if annoyed by his own part in the whole thing – slavery, or perhaps the conversation.

Zeno shook his head, and the conversation moved on. Carne was not the sort of man to insist on anything, except on a blood-soaked deck. But later, when the others were gone and Zeno and I were walking back to our ships, he said, 'Carne is no fool. And if he's correct ...' He looked out to sea for a moment. 'It would be the end of an era. And the Devil to pay in Genoa. And Venice.'

The next day, the Grand Komnenos sent for us, to ask us to demonstrate Western jousting. I suspected our new friend from Nuremberg had suggested it, but it was a feast day for them, and so we went, with our armour, to the main square in front of the palace. I rode Gabriel, and Fiore rode Percival. We ran a really bad course, complete with me losing a stirrup and Fiore almost striking my horse – my lovely Gabriel, who was getting on in years and still my favourite. Jousting is hard without a barrier. It's harder on horses who haven't been exercised regularly, and even harder when you haven't touched a spear in two months.

As we passed each other coming down the list, Fiore shook his head.

'We really need to be better than that,' he said.

The second pass was pretty, as we both struck home high on each other's shields.

The third pass was even better, as both of us struck for the helmet. Fiore's was better, and I was almost unhorsed. Both lances broke, too. There was a little applause from our own people, and stony silence from the court.

Fiore and I met in front of the Grand Komnenos, where he sat on a low chair.

'Would you care to see more, Your Grace?' I asked.

Close up, I could see that he had swordsman's hands.

He cocked his head to one side. 'How does this help you train for war?' he asked. 'Or is it just a game?'

Fiore, never really a courtier, leant forward, crossing his arms on his pommel, as if he and the Grand Komnenos were old companions.

'It is good practice for war,' he said. 'Not as good as a melee, with five or six on a side, but good. Horsemanship, management of the heavy lance, and of course accuracy, and defending yourself against an opponent's lance.'

'How would it help you fight the Turks?' the Grand Komnenos asked. I liked him the better that he wasn't fussed by Fiore's familiarity.

'Oh,' Fiore said, a little too easily, 'we've never had much problem killing Turks. But I trust Guglielmo here to put us where we can make a charge.'

'Your Grace,' I said, 'I've faced some Turks and found them very difficult opponents. To be honest, I would only face them in the field with every possible advantage of the ground and surprise.'

Alexios smiled wryly. 'Ah, messire, I understand from your caution that you really have faced them. But in our narrow valleys and long ridges, your heavy lancer might never make contact. Almost all of our fights are conducted with the bow.'

The Grand Komnenos's Italian was very good. He had wine served, and later, we all went to Mass again.

His German *protospatharios* accompanied us everywhere, and on the beach, at the end, after some gift-exchange, he said, 'There are three Genoese military galleys at Kaffa. If they hear about you, they'll come for you.'

That put the fox among the chickens, I can tell you. I passed the word to Francesco, and he called the captains together.

'Three Genoese galleys can probably take us in an hour,' he said. 'Even with three days to dry our hulls and make further repairs, these ships just keep revealing rot below the waterline, old timber, worn-out fittings ...'

'We would have enormous advantage in a boarding action,' I said. 'They can't be carrying the soldiers we have.'

Carne fingered his beard. 'I mislike fighting Genoa,' he admitted. 'But if we must, we should go straight at them, as the knight suggests.'

'Without talking?' Francesco asked. I could tell he didn't like it. 'We're not at war.'

Carne shrugged. 'If they see the condition of our galleys, they'll stand off, lead us a dance, and then ram us.'

'Let's just try not to meet them,' Francesco said. 'My father is going to be in enough trouble as it is.'

We left Trebizond with hard heads after three very pleasant days. We had a long row into the wind – so long that all of the soldiers and knights took a hand at the oars, myself included, now that all of our Greek ex-slaves were gone back to their homes. We were two more days at sea, with very little sleep, crossing the longest arm of the Euxine. It was late summer. The weather was beautiful, and still, I noted that all of our captains were on deck constantly.

After a pointless tussle with Pilgrim, who'd decided to attack me in the night, I rolled my cloak around me to keep out the wind and tried to get back to sleep.

The two Georgians were standing at the rail. The next day I realised that they had known we were passing the coast of their home.

We made landfall on the coast of Georgia, which I believe is the easternmost kingdom of Christendom, although I saw almost none of it. But whereas Georgia borders the Euxine at its westernmost edge, on its eastern borders it touches Persia. We were very far to the east, and yet the countryside looked like Germany, or Thrace, or even the north of England – high ridges, and dark trees.

Our landfall was Gagra, a small factory, or trading post, of the Genoese. There were two trading cogs anchored off the beach, and a trading galley pulled well up. No one could have been more surprised than the Georgian factor when we hove to off his beach. But there is no roadstead and no breakwater at Gagra, and poor holding ground for anchors. Giorgios made it plain that once we beached our ships, we were at the mercy of anyone who came along after us, but if we stayed at sea, we were at the mercy of the weather, and he insisted we were landing there.

Despite the possibility of three Genoese warships just over the horizon.

We landed. I formed my company into two bands and sent one to watch the market while the other seized the factor and the local commander. And that's where everything grew very complicated very quickly.

I was waiting on the beach, mostly because I didn't want John starting a crusade to free any Kipchaks he found. By his account, Georgia is full of Kipchaks. By this time, instead of acquiring an understanding of Euxine politics, I was confused and irritable on the subject. Or rather, I had now seen that I was being used for some complex ends and not informed as to what they were. Doubly annoyed because I counted Giannis and Giorgios as friends, yet they were completely close-mouthed.

But something told me that Gagra was where they'd been heading all along. The way they spoke to each other. Giorgios's insistence that we land, despite the risks.

All of that vanished when Francesco came back from the castle. His news sent a shock through us.

'There's a Tartar army in the mountains somewhere close, and the podestà has gone to negotiate with them,' he said.

These are the moments when it's really useful to *not* be in command.

'We can just sail away,' I suggested.

'Row away,' Zeno corrected me. But he nodded, as if mine was an excellent idea. He waved vaguely out to sea. 'Wind is blowing straight onshore. But yes. Let's be gone.'

I was clearly never going to make a sailor.

'But Ser Guglielmo is correct,' Zeno said, and nodded. 'It's not our problem.'

Francesco and both of my Greek friends disagreed.

'If we rescue the podestà, we reinforce our Emperor's sovereignty here.' Giorgios said a great many more words, but that's the gist of his argument.

And Francesco was suddenly a contrite Genoese.

'It's not in our interest to leave the podestà in the hands of the Tartars,' he said.

Giannis was silent, but I had observed that his reaction to the words 'Tartar army' had been one of pleasure, not shock.

Damn it, I thought, *they heard about this in Trebizond. Neither of them is surprised.*

We had quite a little debate. I suppose the long and short of it was that only the podestà had the ability to pay a tax from the Emperor, unless we chose to storm his castle in his absence. Which was apparently not in the rules of our expedition. Or that was the reasoning that Giorgios gave us.

While the three captains and two Imperial emissaries were debating the matter, I took John aside.

'Can you find the Tartars and learn … things?' I asked, ineptly. 'Almost anything would help.'

But John took my meaning immediately. 'Tartars. Hmm … Better than Turks. Mongols. Good guards, watch everything.'

He called to Kerchus. They had a brief exchange in Kipchak – more words than I'd heard from Kerchus since I'd known him. I thought he was refusing to go and then, suddenly, they both laughed.

'We'll go,' John said.

Within an hour, they'd swum their ponies ashore, absconded with another dozen horses from the market, and headed inland.

The market at Gagra was more like what Carne had known in the past. There was some Chinese silk in one warehouse. A merchant had resins and spices from as far away as Yemen, and there were local products – beeswax, wood, bark, honey. There was beautiful paper from Samarkand far to the east as well as horses of every type, and slaves. The slaves there were mostly Georgians, with a few Slavs from further north. The spice merchants had lapis and other interesting minerals. One man had emeralds, my favourite stones.

The traders looked at us with more relief than fear. The first evening on the waterfront, I found that even the Genoese merchant captains were far more afraid of the Tartars than they were of me and my two hundred soldiers, however well armoured.

'The last time the Tartars took this place, they killed every male and made a pile of skulls outside after they pulled down the walls,' a Genoese in a long robe said.

'We were hoping that you had been sent by the Bank of Saint George to save us,' another said.

I wasn't convinced that a walled town had anything to fear from an army of horse archers, but then, I didn't understand the full power of a Mongol army back then. In addition, I found it remarkable that these men of the long robes had come back to a place that had been reduced to rubble and skulls. Just to trade. I couldn't decide if they were brave or foolish.

I spent a long night changing my pickets and worrying about John and Kerchus, but in the morning, they rode back in with a whoop of triumph. John slid from his saddle before his pony had stopped moving.

'So,' he said. 'And so. This is a true Mongol, but he is like a bandit chief, not a great one. In fact, he is no one, trying to be someone.'

'But he has the blood of great Chingiz,' Kerchus said with deep respect.

John shrugged, acknowledging a matter of little importance. 'He is one proud bastard,' he said.

'You met him?' I asked.

John nodded. 'With these,' he said, 'it is either war or peace. Either we try to steal their horse herd, or we ride in and talk.'

'We went and made talk,' Kerchus said.

John pointed at the castle. 'He wants the town,' he said. 'He has the podestà and his soldiers. But ...' John raised an eyebrow. It made his face look like a demon's face, which was unfair, because he meant it to indicate deep thought. 'He can no more hold this town than I can hold my piss,' he went on. 'He has maybe five hundred riders. Not enough horses. Some wounded men. He's a bandit who has lost a battle, or so I think. He is desperate. He will risk almost any-thing.'

John, usually so laconic, had plenty to say about a fellow Tartar. That was interesting by itself. He pointed at our ship.

'The Tartar slaves are all his men,' he said. 'And some of them talk.

So I think I know who beat him and where. He wants to command the *Ulus* of the west. He must have faced Mamai, or perhaps the old khan's son.'

'Can we win him over by handing them back?' I asked. 'Can we trade them for the podestà, if that's what Giannis wants?'

John looked at Kerchus. 'Who knows? He is a dangerous man. His name is Tuqtamis.'

'You know him?' I asked.

John made a face. 'You think we all know each other?' he said. 'The steppe is full of his kind. Petty bandits trying to be great khans. I know his kind. He will kill you if you offend him. He cares nothing for the consequences. He has very little to lose. Listen. There are wounded men. There are empty quivers. He lost a fight somewhere north of here, or I am a Turk.'

John had to say it all over again for the envoys and the three captains. Michael des Roches listened, obviously fascinated, but contributed nothing.

'We should try to rescue the podestà,' Francesco said.

Zeno rolled his eyes. 'We should load our ships and row north for Khosta, the next town up the coast,' he said. 'Not even a day's row. This isn't worth the effort.'

The two envoys shared a glance that told me that there was more going on than I was privy to. As usual. But they wanted us to meet with the Tartar chief, and they both wanted to go.

I outlined my reservations.

'There are good horses here, but only enough to mount forty or fifty men,' I said. 'Enough men to be threatening, and not enough to win. If we take too few, he simply grabs us the way he took the podestà. If we take too many, he either rides away or fights us.'

John smiled grimly. 'If he fights you, you lose.' He looked at me. 'Sorry,' he said, spreading his hands low by his hips – a Mongol gesture. 'Five hundred Mongols?'

'So what do you suggest?' Giannis asked.

'Send John back as a herald, with a polite request for a parley. Send three of his men as a gift. Specify a location, like the monastery over there, and each side brings … what? Ten?' I was asking John.

'Twenty,' John said.

221

There was a discussion among the principals. Francesco raised his voice in anger. Carlo Zeno stood with his arms crossed.

I began to wonder if I should have stayed in Italy.

Dawn. The deep river valley that met the coast at Gagra had a monastery about a third of the way up the valley, nestled into the ridge like a bird's nest. A road ran up to it from the town, along the ridge, and then continued past, into the hinterland.

Tuqtamis was punctual, riding like a centaur at the head of two dozen of the ugliest men I've ever seen. They looked remarkably like devils, but then, I'd seen Tartars before. And Tuqtamis himself looked like a prince of demons, in a robe of Chinese silk over enamelled armour. His eyes were slits, his nose short, his arms long.

For all that, his voice was melodious. He spoke no Italian. The meeting was outside, on horseback. I had arranged the escort – John and seven of his men, accompanied by Fiore and seven of my best armoured knights, along with Giorgios, Giannis, Francesco and me. Carlo Zeno had declined to come.

Michael des Roches sat on a mule, trying to look inoffensive, and Kerchus was in the woods above the road with Christopher and a dozen other archers. I wore my full harness, and put on my surcoat of the Order of Saint John. I had no idea whether the red surcoat was known or respected out there.

I sat with John, Giannis and Giorgios, and the others were drawn up behind.

Tuqtamis rode forward alone, leaving his twenty-four men in two neat ranks. As he rode forward, John said, 'He brings a few more to show his power. He is saying, "I have more men and there's very little you can do."'

I noted that John was uneasy. I have seen him terrified, and wounded, but I'd never seen him betray the sort of ordinary fear to which I'm prone myself.

Watching the Mongol leader ride forward alone, I would never have guessed that he'd lost a battle.

He bowed in the saddle, very slightly, and spoke in his pleasant voice, very much at odds with his lacquered armour and demonic features.

John translated.

'He says, welcome to his lands. He says he is the Great Khan of the

Western Steppe.' John looked at me. 'That's crap. He is not the khan of the *Ulug Ulus*. Maybe no one is, right now.'

Giorgios raised a hand. 'It will cost us nothing to call him a great khan,' he said.

John was not a good diplomat. His look of disgust was palpable.

'He is not a great khan,' he said. 'But anyway.'

He spoke a few sentences. His language was fluid, almost elegant, breathy. It was the language that he spoke with Kerchus.

Tuqtamis nodded politely, and then launched into a speech. I didn't know what he was saying, but I know an orator when I see one – head thrown back, arm raised.

'He demands the surrender of the town and the payment of tribute,' John said. 'He also comments that our armour looks very good. He asks, "Does it rust in the rain?"'

'Ask him if he knows about the Emperor in Constantinople,' Giorgios said.

As an aside, let me say that during this whole conversation, Tuqtamis's horse never moved. Mine did – head up, head down, the placement of a foot, various equine signs of impatience. The same went for all of our knights.

Not the Mongols. Their horses stood like statues.

John and the khan had a long exchange, back and forth, a few words each. John sounded heated, Tuqtamis as calm as a man out for a ride on a beautiful day.

'He recognises his cousin, the lord of the stone city,' John said.

'After all that?' I whispered.

'He wants to know why I am with you,' John said.

Giorgios leant out over his horse's neck. 'Tell him that I am an ambassador from the lord of the stone city. Tell him that this town has been held by Franks, and now it is occupied by the lord of the stone city.'

John spoke, and for the first time, Tuqtamis looked uneasy. He spat a comment.

'He says we all look like Franks to him.'

'Tell him that there are many types of Franks, as he must know' Giorgios said. 'As many as there are types of Moslems or Turks. Tell him these are my master's men.'

223

John spoke again. Tuqtamis looked us over. He looked at me in particular, and my warhorse.

He turned away with the sort of sniff that a London goodwife gives to bad fish.

'Ask him why he wants this town?' Giorgios said.

Tuqtamis shrugged.

John said, 'He says it is his already.'

Giorgios raised an eyebrow. 'Tell him that if it was his, we would not be having this conversation.'

'Oho,' said John. 'Now we have some fun.' But he turned and translated.

Tuqtamis had a riding whip made of a horse's tail. He used it to rub his beard. Then he looked at me again. And spoke.

'He says he can come and take it if you insist.' John shrugged.

Giorgios nodded. He smiled. 'Tell him I think that unlikely. Tell him that my master would be interested in being his ally, but not if he claims to hold towns that are beyond his grasp.'

'We are going to fight,' John said.

'Do not touch your swords,' I said. Because when men hear that they are going to fight, most of them loosen their swords in their scabbards. That didn't strike me as diplomatic.

John spoke.

Tuqtamis just looked at us.

'Tell him that we would be happy to return the rest of his men who we liberated down the coast,' Giorgios said. 'And that we suspect he lost a skirmish. John, do you know who he fought?'

John didn't take his eyes off the Mongols.

'Could have been Mamai. He is the war leader, and I heard in Trebizond that he is in these parts. Could have been Toqtaqiya, the son of Urus Khan.'

At each of these names, Tuqtamis blinked. And for the first time, his horse moved under him. An ear twitched, and one hoof left the ground, hesitated, and then was placed. *Click.*

'Tell him that we can feed his men and help them,' Giorgios said. 'Not as tribute. But as an investment in a future alliance.'

John looked at Giorgios with something like pure disapproval. But he spoke the words.

Tuqtamis listened with enviable equanimity. At the end he nodded, and then he rode over to us. He'd been two horse lengths away, and now he rode right up to me, the end man.

He reached out with the butt of his riding whip and tapped my breastplate, hard. But he didn't move fast, and he wasn't particularly threatening, although I had quite a sense of his power as a fighting man, and he was far inside my fighting reach and my area of comfort.

'Hmmm,' he said. Apparently, this is an international sound.

He spoke to John.

'He wants to see your sword,' John said.

I made myself smile. My sense was that we were moving very gradually from provocation to provocation on a road to combat.

'Tell him to give me his,' I said.

For the first time, Tuqtamis and I were eye to eye. He was not short. His stirrups were much higher on his horse than mine, with the result that we were of a height, mounted. His horse was no smaller than mine.

He smiled. I will not ever know, but it seemed as if he was *actually* pleased.

He drew his sword with his left hand. I did the same, and we exchanged swords.

To my surprise, he turned his horse away in one beautiful movement, and proceeded to cut at the air with the Emperor's sword. He rode around in a little circle, his warhorse under perfect control. He cut, and cut.

Best be hanged for a lion, says I.

I rode out to my right, not at him, and began to cut at the air with his scimitar, or sabre. It was a magnificent thing – wider towards the point, yet feeling as light as a feather in my hand, with a strong backbone and a short false edge on a curved blade. The hilt was clumsy in my gauntleted hand, and I took off my steel gauntlet and tossed it to Fiore.

We wheeled to face each other. I saluted him, reasonably sure we were about to fight.

He grinned, raised the Emperor's sword, and turned back to his escort, holding *my sword* over his head.

I looked at John.

John made the gesture with his hands patting the air around his waist.

'I may have used the word *trade*,' he said.

Later that afternoon, we released the rest of the Tartars we had. Tuqtamis moved his camp under the walls into a sort of walled park or garden of fruit trees, large enough for the tents of almost a thousand men and women.

Tuqtamis released the podestà and his six men-at-arms. Over the next few days, the podestà paid us an agreed 'tax', and he also fed Tuqtamis's retinue and provided them with someone else's horses. Tuqtamis sat for a long time with John and Giorgios, negotiating, among many other things, the fate of our Kipchak boys. At some point I was invited to join them. Fiore and I demonstrated the essence of fighting in our armour, and two of Tuqtamis's men wrestled, and then swaggered swords. Tuqtamis was interested in the use of the point. He and Fiore had a spat about the use of the thrust in a mounted fight.

And he asked me, point-blank, for the scabbard.

Look, I'm not a fool. I was not going to demand the return of the Emperor's sword, although it was the finest sword ... no, the finest *thing* that I'd ever owned. But I could tell that this meeting was very important to Giorgios – perhaps the purpose of the whole expedition.

So I took off the scabbard and wrapped the sword belt around it, and handed it over with my best bow. Who knows where that sword is now? His scimitar is hanging on the solar wall of my castle at Methymna.

It was very interesting seeing how the Mongols lived. Their leaders, like Tuqtamis, dressed well, and many had their wives with them, dressed in silks of the finest sometimes, yet other times, wearing a simple deerskin kaftan. They were all much given to drinking wine, despite being Moslems. Several of them swore by Saint George, who, as I have noted before, is very popular among Turcomans. Their women sat with us when we ate, and drank, and made jokes. One of the noble women came to me with a big silver chalice of wine, a cup obviously looted from a Christian church. She handed me the cup, and I drank it off – those are the rules of Mongol drinking. Then she reached out and tugged my beard, and laughed.

And everything was covered in dust. Even the fine silks they some-times wore smelt of horse, and the hems were full of dust. And their horse herd was vast, and consumed grass at an incredible rate. John and Kerchus seemed very much at home.

'Are these your people?' I asked.

John gave me a glare. 'Are you a Scot?' he asked.

And the next day, on the beach, the two Georgian girls knelt and tried to kiss my hands. They'd found a priest and two nuns going back towards their home mountains. We wished them well, although most of the crews of all three ships would have happily kept them as mascots. Francesco and I gave them a gold ducat each. But money cannot fix much.

And Giorgios rode away east with the Tartars. I assume that he went as the Emperor's ambassador – I think he was going to find the Great Khan of the East.

Later, days later, when we were at sea and well up the coast towards Crimea and Kaffa, having already passed the port of Khosta. John and the rest of them tried to explain the situation to me. Tuqtamis was well-born but not very successful – a client, if I have this right, of the lord of Samarkand, one Timur, probably the man Giorgios was riding to meet. And the *Ulug Ulus*, the great Ordo of the western Mongols, was a confederation of all the tribes – Turkish, Tartar and others – who ruled the steppes from a city called Saray, which was located so far from anything marked on any itinerary I had that it sounded like mythology. Despite which, I understood this much – there was a Mongol captain-general, Mamai, and he held most of the land around the Euxine for various khans, who came and went. And he was currently lord of Kaffa and the Crimea, where we were going. And Tuqtamis was his enemy.

'And this *Ulug Ulus*?' I asked. 'Their remit runs all the way to the Euxine?'

Des Roches laughed. 'Do you remember that I told you how the Emperor in Constantinople has an officer entirely concerned with the matters of these people?'

Giannis glanced at him, respectful of the breadth of his knowledge. He nodded. 'For as long as there has been an empire, since the days of Caesar Augustus, it has been our policy to always know what is happening out on the steppes,' he said. 'And to always be friends with the wave behind the wave coming at us. Today, it is the Turks. But behind them are these Mongols, and we need them as friends. There is a new power rising on the Sea of Grass. This is merely one of many gambits to contact it.'

Kaffa, the largest of the Genoese cities in the near-island that is the Crimea, is surrounded by a strong wall and has a small citadel. It is beautifully placed, on ground that rises gently from the sea, and there is a castle on the heights, too far from the harbour to threaten an invader – but, if I still didn't, and don't, understand the politics of the steppe, I am wise enough to see that the threat of Mongol power did more to preserve the city than any wall could do. The Mongols own it, and tax it, and nonetheless have laid siege to it. In fact, they laid a long siege in '46 and failed to take it.

But when we rowed into sight of the land, we were pleased to find a newly built carrack on the beach, a pair of small cogs anchored out, and no galleys, merchant or military.

I was not present for any of the negotiations. I didn't land my men, as we had reason to believe there was plague in the city. Giannis went ashore with Carlo Zeno to make our demands, and learnt about the situation from the Genoese there. They told Giannis that Lord Mamai, the Mongol general, was far off to the north, in Livonia. Lord Toqtaqiya, the ruling khan's son, was somewhere to the south, hunting a bandit – whom we might understand to be our new friend, Tuqtamis.

In other words, the Genoese had no protectors but their garrison, which was riddled with sickness and death. The merchants complained loudly, and then paid a ransom for their ships, which we had taken on arrival. We loaded grain, filled our water and sailed for home.

'Not in a hundred years,' Giannis said, at the stern rail. 'Not in a hundred years has the Emperor's flag flown uncontested in these waters.' He waved back at the coast. 'This is what the Emperor would have liked to see your Count Amadeus do for him, instead of wasting men against the Bulgars.'

'I seem to remember rescuing him,' I said.

'Yes,' Giannis said. 'It was a complicated time. And it still is.'

*

The Euxine is simply too broad for a loaded galley to sail straight across. I confess that our four captains discussed it while we were loading our horses at Kaffa, but the harsh reality of life with galleys was that we had too many mouths to feed, and needed space to sleep and exercise our mounts. In perfect weather, a crossing from north to south would take six or seven days. A storm would be devastating, and we just didn't carry the food for a seven-day cruise, regardless.

So after some discussion we went west, moving cautiously along the coast. No one at Kaffa would tell us anything voluntarily, but we knew those galleys were out there somewhere. And Zeno was worried for the Venetian *muda*, which would be entering the Euxine behind us. Every night we would land, get fresh water, and cook on the beach with John and his people, now including six of the older Kipchak boys, out in the darkness on patrol. We slept on the decks and benches of the galleys. We built watch towers from driftwood to look out over the sea for enemies.

Six days out from Kaffa, men began to fall sick. At first I suspected we had bad water; the barrels looked bad, and we rinsed them with vinegar and drew fresh water from a stream, but even as we were getting water, I could see men fading. By noon on the third day, it was clear we had plague. I'd seen it too often to mistake it.

I know you want to hear about the Chioggia War, and the Great Raid, and Hawkwood. So I'll spare you the long story of that autumn. But it was terrible. I lost more people to the plague in a month than I'd lost to all of the opponents I'd faced since '64. In the end, after considerable argument, I had Francesco leave me and Fiore and all the sick men with the Genoese galley we'd taken. They left us twenty volunteers for double pay, all salted men who'd either survived the plague themselves or been in contact and never had it. Most of them were Greek oarsmen – fishermen, really. Three were Zeno's, and one was my old friend Aldo, who stayed with the Genoese galley. Fiore told me that the plague was nothing to him. Also, it is probably the only reason we made it home alive.

They left us with almost one hundred sick men. Forty died in the next two weeks, and then came the heartbreaking part, where men who'd struggled through the terrible buboes and the pus for five or six days simply didn't get better. They'd linger, and rally ... and die. Men

I loved. Men I'd been with through ten years of campaigns, campfires, arguments, drinking bouts ...

I gathered wood, and hunted, and cleaned shit and pus off dying men. That's what we all did, if we were healthy. And we bathed in the sea every day, sometimes three times a day.

I spent a great deal of time with Fiore, saying nothing. Neither of us ever got sick. And I went for long walks with Pilgrim. A dog, especially an active, bouncy dog, is just the thing when you are losing your taste for life. Pilgrim took more joy in chasing a bird than I did ... in anything, that autumn.

Twenty men of the first eighty made it through. Tommaso died, but Marco didn't. Giannis didn't, and he was one of the first to recover, having survived plague in Constantinople as a child. Gospel Mark died but Ewan didn't, although he was a scarecrow when he recovered. Grice died, and his squire and his page and his archer. Three of Lord Fontana's exiles died, and all their pages. Hector Lachlan died at sea, having left us in good health, with a dozen other men who had seemed perfectly well when they left us. Michael des Roches lingered and lingered. Father Angelo gave him the last rites. I held his hand for a while.

And he didn't die. He was the last one we saved.

Back in Constantinople, Lapot caught it and lived, probably proving he was tougher than the plague. But my three hundred men were reduced to one hundred and eighty by late autumn.

Worse than any battle I ever fought. And they were some of my best – men who'd been with me at Jerusalem, and in Italy for years.

Gone.

It was more than a little like losing Emile again. An enemy I could not fight.

I cursed God. And drank too much. But I'm getting ahead of myself, because when the disease had run its course and everyone was either buried or recovered, we crewed the Genoese galley as best we could and rowed her home. It's a miracle that neither the Genoese nor the Turks snapped us up. We were one under-crewed ship that could barely make way under oars, and had too few actual sailors to risk much sail. We crept down the coast, expecting to be taken by the Bulgarians. We got lost in the mouths of the Danube.

I became a modestly proficient oarsman, and I learnt to navigate. A little. And steer.

We made the Dardanelles more by good fortune than skill, but Aldo was a prince among seamen. Only after our bow was pointed into the narrow outflow of the Euxine did he admit how dangerous it was to miss the opening of the Dardanelles, because, of course, the prevailing wind is pushing you south. If you miss your landfall, you can be wrecked on the coast within sight of the straits. The wind is terrible there, and there's no holding ground for your anchor.

But once we were in the channel, the current saved us, allowing us to coast down the straits with very little effort, a crew of the almost dead. We were almost wrecked again off the Golden Horn, because the oarsmen were too few and too tired to manoeuvre around all the shipping. We fetched a Venetian great ship such a blow that we peeled five paces of painted and gilt wood off her side. We earned ourselves a round of curses, but a pilot boat came out and the pilot saved us, issuing a volley of orders and throwing his own boat's crew into the oar loom. You would not credit how difficult it is to bring a ship into dock off Constantinople. The pilot sent us all into quarantine.

Ewan began to put on some weight. And Peter Albin came from the palace every day. We didn't lose another man.

But I was sore troubled in spirit.

That question was back.

What is it all for?

We were greeted like the returning dead, and there was some hesitancy about employing us at all or letting us mount guard, as the inhabitants of the city had good reason to fear the plague. But Peter Albin passed us as cured after we left quarantine, and the survivors of the company took us into a warm embrace, and we were alive.

We celebrated the birth of the Saviour, worshipped at Hagia Sophia and the church of Saint Nicholas, where you can hear Mass in English in Constantinople. We adored the relics of the Magi for Epiphany and joined the Emperor's court in giving and receiving gifts. Emperor John gave me a fine Italian long sword, much narrower and a little longer than the other Emperor's sword. I suspect he was prompted by Nerio, who was back from Corinth, full of contrition for our losses and for leaving me without much information on such a long mission.

But I explained the taking of the Genoese galley, and Nerio shook his head in mock amazement.

'It will have to be returned, with apologies,' he said.

What that meant to Nerio was that it was towed over to Galata by one of his new Greek-built war galleys, empty of oars, great gonne, or oarsmen, and 'returned' with a note suggesting that it had been 'found' in the Euxine.

That sort of thing might once have been great fun, but I was still in the grip of the loss of spirit from the plague. Nothing much touched me. I felt a little as if I was living someone else's life. I woke each morning, wondering whether life had any purpose at all. Fiore was some help, because he focused on minutiae, and I needed that focus to get through the day. Jousting, swordplay, riding. Lifting stones. Seeing to my guards.

I watched Nerio with his latest mistress, and it didn't touch me.

Sometimes, you must accept your friends as being who they are. Nerio is licentious and duplicitous. On the other hand, he was paying us very well, and the sad truth of it was that, had we not been hit with the black plague in the Black Sea, we'd have had his wages for little enough work.

He'd made a drawing – a very good, detailed drawing – of the town of Megara and its fortress.

'Do you have enough men left to take it?' he asked.

I thought of Gospel Mark and Ewan, clearing the walls at Corinth. I'd lost more archers than men-at-arms, but not a single Kipchak, of whom I now had sixteen. I'd reorganised into a single *banda*, as the Greeks called their small units, under Lapot. Lord Fontana's men had lost so many of their pages and squires that I sent them to see if they could recruit among the various Franks of the city.

'Yes,' I said. 'Will you have any other troops?'

He looked at me for a moment, and smiled. 'No,' he said. 'You are all I have.'

And that was good. Because I focused on Megara, and taking Megara. And it kept me sane.

PART IV

Whilom, as olde stories tellen us,
Ther was a duc that highte Theseus;
Of Atthenes he was lord and governour,
And in his tyme swich a conquerour
That gretter was ther noon under the sonne.
Ful many a riche contree hadde he wonne;
What with his wysdom and his chivalrie,
He conquered al the regne of Femenye,
That whilom was ycleped Scithia,
And weddede the queene Ypolita,
And broghte hire hoom with hym in his contree
With muchel glorie and greet solempnyte
And eek hir yonge suster Emelye.

Geoffrey Chaucer, *The Canterbury Tales*, 'The Knight's Tale'

Spring, in Greece, is as beautiful as it is unexpected. It comes quickly out of winter, as it oft does in England, but places that you will have reckoned a desert – lifeless dusty hillsides and empty waste ground – will suddenly sprout a thousand flowers.

I had not recovered from what the plague did to my companions. While I was not sick myself, I lost almost all interest in ... everything. I didn't spar with Fiore. I didn't make love to a woman, or even watch one. I ran no courses on the tilt that the Emperor placed in the ancient Hippodrome, and I didn't even wish to watch John and his Kipchaks demonstrate their mastery of the horse and bow for the Emperor and his court.

It really was like losing Emile again. I was back in the same dark place. Nothing appealed to me beyond the commission of my duties, and those I took seriously enough. I made sure that my company was efficient. I made sure that they were paid, housed and well clothed, and I used a Christmas grant from the Emperor to give every man a good red cote and hat, keeping in mind the military appearance of those soldiers I'd seen at Trebizond.

Fiore joined me in despondency, as he heard from the Genoese across the channel that his lady love of some years was wed to another.

Nerio, somewhat meanly, suggested that Fiore just find the fellow and kill him.

Fiore sat up. 'An excellent suggestion,' he said.

Wearily, I got to talk Fiore out of it while glaring at Nerio, who found it funny.

Several nights later, after a ceremony where Fiore and I stood guard for the Emperor, we retired to a wine shop opposite the chapel of Saint Mary, buried in the residential neighbourhood of the court and the court's servants. It had been a private house once, with a garden and a well, and Athanasios, a big man who claimed Varangians among his forebears, had trellised the garden so that the grape vines curtained it and gave the impression of privacy. Hung with oil lamps, it was a little like an English inn, with the rafters replaced with leafy vines. If it had a name, I never learnt it. Everyone called it 'Athanasios's', and a great many secrets were exchanged there.

Fiore and I had a table to ourselves.

'It's my fault,' I said.

I'd already had too much wine, but that winter, I was probably drunk every night.

Fiore, much more abstemious and yet a little the worse for wear, looked at me across the table. If I haven't said before, Fiore had a level stare that was quite the most annoying thing. It was always challenging to men and always offensive to women, and no one had ever trained him out of it.

'Yes,' he said.

And that hurt like a sword blow to the arm.

But then he relented.

'I suppose if the plague hadn't taken your lady ...' he said slowly. 'I mean, you were never much help, were you? It was she, in her nobility, who pressed my suit.'

Now, I have heard a great many men, especially priests, expound on the many virtues inherent in absolute honesty, but friends, sometimes a little too much honesty is ... like a violent blow or a sudden sickness.

Yet, it was true. I hadn't done much to press his suit except to tease him, which he hated. I'd virtually forgotten his slim Genoese lady. As I'd virtually forgotten my children.

Fiore leant across the table. 'The person I blame is Nerio,' he said. 'He has contacts in Genoa. He promised to help, and he forgot. Because he is the centre of his own world and the rest of us barely exist, and this has got worse, not better.'

'Nerio loves you,' I said, or something like, to defend our friend.

'Nerio loves my ability to cut through some of his problems.' Fiore tipped over my wine cup. 'You need to stop this,' he said. 'People are talking about your drinking.'

Fiore so seldom dispensed any kind of advice beyond that of his art that I sat in shock, watching my good Nemean wine run through the dust under our feet.

I wanted to be angry. In fact, I probably was angry, somewhere in my head, but I knew he was right.

He leant forward again. 'What you need, Guglielmo, is a woman,' he said. 'A good woman. Emile has been gone for *years*.'

'This from you?' I asked.

He shook his head. 'I don't mean you should play the whoremaster, like Nerio. But you trust women – and, Guglielmo, they tend to remind you of things that otherwise you forget. Eh?'

I had to laugh.

'And ...' Fiore looked at his hands. He was, I think, embarrassed. 'And I'm going to be leaving you in the autumn.'

I grunted.

He shook his head. 'When I found you last spring, you were taking ridiculous chances, putting your trust in that rascal Hawkwood, and ...'

'Rascal?' I asked. 'John Hawkwood?'

Fiore drank off his wine. 'Hawkwood uses you the way Nerio uses me. The difference is that Nerio loves me in his way, and has made me wealthy enough to go back to Udine and make something of myself. I'm sorry, Guglielmo. I hadn't planned on telling you this, but Sister Marie and I talked of it and I promised her to remind you. You need to do something better. Hawkwood will kill your soul, if not your body.'

I probably started to reply. I don't remember, but Fiore put a hand on my arm.

'You are drinking too much,' Fiore continued, 'and you are, as Sister Marie suggested, perilously close to the sin of despair.'

'Sweet Christ,' I thought. Apparently it was obvious to my friends, eh?

'You are going back to Udine?' I asked.

Fiore nodded, accepting the change of subject. 'In the autumn or winter. I have a tidy sum from Nerio, and I am negotiating to purchase a house and a small estate.'

'You are retiring?' I asked.

'I am beginning the life of a citizen,' he said, with all the stuffy petulance that I remembered from his youth. It made me smile.

'Do you know we've been friends for ten years?' I asked.

He smiled – one of the broadest grins I'd ever seen from him.

'Ten years,' he said. 'Before you, dear Guglielmo, I had no friends. So I will always be in your debt.'

Well, there's something to remember in the dark of the night.

A few days later we were summoned by the Genoese bailie, De Merude. In fact, over the winter he summoned us several times. He ruled in Galata, across the strait, as effectively – perhaps more effectively – than the Emperor ruled in Constantinople, but we were not fools enough to deliver ourselves to him. Still, he sent Francesco an order of arrest, which Francesco evaded by going home to Lesvos, and he sent me an accusation of murder of a Genoese subject, in this case the slave trader at Kerasous.

Nerio laughed. 'Empty posturing,' he said.

Sadly, Nerio was wrong.

We stood guard, drank wine at the House of Athanasios, drilled our soldiers and practised the art of arms. And I accepted Fiore's strictures. I worked harder and drank less. I was not sufficiently desperate for a woman's touch to buy one, and otherwise women were in very short supply, as Greek noblewomen almost never appear in public. I saw the Empress and her ladies, most of whom were old enough to be my mother, and no one else.

Despite that, I remember it as a pleasant time. I enjoy practising for war, and I enjoy a well-ordered company, and being paid to be bodyguards to the Emperor gave my lads an edge that we had lost in Italy. In fact, I had never had a whole winter to form my people. Usually, they all melted away into various taverns and brothels at the first snow, and only reappeared in spring, dissipated and lacking most of their kit. Our horses prospered, and our pages grew, and the state of our armour and weapons improved until my company stood on parade like the legion of angels, in glowing red surcoats and sparkling steel armour. I suppose the one thing that had penetrated the fog of my despair had been those 'Roman' soldiers at Trebizond, and I strove to emulate them.

I remember a day when I paraded my whole company in the Hippodrome – I think that we were two hundred and twelve strong, all told. In the Chioggia War I led a bigger company, and we acquitted ourselves well enough, as you may hear, if you sit with me long enough. But on that sunny March day in 1374, in the Hippodrome built by ancient Roman emperors, I paraded the best trained company I ever had, even after the losses to the plague.

And then we were loading our ships for Corinth, and the campaign against Megara. Our first stop was Tenedos, and Zeno had been right. In spring, the place looks like Paradise. Tiny flowers grow everywhere in a riot of gentle colour. I barely noticed.

Megara is not as tough a nut to crack as the Acrocorinth. The town is large enough, on a ridge above the Bay of Salamis where Michael assures me that Athens defeated the fleets of the barbarous Persians before Jesus ever walked the earth. But while there is some change in the ground, and the whole central tower has some elevation, it's not really a strong place. We had a brief look from the sea as our galleys swept west along the coast, alarming the fishermen but otherwise doing no damage. Nerio stood amidships with me, Fiore and Marc-Antonio, pointing to the Catalan tower of the citadel.

One of the wild Scots who'd come out to join Hector Lachlan pointed at the distant tower.

'They took one o' our'n and hanged him frae the battlements,' he said, and went back to oiling his maille. 'Davie Ross. A gude man.'

Nerio nodded. 'The commander is a Catalan gentleman, Francis Lunel,' he said. 'He's very capable, and he's fully aware that I want to take the town.'

Fiore smiled.

I looked at the two of them. 'I mean, it's a fair town,' I said. 'But why Megara? You've put a great deal of thought and money into this.'

Nerio nodded. 'If I hold both Corinth and Megara, I hold the entire isthmus of Corinth and its hinterland.'

Fiore smiled. 'What he means is that it's the logical stepping stone on the way to taking Athens. Nerio intends to be Duke of Athens.'

Nerio sighed, and then grinned. 'I am too secretive with old friends,' he said. 'Yes, I want Megara as a stepping stone to Athens, but it is a valuable town in its own right. The Sicilians and the Catalans are so busy killing each other right now that I want to use the opportunity.'

'Sicilians?' I asked.

Fiore shook his head.

Nerio shrugged. 'Everyone in the West owns a piece of Greece, or claims one. The current king of Sicily – the one the Pope hates – is the current owner. Which, by the way, is merely a convenience for the Catalans, who stole this land from the French fifty years ago, and they, in turn, stole it from the Emperor in Constantinople.'

'Stop,' I said. 'You are making my head hurt.'

'Exactly,' Fiore said. 'So let's just get this done for Nerio and stop asking so many political questions.'

'War and politics are the same thing, I find,' I said. 'To make war, I like to understand the politics.'

Fiore smiled. But Nerio gave me a look – a considering look.

A week later, in his palace in Corinth, Nerio sat me down with a good cup of wine.

'I underestimate you, brother,' he said. 'I think of you as an expert soldier – none better. I made the mistake of assuming you didn't think beyond the length of your sword.'

I nodded. If I have learnt one thing in dealing with Nerio that applies to all the other powerful rich men of the world, it's that the less I say, the more I learn.

'*Alora*,' he began, and sipped his wine. 'I'm not sure where to begin, but the best place is the recent wedding between Frederick of Sicily, which we are now to call Trincaria, and the reportedly very beautiful Antoinette of Baux. The wedding is the seal on an alliance that finally makes Frederick the ruler of Sicily, and for that matter, most of the Morea.'

I sipped my wine.

'The Catalans, who took this place sixty years ago, have no real interest in handing any part of it to a foreign king. Several of them have been fighting among themselves, with a little help from my money. Frederick has succeeded in blackening their names to the Pope, who cares next to nothing about Outremer anyway. In practical terms, this means that right now, in the eyes of the West, no one really has a legal title to any of the great lordships here.' He looked out of his beautifully arched windows, glazed in fine Venetian glass. 'Everyone in Italy is watching someone else. The fools are watching the Visconti, and the smart ones are watching the Venetians and the Genoese.'

Our eyes met.

'It's a good time to grab Megara,' he said. 'No one is going to come and save it, at least if we're quick. But we can't take too much time, because these Catalans will all unite against me if they feel threatened.'

'You said a *coup de main*,' I reminded him.

He nodded. 'That would be the idea.' He handed me a heavy parchment envelope with an outer layer already opened. 'From Sir John Hawkwood,' he said.

I wasn't in the mood to look at a missive from Sir John. I was focused on Megara, because taking it had become my reason for staying ... if not sane, then sober and awake.

We needed to surprise the city if we'd have to undertake a regular siege, which would be expensive and difficult. We had only two hundred men facing almost twice that number behind walls, or so Nerio's spies claimed.

Any road, our attempt to surprise the city started from the moment we landed on the gulf side of the port of Corinth. Our horse herds went to pastures and our men into barracks high on the Acrocorinth, where it was unlikely that their presence would be reported. I stayed there myself for the most part. John and his Kipchaks rode east, past the ancient Hexamilion wall and into the territory of Megara.

After a few days to work up our horse herd and settle our people, and after I'd asked Michael to collect pilgrim itineraries and Greek monks who'd travelled the area, I proposed my plan to Nerio.

I aimed for several layers of misdirection. This sort of thing comes, as I have said, from fighting Turks, because they themselves are so fond of misdirection. I waited for John to return from his scout, and then we all gathered at the top of Nerio's impregnable fortress, eighteen hundred stone steps above the sea.

'We need surprise,' I said. Everyone nodded sagely, as officers do when you say something comfortably obvious. 'But between the arrival of our horse transports and John's new recruits, we have probably provided enough evidence of our presence to put the Catalans on their guard.' I waved at the arched windows in the direction of Megara. 'This Lunel must know we're coming for him, after executing David Ross. Yes?'

Nerio nodded. 'I thought we were hiding you well enough?' he asked.

'You said this Lunel was competent,' I said. 'If he is, he has spies. If he has spies, someone has seen something of us.'

Nerio winced but said nothing.

'Misdirection is as good as surprise.' I said. 'Nerio, do you intend to take Thebes?'

Thebes, as I've mentioned before, is the leading town of central Boeotia, just over the mountains from Athens and Megara.

'In time,' Nerio said, with a hesitant smile.

'Would it shock Lunel if we went for it now?' I asked.

I dismissed their responses to my suggestion.

Look here, gentles. I've laid out almonds and walnuts to show you what I had in mind. At the time we had itineraries and a sketch by Nerio.

'We go in three phases, I said. 'First, we march with the whole force, taking the north coast road across the isthmus towards Boeotia.'

Nerio made a face, but I went on.

'At Egirousa, John takes all the Kipchaks and as many of the pages as he feels he can use, and makes a raid across the isthmus into the marchlands of Megara from the north. According to my sources,' I smiled at Michael, 'there's a good road past the monastery of Saint John the Baptist in a little town called Alepo.'

'Alepochori,' Michael said.

'Sure,' I went on.

'They'll be ready for John,' Nerio said.

'Perhaps,' I said. 'Anyway, John will have orders to fly off as soon as he meets any kind of resistance.'

'Ah,' Nerio said. 'But won't this alert them?'

'Absolutely,' I agreed. 'And their scouts and any pursuit force will find our entire company arrayed on the coast road, a few miles away. And they will report that we are marching north. To Boeotia.'

Nerio shook his head. 'We don't have the men to take Thebes.'

One risk after another. I felt more alive than I had in weeks – and unlike my time in the Euxine, I was the one making the plans.

'We're not taking Thebes,' I said. 'We're marching as far as a little hamlet called Plataea, and then we're turning south, crossing the passes that Michael has marked in his itinerary, and coming on Megara from the north. Over the pass of Erythres.'

'There's a small ancient fort at Oinoi,' Michael said. He was sure of himself, and his information. 'The tower dates to the time of Alexander, or even before, or so the monastery records say.'

'There is a garrison,' John said, stroking his beard, and some of the other men who'd served for years with Nerio nodded.

'We take it first,' I said. 'By escalade.'

'How high are the walls?' Lapot asked, with professional interest.

No one knew.

I pointed to Michael des Roches. 'I think we need to know the height of the walls at Oinoi and at Megara.'

The scholar nodded.

Nerio shook his head. 'It's elaborate,' he said. And then he raised his wine cup. 'But I like it.'

Almost nothing went as planned.

We slipped out of Corinth as quietly as we could, because I didn't want to seem too obvious, but that part of the *empris* went so well that I feared we might actually have fooled the Catalan spies – if, indeed, any such existed. It was June, with short nights and long sunsets, and every chance for men to make noise or take too much time mustering, but none of that happened, and the sun found us on the coastal road headed east along the Gulf of Corinth. Nerio, who accompanied us, and Fiore, both recalled using the same road in reverse for the taking of Corinth.

I confess that my confidence of the day before was gone, annihilated by the rising sun and the complexity. Once we were on the road, all I could think of was the many flaws in my plan. We were strung out on a road that alternated between sandy beach and climbs to clifftops, and Greeks on that coast use boats more than carts. One washed-out bridge would stop my expedition for a day or two. But evening of that long day found us in a nameless village high on the mountainside above the gulf. The village was ill prepared to feed two hundred men, but we had supplies on our donkeys and we made do, and the Greek priest watched us like hawks. Here, just a day's ride from Nerio's Corinth, we seemed to have ridden back in time. The village, which owed its feudal obligation to Nerio, had never heard of him.

The next morning we marched, slowed by sick horses and some sick men. The plague had put its fear in me, and when Lapot took me to the sick men's fire, all I could see in the half-dawn was their dark faces and the splashes of their vomit, and the smell was like the smell when I found Emile. But inspection showed half a dozen pages and archers who'd found a cellar full of wine and drank most of it. I was of a mind to hang the lot of them for scaring me.

We started late. It was long after Sext when our advance guard rode up to the tiny crossroads that marked the way to the monastery of Saint John the Baptist and beyond, to Megara. John was unmoved by my suggestion that he stay the night with us and strike in the morning.

'Night is always the raider's friend,' he said.

He had his original eight – none of the Kipchaks had contracted the plague, God only knows why – and he had his six 'boys'. They were all sixteen or older, and very eager to prove themselves. Too eager, as you will hear. He chose a dozen of our pages – the oldest, and best, with light crossbows and a pair of horses each.

John's plan was simple. We knew where most of the Catalan 'gentry' kept their warhorses. Greece is not a great place to be a sixteen-hand horse, and good horses require grain feeding and shade. He was going to try and steal the horse herd, and spread some fire and chaos.

We marched another mile past the crossroads to Alepochori, and camped under the stars.

The moment John rode away, I felt blinded. It was a nice lesson in how reliant I had become on John's skills. So in the morning I put Lapot back in his old job of scouting, with Christopher and a dozen good archers out in front of us. And I took the rearguard myself, because when John came boiling back out of the plains of Megara, he was going to lead any pursuers straight into our rearguard.

It seemed simple enough, as a plan.

Prime – the first hour of daylight. Michael read morning prayers with Father Angelo as we formed to march.

Terce, and we were well along the beach road to Boeotia, in a little town that our local guides called Psatha. As usual, I'd hired three, and kept them well apart.

Sext, and we were climbing the flanks of a great mountain on an endless series of switchbacks, and there was no dust cloud behind us. I could see, every time I stopped, all the way back to Alepochori, and an hour later, as we crested the tall ridge, I could see the Acrocorinth. Indeed, I remembered this place from my first trip out.

And then we took a wrong turn. I wasn't in the vanguard. I was watching for my friend and invaluable scout John to return with enemies at his tail. Instead, I was watching an empty road below and behind me, sweating into my full harness, which I was wearing because I expected imminent combat, and blind to the errors of our guides.

About Nones, as the sun started to set, we climbed into a village set high on a mountain. By then, I knew we were not on Kitharon, the great mountain that overlooks Plataea. The mountain has such a distinctive shape that I was fairly sure I could see it, a couple of Roman miles to the north.

We were climbing the wrong valley. The last time we'd been here, we'd had local guides as well as both Giorgios and Giannis, who were both important men now.

It wasn't just being lost. We were somewhere in the mountains north of Megara – we weren't that lost. But the chances of a shepherd reporting us increased, of course, and worst of all, John would miss us. And he would be alone, trapped on a narrow coast road between cliffs and the sea, with no room to manoeuvre and no friends.

I sat on my horse in the little square of the town, gnawing on my moustache and trying to decide whether to take the rearguard back down the mountain to the coast road, but it had been a brutal climb, and going back down before twilight would be difficult, and dangerous. And, of course, I'd be splitting my already outnumbered forces.

These are the moments you never describe, Monsieur Froissart – when the great commander doubts everything. When the whole risk seems ill considered and you wonder why you ever suggested any of it. We could have marched on the coast road from Corinth to Megara, moved like lightning, and emerged from the sunrise to try and storm the western gate.

But we didn't. And there we were.

I didn't sleep well. Marc-Antonio went out to check the pickets fairly frequently. Lapot had put the wine-soaked sods of last night's escapade on all-night guard duty, mostly because we didn't think there was much threat of us being surprised, but Marc-Antonio enjoyed tormenting them, and by the Virgin they deserved it.

I was up before dawn. In exchange for an asper, a very kind young man fetched me a bucket of hot water, and I bathed and shaved. Before the little church rang its morning bell for the first light of the sun, which came early up on that mountain, Lapot, who was made of iron, was out with a dozen prickers, searching to the east along the

245

one road. That's because Michael, with his scholarly Greek, had learnt from the priest and the headman that we were quite close to Oinoi.

The sun was just a disc at the eastern end of our valley when Christopher rode up to me, his horse all lathered.

'The tower!' he said. 'Oinoi. A mile, maybe two. A dozen men. Come now.'

And then an infinite delay, the most painful time in war, as ladders were bolted together, donkeys loaded, men armed. Everything appeared to be slow, and the sun rose. And rose.

I cursed a great deal.

'You are feeling better, I see,' Fiore said.

'Christ, brother,' I blasphemed. 'Better?'

'Hmmm,' he replied. 'A week ago, you were slower than an old hunting dog. Now you return to your usual "lose-not-a-minute" self.'

We went forward a mile, and then most of another, with Christopher as our entire vanguard, and when he raised a hand for the column to halt, we did.

Then we were the company I wanted us to be. With nothing but whispers and hand signals, I sent Lord Fontana and twenty lances to block the road into Megara, and I sent Marc-Antonio to block the road down to Erythres. But it was, thank God, still very early, and there wasn't so much as a tinker on the pass.

Lapot came in. We were halted behind a tall spur of rock – rock as smooth as if poured, like the giant icicles I've seen on barns in the north country.

Laconic as always, Lapot pointed. 'Maybe thirty feet,' he said.

We had one ladder that long.

'Leave five lances to bottle them up,' Fiore said.

'We don't have enough lances to leave any,' I said.

'Or lose any,' Fiore said.

I lay behind a smaller rock and looked at the tower. It really wasn't much, except that the stones were huge and very old. It had one door, and that was high on the middle of the south side, with a ladder. Otherwise, it was a squat, rectangular tower on a steep spur of rock that dominated the road.

And had for two thousand years.

'Damn it,' I thought. An hour earlier and we'd just have snapped it up.

'Summon them to surrender,' Nerio said. 'Offer to buy them out.'

'Right now, we still have surprise,' I said.

I wanted to get it over with, and my first inclination – in fact, for a long minute, my *intention* – was to put that long ladder against the tower and try my luck.

I didn't.

'Let's try to do this the way we'd have done it in France,' I said.

When I described my plan, which wasn't complicated but would involve both luck and some serious work, the nearest archers groaned.

Christopher smiled. 'I haven't really been to France,' he said. 'But this is how I would do it in Egypt.'

I was happy that he liked my plan, but where the hell was John?

A little over an endless hour later, a merchant came over the pass with a cart and four laden donkeys. He had a pair of guards and a terrible-looking servant.

The cart had seen better days, and it creaked over the top of the pass and down towards the tower, protesting every foot of the slope. The horses were hitched to the back of the cart to keep it from running away, and the servant cursed like a demon from Hell. He looked a little like a demon, too.

The wagon creaked to a stop outside the tower, and a crossbowman, without his maille shirt and holding his uncocked weapon, came out of the upper door and climbed laboriously down the ladder.

He wasn't chatty, which suited me, as I was the merchant. I was wearing a long robe of Michael's, and I was already dusty and tired and had every doubt about this plan, but I was now committed.

'Where are you heading?' he asked, although without much interest.

Behind him, Christopher darted from the rocks near the base of the tower into the shadow of the base. Behind him, La Motte led the men with the ladder. Ewan had a dozen archers who'd inched their way across the rubble field, with quickly woven hurdles of Greek thorn and straw on their backs to hide them.

I took one of the Catalan's arms and threw him, and put my dagger to his throat.

Now, here's where it got interesting. If they were smart, they had a man watching the man who collected the toll. The thing is, soldiers

247

are lazy, and they'd probably been stuck at this mountain post for months. I thought it was worth the risk.

Christopher was already a third of the way up the ladder. I left the man I'd put down to Beppo, who was playing my servant, and the Biriguccis, my 'guards', followed me up the ladder.

A man stepped out onto the little landing where the ladder ended. He looked down at the cart without curiosity, and took over a long breath to realise that several things were wrong.

He leant out to get a better look, and Ewan put a shaft in him.

Unfortunately, he screamed. Nor did he obligingly fall to his death. He crumpled right there, across the lintel.

Christopher made the platform at about the same time as one of the garrison came to slam the door. I could hear the click-ring of the blades, but I couldn't see a damned thing because I was on the ladder. I was unarmoured, of course, so I got up fast enough.

As my head cleared the platform, I could see that Christopher was wounded. There were two men in the doorway, one trying to pull in the body of the man Ewan had feathered, as he was blocking the door. Both of them were roaring away in Catalan.

One of them decided that it would be easier to throw the body off the tower than to pull it in. This caused me to be in a wrestling match over a corpse while Christopher and the other Catalan cut and parried over our heads. Remember, no armour. I expected to have my hair parted at any moment. I pushed at the dead man and the Catalan pushed him back, trying to throw me over the edge, and the corpse at the same time.

There was a lot of shouting inside the tower.

I dropped my sword. It was doing me no good. I was very near to death every second, and I didn't have a spare hand. Instead, I drew my rondel dagger, and the next time Christopher stepped and cut, I rolled in under him like a dancer, thrusting overhand for the man I was wrestling with.

That was my notion. What actually happened was that Christopher was only feinting a thrust, so that my shoulder hit his knee and took him down. My dagger did slash my opponent, who was crouched in the doorway, and he fell back with a scream.

Christopher's opponent had a clear cut at both of us.

So it was very lucky indeed that there were a dozen archers down there, waiting to loose. He was hit at least twice. I did get a long look at the cutting edge of his *storte*. I was pretty much just lying there, waiting to die, for ... several beats of my heart.

The tower was ours. While they poured men down the internal steps to stop Christopher and me and the Biriguccis from storming the front door, La Motte and his party went up the ladder to the top, unopposed.

Sometimes I make a good plan.

The sword Emperor John had given me was shattered on the rocks below. *Sic transit gloria mundi.*

Some of my lads wanted to string the Catalans up, as they'd done to poor David Ross. I didn't let them. I was glad enough that Christopher and I were alive. I even offered some thanks to God. Since the plague, I'd been a little uneasy with God, to be honest.

An hour after Terce – mid-morning. We had the tower, and we were almost certainly undetected.

We had no idea where John was, and it was still two days to Megara.

Nerio nodded. 'This,' he said, 'is what risk feels like.'

We 'camped' that night – if camp is a word for no fires, no beds and very little food – in a tiny village high above Megara. At least, I hoped that it was above Megara. What Michael's pilgrim routes and monkish itineraries had hidden from us was the bewildering number of dirt tracks that covered the hills like loose threads on the floor of a spinning room. By the time we made 'camp' we'd made a dozen guesses. Our little team of guides – now five, including a young shepherdess who was fearless and who had a legendary command of Greek invective – couldn't agree among themselves as to which dirt track led to the monastery. A peasant woman admitted that there was a *convent* of nuns below the town.

Michael's face was a study in the moonlight.

'A convent,' he muttered. And then, to me, quietly, 'I have no idea. It might have been a convent that we were looking for. I may have made a mistake with my Greek.'

Well ... We all know about spilt milk.

I was deep in enemy territory, I'd lost my scouts, and I was myself lost. My right shoulder hurt like fire because in attempting to throw myself up a ladder with a dagger strike, somehow ... I'd done something ...

Sleep was slow coming.

The bronze bells of the convent woke us in the middle of the night.

Michael was awake beside me.

'Vigil,' he said. 'Tomorrow must be a feast day for them.'

'You know the canonical hours of the Greek rite?' I asked.

Michael gave me the same look Fiore would have given me if I'd asked him about swords.

'Yes,' he said.

'Where do you stand on the Union of Churches?' I asked.

I found it amusing that we hadn't discussed this subject before.

Michael chuckled. 'It's my current subject,' he said. 'That is, after all, why I'm here with you.'

That's the sort of thing you talk about, in the dark, in whispers, on campaign.

But I realised that if this was our 'monastery,' then we had to get up in the dark to make it to the gates at dawn. Our only piece of good fortune was the bright three-quarter moon.

I went and woke Ewan and Christopher.

'I need a route down to the plain,' I said. 'I'm going to wake everyone in an hour.'

Ewan muttered something about my parents that was unkind. Christopher pulled his blanket tighter around him and tried to go back to sleep.

But in the end, they went.

An hour later, I was waking my people. I had a hollow feeling in the pit of my stomach and I had that light-headedness that comes with too little sleep, too little food, and dirt. No, it's true ... bathing can replace sleep, up to a point. I learnt that from the Order of Saint John.

Gritty, tired and full of doubt, I nonetheless woke my people and got them armed and mounted. The bells rang again as the sky turned grey. A line of pink appeared in the east. I wondered if the mother superior of the convent below us on the mountain was a tyrant. She'd certainly sounded Prime about twenty minutes before the rim of the sun rose above the mountains.

I had plenty of time to think it was all foolishness.

And then we were moving, led by Ewan. We went down the mountainside by way of an endless series of switchbacks – at least, they seemed endless to me. The sun rose above the mountains in the east, and cocks crowed in farmyards.

Dogs barked at us as we came down the steepest path I can ever remember using, so steep that I was leaning all the way back and my stomach muscles felt like iron bands, the high back of my saddle pressing into me and my seat precarious.

We came down into the back of a farm, through an olive grove, and the farmer stood in his yard, watching us.

His farm road met a very slightly larger track and we turned west, away from the rising sun, and our pace increased.

And I already knew it was too late in the day. That's the problem with making plans based on travellers' tales. One glance down the valley we were descending, and I could tell that the walls of Megara were still a mile away. We were going to cross a mile of open ground in morning daylight.

The Catalans weren't that bad. They would not be asleep.

'Halt,' I said.

Everyone was in armour. The first rays of sun to strike us in the line of sight of the gate towers would give us away. I took my big dun-coloured cloak off my saddle and put it on, and rode forward with Christopher to the head of the valley, where it drained into the plain of Megara. In spring, there was no doubt a torrent running in the now empty gully to my left.

We were short on food. And we'd lost John. I knew nothing, and it was possible that I was heading into an ambush.

I gathered Lapot, Nerio, Fiore and Fontana, and put it to them.

'We have no chance of taking that gate today, much less getting the tower,' I said. 'If they didn't see us coming down the mountain ... if no one from that village tells Megara that there's an army creeping up on them ... maybe we can take the gate tomorrow at dawn.'

'Or they can come and cut us off here,' Nerio said.

'You propose camping on this poor farmer's land? He might have enough eggs for five of us.' Lapot glanced down the valley. 'No feed for the horses.'

'Not enough water,' Christopher reported. He'd already put a bucket down the man's well.

Nerio looked at me. 'Your call,' he said.

And there it was. We'd piled up the risks, and now we were going to pay. It was my fault. I was in command, and I'd based my risks on news collected at second hand.

'We could try the merchant wagon trick again?' Fiore said.

'We don't have a wagon any more,' Lapot reminded us. It was many miles of mountain track behind us.

I have never hated being in command more.

'We will go a day without food,' I said. 'As far as I can see, it's our only hope of seizing the town.'

'Christ almighty,' Lapot spat.

'Ration the water and get it to the horses first,' I said. 'Give the farmer some gold and buy everything he has. Put everyone under cover, no fires, and tell them to sleep all day if they can. We will move at full dark.'

'You're sure?' Nerio asked. 'For my money – and it is my money, Guglielmo – we can race across the plain ...'

I was tempted. There's a certain brave cowardice in my mind that always wants to 'get it over with'. And Nerio wasn't wrong. There was a solid chance that we could gallop up the road, put the ladders against the walls, and get in.

But that left no way out if it was a trap – if they'd captured John and they were waiting for us. One smart sortie and we'd all be taken.

Fiore looked at me. He tilted his head to one side as if examining me very carefully.

'I'm open to your views,' I said.

Fiore narrowed his eyes. 'No,' he said firmly. 'You are better than I am at this sort of thing. There are too many imponderables.'

I swear, until that moment, Fiore had never told me I was better at anything. It gave me an odd lift.

Lapot just shook his head. 'Lads will hate it.'

I nodded. 'I'll survive that.'

I spent far too much of that day watching the west gate from a low, rocky promontory at the opening of the farmer's small valley. I'd taken off my armour, and I could reach the edge of the rocks by a sort of goat-path that kept me out of sight of the town until the last moment. I think I climbed up there a dozen times.

Of course we had sentries. I was just unable to leave it alone, like a sore tooth.

Michael shook his head and apologised for the faulty information. He was sitting in the farmer's hut, helping Christopher and two other men cook. Michael was a very good cook, as I had reason to remember, and we'd decided that the smoke from the man's fire wasn't out of place. Our four 'cooks' turned every piece of food we had on our donkeys, plus what the farmer could provide, into a stew. At Vespers – we could still hear the bells from the convent – everyone got a cup of stew. I waited with the officers. We ate last, in case there wasn't enough. Standing in the gathering twilight, surrounded by my company and the smell of that stew, was one of the longer waits of my chivalric life. A hundred and seventy-two men had to get a cup of stew, with Michael measuring it like an Armenian merchant in Smyrna measures gold.

We all got fed. The horses were restless, but the water had held out – a minor miracle.

I knelt on the rocky ground and prayed. The last light left the sky, and an hour later, the moon rose. Not enough light, but better than no light at all.

Ewan and Christopher were already out ahead. I had the ladders already assembled on pairs of horses, and every man knew his place on his ladder. We formed in two long files, with me at the head of one and Lapot at the head of the other, despite Fontana's protests that he should lead.

In the moment, I was finally calm. We'd made it over the mountains and we'd waited out the day without being attacked. If it was a trap, it was every bit as elaborate as my over-elaborate plan of attack.

In the dark, everything takes longer – every unbuckled buckle, every right or left turn, every hedge you have to pass, every bridge. We had a little more than a mile of open ground to cross on a fair road. On horseback.

It took us more than an hour. And we lost our order. Horses threw shoes, and one man fell off his horse into a ditch. A Gascon man-at-arms, Bertran Lavout, led his entire lance down the wrong farm lane and didn't catch up with us for hours.

Despite which, we arrived at the gate. There was no outwork, which had been one of my fears. A small projecting wall or a couple of detached towers can wreck an escalade before it begins. But there were just two towers looming out of the darkness, with a closed gate between them.

We put the first two ladders to arrive against the walls about fifty paces to the west of the gate, and there was no point in waiting. I started to climb. I wasn't first – Lapot was. Accident of chaos. I was about halfway up when there was a loud challenge over by the gate – a shout that split the night, and the flash of a lantern.

'A l'arm!' bellowed a sentry.

So much for surprise. On the other hand, I got a foot on the wall unopposed, and Lapot was already running along the parapet back towards the gate towers.

A bell began to ring. The Catalans were good, or they were ready, or both. Let me pause here to explain that we were good, too. We'd got two hundred men under their walls undetected.

Or it was a trap, of course.

But once you're on the wall, there's nothing to do but fight.

Whoever had built the gate a hundred years before knew I was coming. There were no doors from the parapet into the towers. On the other hand, the Catalans assumed we were still outside. God knows, enough of my company was now in a state of complete confusion outside the west gate, milling around in the market space there. This is what really happens in battle. You practise something, the crossbow bolts fly, and everyone forgets everything.

Which is why the Catalans in the tower were concentrated on the men in front of the gate, and had left their wooden stairs from the gate yard undefended and the oak doors open. The problem was that there were no steps down from the wall. I could see the candlelit interior of the gate towers, and the wooden steps from the gate yard, beckoning like my hope of Heaven, but I myself was standing twenty feet or more above the pavement, and if you think that you can jump that distance in plate armour ... well, you can't. At least I can't. I'd break both ankles.

There were a dozen men with us, and by luck and a little bit of planning, one of them was Witkin, who tended to stay close to me. He was an odd man, as I've said repeatedly, but he had a length of rope tied around his waist, because I'd told him to bring it. In less time than it takes to tell it, Greg Fox and I were on the marble slabs of the gate yard, with the rest of them coming down as fast as they could.

I waited until Fiore was down. I could hear the alarm in the citadel behind me, and I worried that we were in a trap, but getting the gates open was the first requirement to any further plan.

I pointed Fiore at the far tower.

Lord Fontana sprang in front of him and ran, his sabatons clicking on the marble, for the wooden steps up to the floor above the gate on the far side.

A Catalan wearing nothing but a nightshirt stepped into the light, raised a crossbow, and shot.

Fontana took the bolt in the aventail at his neck, and went down. Fiore ran like the wind and leapt over the fallen Italian knight. The man in the nightshirt was spanning as fast as he could, shouting in Catalan.

Then I lost track of all that, because I, too, was running as fast as my leg harness would allow. The wooden steps shuddered under my weight, and that of Greg Fox behind me, and four more men-at-arms behind him.

It was all in one flash. The man filled the doorway above me, his hair as red as mine and wild from sleep ... The crossbow – the impact of the bolt dead centre in my chest ...

I fell back, hit Greg, and we fell together off the steps. I hit my head, smashed my plumes, as I found later, and lay stunned. But not dead. My breastplate held. It was dented in, and I had a broken rib.

Lapot took the tower without me. Fiore and Ser Antonio di Piacenza, Fontana's lieutenant, took the other tower, and Beppo, bless him, got the gate open. Someone remembered why we were there.

Nerio gave orders, but it was too late. Men were hungry, thirsty, tired and scared. The Catalans had wounded half a dozen and killed some horses. And there were riders coming at us from behind on the road.

The whole company bolted in through the gate. I know, because they rode right over me. By luck, and good horse training, none of them finished me off, but I had an uncomfortable time in the fire-streaked darkness as hooves landed all around me. I lay, unable to breathe or fully understand exactly what was happening.

Eventually Greg Fox recovered enough to rise. By then, most of my company was riding through the darkened town. Nerio was shouting himself hoarse. Beppo had closed the gate behind our rearguard and someone was outside, pounding it with a sword hilt. Everything that could have gone wrong had, except that we had taken the gate. But remember that we'd taken the gate to the outer wall, not to the castle at the centre of town. The Catalan garrison would be in that castle – and it was probably a larger garrison than my whole company, which was currently riding riot through the darkened streets of Megara.

My head felt as if it was on fire.

But we had one piece of luck – one thing that saved us from disaster in the darkness.

My young trumpeter, Giorgios, sat on his mare near the steps, watching me.

Something familiar about the shouting outside the gate, too.

'Giorgios!' I called. Maybe I mumbled, as it took a surprising amount of time for the lad to come to me. Fiore was waving from his tower by the gate. Greg Fox was looking at Lord Fontana.

The boy came.

'Sound "Rally on me"!' I said. 'Sound it over and over.'

I was recovering. The heavy lining inside my helmet had saved me – that, and the muscles in my neck. My neck hurt, and my shoulder ... Good saviour Jesus, my right shoulder felt as if the bolt had gone right through.

Somewhere outside the gate in the dark was my Percival.

The trumpet began to sound *Rally*.

Fiore was shouting something. I tottered over to Lord Fontana and Greg Fox. My mouth was as dry as a bone from too long without water, and my head hurt, and my shoulder ...

Fontana had a crossbow bolt through his neck. And he wasn't dead.

'Father Angelo!' I roared.

Fontana wasn't dead, but he would be very soon. The amount of blood around him on the marble stones was like a lake, a spilled tun of wine.

I knelt in the blood.

Fontana's gauntleted hand came up for my face. I flinched. But he caught my neck with surprising strength. And it hurt, of course.

'... sister!' he said.

'Lie quiet, my lord,' I said. 'I have sent for Father Angelo ...'

'... my sister!' he said again. His eyes all but bulged out, he was so insistent. Well ... he knew as well as I did he was going.

'Would you care to pray?' I asked.

I had a rosary on my knight's belt – I always do. I dropped my gauntlets and got it off my belt clumsily, and he grasped it. I could see in his eyes he knew what it was.

But he said, '... beg you!'

Greg Fox looked at me. He's a very intelligent man, if not as given to long speeches as Nerio or I.

'I think he wants you to take care of his sister,' he said.

'Hauuh!' grunted the dying man. He couldn't nod.

'Yes,' I said. 'I promise.'

'Ahh,' he said.

'Who is it?' Father Angelo said. 'Let me in.'

He pushed my right shoulder. I may have screamed, but I forced myself to my feet to give him room with the dying man.

Fiore was above me on the wooden landing of his tower.

'It's John!' he said.

'Who's John?' I probably replied.

I remember a moment of complete confusion – nothing made sense. And then, gradually, with various people shouting at me, and the ring of our trumpet, I understood that the man beating at the gate with the hilt of his sword was John the Turk.

Well ... the good news was that I hadn't lost John or his people. The bad news, as I learnt over the next hour, is that we'd taken the outer gate and never come close to grabbing the inner gate or the citadel.

My chest still hurt when Nerio came up. By then, my trumpeter had worked his miracle. I had most of my lances back, in order. Discipline held.

But we were two hundred men holding the outer wall of a town of eight thousand souls, with a garrison the size of our whole force in the citadel.

'What do we do now?' Nerio asked me.

I was looking at the citadel, which sat on a low acropolis, nothing like as impressive as the acropolis of Athens or Thebes. The walls of the citadel were relatively new, and well built. Beyond them to the south, the water of the harbour glittered, just a league or so away.

'This will require a siege,' I said.

Nerio bit his lip. 'I do not think I can afford a siege,' he said.

The near-despair that had seized me since the plague struck still had me in its grip. Now that we'd fought an action, it was worse. Lord Fontana was dead at my feet, with a few other men, half a dozen in all – too many for a failed attempt. I felt incompetent and I just wanted to lie down and sleep. The blows to my breastplate and head probably didn't help.

I looked up at the citadel. The sun beat down, and sweat made me feel prickly.

'Then we're done here,' I said, or something equally final.

Nerio looked at me. 'What? You're just going to give up?'

'We don't have the men or the machines to take the place,' I said. I was thinking of Piacenza, and the wasted victories of the last year. 'If I had more ladders, I might at least threaten an escalade. But we don't have the ladders. And,' I added bitterly, 'I don't have the men who died of the plague in the Euxine.'

'And from your tone you blame me for that?' Nerio snapped.

A short sea voyage. Isn't that how Nerio had described it? I did blame him. Which was ridiculous, really.

Fatigue. Despair.

I was considering my reply, struggling with a desire to spit out all the anger I felt, aware that to do so would be foolish, or worse.

Fiore caught my bridle and turned my horse.

'Breathe,' he said. 'Nerio can be an arse.' He shot a look at Nerio.

It doesn't sound like much, perhaps. But it was the act of a true friend. I did breathe.

And I swear, when I breathed in, I caught the smell of sulphur. I swear I did. And it was all right there.

I took three breaths, and then I said a little prayer to myself, as if I was going to fight. And I smiled at Fiore, and then at Nerio, who probably was getting ready for a sermon or a diatribe or an angry rant.

Usually it only takes a few breaths to separate a pointless rage from an intelligent comment. Sometimes, you need a friend to buy you those breaths.

'Let's have a look at the walls,' I said.

So we rode all the way around the citadel. Twice, someone high on the walls above us tried a shot with their crossbow. One rattled against a house roof quite close to me.

The citadel was a typical square tower, if larger than most. It rose three storeys tall, squat and powerful, with sloped walls and covered sentry posts at each corner of the top, which, with the battlements, made it look like some sort of beast. An inner tower thrust up from the outer, another two storeys from the centre of the squat outer fort, with a handsome conical tile roof. It was very modern. On the other hand, it didn't command the whole town because of the slopes of the acropolis. There were big stone houses and a pair of fine churches right against the fortress that blocked their sight of the lower slopes of the hill, a big parade ground, or perhaps a market square, directly in front of the citadel's gate, and then a couple of very Italian house towers and some more good stone houses beyond the citadel and, if anything, a little higher on the shoulder of the acropolis. It was a strong place, but, even with my relative lack of experience in these things, it looked badly sighted.

Nerio remained silent as we rode around the walls. I told Lapot to organise patrols – I didn't want a rising from the people of the town.

'I think I can take it,' I said at last, and felt a heavy burden fall on me as I said it.

Nerio immediately smiled. 'How long?'

I wanted to shout at him. I had taken part in a dozen sieges – some serious, but mostly failed sieges that had never really amounted to a close attempt. In Bulgaria we'd taken a few towns, but we lacked a really good siege train. Still, riding with the Green Count, who had professional engineers to direct his sieges, had given me a cursory education. Otherwise, mostly I'd ridden with routiers who stormed places at night. Against a garrison of two hundred Catalans, any such storming action was going to be doomed.

But I did have an idea.

'Two weeks, or never,' I said. I tried to sound like Hawkwood – authoritative, firm.

Nerio nodded.

'I will need things,' I said.

'Anything I can get, you will have,' Nerio said.

'I need the bronze gonne from the Genoese galley,' I said. 'It's currently ballast in one of your new Greek dromons.' I was looking at the corner of the citadel that projected out over the stone of the acropolis. 'I need a hundred marble balls chipped for that gonne. I need all the powder you can find me.'

'A trebuchet would be just as powerful, or more so,' said Fiore.

I looked at him. Good friend as he might be, he was not helping.

'What do you suggest as a torsion arm?' I asked, waving my hand in the direction of all of the Morea. Big trees are very rare indeed in Greece. I thought of the deep woods of the shores of the Euxine. 'Get me the bronze gonne.'

Nerio nodded.

'And you may as well summon the garrison and see if they'll just surrender,' I said. 'Bribery and a fair offer now might make them capitulate sooner when we start shooting.'

Nerio looked thoughtful.

As it proved, we sent Marc-Antonio with the summons. He was treated courteously, but the Catalan commander, Francis Lunel, was adamant that he would not surrender the place for love nor money. The civilian governor, Demetrios Rendi, a Greek, demanded that we quit the town.

Marc-Antonio came back to us looking crestfallen.

'They believe they are in a very strong position,' he said. 'And they expect to be relieved from Athens or Thebes.'

Nerio sighed.

I was becoming interested in the challenge.

'Let's try,' I said. 'We have the outer walls. We don't need to do a thing until the gonne arrives except hold the gates.'

Lunel made a sortie that night, trying to retake the main gate. It was well led and relatively silent, but I had a dozen archers out in the town as a tripwire, and we caught his sortie in the streets and shot them up. We captured half a dozen Aragonese gentlemen.

Then passed three very hot days with almost no action. Ewan and Christopher moved archers into the town, and with some care we chose three of the big stone houses to use as bastions. With a mixture of loopholes and heavy wooden shutters, the three houses were fortified in full view of the tower.

The tower didn't have an engine of any kind – not a mangonel, not a catapult. That was important.

Ewan's archers began to exchange shafts and bolts with the Catalans. The Catalans had the advantage of height every time, but Ewan could put five archers up against a single embrasure in the castle. We didn't do the garrison much damage, but we kept them entertained. We had a try at their gate with a ram, but they had heated oil and several embrasures covering the gate. Only darkness and luck got us away with nothing more than László, our Hungarian knight, twisting his ankle.

The next night they tried to storm Ewan's house. That was almost a battle – about fifty men on either side. I think we surprised them with how many men-at-arms were in that house, but they surprised me with their desire to take it, and only daylight ended the street fighting. We'd lost six men, and they'd lost twice that.

The next night, we were all in the three houses. From the loopholes and windows we could see every inch of the base of the castle. The Catalans couldn't get a sortie out.

John and our pages were out in the countryside, watching the roads for a relief column. And bringing us food.

By the seventh day, we were running out of spirit for the whole thing. The archers were low on sleep – it was dangerous all the time at the loopholes. I was moving from house to house, trying to keep everyone encouraged.

The three houses were all a little different. On the lower side of the acropolis, the western side, we had the biggest house, with thick stone walls and heavy shutters and a heavy beam roof supporting red tiles. We called her the Red House. The Catalans were close enough to toss stones from their highest battlement, and when they hit our house the stones would smash the tiles and carry right through. It was a very difficult shot for an archer to lean out, exposing himself, and shoot up into the tower. However, I had plans for this house, as it was ideally situated for my gonne. I was preparing a bed for the bronze tube, at an angle, built into the wall of the house so that it would fire through a shuttered window at the corner of the castle that protruded out over the bare rock of the acropolis.

The second house was above the citadel – that is, it was physically above it, but much lower, of course, than the walls of the castle itself. Still, from the upper windows, Ewan and his best archers had relatively safe positions from which to pepper the defenders in the castle, at least on their lower level. Ewan had most of our crossbows there. Sieges aren't always a good place for the English war bow, because holding a heavy bow at full draw waiting for an enemy to poke his head out is very tiring compared to cocking a crossbow and waiting all day. Anyway, the second house we called the High House.

Our third house was across the market square from the castle gate. It didn't offer us much in the way of shooting at the defenders, but it completely covered the one exit from the castle, and there we concentrated our other archers, and they waited for a sortie to develop. It had blue stucco over the stone of its construction, and we called it the Blue House.

It was an odd sort of siege, as we dug no trenches and had no engine. We did try to set fire to their roof, and they did the same to us, and they did some serious damage to the lower house with hurled stones, as I have mentioned.

It may surprise you, but most of the citizens stayed in their houses. They didn't make trouble for us, and I told every man, to his face, that thievery or rape would be punished by death with no hesitation. I needed the town to remain quiet. I arranged for a market outside the main gate, which I called the 'Athens' Gate because it opened on the road to that famous city. I lacked the soldiers to make sure of the market, or to force the farmers to sell there, and I had to count on their duty to their fellow citizens, or their greed.

In fact, I was taking risks in every direction. My use of the three fortified houses in the place of regular siege lines was forced upon me by circumstance, and I misliked it. I was sleeping very little myself because I could imagine my opponent mustering his full strength – which, I will remind you, was reputed at two hundred men – and pouring out of his main gate, assaulting any one of my three defended buildings, which, in my imagination, he would then take, ending the siege, breaking my company, and perhaps ending my career or even my life, not to mention Nerio's run of fortuna.

I have a very active imagination, as I believe I have mentioned ere this.

The morning of the eighth day dawned, and the harbour was suddenly full of ships. I recognised Nerio's Constantinople-built galleys immediately, and there was a cog flying the Lion of Saint Mark.

Before I'd had my morning cup of warmed wine, Michael des

Roches was standing by me. I was in the main hall of the Blue House, nasty and unshaven and unwashed, watching through the door as my enemies erected wooden hoardings like screens across the castellations of the castle's middle level.

'Gon'a make tha' shootin' harder,' Ewan said.

Behind him, Dick Thorald nodded, his grizzled chin going up and down rapidly. The older man said something, but his thick Cumbrian accent and the sound of the hammering caused me to miss it.

And anyway, my attention was on the scholar.

'I'll have your gonne up here by Nones,' Michael said. 'I found a drawing in one of the Greek texts of Vitruvius. The drawing was far cruder than the text, but it illustrated a way of moving a very heavy stone.' He smiled. 'Shall I explain?'

I shook my head. 'No. Just get it here.'

'It's really quite brilliant,' he insisted.

'Show me when you get it here,' I said. 'Dick, see to it that Master Michael makes it back to the ship without accident. He may give you one – and only one – cup of wine. Then see to it that he comes back here with dispatch. By which I mean, as quickly as he can, with the gonne.'

Dick nodded. 'Aye,' he said. 'A cup o' wine will go down easy.'

At least, I think that's what he said.

I had almost convinced myself that the Catalans would attack before the gonne reached me, and I was not so wrong, either. The sun was setting, and there were sounds from inside the castle. And no gonne.

Thorald came in the back of the Blue House after I'd made my rounds and returned. A young archer who'd joined us in Italy, Sam Turpin, had taken a crossbow bolt in the thigh, and was bleeding out, despite every effort from Magister Albin. I was standing by the two of them, feeling useless and dirty.

'Gonne's stuck in t'a street.' Thorald said.

He jerked his thumb over his shoulder. I could smell the wine on his sour breath even over the smells of blood and faeces and old plaster.

I cursed. I own it. And then, leg armour and all, I followed Thorald out into the dusk. We trotted and hobbled, just the two of us, down the main street which ran to the Athens Gate, and there, at the steepest part of the hill, was my gonne.

Michael was right – whatever ancient had come up with this method of moving a heavy object was brilliant. I didn't require an explanation, either. The gonne had been made into an axle, and had wheels attached. It looked as if it rolled fairly easily. Unfortunately, it had become wedged between two houses, each of which encroached on the street with projecting stone corners.

I don't know what that bronze tube weighed, but I guess it weighed as much as three warhorses. In other words, there was no manoeuvring it past the houses.

Michael des Roches looked crestfallen. 'I'm so sorry, William. I was so sure ...'

'We'll knock down the houses,' I said. 'At least this one. I'll need ...'

'*Libratores*?' asked Michael, in his elegant Latin. 'That's what Maestro Vitruvius calls the men who work on siege engines.'

I took several deep breaths, because Michael did not deserve my torrent of temper, but honestly, why do I surround myself with pedants?

Because I am one myself, you'll say, Master Chaucer, and you have the right of it. But at that moment, I didn't care a fig seed for the Latin name for someone who works on a siege machine.

'I'll need sailors,' I said. 'I don't have any soldiers to spare. Where's Nerio?'

Michael didn't know, and that meant he'd have to go back to the ships in person, with the consequent delay. He had four men and two mules with him. I kept the four men, and Thorald, by a miracle that only old soldiers can invoke, found a pickaxe, and we went to work on the corner of the house after knocking at the door and casting the inhabitants heartlessly on the mercy of their neighbours. Indeed, I tried to be kind, but I was in a tearing hurry. I promised full restoration of the house, but I lacked Nerio's excellent Greek. There were tears and entreaties, and it all took time. And through it all, I worried that removing a corner of the stone would, in fact, cause the whole house to collapse.

I was so close. My gonne was perhaps eighty paces from its prepared cradle.

I thought of a mistake I'd made. I hadn't considered that the gonne tube would have to cross the market square in front of the castle.

I froze, the pick in my hand. I probably unleashed a string of blasphemies that I still regret.

'Dick,' I said. 'You know the Red House?'

''Course I do,' he said.

'I need you to find a route for this monster to get from here to the back of the Red House without passing through the parts the bastards on the walls can see or shoot at.' I waved at the castle.

It was then that I realised I could hear shouting from above me.

Quite a bit of shouting.

Like, a sortie from the castle attacking one of my houses.

Before that moment, I wouldn't have said I had enough energy to walk back to the Blue House. But once I understood our danger, I ran right up the hill. And there before me in the last twilight of the day unfolded my worst nightmare. What looked like the full garrison of the castle was assaulting the Blue House, held by perhaps forty archers and five men-at-arms.

The attackers were all around the house, trying every opening, doors and barricaded windows. I knew from a week in the place that there were three practical entrances on the ground floor – the front door facing the castle gate, a side door on to an alley, and the back door that faced the Athens road. Panting my way up the hill of the acropolis and cursing my sabatons and leg armour, I saw men in maille and heavy cotton gambesons all around the back door. In the door was Fiore, and he had a wounded man at his feet trying to grapple his legs. Even as I watched, he parried an incoming blow, allowed his opponent's sword to push his down, rammed an armoured elbow into the man's face over their hilts, and then, in the same tempo, used his lowered sword to kill the man at his feet with a thrust through an eye socket. He recovered his sword by punching his immediate opponent, the man he'd embowed, with the pommel of his sword, and teeth flew.

I confess, despite Fiore's expertise, it looked hopeless. The Catalans were doing exactly as I'd feared. And my first temptation was to hurl myself like an armoured thunderbolt to the rescue of my friend and my archers.

But, as I have said, my opponents were doing exactly what I'd feared, and I had taken a few precautions. And Fiore, God bless him, was not going to fall quickly to a handful of Catalans, especially as he was using the doorway against them, darting back, forcing them to come into the narrow space on his own tempo.

I turned and ran for the Red House. My plan had been to use Giorgios, my trumpeter, to summon help, but he was inside the Blue House and I was outside, thanks to bad luck, or maybe bad planning. In truth, if you have a trumpeter, he should be with you at all times.

Lesson learnt.

Someone saw me crossing the market square, because a bolt rattled off the peak of my helmet and I stumbled. Running in near darkness in leg armour is difficult enough, and a week of the enemy showering the square with broken tiles and pieces of masonry had made it a nightmare to cross. It was a second miracle that I made it to the side of the Red House without turning an ankle.

No enemy awaited. The Red House was free of assault, although the whole garrison was awake and armed – almost fifty men.

I took all the men-at-arms, leaving Marc-Antonio to command the archers and pages. I was afraid that the enemy would make a grab for the Red House once I led a counter-sortie, but it was getting really dark now, and that didn't seem very likely.

I had the Biriguccis and Beppo and László the Hungarian. La Motte was up at the other house, but I had enough men. Marc-Antonio gave me a clay canteen of water which I drank away, and then we were off. But this time we followed Dick Thorald, who'd found a way through the web of alleys below the crest of the acropolis. We missed our way once, and I was almost glad of it, panting with fatigue while Dick cast about like a hunting dog on a scent, but he found his way and we were off again, out into the Athens road and then back up towards the back door.

Fiore had held that door for fifteen minutes. He'd changed his long sword for a short poleaxe, and he'd put seven men down. The attackers had sent back to the castle for crossbowmen and were waiting, backed around a corner to avoid the accurate archery from the house. But there were men on the tiled roof, and they were trying to fight their way into a hole they'd made.

The men on the street never saw us coming, so focused were they on Fiore. I wasn't in the lead – that was Claudio Birigucci. In five heartbeats we were all at it – a melee that started at the corner of a street and then spread rapidly as both sides threw in more men. Men came around the house from the front while more of our men-at-arms came up from behind me.

It was dark. A few fires flickered. The Catalans had lodged a fire in the second floor of our Blue House, and someone had set another house on fire, close enough that the smoke made things even more confusing. A woman was screaming. A man with a sword in his guts was roaring his despair, writhing on the paving stones of the market square.

I thanked God for full harness. I took more blows there in the time it might have taken to say the Paternoster than I had taken in two years. I just couldn't see – I couldn't see who was on my side, and everyone was in armour. Reinforcements joined from alleys and doorways, and the swirl of the melee moved from the back door of the Blue House out into the main square without plan or strategy. The enemy soldiers on the roofs of the houses threw paving tiles without heed of their friends. My archers weren't much better, as Benghi Birigucci's arrow wound would later prove.

But there were clues, even in the smoky darkness. Beppo, bless him, wore a dark smock over his breastplate, and I knew it immediately in the whirl of the melee. I got next to him, and László knew the beak of my faceplate the same way and joined us. Then Fiore was there, like the Archangel Gabriel.

And, out in the square, we could see – at least a little. And the big stuffed gambesons that the Catalans wore, with heavy collars in place of visors, gave me a target. By then, the melee was five minutes old. Men were gasping desperately for breath, and we were settling out of the chaos into something like lines.

It was a little like watching a stone roll downhill – slow at first and then gathering speed. We sorted ourselves out, and then we went at it again, but now our better armour and better training began to tell and, like the stone racing down, we gathered momentum, pushing them back and back.

I fought one small man whose magnificent moustache showed even with the high collar of his gambeson. He was smaller than me, but quick as lightning, and he knew how to play with a sword. We both landed blows, but they were mostly inconsequential, and then I tried to play close and he almost got the point of his sword inside my visor. My knee met his. I reached for his leg to throw him, and instead found his hand with a dagger in it.

I snapped a punch at him. Most of it was caught by that high collar, but my steel gauntlet clipped his face, and his head went back, and I dropped him with a shove. Over my shoulder, Greg Fox put a spear point to the man's nose, and he raised his arms in surrender.

It was then that I realised that I had no more opponents. They'd broken for their sally port, although they'd had to cross the worst of the broken tiles and dropped stones, and there were half a dozen Catalans lying there, cursing broken ankles or worse.

Crossbow bolts were already rattling on the paving stones. I got a thigh full of splinters where one exploded just behind my leg.

I grabbed my capture under the arms and began to haul him back towards the Blue House. The last survivors of their sortie got in the small sally port that was set in the tower-castle's main gate, and I heard it slam shut like a thunderclap.

They'd left quite a few men outside – half a dozen on the roofs, and another dozen who'd gone to set fires. We had an uncomfortable night, because those few men made as much trouble as the whole original sortie. The Catalans were brave and tough and smart. They moved from house to house, they killed men going to the jakes or getting water from the wells, and finally, Lapot and I had to lead a dozen of our exhausted men-at-arms to hunt them down. We were aided by the screams of townspeople, but the real hero was Pilgrim, In the end, and with the help of an abandoned helmet, he led us to a basement with an outer door – some merchant's warehouse, perhaps, in the lower town. Dawn was breaking in the east.

Pilgrim began barking. It was an angry bark, as if all of our fear and battle rage was translated to my nice dog. I'd never heard him make a sound like that.

Lapot looked at the warehouse. It was really a shop where two streets met – mostly wood.

'Let's just burn it,' he said. 'Kill anyone who comes out.'

I just wanted to get it over with. And to lie down in the dusty street and sleep. And to have Pilgrim go back to being a happy dog. I was sorry he'd got involved.

Instead, I walked forward to the entrance. Steps led down into darkness. There was no door.

'Surrender,' I said, 'and you will not be harmed.'

'You surrender,' came a Catalan-accented voice. Men laughed.

'Our army will be here in two hours,' said another. 'So fuck off.'

'If you don't surrender right now,' I said, 'I will burn this wooden building over your heads and kill you all.'

Lapot, behind me, snorted. I don't blame him.

There was something of a heated discussion. I don't speak any Catalan so I couldn't follow.

'Torches,' I said, and La Motte sent his page running for torches.

Yes, it's true – my little band was basically all officers. No one else was willing to move. I had to pray that the Catalans were no better off, and I didn't like the sound of an 'army' coming to the rescue.

'Let us go back to the tower, and we'll go,' a voice shouted in pretty good French.

'No,' I said. 'Disarmed, as prisoners for ransom.'

'You'll never take the tower,' the man said. His French was very good, and that led me to wonder. 'Let us go back to the tower. It'll all be over when the marshal comes with our army.'

'All the more reason for me to hurry,' I said.

I could see the torches coming. The page was running, and the flames blew out behind him in the early morning light as if he was a herald of the old gods of Greece.

'Please allow me to consider,' he called out.

I could see he'd come to the base of the steps. He was in good white armour, not the heavy gambeson his countrymen favoured.

'Messieur Lunel?' I called out.

'*Oui!*' he responded, and then I heard him curse. 'Ah, well. You are Guillaume le Coq, yes?'

'Yes,' I said. 'And you have until the torches reach me to surrender. I am aware that you are the commander. I promise you on my word as a knight that you will be ransomed.' I had guessed he was the commander – the French, the armour ...

He laughed and showed himself, apparently unafraid that I had archers.

'I propose something else,' he said. 'I will come up the steps and you and I will fight with swords. If you win, we are all your prisoners. If I win, we go back to the tower unmolested. If you dare.' He was teasing, testing my manhood.

'Let me fight,' Fiore said.

I shook my head. 'He wants me. Commander to commander.' I leant down. 'I agree.'

'We fight to the death, or until one cries quarter,' Lunel said.

'I agree. If I cry quarter, you do not take me prisoner.' I leant down. 'As you have me at no other disadvantage here.'

'You bargain like a tradesman,' he said. 'But then, I hear you were a cook.'

'You agree?' I insisted.

'Ah!' he said, and sprang up the steps. Either he was not as tired as I, or he was a great actor.

'Bring up three of your men,' I said. 'Let's have witnesses.'

'You are a man of good honour,' he said. 'Raoul!'

As it proved, two of his household knights and his squire came up. They looked like I felt.

Fiore took over the proceedings. He sketched out a fighting ground with his heel in the dust.

Lapot handed Lunel a canteen full of water.

'Drink,' he said in his Norman French. 'You've had a hard night running away from us.'

Lunel snorted, but he drank the water. The sun rose, casting a rosy glow over the buildings and our armour. I had Greg Fox take my visor off. I wasn't being particularly chivalrous – I wanted to be able to see and breathe.

Lunel drew his sword, which was very long, and saluted. It was an interesting sword, with down-curved quillons, a long hilt and a very narrow blade.

I had a heavy, broad-bladed sword I'd taken off one of the Catalans in the fight at the gate. The blade was broad and the quillons had little drops at the ends that I liked.

I saluted in my turn, and immediately grabbed my sword blade about midway down. This is called 'half-swording', and if you aren't a man-at-arms it may seem odd to grab your own blade, but it's almost perfectly safe. I sharpen different parts of my blade in different ways, which is why I usually sharpen my own sword – very sharp at the tip, almost completely dull in the mid-blade and all the way down to the hilt.

This is probably not the part you wanted to hear, eh?

I stepped forward. He wanted to circle, and I wanted to get it over with. In addition, I'd already decided that I was the better knight. It's difficult to describe, especially as he clearly had a good spirit and plenty of *preux*. But he had not trained the way I had trained. I could tell.

Still, he wanted to probe me, to circle, to drain me of my spirit and maybe break a finger or stab my palm. He flicked blows from his own half-sword garde, aimed at my hands. His attacks were accurate, if not as fast as they might have been.

The third one was deceptively slow. I missed my parry, but his blow was almost out of distance. Almost, but not quite. His point went between the third and fourth fingers of my left hand, cutting both quite badly.

The pain was sudden, and he knew he'd hit me and passed forward, looking to overcome me in one rush. In fact, in the moment of pain, I'd let go of my blade with my left hand. Only my speed and good armour saved me from a fight-ending fall or a stab to the chest. His point scraped across my breastplate, and my back heel skidded and then I was around, clear of his weapon.

My hand worked. The pain was manageable. But now, having wrenched myself around to avoid his rush, my shoulder burned as if hot oil was flowing through my armour.

Now he was eager to play close, sure that he had me.

'If you would care to surrender,' he said, and launched a heavy, overarm thrust with both hands.

Now it was my turn to back and circle. And I was tired. But I turned his blade.

'No,' I said.

'So be it.' He grinned.

He made the same thrust, his arms high, the sword coming down on me from above like a striking serpent.

This time I didn't retreat. I crossed him, not with the foot of long sword that protruded, dagger-like, from my bleeding left hand, but with the *forte* of my blade between my hands. I lifted, rolled his sword off to my left, and clipped his face with my pommel. His head snapped back and I stepped forward, hard and long, looking to get my knee behind his for the throw, but he was fast and well trained. He literally sprang back, despite the weight of his armour, stumbled, and fell flat, his head hitting the dirt of the street with a hollow thump.

Fiore looked at me.

I stood back. It is one of my proudest moments. I hadn't thrown him, and this was public combat, like that in the lists, not some desperate fight in the dark.

'Let him up,' I said.

Lapot grunted disagreement.

I flexed my left hand. His slim blade had gone between my armoured fingers, cutting both, but despite the amount of blood, the fingers worked.

Lunel's squire got him to his feet. He saluted.

I saluted.

Again, I went straight at him. This time, I attacked. I had my sword down by my left side, still at the half-sword. He held his point forward, at the half sword, his hilt on his hip. I swept my sword up so that again I crossed his point between my two hands. He threw all his strength against me, and I allowed him to, letting his point whistle harmlessly past my chest as he over-parried, and stabbing him up under the arm. My broad point never penetrated his maille, or he'd have been dead on the spot, but the pain must have been incredible as about a finger's width of my point went into his underarm. He screamed, and I slammed my pommel into the side of his helmet, turning his head. Even then, he threw a weak but accurate blow, one-handed, as he tried to turn away. The point of his sword slashed my cheek, missing my eye by the width of an arrow shaft. I got my pommel hooked over his neck, my armoured knee behind his thigh, and I threw him quite hard to the street.

This was a fair throw. I put my sword to his open face.

'Yield?' I panted.

'Damn it,' he said. 'I yield.'

He was not the greatest knight I've ever faced. Nor was I incorrect in my belief that I was better trained. But I offer his two blows – the thrust between my fingers, and the half cut at the very end – as examples of why you must never allow yourself to believe any opponent is incapable of putting you down.

And, in the long run, I'm quite glad I didn't kill him. At the time, so much of me hurt that I feared I was worse wounded than I was. And I had no time to savour my victory – not that I would have been allowed to do so – as, the moment the prisoners were under guard, Fiore began to point out the many faults I'd committed.

'Really,' he said, 'it's a shame on me that you were almost beaten by a man so much your inferior.'

I hoped Lunel didn't hear that.

An hour later, and I hadn't managed any sleep. Go ahead – you just try to catch a nap after fighting for your life. I had drunk some water, issued it away, and Albin had washed my hand and my face. He'd poured boiled wine over both, and told me that we had twenty-three wounded from the night's fighting.

You may well ask why I was not more concerned about this 'marshal' and his army. I had reached a place of fatigue and tension where the best I could do was stumble from one decision to another, one crisis to another. I was sure of John the Turk – sure that he would tell me if there was an army on the road.

Nerio appeared with twenty sailors. He was clean and neat in a superb harness that made me feel poor and underdressed for battle.

'Michael is moving the gonne,' he said. 'Where is this army?'

'Army?'

'Lapot says that John de Llúria and the whole feudal host of Athens is coming for us,' he said.

'Lapot is tired,' I said. 'We're all tired.'

'Damn it, Guglielmo! I am risking my fortune ...'

'We are risking our lives,' I pointed out. 'Is it nothing to you that we have their captain? Lunel? We beat their assault. Their spirits must be very low.'

Nerio relented. 'I will certainly pay you double for this night's work,' he agreed. 'I'm sorry, Guglielmo, but we are so close! Even now, my sailors are putting your bronze monster in her cradle.'

'Take no thought for the morrow, brother,' I said. 'Sufficient unto the day is the evil thereto.'

'*Quid sit futurum cras, fuge quaerer,*' put in Michael des Roches. 'Or in the Greek, ἀρκετὸν τῇ ἡμέρᾳ ἡ κακία αὐτῆς.'

Nerio rolled his eyes. 'I'm so glad we're all so well educated.'

At his insistence, we sent Marc-Antonio to the tower with another summons to surrender, including a mention of the capture of their captain, Lunel.

The Catalans refused to surrender. The city's governor, Demetrios Rendi, sent a note promising that he was going to hold until relieved.

While Marc-Antonio trudged back and forth, I was in the Red House, watching a dozen sailors rope our bronze gonne tube to the carriage I'd prepared. Our Greek carpenter had had to make adjustments. The whole thing looked not so much like a weapon as like the wreckage of a small ship on the ground floor of a house.

Marc-Antonio returned at about the same time that I discovered that we only had about ten pounds of prepared powder for the gonne. I'd spent enough time shooting with Carlo Zeno, who was really expert, to know that the powder had to be thoroughly mixed. I sent pages out into the town to find wooden mixing paddles and churns, such as women might use in making butter or stirring cream.

'This is only good for two, or perhaps three shots,' I said. 'It's not enough.'

Nerio started. 'That's not possible!' he cried, and his frustration was plain. And then, 'I promise you, this is all I have.'

I had perhaps as much as would cover the palm of my hand, in a little horn bottle, for a hand gonne.

I do not mean to bore you with the intricacies of command. In fact, if I haven't already said so, La Motte and Lapot and Ser Antonio di Piacenza and Marc-Antonio and Tom Fenton and Ewan and Christopher were all working as hard as I. They made sure men rested in shifts, sent patrols out into the lower town, in case there were yet a few Catalans loose, and watched the gates we held with just a few men each. But we were deep in good leaders, and that counted for us as the eleventh day dawned on our siege, because I didn't have to think about every element of what we were committed to do. I mostly only had to direct – I mean, when I wasn't fighting, or running back and forth.

So I allowed my officers to do their jobs, and I concentrated on the gonne, because that was my business. And my foremost problem was that I didn't really know how to load it. That is, I knew what to do – powder first, then a clod of earth or a wad of cotton or wool, then a marble ball, then a little of my good powder in a goose quill in the touch hole, and bang ...

But how much powder? And would it actually burn? I had very little, but I tested a spoonful and it burned right merrily, with a stench like Hell's own fart. Too little and ... I had no idea what would happen.

I'd heard, from Italians, that too much meant the whole thing would explode.

It is remarkable how good an idea can be, seen at a distance. A week before, the idea of using the gonne to put a breach in the tower had seemed brilliant, or at the very least, workable. Confronted with the reality of the gonne, wrapped in hawser so many times that it looked like a broken sword hilt left in the rubble by a giant, I was ready to despair.

And the worst of it was that there was no one else to lean on. I confess that I enjoy working with other people. All of my life in chivalry, I have had men – aye, and a few women – to whom I could turn. I think of Father Pierre Thomas, Fra Peter Mortimer, Sister Marie, Nerio, Fiore, John Hawkwood, Richard Musard, Count Amadeus, and perhaps most of all, Emile. It may seem a small thing to you, but there I was, tired, gritty, and with the expectations of two hundred men riding on my actions, looking at a device whose mysteries I only barely understood.

Fiore was the most help, as you may expect. He had a long look at the machine, and then pulled at the ropes holding the gonne tube to the carriage, which is a fancy name for a big wooden structure very like a keg stand writ large.

'They're not tight enough,' he said.

It was true – he could get his hands under some of the coils. So, with the carpenter and a dozen sailors, we drove wedges in under the ropes. That took several hours. Down in the lower town, bells rung. I had a nap, as I'd lost count of days and couldn't remember when I'd last been asleep. When I awoke, the carriage was strengthened.

'Bastards ain't shootin' much,' one of my archers mentioned. 'I h'ant seen a head all mornin', like.'

Another curious fact of a siege – this evidence of a failure of the enemy's morale helped my tired lads. It gave them a lift. Suddenly I heard some chatter. Witkin began complaining about the food. Young Blaise Kentman, a page in La Motte's lance, showed his bare arse to the tower and got a gale of laughter from all three defended houses.

Which was good, because one of the sailors – an older man who might have been a Tartar, with his slanted eyes and sallow complexion – finally shook his head. He turned to me and spoke in almost perfect Venetian Italian, which was not the accent I was expecting.

'Rope's too loose, messire. This will fail ... It will fail in a ... spectacular way.' He threw his hands in the air.

'Have you seen a gonne fired?' I asked.

He shrugged. 'No. But I hear tales. And anyway ...' He pulled at the rope. Even with wedges in the loops, he could pull a bit. 'This wouldn't hold a mast in a storm. The powder comes from Hell? Yes? So it is more powerful than a storm.'

We unwrapped the gonne. We stripped off the whole length of cable, which, I promise you, is a terrible job even with a roof to block the sun. In the end, and with Michael des Roches taking charge, we canted the gonne up on an angle with heavy blocks and then unwound the rope. By sunset, we were back where we had started.

Des Roches hung lanterns. We had the big oak doors closed. There wasn't anything the enemy could do to us – not that they'd been active all day. Nonetheless, I got to my feet and pushed myself out of the back of the Red House and around the web of alleys to the Blue House, then up to the top of the town and the High House, checking on sentries, making sure we were prepared. During the day, Ewan had 'borrowed' a church bell – cleverly. He'd taken it from the tiny Latin church and not from the Greek church. It was a small bell, but it made a good sound, and now we had a way of sounding the alarm. And now I kept Giorgios, my trumpeter, with me at all times.

I had now been in my armour for four days. Every strap hurt. There were particles of grit – sand, wool, hairs, I have no idea – but they were everywhere, so that I would stop in the middle of a task and try to scratch something deep inside, under the plate, the chain, the gambeson, the linen shirt ... Good Christ, it was miserable. And so, what I remember best is getting back to the Blue House, and finding that Greg Fox had a cauldron of hot water and a clean shirt waiting for me.

I even got a cup of wine. Friends, it was heaven just getting that shirt off, and there were weals on my body like wounds.

Also, it turned out that some of the 'sores' I'd been scratching for days *were* wounds. Somewhere in the fight in the darkness I'd taken a cut up on my thigh under my cuisse. I know that shouldn't be possible, but there it was, a long, livid line.

Albin came and treated me, rubbing a concoction that was mostly olive oil into everything after it was clean.

I put on a clean shirt, and I really, *really* didn't want to put my harness back on.

Let's be brief . . . I did. And all the straps bit down again.

Despite which, I felt much better. I can't stress this enough – when you can't have sleep, food and cleanliness can help. We had something with a lot of chicken in it that Lapot had cooked down in the town. Greek boys brought kettles of the stuff up and everyone ate as much as they wanted.

I'm telling you these details because that's all war is. It's details. On the evening of the eleventh day of the siege, we all got a rest and a hot meal. I think it made a difference.

I went back to the Red House.

Des Roches was no longer staring at the problem. He was drawing. There was a man I didn't know, obviously a local. Beppo was sitting on a chair, looking pleased with himself.

'Blacksmith,' Beppo said. 'Beppo finds him while others talk too much.'

'Beppo is very clever,' I said.

'Also handsome,' Beppo agreed. 'It wasn't that hard.' He grinned.

For gold, paid on the anvil, so to speak, the smith made four heavy iron straps, the kind that we use to hold a bracket to a beam, or to bind a ship's mast. He spent all night going back and forth to his forge down in the lower town, heating, banding, fitting, and then, before our very eyes, he fitted them and riveted them home, with four men stretching them with levels and little clamps. He had to build the clamps with Michael's help, from drawings. As Michael later explained, they were the same sort of clamps he used to draw wire, simply made much more robust.

And yes, you might not credit it, but you can stretch iron. And that meant that when the rivets went home, the gonne was held tight to the carriage.

I got about four hours of sleep, despite the constant tapping of the smith, and woke to a new day. We hadn't been attacked in the night.

Perhaps it was cleanliness, or the energy of sleep, or even just a cup of wine and a good meal. I weighed one of the marble balls in my hand. It weighed roughly what my good helmet weighs with the aventail on – about sixteen Tower pounds. I know, I had it weighed.

My hell powder was badly mixed. I could see that it had separated during its various journeys. It had probably been made in Italy, and it had travelled all the way out to Constantinople and back. So I took the paddles that my archers had found and began to mix the stuff, myself, in the alley behind the house. I weighed it on a balance beam against my helmet and aventail, and then against the ball. I had about the same weight of mixed powder as the ball.

I had three nicely chipped round marble balls, and two more that were ... not round.

I mixed the powder some more, with my wooden tools. It was bad, in a slow, anxious way. Everyone else hid. No one volunteered to mix the noxious stuff. I turned it and turned it with a broad butter paddle until it appeared the same dusty colour all the way through.

I left the powder barrel out in the alley, and went back to the gonne. It was still early morning. Our adversaries were either not awake or still licking their wounds.

It is often surprising to me how, after you dread something, and worry at it, when you actually come to *doing* it, the labour can pass so quickly. In what seemed like heartbeats, Michael and Fiore and I got the tube aimed at the base of the castle, right where the angle of the tower extended into the street in front of the Red House. We did so without opening the oak doors, because Michael had made marks on the door to indicate our target.

Then I loaded it. Well, I'm still here, so you know it didn't explode. I put the charge down, and packed it with the pole from a butter churn, trimmed by the carpenter. Then I put a big wodge of new wool down the tube and hammered at that a little, terrified every time I thrust my rammer into the wool that the whole thing would ignite.

Nerio came into the chamber where we were working the gonne.

'You weren't going to fire this thing without me, were you?' he asked. 'Here, let me put in the ball.'

'It's dangerous,' I said.

Nerio grimaced. 'If this blows me up, I won't have to watch the destruction of my little realm by the Catalans,' he said.

I gave him the best of the three marble balls. It didn't quite fit down the tube. In fact, it went in about a third of the way and just stuck. Nerio smacked it with the butter churn and then leapt back as if he expected it to bite him.

I just hope that you can picture this, my friends – Fiore, me, Michael

278

des Roches, Lapot, Nerio Acciaioli, Greg Fox and Marc-Antonio – a wall of good knights, brave men who'd seen a hundred battles – all whimpering and flinching from this inanimate thing that sat there.

Des Roches made a sound that just might have been a grunt of contempt, and went to where Nerio had dropped the butter churn as he leapt back. He slammed the implement into the wedged ball, not once but two or three times. Then, as if this was a matter of no moment, he went and fetched one of the blacksmith's hammers, and with two hard taps, drove the stone ball down tight against the powder. He gave us all the sort of look my Emile used to give other women when she picked up a dead mouse and threw it into the fireplace. *She* would never have shown fear of that machine.

Ah, well.

With trembling hands – I admit it! – I put a little of my good powder into a goose quill. I put the quill into the touch hole at the breach of the gonne, forcing it down until I could feel it bite against the grainy hell powder deep in the breach.

The whole process had taken perhaps five minutes.

No one, not even Michael, was eager to touch it off.

'This is my *empris*,' I said, after a longer hesitation than was quite right. 'I'll do it.'

I ordered them all out of the room. In fact, I sent everyone into the alley behind the Red House. While they were clearing out, Marc-Antonio attached a long beeswax taper to a spear shaft. Des Roches and the carpenter opened the oak doors facing the street and the black wall of the tower. We weren't going to miss.

Finally, they were all gone, and I was left alone with my lit taper. Outside, the sky was a beautiful blue. Down in the town, cocks were crowing. Somewhere, a dog barked. Pilgrim was safely tied up down at the gate.

I had wax in my ears, like the wily Odysseus, and I was in full armour with my helmet on and my visor down. I leant out . . .

And the taper went out. I had probably moved it too fast.

I had to go outside and have it lit again by Marc-Antonio. There was some nervous laughter.

I went back in, shielding my taper. I had that feeling that I just wanted to get it over with. I leant out, and moved the taper to the quill . . .

There was a fizzing sound, and fire spat straight up out of the quill. And then a delay that seemed eternal ... I swear I could have counted to ten, although Marc-Antonio said it was immediate.

And then a sort of long bang. The room where we'd put the gonne filled instantly with smoke, shot with fire, and something hit me, hard, in the faceplate. I was knocked flat.

Our marble ball blew a big hole in the foundation of the tower, undermining the corner and shaking the whole structure. But, apparently, a piece of our ball bounced back, taking out a big section of the room in which we'd lodged our gonne. After all, we were shooting across an alley perhaps ten feet wide. Pieces of dislodged stone hit me. The one that hit my visor hit me pretty hard, but that's what armour is for.

The gonne itself had become dislodged from its carriage, bending the hoops that had bound it like a devil escaping from Hell. The bronze tube had shot across the room and bounced off the stone steps, wrecking them. Plaster and lath and bits of fresco continued to rain down.

And that was one shot.

I find it fascinating that I now have Master Chaucer on the edge of his seat while you, Monsieur Froissart, look bored. But it is my tale to tell and I will tell it.

It took the whole rest of the day to rebuild the carriage, the hoops, and the room from which we fired. Nerio's sailors became the stars of the siege, because they seemed to know how to do everything. The one who looked like a Tartar was Giacomo, who was apparently born in Syria somewhere but considered Venice home. He was their leader, and he seemed to be the embodiment of a 'jack of all trades'. With our carpenter, the smith and three archers, he cleared away the rubble that had been the stairs, and used levers to move the carriage and then the gonne tube.

By this time, the defenders were awake to their new peril and had begun to fight back, shooting crossbows down at us to the best of their ability. The late afternoon had developed into something like a skirmish, with Ewan and his best archers trying long bowls against the crossbowmen up in the tower. Christopher got into it, with the two best pages using their crossbows against the garrison from the far side, but the tower had all the advantages of height. Our carpenter refused to go back into the Red House until the crossbowmen stopped shooting.

I wasn't accomplishing anything at the Red House, as Giacomo and Michael were in charge, so I went back to the Blue House. I ate a piece of mutton and a big chunk of bread, and then had a look at the shot-stour from Ewan's perspective.

He and three other excellent archers were taking turns to loose from what had once been the balcony of the house, now fortified with old doors and a slab that might have been a grave marker. At this range, men moving in the tower were just shiny dots as their helmets moved along a distant parapet.

'I don't think I've hit a damned thing all day,' Ewan said.

'Nor I,' muttered Dick Thorald. 'Waste o' shafts.'

The garrison had put up wooden hoardings on the tower, so that they were protected from arrows even between the crenellations. I watched a crossbowman, in flickers. I knew where he was as he moved back and forth, and then stood, spanning his weapon. Ewan, one of the best archers I've ever seen, lofted an arrow at him, and it was well shot. It just cleared the hoardings by a finger's breadth, and we heard it rattle around on the stone of the parapet.

But the crossbowman finished winding his weapon, and then, as if he had all the time in the world, he took his shot. I heard the scream.

One of the sailors was hit.

There are some things you have to do yourself when you are in command. I walked back across the dangerous rubble to the Red House, where I encouraged the sailors and begged the carpenter to finish re-laying the gonne. Nerio promised money – they all agreed.

And then I went back to the Blue House, moving like a sore old man, which I was, to all intents. There I sent Giorgios for my baggage, which proved to be in a good room upstairs – the room in which I'd bathed, in fact. And there, having followed me around for a year, was my little hand gonne. Not so little – about the size of a good poleaxe.

I went back to the armoured balcony and loaded my hand gonne. Already, the adventures of the morning had made me surer with my loading. I wasn't as afraid of the hell powder as I had been on board ship.

It really wasn't that far across the market square – perhaps thirty paces. And I could rest the stock of the hand gonne on the stone slab that acted as a wall for the balcony.

We'd done a fair amount of shooting on the ship, but not at thirty paces. On the other hand, my target was almost at my level, and I was aiming at the hoarding. The man appeared, as I say, in flickers. He wore a dusty blue gambeson, and sometimes the Greek sun shone on his kettle helmet. I certainly knew where he was.

He began to wind his weapon. Over to my left, I heard Giacomo shouting at someone to *push harder, dammit.*

I had a little length of match. It's just cotton cord, impregnated with hell powder and a little urine. It occurred to me that I should be using the match to light the goose quill on the gonne, and then my hand moved. I touched my burning match to the touch hole on my gonne and she barked like an annoying little dog. Very different from the noise of the great gonne.

'Ya missed,' Ewan said. 'You turned yer head away. Yer whole body flinched. My lord.'

In fact, I'd missed the tower. I know it doesn't seem possible, but then, I'm a knight and not an archer.

'Let me,' Ewan said.

I loaded it for him, and he rested it on the slab as I had, took a long breath and then let it out.

'Light it,' he said.

I did, pressing the match at the touch hole.

Ewan, not used to the damned thing, got a face full of vented flame that singed his eyebrows. I supposed I should have told him *why* I'd turned my head away, but his comments rankled.

Thirty paces away, the crossbowman was flopping like a gaffed fish – a gruesome sight. He took too long to die, and we both felt ... guilty.

But Ewan shot him, right through the wood of the hoardings.

No more crossbowmen came up to challenge our gonne crew.

A little after the Greek church down in the town rang its bell for Vespers, we had the gonne loaded again. I think that I was more afraid for the second round than for the first. Even a cursory examination of the damage had shown me that I'd missed being killed by a piece of ricocheting marble by about two feet. My afternoon's adventure with Ewan had shown me how unreliable the damned things were.

The future of warfare, my arse.

Regardless, when we were ready, Nerio insisted on touching her off.

'This is my little empire to win or lose,' he said. 'You gentlemen have done all the work and taken most of the risks. Let me do this one thing.'

Neither Fiore nor I argued so much, either.

We went out in the alley, and Nerio used my dwindling supply of slow match to touch off the gonne.

This time, because of Giacomo's efforts, the gonne didn't leave the cradle, or carriage. The whole thing, according to Nerio, hopped like a frog.

The twenty-pound stone ball slammed into the corner of the castle tower, just to the right of the first hole. We were precise, because the range was fifteen feet.

I saw it happen. The powder smoke, the smell, the noise, and then a second motion, from the tower. There was some dust, and the corner of the tower subsided. There's no better word. It just slid down a little, and stopped, and then slid some more, until about a ten-foot gap had opened all the way up the wall, so that we could see into the garrison quarters on the second floor.

A woman screamed, and then was silent.

So, just so you understand. We'd opened a breach, something like a huge crack, all the way up the tower. But that meant that the breach faced across fifteen feet of alley to our gonne, with nothing between them but smoke.

Luckily I had a dozen of the best knights in Outremer right there, watching the action. We went immediately to the breach and stood there, protecting our gonne for as long as a Mass might take. They tried two attacks – one through their main gate, that failed before it started, and another, bolder sortie through the breach towards our gonne. But the breach was so narrow and so irregular in shape that men could only come out one at a time.

Eventually, Witkin got a ladder and got three archers to the ruined upper storey of the Red House, where they could sweep the breach with war bows. The sortie gave up and retreated, leaving two wounded men behind.

I was leaning on my poleaxe, wondering if I could get them to surrender, when Marc-Antonio said there was a messenger from the gate. It was the boy, Blaise Kentsman.

'My lord!' he said. 'John – that is, John the Turk! He is at the gate! He says there's an army marching for us.'

Just getting down to the gate was about all I could force my body to do. It was full dark by the time I walked down to the outer wall. I remember that all the way down the hill I cursed myself for not taking off my shoes and emptying out the gravel from the rubble around the gonne.

War! Glory! Honour!

Gravel inside your arming shoes.

I went out through the sally port, a small side gate set into an angle in the outer wall.

'John,' I said.

He was sitting on a steppe pony, and he was alone.

He turned slowly and nodded, and for a moment I thought he was wounded.

'Yes,' he said. 'By the good God, William, I am tired.'

'Me, too,' I said, or something like it.

'Our enemies have purchased themselves a small army of Turks,' he said. 'Perhaps two or three hundred. You remember a red-haired bandit called Everenos Bey?'

'How could I forget him?' I said. 'He was like my brother.'

John grunted, or perhaps chuckled without mirth. 'I ambushed your brother yesterday, under the mountain by Vlachada,' he said, and shrugged. 'What are my chances of getting a cup of wine?'

I sent my trumpeter for wine.

'I didn't hurt him much, but I embarrassed him, maybe.' John looked sly. 'I think Greece makes the Turks lazy.' He looked out to sea. 'Maybe it is just fighting Franks.'

'Everenos Bey is commanding the Catalans?' I asked. I was tired, but the Morea was fucking complicated.

John shook his head. 'No, no. John de Llúria commands. He has perhaps a hundred men – a few knights, mostly crossbowmen on good horses. And he has hired Everenos Bey.' John smiled grimly.

Giorgios appeared with a wine skin. 'The men inside say it is terrible wine,' he ventured.

John and I produced our cups and filled them. By the gate's torch-light, the wine appeared to be brown, not red, and it had an acrid tang. It was indeed terrible.

We drank it anyway.

'How long can you keep them off me?' I asked.

John looked down the plain of Megara towards Athens, and his craggy face was a profile against the sky and the rising stars.

'Maybe tomorrow,' he allowed. 'If I am *fucking* clever. Can you give me any men?'

'Perhaps twenty,' I admitted.

I wasn't really eager to give away any of my precious men, but I could, in my endless series of gambles, wager that the garrison was not going to make another sortie.

'Twenty could be enough,' he said. 'Knights?'

'*Certo*,' I agreed, and went back to organise it.

La Motte and twenty men-at-arms rode off with John across the plain of Megara. I was left with a few over one hundred unwounded men.

Around midnight, I sent Marc-Antonio to the tower under a flag of truce. After some negotiations, the mayor, or governor of the place, Rendi, agreed to meet me for breakfast, in the open market square. Each of us was to bring two men.

Demetrios Rendi didn't look Greek. He was tall, well-built, and his skin was a deep brown, but his eyes were green. In ten sentences I could see why the Catalans had a Greek governor here. He was well educated, with fluent Italian and educated Greek, and far more Latin than I'd ever manage. He brought with him a woman, who proved to be his daughter, Maria, and a priest, who proved to be Fra John Boyle, a Dominican priest from Ireland.

I brought Michael des Roches and Nerio. My intention had been to show how civilised I was. My archers had the square covered from three sides and the gonne was loaded. I had little fear for my safety. But as it proved, I'd made a brilliant choice, because Rendi took to Michael immediately.

We had warm bread and olive oil, some cheese and a copper of hippocras, sitting at a narrow table that was really just some boards thrown on wooden horses. My pages had found us benches, and we sat in the morning sun and ate with relish. The young woman was beautiful – I probably should have said that immediately. She had translucent skin, slightly slanted eyes and jet-black hair, and Nerio could not take his eyes off her.

'What do you offer as terms?' Rendi asked.

'The garrison may take their personal belongings and march away to Athens,' I said.

This had been discussed in advance with Nerio, of course.

Rendi nodded. 'I live here,' he said. 'This is my city.'

Nerio kept looking at his daughter. 'You fought well,' he said. 'I can be a good lord. I'm not planning to punish you.'

Rendi looked away. And then back. 'I brought my Maria to show you that I am tied here. May I have five days to wait for relief? If I am not relieved in five days by my feudal lord, I will surrender on these terms.'

Nerio looked at me.

I got to play the bad mercenary. That was my role, and I'd certainly seen John Hawkwood do it well.

So I tried to play it like Hawkwood. I smiled and leant forward.

'Messire,' I said, 'if you turn your head just a little, you can see where our great gonne is emplaced at the base of your tower.'

He looked, and he was a little paler under his brown skin.

'Yes, I see,' he said.

I sat back. 'I'm glad you see. Because we don't have to wait five days. My men are tired and hungry. When I fire that gonne, which is loaded, more of your tower will fall. You understand, yes? Because then we will storm it.'

Maria turned absolutely white. '*Theo mou*,' she said. I knew enough Greek to understand 'My God'.

I nodded. 'We have better armour and better weapons, and your tower is no longer defensible.' That was quite an exaggeration. And he had at least as many men in the tower as I had outside.

Rendi glanced at me with hate, and then at Nerio. 'My lord, I was given this place to hold by Roger de Llúria, and I will be punished if he feels I did a poor job.'

Nerio tore his glance away from the beautiful maiden and looked at Rendi.

'Ah, messire, but you aren't thinking this through,' he said. 'If you surrender today, you will be under my protection. As will your daughter.' He nodded in her direction. 'And if you do not … Why, we can all try the fortunes of war.'

Rendi, who was obviously a brave man, winced. Because he had his daughter with him in the tower, and he was not willing to risk her.

I didn't much fancy my role here, and I was thinking of my own children. Suddenly, amid the emptiness of the last few weeks, I discovered a longing to see them again.

'Give me until tomorrow,' Rendi said. 'I beg you. So I may be said to have defended my castle for two weeks.'

Nerio glanced at me. He had everything riding on this.

I didn't want to storm the castle. I would lose men, and other men would do foul things, and I'd have to bear the weight of it. John could probably buy us a day.

'I will expect your surrender at dawn tomorrow,' I said, 'as the rim of the sun touches the mountain.'

Nerio gave me a little nod.

'Until then, I give my word not to attack the castle, if you will give your word not to attack me. If you do not surrender at dawn tomorrow, I fire the gonne, and storm you.' I tried to sound as deadpan as Hawkwood would have done.

'May I speak to my captain? I know you have him as a prisoner.' Rendi looked at us. 'I know I can expect no quarter from you gentlemen, but I am not a professional soldier and I don't know what my responsibilities are.'

Damn it, I liked him.

Nerio was eating Maria with his eyes, so he was no help at all.

I left Michael to make polite and educated chatter, and I went and fetched Lunel.

Lunel walked off about ten steps with Rendi. They spoke for two minutes, and then embraced.

Rendi came back. 'I agree to a truce until dawn. If I am not relieved, I will surrender.'

Nerio nodded, rose, and bowed to Maria, most graciously.

Lunel leant over to me. 'I just did you a favour.'

'How so?'

'I told him the truth – that Llúria and his Turks won't have the *cojones* to come and winkle you out of this place. They might ride around outside, but the Turks are useless in a siege and they won't die for Llúria anyway.'

'And you did me this favour,' I said, 'which I agree is a favour, because ...?'

Lunel shrugged. 'Oh, I suspect I'll need a job, now.'

As usual with the siege of Megara, nothing was easy. About an hour before the bells should have rung for Vespers, one of the older pages came riding up to the gate. By a stroke of rare *good* fortune, I was at the main gate of the outer wall, visiting my outposts and discussing our next moves with Fiore, who had the gate guard.

The boy, almost a man, was tall, gangly, and both tired and proud. He was one of our Italian pages – Andreas something or other.

'Ah, Ser Guglielmo! *Illustrio!* Captain John says you must come with all your strength – that he has chosen you a battlefield.'

'*Chosen me a battlefield?*' I muttered.

I looked at the boy. 'Chosen me a battlefield for what?' I asked.

Andreas's eyes grew wide. 'Captain John sent you a message this morning, *Illustrio*. The Turks have got past our little trick and now they will be marching here. John asked that you bring the Company out to fight.'

Sweet Saviour of mankind, I thought.

'How long ago did you send me this message?' I asked.

'Five hours,' the boy said. 'Oh, by the blessed Virgin, messire, do not tell me you never received it? That was my friend ...'

It had been a long two weeks, and many things had gone wrong. One of the positive elements in having a long, hard siege and a friend like Fiore is that you start discussing every possible scenario.

'Very well,' I said. 'Andreas, I'm going to need you to change horses and ride straight back to "Captain" John.'

Of course, John deserved rank. He was perhaps the most indispensable member of our force, and sometimes Fiore and Nerio and I agreed that he, not we, should be in command.

But that was not the crisis facing me.

Fiore, who was standing by, brought the boy one of his own Arab horses, a dark mare with powerful haunches.

'Tell John we never received the first message,' I said. 'And tell him that I need to play a little trick here. So we won't reach him until midnight. I'll need guides. Where is he now?'

Andreas pointed back east. 'Most of the way to Elefsis,' he said, 'over by Athens. We hit their flocks and burnt barns last night.'

The boy was proud. He'd probably ridden fifty miles in a day.

And now I knew how John had bought us time to win the siege – by attacking Athens, or, at least, burning their farms.

Poor peasants.

'I need to understand,' I said. 'You raided into the territory of the marshal, and drew the Turks and the Catalans away?'

'Yes, my lord. But when I left Captain John, the Turks were beginning to understand how few we were, and were getting bolder. And John said, "Tell Guglielmo that I will find him a battlefield in the Pass of Megara, between the mountains and the sea."'

It's another of Hawkwood's sayings – always make messengers repeat their messages several times. Do you note that there was a great deal more information in the second repetition?

'Right,' I said. 'Now I understand fully. Tell John "midnight".'

Young Andreas saluted and turned his horse.

'Give the boy some food and a canteen of water,' I said.

I had a great deal to arrange, but thanks to several conversations with Lapot and Fiore, we already knew what we were going to do.

My people had a busy evening, but this is where all the training of a winter in Constantinople paid off like gold in your hand. Men marched around in all directions in the town. I hadn't promised my adversary not to move men, only not to attack him. My men moved around so much – helped by some donkeys towing branches – that they raised dust in the evening air.

In fact, I moved a light garrison of twenty men into the Red House. And I abandoned both of our other positions. Then my whole force slipped away, down the back of the acropolis to the gate, where I left ten men under Nerio. Why Nerio?

Because if my ruse was successful, he was going to accept the surrender of the garrison in the morning.

Our whole plan was held together with catch and clay, as my mother used to say. But I didn't have another army, and I was so desperate that I pressed Nerio's sailors into service holding the Red House, although they were patently not interested in fighting.

And then, in full darkness, I mounted one hundred and seven men in the ground in front of the gate, which wasn't visible from the castle, or so I had to hope. We had almost no pages, because most of them were away with John. It could have been chaos as we sorted out the horse herd. It might have been chaos just getting the whole company armed and equipped in darkness and silence.

Here's what you get for a winter of training. Not only were they all ready, but Ewan and Christopher had decided that they should appear as if on parade in Constantinople, the better to overawe our opponents. Extra time had been spent polishing, and every man had his surcoat on.

You do not need to be a great commander when you have such people serving you.

We rode off as the convent, now high above us to the east, rang Compline. I was all too aware that the Turks might already be on the plain of Megara, and that I was taking yet another enormous risk, but I remained confident in John. If the Turks had got past him in the valley, he'd have told me. Still, bereft of my Kipchaks and all my trained pages, I had to send Christopher and some veteran archers out as scouts.

To our immense relief, they found a Kipchak guide waiting where one of the mountain monastery roads crosses the road from Megara to Athens. It was one of our boys from the slave market, now carrying a fine sabre and wearing a good Spanish basinet with a long spiked top and an aventail big enough to be a shirt of maille on the young man.

He had no Italian or Greek or English, but simply waved and rode off. We followed, riding under the magnificent whirl of stars that is a night in Greece. Dogs barked in the villages we passed. The sea hissed against the shore to our right, and after an hour or so, we could hear the ethereal sound of the Greek nuns singing another praise to God high above us.

Shortly after, we met a second guide, no more verbose than the first. He pointed us forward, and we rode into the throat of the pass. The road from Athens to Megara passes along the foot of a great ridge, or series of conjoined mountains that loomed to our right, blocking off the stars. High above, a few lights flickered – shepherds, perhaps, with fires.

We climbed a ridge in moonlight, and there was John, sitting on his horse like an ancient centaur in the darkness.

'So,' he said. 'I sweat blood and you have nice ride.'

Since his Italian was as good as mine, I assumed he was on edge, or excited, or both.

His chosen battlefield was excellent. It also demonstrated to me why Megara had never been taken by Athens in the ancient world, at least according to Michael. He was reading several texts all together, and telling us the tale at our campfires, event by event, so that my archers were living the Peloponnesian War even as we tried to take Megara.

But I've left my road. We were atop a low ridge, a finger of the great mountain beside us that ran down to the sea, so that the beach-side road had to climb up a double switchback to reach the top. Best of all, the top of the ridge was crowned in deep pine woods – ancient trees, tall and hale, with a soft carpet of needles underfoot and no undergrowth. A mailed knight could ride among the trunks without fear of being dismounted, and archers could wait concealed, in shade. The ridge was only about five hundred paces from end to end, but the last two hundred paces on the left, or mountain side, were so steep and precipitous as to cover our flank against any but winged angels.

A three-hundred-pace front. We had about two hundred men. The road crossed the ridge almost at the sea.

I didn't prepare the way I would have to face the French, or even Italians. My opponents were, according to John, about a hundred men-at-arms in somewhat antiquated armour, meaning maille and leather, and three hundred Turks with very dangerous bows and superb horsemanship. They'd have some good light armour, too.

But I didn't think they could get around us, and that meant they'd have to come up the ridge. And I thought that my men-at-arms were the match of theirs, by means of training, and by quality of armour. And I thought that my English, Hungarian, Picard and Italian bow-men – and one Mamluk – were, in this situation, a match for the Turkish archery.

Maybe.

The moment I made my dispositions, I set a forward picket of pages, and ordered everyone else to gather some sleep. The Kipchaks and pages, who had been awake for two days, were out before I was done speaking.

If you're interested, I heard a bit of the story from John later. Sadly, he is so modest that he won't embellish it to make a better tale, but you can just ask him yourself, Monsieur Froissart. Anyway, John opened his campaign with a daring raid on Everenos Bey's horse herd and led him a merry dance through the rough ground of western Attica, burning barns and stealing sheep and horses until the Turks finally reacted with their whole force. Then wily John slipped away over the same tracks we'd used to get into Megara in the first place – tracks that the Turks didn't know.

And Marshal Llúria apparently lost his temper, recalled the Turks, and ordered the whole force into motion to attack Megara, having lost days chasing John around Athens.

So when I tell you this whole tale, remember that all of the knightly contests and deeds of arms of which I tell you were enabled by a double dozen Tartars and as many Italian pages, riding through nights and days.

So, there we all were. I drank a cup of well-deserved wine and slept for six hours. I rose to find that Marco had a fire going behind the ridge. I got a cup of warm wine with spices.

It was a magnificent morning, with the sun just rising across the bay that lay between the isle of Salamis and the mainland. There were fishing boats just setting out into that bay, and I wondered, as I sometimes do, what it would be like to have a simpler life and not be risking death that morning.

The Catalan 'army' of perhaps four hundred and fifty men appeared at mid-morning. Thanks to all that training about which I keep bragging, my people were fed and our animals watered. They were all sitting or lying flat, and everyone was in full shade. I was well up the 'finger' of the ridge, a little north of the middle, where I had the best view. I was mounted on Artemis, with Pilgrim bouncing around the ancient woods, chasing squirrels and anything else that moved – sunbeams, probably.

Behind me, in Megara, Rendi had either surrendered to Nerio or he had not. I couldn't affect that. If I won this very small battle, I'd have a free hand to take the damaged castle. If I lost, it wouldn't matter a damn whether Rendi had surrendered or not, because the Catalans would just take it back.

I had plenty of time to enjoy the morning, and my relative freedom from the dark despair that had dogged my last months. I didn't agree with Fiore about Hawkwood, but I did agree with both Fiore and Sister Marie that it was time I did something useful with my life. Win or lose, I'd need to recruit some new men, and I was determined to see my children, and even play a role in their lives. And I'd promised Fontana I would look after his sister, and I had the idea that maybe she'd be pleased to be a governess. If you think these are odd thoughts for a commander on the day of battle, they were. I was curiously calm, even confident. It wasn't the absolute confidence of victory; more the knowledge that what could be done, had been done.

When Fiore joined me, I had just finished arming, with Marco hauling my kit out of the baskets that a very annoyed donkey had hauled up the ridge. I was clean and neat and I'd shaved.

'You know,' Fiore said, 'Nerio likes to mock me for failing to observe things that aren't about fighting.'

That was a typical greeting for Fiore, by the way. He never had any small talk of any kind.

'That's true,' I said.

Fiore nodded. 'I know it. So I will content myself in saying, you look better, Guglielmo.'

I took his hand. 'Thanks, brother. I feel better.'

He nodded. 'They outnumber us stoutly,' he said.

I grinned. 'I think I will risk a boast,' I said. 'And I say that, despite every disappointment of the last two weeks. Unless the Turks have horses that fly, or our old companion Everenos has the wisdom to send a party through the hills to outflank us, there is no advantage in numbers that will take this ridge.'

Fiore smiled. And he put a hand on my arm – a rare gesture from him, as he was not a man who liked to be touched. 'I like it when you are like this, Guglielmo,' he said.

We watched Llúria's banner move forward until they were perhaps half a mile away. And then, after a half an hour's wait, during which his men sweated on their horses and my men reclined in the shade, three black dots detached themselves and rode forward.

'They'll come to the road,' I said. I assumed it was a herald. 'I'll ride down. Care to join me?'

'Of course,' Fiore said. 'Do you know what worries me?' he asked.

We were riding through ancient woods so magnificent they might

293

have been made in the dawn of the world, under a sky of heart-aching blue. Not a bad day to die, if it came to that.

But I didn't think it would come to that.

'No, my friend,' I said. 'I never know what would worry you.'

Fiore ducked under a branch and pointed at the distant Catalans. 'It worries me that when I'm a small-time lord in the hills above Udine, I will miss all this.'

I didn't need to answer. No one, except a madman, thinks war is good. But the time before – the camaraderie, the training, the preparations ...

We came to the back of our position on the road. The pages had taken down just two of the great trees and dropped them across the road. We had to ride quite a way to go around them.

Soon enough, three men rode up the ridge to us. One was Everenos Bey. The other two were strangers. As one carried the banner of Marshal Llúria, I assumed the other was the man himself. He'd had smallpox as a boy and his face was badly marked. Otherwise, he was a well-armoured gentleman of middling size.

He reined in perhaps ten paces away. I thought of my last armoured parley, with the Tartars and Tuqtamis. Llúria was not as impressive, but he had something of the Tartar's calm. And his horse was damned good.

Everenos Bey didn't rein in. He gave a whoop and rode right up to me.

'It is a long way from Didymoteichon,' he said.

I embraced him. 'Have you come down in the world, brother,' I asked, 'that you are fighting for this infidel?' I knew he understood Italian.

He smiled. 'I do the will of my Sultan in all things save where it touches on my religion,' he said.

Everenos Bey is a Turk, a man of honour, a great captain among his people. We had met before, at a tournament at Didymoteichon, one of the cities that the Turks have taken from the Romans, or Byzantine Greeks.

'You two know each other?' Llúria asked. This was clearly not a turn of events that he expected, or relished.

Everenos Bey nodded sharply. 'We do,' he said, without elaboration.

'Have you come to parley, or merely look over my arrangements?' I asked Llúria.

His eyes narrowed, although perhaps it was just the glare of the midday sun.

'I came to order you to desist and go back to your bolt-hole in Corinth,' he said. 'We don't need your Florentine gold here, and you will, if I have my way, be punished by the King of Aragon.'

I waited a bit, to be sure he was finished.

'For my part, my lord,' I said, 'the city of Megara and its castle surrendered to us this morning, at the end of a period of truce that we negotiated with your captain and your governor. As to your King of Aragon, my lord Renario Acciaioli is Duke of Corinth under the Prince of Achaea and the King of Jerusalem by right of tenure, and also has the blessing of the Emperor in Constantinople. And finally, my lord, I can't imagine that you have the soldiers or the time to break through my men to Megara and lay siege to it, so why not save blood and treasure and ride home?'

Llúria sat calmly, leaning slightly forward, with his arms crossed on his high saddle bow.

'You are not this Renerio Acciaioli?'

'I have not that honour,' I said. 'I am Sir William Gold.'

I'd love to tell you that he quailed away in fear, but instead his lip curled and he shook his head.

'Never heard of you,' he said, and I'm pretty sure that was an honest reaction. 'How much would I have to give you to move out of my way?' he asked.

I shook my head. 'I am not available for sale, my lord,' I said. 'Perhaps it will save time in these negotiations if I say that Lord Renerio is one of my firmest friends.'

'Bah,' he said. 'You Italians all sell your friends on a regular basis. How about one hundred ducats of Venetian gold?' He smiled. 'Paid immediately?'

'My lord couldn't buy my horse for this amount,' I said, which was true. I was on Gabriel.

'You seem determined to insult me, and yet I am offering you every consideration,' he said, very reasonably.

I thought of a few really stinging replies, but I was mature enough as a commander to realise that if I could bring him to refuse battle by any means, I was saving my men's lives. No position is so superior that some wouldn't die to hold it.

'I mean no insult, my lord,' I said. 'But I will not be bribed, and you cannot force this road.'

Everenos had listened patiently. Now he looked at me with a raised eyebrow.

'You have not faced us before,' he said. 'You may find us a more difficult foe than you expect.'

I bowed in the saddle. 'My lord Bey,' I said in my best Italian, 'I agree, and every battle is a test of fortune, is it not? And the will of God? But I might also say the same of you, Everenos, my brother. You have never faced us. Except in a tournament. And think of how that went.'

He flushed. 'Games,' he said.

Me and my mouth. I had angered him.

'We shall see how long you can hold this ridge,' Llúria said. 'Don't tell me, when your corpse is picked by crows, that I didn't warn you. The Turks are deadly, and I will give no quarter. As you are mercenaries in service of a pirate.'

I nodded. 'Of course, in that case, I'll be dead,' I said. 'And not telling you anything.'

Everenos laughed. He flicked his riding whip, a debonair gesture, as if acknowledging my wit, which made me smile. Llúria frowned and rode away with his banner.

Fiore grunted. 'You are not particularly diplomatic, I find.'

The Turks came first. They rode up the ridge in a loose line, two or three horsemen deep, and they came up steep spots I wouldn't have thought a rider could cover. But their horses were not magical, and they slowed as they came on.

Perhaps a hundred paces from the top, when most of them were riding across bare rock, orange-white in the brilliant sun almost directly overhead, Ewan led fifty archers out of the woods. They were also in a loose line. Most of them took their time putting a few shafts into the light soil.

At about seventy paces, Ewan's line let fly.

The Turks took a few hits, and rode back down the ridge. Ewan's archers walked forward, collected the wounded and picked up their shafts.

Before a slow priest could have said the Mass, another party of

Turks tried the highest part of the ridge on my far left. Before they were halfway up, John and his Kipchaks were dropping arrows on them from the heights above. I'm not sure we hit anything, but the Turks rode away.

Well beyond long bowshot, from my high vantage point, I saw Everenos ride up to the banner. In my mind, he was saying 'This is not practical' to Llúria. Llúria, of course, demurred.

Eventually, in my mind, Everenos told his paymaster to have a go for himself. I only say this because as the bells rang in the high convent for Nones, and the sun began to slant down from behind us, right into the eyes of our attackers, the Catalan horses came forward. They weren't in any hurry, but it was clear they planned to force the ridge at its lowest point, by the sea.

And that's where all my men-at-arms waited. I rode down to join them, and met Nerio.

'He surrendered at dawn,' Nerio said. 'If you can break contact and withdraw, we can hold the city walls forever. His Turks will just ride away.'

I nodded. 'About thirty minutes too late,' I said. 'Now, will he try for the beach, or the road?'

Indeed, at the lower end of the ridge, the road ran into a man-made gully carved right out of the rock. We'd filled it with trees. But if Llúria was really bold, he'd have a go at the beach, which was flat and open.

He had about a hundred men-at-arms, some of whom wouldn't even have qualified as 'light horse' in Italy. I had fifty of my men-at-arms, and most of them were in steel cap-à-pie. Our horses were superb, if I may say, and we'd trained all winter.

I nodded at Nerio. 'If he comes in the beach, I'll meet him on horseback,' I said. 'You and your squire would, of course, be welcome.'

Nerio smiled. 'I wouldn't miss it,' he said. 'Damn, my friend. If we can take Llúria, you could save me a lot of time in taking Athens.'

'Shh,' I said. 'No tempting providence.'

The beach was a narrow strip, with gravel on the upper reaches that was soft and not really good footing for a warhorse. The centre of the beach was good sand – soft, but not too soft. The last fifteen or twenty feet before the sand met the water was wet, and hard enough to hold a horse's hooves.

In other words, it wasn't good ground for a cavalry fight at all. In fact, I was very tempted at the last moment, when I could see Llúria fling his horses down on to the beach, to order my people to dismount. I had archers above us in the rocks, although not as many as I'd have liked. Fifty longbowmen would have made my men-at-arms unnecessary. I think we had eight or ten, and a few pages with crossbows. We were spread thin, like not enough butter on too much toast.

Llúria formed his horses into a wedge with his best armoured men at the tip.

I formed mine into an angled line, with the gentlemen on the gravel at the top of the beach on our left, well forward. The line echeloned back to me, Fiore, Nerio, Greg Fox and the Biriguccis, with Tom Fenton leading a handful of mounted pages and Beppo behind us as a tiny reserve. We were on the hard sand.

We let our opponents advance. They came on, from long bowshot, and the archers and crossbowmen played on them from the moment they were within range. The archers didn't score many hits, but they didn't need to. After two horses went down, the whole mass of our adversaries began to stretch out into a gallop. Immediately, their wedge became a mob, and the mob was fastest on the seaward side and slowest in the gravel at the top of the beach.

And my company sat as still as statues under our banner, which La Motte had.

Nerio had already closed his visor, but he snapped it back open.

'Well, gentlemen,' he said to me and Fiore and everyone in earshot. 'Here we are again.'

The ground shook. A hundred Christian gentlemen on horseback have that effect, but then, so do a hundred Moslem gentlemen.

Fiore nodded, his face serious. But then he said, 'What Count Amadeus would have given to be in this fight.'

Which was true.

'For what we are about to receive,' I said. And as if we'd practised, the three of us put our visors down together.

Our dozen or so archers and crossbowmen had now begun to score regular hits. The less armoured Catalans suffered the worst, and they were packed up on the soft gravel and easy to hit.

Llúria led twenty or so well-armoured men in a gallop down the hard packed sand.

I turned to Giorgios, my trumpeter.

'Sound "march",' I said. I'd never had this much control.

Our whole echeloned line began to plod down the beach.

Fifty paces out, Giorgios sounded 'march-march' or 'trot'. We went a little faster.

Twenty paces out, Giorgios's trumpet ordered the charge.

It was far from perfect. I'd actually underestimated the effect of the gravel. Some of our men-at-arms at the top of the beach had come to a virtual stop, unable to ride forward as their horses balked. But for the most part, our angled line was intact, and the enemy had no formation whatsoever.

I unhorsed my man, and Fiore his, but the nature of their charge and our response meant that instead of punching out through the back of their formation, we simply rode deeper into their hundred men. I hadn't expected his whole force to migrate down the beach to the hard sand. Maybe it was just the horses seeking firmer footing, but, as is so usual in war, nothing came out quite as expected.

On the other hand, the immediate result was that while Nerio, Fiore and I, and our immediate companions, broke the front of their charge and plunged ever deeper into their array, the rest of our angled line began to outflank their whole section of the beach.

None of that was apparent to me. What I saw from inside my helmet was a series of vignettes. My first opponent going back over his crupper, then a dense body of men, and Gabriel picking a way through, then brilliant flashes as I was surrounded by men hacking at me. Someone got me in the back – a thrust that went in through my maille. But whoever that was didn't press his advantage or throw me from the saddle, and the spike of pain vanished in the fear and the spirit of battle.

Gabriel turned and turned, hooves lashing. I parried what I could on my sword and cut back, looking for open-faced helmets and textile armours, places where I could hurt a man. The sun was like an additional opponent, blinding me as it flashed off sword and helmets.

More by luck than intention or skill, I got my pommel past a man's helmet, cocked to his neck and threw him from his mount. He splashed into water, and only then did I realise that everything had changed. My horse was chest deep in the sea, and the whole melee had moved down the beach and back towards the Catalan lines. Llúria's banner was gone, and the Catalans were, for the most part, trying to get out of a trap that nature more than my cleverness had forced upon them.

But I couldn't see Nerio anywhere. I could see Fiore and La Motte and Greg Fox, almost a hundred paces away, still sweeping along the beach as the Catalans broke. But in what you might call the 'pocket' of the beach, almost directly under the pass of the road, we were still fighting, and the action had moved into the water.

I was hardly alone. In fact, while I flipped up my visor ... Let me take this opportunity to again praise a helmet where the visor stays up when you push it up and locks down when you want it down, and can be operated by the armoured thumb of a tired, fearful mortal. As I say, while I flipped up my visor to try to read the action, Tom Fenton came up along the strand with my reserve of armed pages, clearing away my prospective opponents.

It was a very odd action. The sand, the gravel, the water – and perhaps the steep slope of the beach – all acted to push the fighting into the water. But in the water, a knight unhorsed could drown in his harness. And because of the wet sand, there was no dust, so that every element of the melee was laid bare, as if in a painting.

And I couldn't find Nerio.

I was free of opponents, still. Even as I watched, the Catalans nearest me saw Fenton and broke away like frightened birds.

I couldn't find Nerio, but I was almost positive that I was looking at Achille's horse, just down the beach, riderless and up to its fetlocks in water. I put Gabriel at the riderless horse and discovered that my latest long sword was broken at the midpoint of the blade. I have no idea when that happened.

Achille's horse was perhaps twenty paces from mine, but in the time it took me to get Gabriel to take me there, another horse burst up from under the water, like a sea monster. The trappings, black with seawater, were unmistakably Nerio's.

In ten beats of my heart, I was looking down at Nerio. He was on the sand, perhaps four feet under water, unmoving. I knew his harness immediately.

And for a few moments, I thought very, very clearly.

I turned in my saddle and slipped into the water. It came up to my armpits. And then I went down into the water, still holding Gabriel's reins. I had to open my eyes under water – not as hard as it sounds, I suppose, but I remember it as an effort of will. There was Nerio.

I closed my gauntleted hand on his visor, which was open, and lifted. And then I got a hand on my saddle bow and told Gabriel to go.

He went. He went strongly, ploughing the ocean like a farm horse ploughs the land. He dragged Nerio's armoured body up the beach until Nerio was lying clear of the water on the hard sand, the sand itself ploughed to a slurry by hundreds of hooves striking it over and over.

I felt as if my right arm had been pulled out of my body, but I was still thinking. The cavalry melee was won and lost. The Catalans were scattered or taken, and my archers were coming down from the road to loot.

I got my gauntlets off – harder than you might think when absolutely soaked with seawater. I wanted my helmet off, but that was impossible for me alone, and I had neither squire nor page. But I remembered Aldo's tale of rescuing the drowned man, and I got down next to Nerio in the sand, and I forced him to sit up, rocking him as hard as I could.

And sure enough, exactly as Aldo had described, some water shot out of his mouth.

I laid him flat and forced him forward again, this time right over his legs. He spat water, and then gave a weak cough. And nothing.

I let him flop back. We were both coated in wet sand. I got him up again, forced his torso forward over his legs. More water. Another cough. This one was stronger. His eyes moved.

Again. Faster. Less water. More coughing. My right arm and shoulder burned as if I'd taken a great wound. Something was really wrong, but I slammed Nerio forward, desperation powering my attempt. He was hacking away like a man with a winter illness, or an old man on his way to the grave.

Suddenly he threw up all over both of us, and his gauntleted fist caught me in the side of the head as he scrambled in some sort of waking panic.

I went out.

When I came to, my first thought was that I'd been taken. There were armoured legs all around me, and no one was paying me any heed, and I actually got my hand on Charny's dagger. But the legs to the right of me weren't armoured, and they emerged from long brown robes, and they belonged to Michael des Roches, who was speaking softly.

'Hello?' I managed, or perhaps I cursed.

Well. Of course we'd won the melee. We'd won it before I went down. And Michael, who apparently knows everything, knew far more than I did about saving a man with lungs full of water. Nerio was alive.

And I was alive.

Achille, Nerio's squire, was dead. We only lost four men, and he was one of them, trying to save Nerio from drowning. He was, we heard later, holding Nerio on his saddle after his master was knocked unconscious by a blow, and a Catalan rode up and stabbed him under the arm. Or so we guessed.

As battles go, it was one of the smallest in which I've participated. And that was the end. Llúria and his excellent cavalry won the horse race, having lost the melee, and rode away. I gathered later that he had ordered Everenos to attack, and Everenos declined politely. A week later, I met Everenos not far from there, on the road. I exchanged some Turkish horses and two of his people that John had captured, for a Kipchak boy and three of our pages that Everenos had snapped up during John's raid in Attica.

Everenos shook his head. 'If you infidels keep fighting each other,' he said, 'how will you ever stop my sultan from taking all your lands?'

'My lands?' I laughed. 'I suspect Nerio will take all of this.'

Everenos nodded. 'Yes. I tell you no great secret when I say that I will be recommending to my master that a close eye be kept on our friend. He is too dangerous.'

We clasped hands and rode away. I haven't seen him since, but I expect that he remains the very best kind of Turk – honest, capable, with a streak of humour and a strong sense of honour. I hope the sultan values him as he deserves.

For my part, I took a month to recover, and even now, five years and more later, my right shoulder has never been quite the same.

Nerio paid us magnificently, which is to say that he paid us not one but two double pay months for our victories, and he paid cash, as well as my own stipend.

'You saved my life, brother,' he said.

We were, by then, standing on the beach at the Bay of Corinth side of the isthmus. I was preparing to board a Venetian carrack sailing for Venice. I was leaving my company well paid, under Lapot, with Nerio. I took only Greg Fox and the Biriguccis, László the Hungarian and Beppo. At the last moment I was joined by Father Angelo, who was going home to deal with a civil law case in his family. I was going to my estates in Savoy to see my children. I'd sworn an oath, there, before the battle.

I assumed, then, that I would be back in Corinth before the sailing season ended. Little did I know that it would be four years before I saw Nerio again.

PART V

Venice

And al was conscience and tendre herte.
Ful semyly hir wympul pynched was,
Hir nose tretys, hir eyen greye as glas,
Hir mouth ful smal, and therto softe and reed.
But sikerly she hadde a fair forheed ...

Geoffrey Chaucer, *The Canterbury Tales*, 'The General Prologue'

On the fourth day of October, the feast of Saint Francis in the year of Our Lord 1374, I arrived in the lagoon of Venice where, despite being in the peak of health – or rather, as healthy as a thirty-four-year-old warrior can be – I was held with the entire crew on suspicion of having the plague. We stayed in the cramped quarters of the old plague island for forty days. I had the most remarkable collection of mixed bites – bed bugs and mosquitoes.

I read Sir John Hawkwood's letter. It was almost a year old by then, written from Bologna in the last winter.

I'll just sum up. Hawkwood didn't apologise. In fact, he didn't refer to our last meeting at all. Instead, he wrote a long and detailed letter concerning the politics of Italy and his place in it. He summed up by saying, 'You are not missing anything by your absence, most noble knight, because as the Pope cannot or will not pay us, we are no longer making war of any kind, and my soldiers, those who are still with me, behave more like routiers every day. And who can blame them? They have not been paid.'

I gathered from his letter that the Green Count had been handled roughly by the Milanese in the north, and that otherwise, the war had come to a stop.

And I gathered that Hawkwood wanted me to return, although, just as six years earlier, he was in no hurry to have me. Or need me.

There was no note from Janet, where I might have expected one.

In Venice, I also received mail. I had two letters from Richard Musard. One was about the aborted campaign in the Tyrolean valleys north of Milan. The other brought news of court, and of the rapidly expanding career of one Robert of Geneva, now a Cardinal of the Church and holding powerful benefices in England and France.

Richard said that he had been mentioned as a possible papal legate for the war against Milan.

After forty days of bad food and insects, I took a boat to the city with my baggage and my small household. I had a letter of credit on Nerio's bank, but my credit in Venice was excellent, as I discovered on my second day in the city, when a messenger brought me an invitation to dine with Vettor Pisani and his family. That evening, Greg Fox, Benghi Birigucci and I dined with Lord Pisani, and Beppo waited on us as if he was actually a servant. Pisani, who had just passed his fiftieth name day and looked as thin and hale as a young man, although with a fuller beard, was an excellent host. You may recall that we'd stayed with him the year before, or rather, Lord Fontana and his sister stayed and I visited.

'Tell me of Carlo Zeno,' he said. 'I hear you two had great adventures in the Euxine and I'm jealous.'

I told him the tale, but in truth, he seemed to know everything before I said it, and some of his questions were very carefully targeted. He was mostly interested, in fact, in the relations between the Emperor's ambassadors and Tuqtamis. I was cautious in my reply.

Greg Fox ate a great deal and looked carefully at everything, from the wall hangings to the dishes served. I think it's the first time I'd taken him to a great lord's house, if you except the Emperor in Constantinople, of course. Benghi listened to Pisani as a monk would listen to a great sermon. I watched my step. But as far as I'm concerned, Pisani's questions confirmed my suspicions that most of our actions in the Euxine had been on behalf of the Serenissima. We were proxies, if you will.

After dinner was over, and as Pisani's wife and sister left us, his wife, Maria, smiled. I bowed to her. Now let me add that women do not usually directly address men in great Venetian houses. Indeed, a singular honour had been done with me that the women of the family dined with us.

Lady Maria smiled. She wore a veil, but it was pulled back for dinner. She was perhaps forty, and striking, with very dark hair shot with grey.

'Perhaps it would not offend if I were to ask after the most noble lord Fontana?' she asked in a low voice.

To be honest, I was instantly on my guard. In the entire time I had stayed in this palace a year before, she had never addressed me directly. She was a great lady, from the famous Venetian Trevison family, and such interactions were very rare.

That said, Pisani was a well-travelled and modern man, for a Venetian. He nodded at me, a sort of 'Go ahead, I'm impatient with all this etiquette' nod.

'My lady,' I said. 'Lord Fontana was killed in the fighting at Megara.'

And this is where one's social life becomes very complicated. I knew, if not in that very moment, then certainly not long after, that she already knew Fontana was dead.

'Ah,' she said. 'Will you perhaps inform his sister?' She smiled. It was genuine enough. 'I quite liked having her here.'

'My lady, I promised her brother as he lay dying that I would take care of his sister,' I said. Perhaps I said it with a little less drama. I certainly hope so.

Instead of smiling, her eyes grew a hint of steel. 'You'd best do so, then,' she said.

I caught the hint of an aristocratic sniff as she moved off to the women's quarters.

Pisani watched her go. 'They lead different lives from ours,' he said suddenly. 'Women, I mean. But no less complicated.' He had been watching his wife, but now he looked at me. 'You know she's telling you to go and see the woman.'

'I gathered that.'

Pisani nodded. 'Tell me if I can be of help. In the meantime, allow me to say, unofficially, that you have been of signal service to the Lion. Is your company available for hire?'

I bowed again. 'You are most gracious, *magnifico*, but my company is well situated, guarding Messire Nerio in Corinth.'

Pisani smiled. 'Good for you, my dear knight. But Venice would like to offer something. One might take it as a reward, if one were not loud about its origins.'

Beppo, who was helping clear the table, managed to stifle a guffaw, but I caught the roll of his eyes.

'My lord is too generous,' I said, or something flowery and appropriate.

Pisani nodded. 'We have in mind a sort of *condotta in aspeto*, a contract in waiting. And perhaps, in the event of this war we all fear with Genoa, you would come and serve us. Until then, we would pay you something. You see?'

I walked out of Pisani's palace, or rather, was rowed out, a richer man.

The next day, with a livery boat borrowed from Lord Pisani, I was rowed out to Murano to ask after Fontana's sister. My problem was that I didn't know what convent she was in – and the whole system is so close-mouthed that no one in Venice would tell me.

That's not precisely true. No one would tell me initially, so I began, as Greg Fox put it, to beat the bushes. I went to each of the fashionable convents in the city. I was quite sure she was on an island, but I thought I'd start with the simplest solutions. After midday, I walked over to the Bailie of the Knights of Saint John, where I was well received, as ever, and I put my problem to the prior, who promised me his support.

'It's a scandal,' he said. 'Venetian fathers force their daughters into convents to save the cost of their dowries. Half these girls have no profession. Some of them scream when they are taken. It is a shame on the religion. But the convents are secretive because they fear retribution, or rescue attempts by lovers, I suppose.'

'The poor woman's brother is dead,' I said. 'She'll want to know.'

The prior embraced me gently. 'We'll find her,' he said. 'Give me a few days.'

I spent three days looking for her, and added mightily to my collection of insect bites. Autumn is not the best time to visit the lagoon, and they had had a wet summer. But none of them had heard of Lady Fontana, and indeed, several convents insisted to me that they would not take a 'foreign' lady.

I was also thrown out of one, but that's another story, and I promise you, gentles, that I had committed no sin.

In between these expeditions into the lives of nuns and lay sisters, I went shopping. Marco had new livery. Greg Fox and I had new clothes and boots. A year is the death of many a boot, and many a fine linen shirt as well, I promise you, especially a year such as I'd spent.

On Sunday I went to Mass at the chapel of the knights, because I knew people there and Venice can be a little hostile to foreigners.

Feelings against Genoa were running high, and I thought I'd go to church with friends.

After Mass, the prior took me aside and said, 'I believe I've found your friend's sister, but I have to tell you that she's been a burden on her convent and ...' He looked away. 'She is not a proper woman of religion.'

'I think her brother forced her to the convent,' I said.

'No behaviour of her brother's can justify her,' he said, with conviction. 'I don't know what you can do with her. But here is where she is – the Clares' convent on the island of San Francesco del Deserto.'

His disapproval was absolute. As he was generally very much a friend, I was not happy to see him so distressed.

I remembered Maddalena as a woman of spirit. I could see how she might fall foul of a strict mother superior, but I had a difficult time imagining her as causing a real difficulty in any community. And the prior was angry.

On the other hand ...

On the other hand, this woman had probably saved my life, and she wasn't a harridan by any measure.

'My lord, I don't know of what she stands accused,' I said carefully, 'but she is a good woman, and I know her well. I can't believe she would ...'

'She struck a priest,' the prior said. 'A Franciscan, Father Stefano. After attempting to seduce him.'

I remember this well. I stood there, in the library of the priory of Venice, and I thought carefully on my words, because the prior was a good man, and had been, if not a patron, at least a guide. And I have learnt that many men, especially men in the religion, cut off from the lives of women, can believe things, as if women are alien beings.

'My lord,' I said, 'the woman I know would never do such a thing.' I met his eyes. 'My lord, you know me, and you know I have a good eye for men. For what they will do.'

He met my eyes, and then looked away. 'Guglielmo,' he said softly, as if he was giving confession, 'In this case, you are wrong. She was your lover?'

'Ha!' I said. The explosion wasn't mirth, or anger, but something in between. 'No, my lord. She is not a lovesome woman.'

The prior looked at me for a long time, and I held his gaze.

311

'You disturb me,' he said. 'Go and see her. Here, I will have the archdeacon write you a special pass.'

'The archdeacon?' I asked.

'The prelate who has charge of the punishment of the clergy within our diocese. An officer to whom you and I, belonging to the Order, owe nothing. But he is a good man, if strict, and he is a friend of our order.'

He wrote me a note, and I took it across the city to San Marco, where a clerk passed it to a priest, who led me through a warren of offices I didn't even know existed, to a sumptuous room on a side canal.

The archdeacon was a very fat man, but his smile was winning, and he didn't wear rings or jewellery, which I always take as a good sign in a clergyman.

'My son,' he said, and gave me a blessing. 'My brother the prior asks that you be allowed to see a cloistered laywoman among the Clares. Is that correct?'

'Yes, Venerable Father,' I said.

He nodded. 'The prior says that you are aware she attacked a priest. This is a serious matter, my son. Can you tell me a little of why you take an interest?'

'Her brother died in my service,' I said. I decided it was time to play my various Venetian political cards. 'I believe that the Lord Pisani would speak for me in this – that he died in the service of Venice.'

'Ah,' the archdeacon said. He conveyed a great deal with that sound. He made clear that he understood immediately that I had a patron, and that he would, indeed, have to take my request seriously.

I love Venice. Mostly.

'Venerable Father, Lord Fontana's dying request was that I should see to his sister.' I didn't glare, but I went from a humble downward glance to a straight eye-to-eye stare. 'I gave him my word.'

The archdeacon looked as if he was in real pain. 'I see,' he said.

'The prior suggested that you could arrange for me to interview her,' I said, bearing down.

'I'm not sure what that would serve,' the archdeacon said slowly.

There were a lot of different ways to play this, and I was, frankly, too inexperienced at dealing with Venetian politics, especially Church politics.

But the fact was I'd given my word to a dying man – a man who, despite being something of an arse from time to time, had been my friend and companion. I was eager to get this done and get to my children. But the unexpected difficulty did more to fuel my interest than kill it.

'It would serve me, Venerable Father. The prior informed me that the woman in question is accused of striking a priest. And perhaps attempting to seduce him.'

'These are not matters for you to deal with,' the archdeacon said gently.

'Venerable Father, I find these matters to touch directly on an oath I have given, and thus on my own honour.' I smiled my 'man-of-the-world' smile. 'May I speak plainly, Venerable Father?'

He winced, but said, 'Of course.'

'I don't believe the charges,' I said.

That sat between us for a moment.

Let me say a difficult thing – and Master Chaucer, stay quiet.

Not everyone in the Church is a good man, or a trustworthy clerk, or a pious monk, or a gracious nun. Now, in ten minutes of formal conversation, I had come to an understanding that the archdeacon was a hardworking man who was honest enough, if you take my meaning. If I had found him venal, I would have tried other options. If I had suspected him of malice, I would have used another kind of patronage against him.

But he had something about him that suggested that he took his job very seriously.

He pursed his lips, which made him look a little too much like an amiable cherub, but to think that would have been to miss the mark. He was a stern man.

'For that to be true,' he said, 'a priest would have had to lie, with malicious intent, about an innocent woman.'

We looked at each other. Master Chaucer is laughing, and I know why, and cynicism comes easily, does it not? Because we both know how often friars and frocked priests pursue innocent women, aye?

The archdeacon looked straight at me. 'If I refuse you, what will you do?' he asked.

'I'll go to Pisani, and various other gentlemen of Venice whom I know through my military profession,' I said.

He nodded.

'You are a Franciscan, I think,' I said.

'I have that honour,' he agreed.

'I served Father Pierre Thomas for a few years,' I said. 'He was the greatest priest I've ever known. I am not some son of Belial, who despises the Church, Venerable Father.'

He nodded. 'I don't like this. I don't like the thoughts that you have put in my mind. Not the least of them, that I took this story at face value without a qualm.' He shrugged. 'My son, I find it ... unlikely ... that this woman is innocent. No one from her convent has spoken for her. Not one.'

He glanced out of the window. A passing boatman was singing out '*Haaaooo*' as he came to the turn in the canal below.

I could feel the 'but' coming, so I stayed silent.

'But you have shaken my conviction,' he said. 'And you have powerful friends.' He wrote on a piece of parchment. 'Here is an order for you to be allowed to interview the woman Anna di Piacenza at the Monastery of San Francisco del Deserto.'

Anna? I thought.

'Fontana di Piacenza,' I said. 'A very noble family.'

His look of concern, if anything, increased. 'She is a noblewoman?' he asked. 'How could that not have been noted?' His eyes narrowed. 'Yes. This should be looked into. I have been remiss.'

I took my leave

The next morning, I borrowed a liveried boat from Lord Pisani, and took Beppo and Father Angelo – Beppo, in case I had to do something desperate, and Father Angelo, in case I had to do something religious. Both of them knew as much of the story as I knew myself.

'Bah,' Beppo said. 'Beppo remembers this lady, when the boy lay dying. Eh? So fuck the priest.'

And Father Angelo looked out over the stern of the boat at the glories of an early morning on the lagoon.

'My Church is full of sinners,' he said, slowly. And shook his head. 'Like you, I cannot believe such ill of her.' He shook his head again. 'Priests in convents are exposed to many temptations, and not all of them come from his charges.'

'Just imagine a bad priest let loose in a convent,' I said.

'You convict him unheard,' Father Angelo said.

Now, here's the thing, gentles. I would not have said, amid the smoke and dust of the siege of Megara, that I cared much more than a whit for Maddalena Fontana. Or perhaps a whit or two, if you take my meaning.

And yet, I found that I was utterly her partisan. I was not going to let this go.

It was a long trip across the lagoon – several miles north of Murano, on a very small islet that had apparently been visited by Saint Francis himself in the last century. The convent was small, right against the back of the monastery, but with its own chapel.

We landed at the pier. I think we were expected. What the good monks had not expected was Father Angelo, one of their own, and one with a heavy build and a powerful voice. He took command as easily as I might have if we'd been in battle.

'We are here to see Donna Fontana of Piacenza,' he said to the two monks who awaited us on the pier.

'Yes,' said the shorter of the two. He bobbed his head. 'I'm afraid there is some difficulty—'

'No,' Father Angelo said. He wasn't loud. He was more … large. He pushed through them without pushing anyone, if you take my meaning. 'There will not be any difficulty. Let us proceed immediately.'

The two monks – Franciscan friars, of course – glanced at each other.

'Really,' the taller one said, 'it would be better if you returned—'

'No,' Father Angelo said again. 'It would be better if you produced Donna Fontana immediately.'

'By the Virgin,' Beppo said quietly. 'If you ever take a bolt, he can take command.'

I was of a mind with Beppo but I often am, for my sins.

'We were told …'

Father Angelo seemed to swell. 'Brothers,' he said, loudly but with infinite kindness. 'Either you have nothing to hide, in which case the sooner we see the lady, the easier it will be. Or you are hiding something, in which case, it will be the worse for you if you delay us.'

Again, the two of them were confused, but by that time, Father Angelo was walking up to the sea wall. At the top of the steps, he turned south and headed for the convent gate.

315

'No, brother!' shouted the taller monk, and then, as if embarrassed by the sound of his own voice, he scurried – I can use no other word ... He scurried after Father Angelo.

Beppo and I followed along behind.

'I'm already inclined to take the lady away with us,' I said.

Beppo nodded. 'With you, Capo.'

We followed the two monks, who were following Father Angelo, who was proceeding like a big war galley under sail.

He was angry. He hadn't seemed angry in the boat, so I have to assume that the two idiots on the dock had set him off.

'The convent gate will be barred,' the taller monk called after him.

'Interesting,' Father Angelo said.

He had arrived at the gate. He rang the bell.

There was silence. Over on the other side of the wall, the monks' side, we could hear sandalled feet scraping on a walkway. Were they lining the cloister? Leaning out?

'I can get the gate, Capo,' Beppo said. 'Not my first convent.'

As good as his word, he went up the stuccoed brick wall as if it had stanchions set into it, and we heard him drop down on the other side. He shot the bar back. – we heard that, too.

'You are in defiance of the Order!' hissed the smaller monk. 'You are breaking your vows!'

This was clearly meant for Father Angelo.

I smiled and thrust the archdeacon's letter in his face, somewhat aggressively, I will admit.

'I have an order from the archdeacon of the diocese, and another from the head of your order,' I said. That last was a flat lie, but a very effective one. Both monks turned white, as if I was a very demon from Hell, and flinched away.

'But, we were told ...' muttered the tall monk.

'Silence!' spat the shorter monk.

I walked through the gate. It gave on to a pretty courtyard, with fruit trees trained on trellises along one side of the cloister, and a rather elegant brick dormitory set back from the main building, which looked something like a small version of the Hospital on Rhodes. It was all very elegant, and somewhat Venetian.

I stopped in the gateway and rang the bell again. I rang it hard and long – I was, if you like, rude.

No one came.

So I walked into the middle of the courtyard, and raised my voice.

'I am here at the order of the archdeacon of the diocese to see one Lady Fontana of Piacenza.' My voice echoed around the yard, off the chapel and the dormitory. Someone could hear me. 'If you do not produce her, I will come and find her, and it will be the worse for you.'

Beppo nodded once to me and slipped in under the trees, and was gone like a shadow at noon.

I moved straight to the dormitory, because I imagined she was there. The door that I approached was locked. I could hear people on the other side.

'Please open this, or I will have it broken down,' I said.

'You cannot be here,' came a voice from inside.

'You cannot stop me,' I said. 'And it might be dangerous for you to try.'

However that might have come out, there was an altercation behind me, in the gate. I turned back to find Father Angelo face to face with another Franciscan, as tall and broadly built as he was.

'You must leave,' the man said in a powerful, serene voice, if a trifle nasal.

He turned to me as I walked up, and I saw that he had a black eye and a laceration on his neck. And someone had broken his nose. Otherwise, he might have been quite handsome.

'I have a licence to be here,' I said.

'No, you don't. Leave before I ...'

I walked straight up to him. 'Before you what?' I said. 'Someone beat you pretty badly. It would be a pity if that were to happen again, eh? I hear it hurts more with the second beating.'

He was a big man, and very used, I think, to physical intimidation. You can be a very dangerous fellow, in a monastery, and yet not be so very dangerous as all that. And there was something about him that struck me immediately – something that I noticed ... sort of noticed under the bluster and the bruises. I couldn't put a finger on it, but he was ...

He was ...

Well, he was sputtering, his cultured voice now more nasal and less effective. 'Are you threatening me?'

317

It's very difficult to bluster through a broken nose and bruises. It's hard to be imposing. We were of a size, but I had every advantage if it came to violence.

'Are you threatening me?' he repeated.

I snapped my fingers under his nose – a very rude gesture.

'Got it in one, little man.' I don't do this often, this loutish version of a storybook routier, but I know the archetype. And I had it – his accent.

He was from Piacenza. He had the same accent as Fontana.

That made me smile, because I was sure I had him.

'You are the priest who levelled the complaint against Donna Fontana, eh?' I asked.

'None of your—'

I didn't touch him. I just moved very close to him, and he stepped back into the gateway, and almost tripped over Father Angelo, who was behind him.

'You are from Piacenza, are you not?' I asked. 'The archdeacon will be very interested in that small fact. I think you omitted to inform the Church authorities that the woman you accused was a gentlewoman of Piacenza. Eh?'

'She attacked me,' he said. 'And who will accept the word of a harlot over mine?'

At the word 'harlot', I had a flash of Donna Fontana in the tent with the dying knight.

I fought down the urge to strike him.

'I think you had better come back to Venice with us,' I said. 'Don't you agree, Father Angelo?'

Father Angelo smiled a nasty smile. 'Ah, so much makes sense already,' he said. 'And to think, Father Stefano, that in the boat coming here I tried to defend you.'

Father Stefano spat. 'You think because I am from Piacenza that I lie?' he asked. 'Everyone there knows what kind of woman she is.'

I nodded. 'Fascinating,' I said. 'Now, have one of your lackeys fetch the woman, and we'll be gone.'

'No,' he said.

I nodded. 'Very well. Any damage we do to the fabric will be laid to your account.'

He didn't budge. 'I am being punished as a martyr for my faith …'

'Father Angelo, I leave your brother priest to your tender care.'

I nodded and turned away, because I wanted so badly to re-break his nose.

'Keep him here, Father,' I said. 'Or take him down to the boat. Feel free to knock him unconscious if he resists.'

'You imperil the souls of every woman in this place, you ... bandit!' Stefano shouted behind me. 'You will burn in Hell.'

'Possibly, but not for this, Father.'

I nodded coolly to him and went to the big building.

The side door was unlocked – a bit of an anticlimax, but if my guess was right, this man was a monster and his control couldn't be absolute. Our arrival must have signalled the end to someone.

I was right. Inside was a broad passageway, almost a hall, with three wimpled women standing there.

The oldest was perhaps forty. She looked at me.

'You are from the Church, my lord?' she breathed. She spoke in broad *Veneziano*.

'I have a letter from the archdeacon ...' I began.

I didn't know my Church costume. I had no idea if this was the mother superior, the abbess, the prioress ... The three women had hard, red hands and the lined faces of working women, but I wasn't sure.

She glanced back at the other two women.

'He's a demon from fucking Hell,' she said. 'An' this foreign lady stood up to him, like.'

In fact, as I found later, they were lay sisters – lower-class women who did most of the heavy work. But they were most emphatically not friends of Father Stefano.

'We told the bishop when he came,' she whispered. 'And he just walked away.'

'Aye,' said another woman. She was younger, and hid her face.

'Good Christ', I thought, 'What have I walked into?'

Beppo found Maddalena. She had bruises on her face, too, and she was locked to a post in the hall of the dormitory where all of the good sisters could see her, which should tell you a thing or two about the convent and the Franciscan Stefano. She smelt bad and looked worse, but when she saw me, and Stefano over my shoulder, at Angelo's mercy, she smiled. Oh, I'll never forget that smile. 'Ferocious' is my best description.

'I'd rather not ride in a boat with that man,' she said carefully. She had a split lip and her cheek was swollen. 'But if I must, to get out of here ...'

We left the pier with a silent row of hooded figures watching us from the sea wall. The beautiful day seemed darkened – I shivered. I didn't want to allow myself to consider what the women there – aye, and the men – had probably lived through. Isolated, under the thumb of a tyrant with religion and size on his side ...

When we were out on the lagoon, Father Stefano spat at his feet.

'You are going to believe this whore over me?' he said.

Beppo, who was helping the Pisani men row, caught a crab. His oar skated across a wave top and slapped Father Stefano in the head, and he fell into the bottom of the boat without a cry.

Beppo grunted. 'Beppo is sorry, mates. He missed his stroke, eh?'

The other three sailors grunted and continued to row.

Maddalena wept a little, and then watched the gulls, isolating herself from us by turning her body away. She didn't say anything to us for an hour, as we rowed steadily across the lagoon down towards Murano. I tried not to stare, but I watched her, and she watched seabirds, and fishing boats, and a farmer on the Lido picking fruit.

And then, as if she'd finished a difficult subject, or perhaps just written a long note, she turned in her seat and looked at me and Father Angelo.

'*Alora*,' she said, with her usual asperity.

I handed her my handkerchief.

She sighed. 'He knew me from my city,' she said. 'I expect we are going to deliver him to the Church authorities?'

'Beppo says we could have an accident and lose him over the side,' Beppo contributed.

Maddalena smiled like a winter sun. 'Yes,' she said. She looked at me. 'I would rather have rescued myself, you know.'

'I'm sure, that, given time, you would have managed something,' I said.

'My brother is dead. That part is true, yes?' she asked.

'Yes,' I said. 'He died in my arms. And he asked me to look after you.'

'Christ,' she said, and looked away. And then, in a steady voice, she said, 'When I was very young, I did something foolish, and lay with a man. The wrong man.'

She looked away, and then at me, gauging my reaction.

I wished that she had Emile sitting here in the boat, instead of three men.

She looked away again. 'It came to light – the foolish boy bragged about it. Too many people knew. My brother killed a couple of men in duels, and then he arranged for me to be sent away.' She smiled that wintry smile. 'I was christened Anna, you know? Not Maddalena. That's what the nuns made me call myself.'

'And this Father Stefano knew all this?' Father Angelo asked.

She nodded to him. 'Oh, yes. Just a day after my brother left me there, and I, for my sins agreed to it, this bastard appears. He was, at first, solicitous. It only took me a day or two to discover that he expected me to be ... light.' She shot his prone body an icy glance. 'Can you guess how many of the women in that convent he has forced? I broke his nose, and I told him that if he came back I'd kill him. He's a fucking coward, Guglielmo – he was afraid of me. And he had me shackled to that pillar ...' She breathed deeply. 'Fifteen days.'

I leant forward to the stoic boatman. 'Let's visit Ca' Pisani first, my friend,' I said.

Ah, Monsieur Froissart, I'm shocking you. And you only want to hear about battles, eh? So let me say that Father Angelo and I decided between us that we would put a sword into the balances of justice, as the Venetians say. We left Maddalena, or Anna, in the care of Lady Pisani, and we had her tell her tale to Lord Pisani, in some detail, albeit with a few bits of past history left out.

Father Angelo had noted how many daughters of the patrician class might be victims of this Father Stefano. Vettor Pisani took notes, swelled with rage, and was rowed away to the Doge's palace.

And *then* we dropped Father Stefano at San Marco. In fact, Beppo and I helped him walk all the way to the archdeacon's office.

The archdeacon gave me the same kind of look that Pilgrim sometimes gives me when I'm late to feed him – a sort of gentle reproach that goes straight to my soul.

'Was it necessary to mistreat him?' he asked. 'Would Father Pierre Thomas have beaten him?'

I bowed. 'I haven't touched him, Venerable Father. One of the boatmen slipped and hit him with an oar.'

The archdeacon was Venetian, and had not been born yesterday. He sighed.

'Very well,' he said.

We were still standing there when a messenger came, in the Doge's livery. A note was delivered, with no seal. The archdeacon read the note, and paused to pray before addressing me.

'I gather that I will be investigating this in person,' he said. 'Despite which, gentlemen, I probably owe you a debt of thanks.'

'Justice is part of the duty of a knight,' I said.

'Hmmm,' the archdeacon sighed. But he blessed us, even Beppo.

Donna Fontana declined to be a governess.

'I don't particularly like children,' she said. I gathered that she might, eventually, say more.

On the great balcony of Ca' Pisani, Donna Fontana and I were left alone. Maria Pisani walked off, motioning to her maids to attend her. It was very obviously contrived. And well meant.

Maddalena rolled her eyes with some of her accustomed spirit. But when we were alone, she said, 'I should thank you.'

'I need no thanks ...' I began.

'Please,' she said. 'Some day, perhaps, I will thank you. I am not unhappy to be alive. But by the risen Christ, sir, I am tired of being an object to be judged, rejected, wooed, raped or rescued.' She shook her head. 'I am ungracious. But, by the Virgin, sir, I feel rather ungracious.'

I smiled.

'You are mocking me,' she spat.

I shook my head. 'No, my lady. Merely glad to see your spirit unbroken. May I say something?'

She looked at me, and I believe that was the longest our eyes had been locked. That look went on for a surprisingly long time.

'No,' she said. 'Another time, perhaps. But today I need nothing – neither a moral story, nor a powerful memory. And you are given to talking too much.'

I bowed and took my leave. Still smiling.

I left her with Maria Pisani, who seemed very fond of her, and when I tried to offer some housekeeping money to Lord Vettor, he spurned me with all the annoyance of a rich patrician.

A month later, I was at court in Savoy. I saw Richard Musard, and the count, who treated me like a prodigal son, and I promised to return to court for the hunting and for Christmas, but I wanted to see my children – an excuse, to any aristocrat in the world.

They ran to me across a courtyard that had once been Emile's and was now their own. Edouard was almost a young man. And little Richard was four, and could walk, and didn't remember me at all, but was clearly happy to have a fine Venetian glass of his very own, and a small toy knight. And Magdalene, Emile's first child, was fifteen. She was pretty, verging on more than pretty, with a heart-shaped face and a head of dark red hair that seemed to have a bit of a mind of its own. She wasn't as fast to come out to me, but watched with a distant smile as Edouard embraced me and Richard played with his knight.

'I thought you'd forgotten us,' she said later. 'Do you know, my clearest memory of you is when you came in out of the dark when Mama was dying?'

'Did I scare you?' I asked.

She shook her head. 'I know you saved me,' she said. 'But somehow, all I remember is Mama dying.'

And then she gave me a hug – brief, almost elusive. But over the next few weeks, there were more hugs.

Well, you don't care about the good times – the happy times. So I won't burden you with two months with my children, getting to know them. I fenced with Edouard, which was wonderful. I danced with Magdalene, or played cards, and Richard followed me about as I went to the stables or out to the barns. Edouard was lord of his own estates now. The count was his regent, but Amadeus had a surprisingly light hand, and Edouard was learning to manage it all. Nor was Edouard's steward a bad man, or hesitant to see me. And I spent time on my own estate near Chambéry, which was smaller and lacked the children, but needed a visit from time to time. I went to court, and danced with some fine ladies, and thought a great deal about Emile.

Father Angelo wrote to me from Verona about the scandal in Venice, whereby the archdeacon and some Dominicans and a Franciscan officer had purged the monastery and closed the convent.

The nuns were sent elsewhere. God send, they went to better homes.

The Biriguccis wrote to me from Umbria, to say that the Pope meant to make war on Florence, once his closest ally, and would I be fighting in the spring?

Greg Fox danced and sang with the count's court, and seemed utterly at home.

And Fiore wrote to me from Udine and Friuli, to say that he'd purchased a small estate and was a landed gentleman now. He said he'd begun work on a compilation of his thoughts on *armizare*.

I sent a letter to my sister in London, and received a reply before Christmas, to my delight. Sister Marie rode up one day, and settled into a nearby convent – the one the count had offered her back in '68 or '69.

And Nerio wrote to me from Corinth, to say that he was beginning to think of taking Thebes from the Catalans, if the Emperor could only hold on in Constantinople for a few more years, and the Venetians and Genoese maintained their uneasy peace.

Christmas came and went, and we went hunting, and we took sleds down the streets. I was a little old for the sports of the younger men, but I rode in a small tournament at Chambéry, on the count's team. I had a good day, and I won the prize, which was a superb long sword. I wear it still – this one here.

All in all, it was a fine winter, and I was happier than I had been in years. Women began to appeal to me, and there were some fine ladies at court who thought of me as something more than a cook's boy. And I had Sister Marie for conversation, and Richard Musard.

I might have retired then. But as winter turned to spring, the ice in the streets became mud, and a messenger struggled over the passes with a letter from Sir John Hawkwood.

It was the spring of the year of Our Lord 1375.

EPILOGUE

It was again very late, and Aemilie had brought three candles for Froissart. Chaucer had leant his stool so far back that it looked as if he might crash over, but he held his place by what appeared to be an act of magic.

'The Church,' he muttered. 'How many women – aye, and men, too? Wasted lives.'

'But we have not yet reached the Great Raid!' Froissart said. 'And these two battles? I've never heard of them. And your friend Nerio ...'

Chaucer laughed. 'Ah, Renerio Acciaioli. I promise you, he is everything that William says. A great rascal and a great noble, too.'

'High praise from you,' I said.

'But you have still said very little of this Chioggia War,' Froissart insisted. 'The greatest war of our time, you said, and all I hear of is this little island of Tenedos.'

Sir William waved at his friend John, who had come in hours before, and now sat close by, sewing.

'John signalled me that we weren't leaving tomorrow, either,' the red-haired knight said. 'So I promise, the Great Raid, and the massacre of Cesena, and the War of Chioggia, and Nerio at Thebes, all tomorrow. The worst of times, and the best.' He held up a slip of parchment. 'And it appears that I have a ship, and a *sauvegarde*, but not until Wednesday. So drink up, my friends.'

Aemilie poured him a cup of wine.

'And the Lady Fontana?' she asked. 'I feel for her. What of her?'

Sir William smiled. 'Why, I married her, of course. But that's another story for another day, lass.'

He kicked his long sword out behind him as he rose, and nodded to Froissart.

'I'm for Mass,' he said.

325

Froissart was still writing.

Chaucer, on the other hand, picked up his own pen case and his rosary.

'I'm with you,' he said. 'And the rain's stopped.'

Together, they walked out.

The End

The 'Chivalry' stories will continue in book seven,
Captain of Venice

AUTHOR'S NOTE

Historical novels, especially those centering around adventure, are a daring tight-rope act between a ripping yarn and a good piece of history. In this installment, I let my love of history run away with me for a while.

Patrick O'Brian (whose books I fairly worship) once said that if he'd known how popular Jack Aubrey would be, he'd have started his adventures in an earlier year. For my part, I found that I couldn't send my hero forward from 1372 all the way to 1378 and the War of Chioggia without at least visiting some of the major incidents of the 1370s, and once I got to research, I discovered more (and then more) of interest. In this volume, I wanted to show the reader some of the causes of the great war between Venice and Genoa while also continuing narratives about the decay of the 'Byzantine' empire, the rise of the Ottomans, and the failure of the Union of Churches. In the end, what was supposed to be two hundred pages in my outline turned into a book of its own, and I'm a little afraid that this will happen again for 1375 and 1376. We'll see this summer when I start writing book 7.

I will say that the two battles in the first part of the book really happened, although they are hardly ever mentioned in Hawkwood's hagiography; that the Emperors at Constantinople regularly worked with the various peoples of the far Steppe, including the Mongols; that Andronicus did work to unseat his father and make himself master of Constantinople, and that Nerio really did grab Megara in 1374 (although one source says 1381). Was William God at the taking of Megara? I suspect not, but my own love of Medieval Greek history keeps taking me back to the area.

As usual, I owe a debt of gratitude to William Caferro and his brilliant biography of John Hawkwood; to Kenneth Setton and his superbly researched series on the Papacy and the Levant, and to dozens if not hundreds of other authors and academics whose work informs mine. But I also owe a debt of gratitude to my reenactment and SCA friends in Canada, the United States Italy and the Czech Republic, whose efforts at Living History make it possible for me to write about Medieval life and warfare at such a fine-grained level of detail. In my opinion, there is no substitute for the direct experience of wearing armour, cooking over an open fire, staring at frescos and art ...

And finally, thanks Nancy, my sister-in-law, first reader and first critic, to Sarah, my partner, and Beatrice, our daughter, for putting up with vacations that are thinly-veiled research trips, and a lot of dinner-table monologues that begin with the words, 'So, I found out today that in thirteen seventy-two ...'

Christian Cameron
Toronto 2024